THE FAUST LANE

MARCUS BOLT

VIA BOOKS • ENGLAND

A VIA BOOK

First published in
April 2016 by VIA Books
through www.lulu.com
Copyright © Marcus Bolt 2016

ISBN: 978-1-326-63527-5

Cover and book design by Creative Concepts, Bristol
Typeset in Eveleth Clean Thin & Plantin
Produced through www.lulu.com

VIA Books
England

*For my grandchildren – Raven, Aaron, Rose,
Eli, Ariel and Dahlan*

one

AS THE INCLINE grows steeper and the geriatric donkey begins to wheeze, David not only feels sorry for the animal, but decides it's probably less of a torment to walk anyway. The dirt track is pot-holed and rutted and the cart's springs appear to have petrified over their hundred-year lifetime.

He slides off the back of the cart and overtakes, calling up, 'Gracias, Senor,' to the walnut-faced driver, who'd picked him up just outside of Orgiva. The man raises a hand in acknowledgement and continues to stare ahead, saying nothing. Foreigners are tolerated but never fully embraced in Andalucia.

David follows the steep track up, panting with exertion in the dust-laden air, sweat trickling between his shoulder blades. The day has been blisteringly hot, as usual, the stark sun dry-roasting exposed skin.

After three more twisting kilometres, he finally reaches the left fork that angles down to the extended *cortijo* he calls home. As he approaches, he admires again its elegantly simple construction. Moorish influence. A basic tree trunk frame with in-fill panels of rough stone – the roof domes and walls, both inside and out, covered by a thick layer of plaster that always reminds him of icing sugar. The really hard, pure white stuff you get on wedding cakes. The exterior walls dazzle with reflected sunlight and shimmer in the heat-rising air. Inside, a leaf-dappled light dances all day, giving way to the TV's gaudy flickering at night.

It is so cool inside, he shudders as he enters. He drops his bag on the tiled floor, heads for the kitchen and takes a litre bottle of water from the refrigerator, glugging half of it down in one go, tipping the remainder over his head. The shock is almost painful and makes him wince.

Towelling his hair, he returns to the sitting room and collapses on an old leather sofa, kicking off his sandals, placing the soles of his feet on the cool, terra cotta tiles as portents of old-age pulse up and down his legs.

Stretching, he tells the room, 'I am *totally* knackered,' then calls out, 'Hi, Michelle. Any mail?'

The house computer wakes and replies, 'Welcome home, David. I'm afraid there have been no communications while you've been away – electronic or otherwise.'

'Ten billion people in the world and not one of them wanted to talk to me today. What a relief.' He next asks if there's anything new on the Trust's website.

Michelle illuminates the wall-hung screen. 'Nothing on the message board. There are a couple of interesting new articles. Shall I read them to you, or print them out?'

'Later.'

As a Trustee, he is obliged to visit the Trust's headquarters several times a year. Mind-numbing trips that involve a two hour taxi drive to Malaga airport and a similar length flight to England – followed by meetings that become more and more tedious as the years go by. But at least he gets to see his grandchildren.

His own children, three girls and a boy, are married now, all with kids of their own and he is Grandad to nine with more on the way.

– *Enjoy being a grandfather more than I enjoyed being a parent...* he muses.
– *Wonder if that's true for everyone, or am I merely a late developer...?*

When their parents go out, taking advantage of his presence, he baby-sits, fascinated, watching his grandchildren at play, occasionally sorting disputes, making or mending toys, inventing games. At these moments, listening to their laughter, or having an in-depth one-to-one with a tear-stained, hurt or thwarted toddler, the proffered ice cream more efficient therapy than his words of wisdom, he experiences a profound contentment.

– *Life doesn't get any better than this...* he thinks.

David hasn't seen his ex-wife in years. He asks his offspring how she is, but doesn't really listen to their animated replies. She has married again – to 'a nice guy, an accountant', lives near Windsor and is very happy – is all he knows. He did make tentative overtures about their getting back together, but they both knew his heart wasn't in it and, by then, hers was already elsewhere. And anyway, far too many years had gone by to stop and reverse time's unpicking of their knitted-nerve-ending union. At least they parted cordially and on a note of honesty he is glad to recall.

– *We had closure, I believe they call it...*

'Would you like today's paper, David?' Michelle asks.

'No. Too tired, thanks.' He has the *Times* downloaded each day, but it's more for the crossword than news or editorial comment. He doesn't feel like an ex-pat any more; no longer English, but certainly not yet Spanish – he can't even remember what prompted him to settle in Spain.

– *Cheap and warm, I suppose...* He has, more or less, isolated himself from the world, become neutral, a non-citizen.

– *Quite easy to do when you've got a private income...*

The income is in the form of an index-linked pension augmented by a dribble of royalties from *The Purpose of Life*, a self-help book he authored. Not exactly a best seller, but adequate. He never quite understands why, though, feeling at times like a charlatan.

– *Can't see that there's much purpose to my life, nowadays...*

But he accepts the fortunate accident and its pursuant contentment as payment for the battering life gave him and for the time and effort of physically wrestling it all onto paper. The first half was laboriously typed with one finger, he remembers, until he discovered and installed the latest voice-recognition technology available at the time.

He calls, 'Off,' and the plasma screen blanks. Standing and stretching he walks stiffly to the bathroom, where he orders, 'Cool shower,' and water at the correct temperature begins to cascade as he slips off his shorts and top.

His home, which he bought and refurbished for the price of a small flat in suburban England, is governed by a central computer. It controls temperature, lighting and security, as well as monitoring work files, finances, diary and all his telecommunications. The computer is of the latest 'fuzzy logic' generation and over the months has analysed and learned his lifestyle requirements solely from their interaction. Michelle, as he calls 'her', is running at about ninety-eight percent accuracy, so he rarely has to use the touchscreen keyboard. He rather enjoys the incongruity of this ancient, hand-built peasant dwelling packed solid with the latest digital wizardry, which he has wholeheartedly embraced. He thinks of the house as an old, old woman rejuvenated by a transplanted teenager's brain.

Stepping out of the shower, he scrubs himself dry, one handed, with a rough towel, mistrustful of the warm air body-drier – a praxis imprinted in childhood by a worrier-queen mother steeped in old wives tales. Using the mirror, he examines the rounded stump of what was once his left arm. The fleshy hemisphere never fails to fascinate him with its taught, pink smoothness – the scar tissue never taking a tan. Out of habit, he presses it with a finger nail, but after a dozen years the stump still feels numb;

then he stands sideways to the mirror, flexes a few muscles and feels fairly satisfied with his still lean body.

'Not bad for sixty…' he tells his image, smiling and winking at it before ambling naked into the bedroom. He selects and dons slacks and a sweater, then returns to the kitchen to pour himself a glass of white grape juice. He no longer drinks alcohol, disliking chemically induced feelings nowadays, and no longer misses it, realising he has at last quit.

'I'm not a dry drunk any more. Cheers…'

He asks for the French windows to be opened. They slide noiselessly apart and he walks through the opening. The oven-hot, late afternoon wind gusts as he stands inspecting the garden. His land, all five hectares of it, continues to angle down the valley's southern slope to the summer-dried riverbed. The loosely bordered plot is planted with lemon, olive and almond trees. A local farmer husbands the site and maintains the ancient irrigation system in exchange for half the harvest. A satisfyingly sensible deal all round. He is convinced the farmer cheats him, but he doesn't particularly care as long as the work is done.

– *Not worth hassling over a few Euros…*

Fig and grape vines cover the rear of the house in a shaggy, hippie hairstyle and David half-heartedly collects baskets of their fruit which he always intends to sell, but never quite gets around to lugging down the mountainside to the local market. He has caught a very bad dose of *man̲ana*.

'Must do something about that,' he admonishes himself, noticing the piled, brimming baskets cluttering the shady veranda. 'Tomorrow.'

All day he looks forward to the evening when the temperature goes down with the sun and the cicadas cease their day long rapping. Sitting on his veranda, under the vines – the moon rising high over the Sierra Nevada, constellated house lights twinkling orange and yellow over the valley sides – a palpable calm descends as the night closes in. A tranquillity that seems to emanate from the ancient, terraced landscape and is borne on the perfumed air he breaths in, and out, in and out until he too is filled with its peace.

Spain has been his home for ten years now, and he has lived here alone all that time. He has a woman friend – Juanita, a widow, living nearby. He takes faltering Spanish lessons from her once or twice a week and helps with her almost perfect English. They have dined at each other's houses, been to concerts and the cinema together, driving into Orgiva or Granada in her car – he hasn't owned a car in years. So far, their liaison is platonic. David divines correctly that she would be open to more intimacy, more physicality. He enjoys her company, very much, and she is still a beauty, but he is not sure yet if he's ready for, or even capable of, another, probably final, in-depth relationship.

– *Maybe, he thinks, Maybe, one day...*

'David. May I remind you Juanita's coming to supper at eight?' Michelle interrupts as though reading his mind.

'Christ! Thanks, Michelle. I forgot. I'd better get supper ready now.' He involves the computer in the minutiae of his life, talking his thoughts out loud like a latterday Crusoe to Man Friday. 'I can re-heat it later when we're ready.'

Shuffling back to the kitchen, he stoops to re-open the fridge. He finds a plate of seafood and a large bowl of cooked rice and hoists them one at a time to the work surface. He begins to prepare a paella, scooping rice from the bowl, adding peas and pre-diced vegetables from a catering pack, tossing it all into a wok, scraping in the sea food, adding oil, stirring with a wooden spoon. He has become a competent cook over the years of living alone despite having only one arm. The house computer could do it all for him, of course, but even he, a committed technophile, draws a line.

As the cooking seafood smells rise from the pan, his mouth waters. He usually only has one main meal a day, and he is very hungry.

'Would you like some music, David?'

'No thanks, Michelle. Tell you what, though, while I'm rustling up a deliciously creative dessert, could you read back the first part of my manuscript again?' he asks, adding more oil to the mix, testing taste and temperature off the end of the wooden spoon. 'Up to where Juanita and I left off last time. I need to see if the changes work.'

'With pleasure, David. "QWERTYUIOP. A novel by David O'Connor, copyright July, 2020",' enunciated in a clear, too perfect voice – the only way you'd know she wasn't human. 'David, a search has revealed that over the last twenty years there have been eleven books using this device as a title.'

'Yeah, well. It's only a working title. First thing that came into my head.'

'May I also point out the year is twenty nineteen, not twenty twenty?'

'I know. I just like the idea of twenty-twenty vision. It's a pun. A joke?'

'I'm afraid computer technology is not yet advanced enough to grant me a true sense of humour, David.'

'Yeah, forgot. But it'll be years before the damn thing gets published – if I ever get round to posting it on the net, so don't worry yourself. And anyway, I'm only doing it for amusement.'

'Yes, David. Also, wouldn't it be advisable to use a nom de plume?'

'Michelle,' David calls, exasperated, 'Please switch off your crit programme and just read, will you? From the beginning.'

'Certainly, David...

ROAD RAGE

As he unlocked his car, Jon slipped out of fretful daydreaming, becoming sharply aware of the world around him, surprised at having been so self-wrapped for so long. As he lowered himself in, he wondered if it had anything to do with the approaching anniversary of his father's death.

– *I really miss the old sod. Strange, really. We didn't get on that well when he was alive...* He poked the key into the ignition.

– *Or p'raps it's because business is so dire...* The starter whinnied and the engine fired.

– *Or because me and Yvonne aren't exactly happy at the moment...* He reached for, pulled across and clicked home his seat belt.

– *And I'm so very, fuckin' bored all the time...*

Easing the car on the clutch between the graffiti-covered walls lining the access road to his office, he forced a gap between scurrying pedestrians and poked the car's snout into the dense one way traffic. A driver, unable to squeeze his van past, signalled him in crossly. Jon flicked acknowledgement and joined the creeping convoy.

To right and left, up and down the length of the High Street, brightly lit shop fronts prematurely darkened the twilight sky, their stacked-to-over-brimming wares visually tumbling out onto pavements chock-a-block with harried, hurrying shoppers. Banks and fast food outlets, estate agents and clothes stores, newsagents and chemists – contemporary barrowboys mongering all the must-have paraphernalia of a late twentieth century lifestyle.

– *It's all so overblown, kind of tumescent – morose...*

The traffic crawled towards the High Street's grande finale – a new library complex and sour-faced council offices towering above the cross roads. As he approached, traffic lights switched in concert to amber, then quickly to red. Jon zipped across the white lines in tandem with the car in front, a yard off its rear, his throttle foot impelled by impatience.

The road widened, lined with four-storey, Regency terraces, their once elegant facades now despoiled by a plethora of company name-boards and *To Rent* signs. Virtually all of the accommodation in this part of the old market town had been made over to offices and showrooms and, at night, the once thriving community was desolate, its ghosts only disturbed by late night rowdies and an occasional patrolling police car.

Despite the nose-to-tail parking lining the road, the one way system facilitated a picking up of speed and, as he pressed the accelerator, Jon experienced a fleeting moment of freedom. But, within a mile, the road narrowed again, where a grey-metal viaduct carrying the Metropolitan line crossed obliquely overhead.

A sign warning *Low Bridge* winked into Jon's consciousness as it sped past, triggering a synaptic search engine that crackled to life, connecting neural pathways, downloading stored data. As he passed under the ominously rumbling structure, flickering images coalesced in his mind – half seen, half felt – and a frequently played, angst-tinged memory began to screen.

A college blues band, shuffling home stoned after a gig; around two in the morning; horizontally driven snow...

The five young art students leaned into the wind, hands in pockets, coat collars up, chins tucked on chests, experiencing the snow blizzarding in their faces as torture after the womb-like warmth of the club. They began to cross the High Level Bridge that spanned the river valley to guide the London rail link through the suburbs, into the city centre and back out again. Alongside the electrified rails to their right, a footpath ran, open to the elements. Continuing their silent, head-bowed trudge, each encapsulated in his own discomforted world, they reached the bridge's centre, where they synchronously stopped, lined up and pointed their penises through the diamond-latticed guard-rail. One by one, they began to hiss steamy arcs into the River Medway coursing darkly fifty feet below.

'Jesus! It's cold enough to freeze your piss,' one remarked through chattering teeth.

'Imagine bloody great icicles hanging off the end of yer dick,' another suggested, his white-breath words whisked from his mouth by the wind.

'You could snap 'em off and make sculpture...'

'You'd need a massive refrigerated studio, though.'

'And transport.'

'Yeah. And the gallery'd have to be a massive cold store.'

'You could hire out fur coats to visitors...'

'What are you two on about?' a third challenged, shivering, shaking the last drops and zipping up. 'Who'd wanna work in piss, for Chrissake?'

'Jon would. His work *is* piss... Ow! Fuck! You bastard!' yelled as Jon smacked home a handful of snow from close range, ramming it down his insulter's neck.

Revitalised, they became kids again, laughing and whooping, throwing and ducking, bending to make snowballs, lurching along the footpath, away from the river towards home.

Levelling with the upper floors of a cuboid factory glowing neon-dull some twenty yards to their left, they slid to a halt and stared in, captivated by the silent formicary of the overalled workers busying themselves over lathes and strenuously pulling component-laden carts.

'Looks like they're in prison. Poor bastards.'

'Like the machines are running them.'

'It's a scene from "Metropolis"...'

'You could stick this in Tate Britain; the biggest installation in the world...'

'You could turn it *into* a Tate; first show "Contemporary Futurism". Nice concept.'

'Bollocks to conceptual art!' Jon yelled, hurling a snowball. It smacked into a window pane with a resounding, hollow 'doompf'.

An inquisitive inmate ambled across, pressed his face to the begrimed window and peered out, shielding his eyes from the interior neon lights with both hands. Another snowball – doompf – and the man started, jumping back in alarm. The young men on the bridge convulsed with laughter, instinctively sensing a new game. A hail of snowballs thudding into windows bringing other workers scurrying over, eager for diversion from the humdrum night shift. They swivelled open lower window sections to their forty-five degree limit and began to jeer out good-humouredly into the night air.

'Wank-ers!'

'Get yer 'air cut!'

'Art school poofters!'

In response, a cannonade of snowballs – some exploding through openings, spray scattering the enlivened, laughing factory hands.

'Missed, you tossers!'

'You couldn't 'it a fuckin' barn if you was standin' in it!'

'Arse'oles!'

14

A foreman in a diarrhoea-brown coat bustled into view, testily ordering the men away. They sloped back to their machines mouthing curses. The laughing students observed the men sneering, making V-signs at the balding, bespectacled figure's back as he turned to face the source of the disruption and approached the opened windows.

'That's enough of that. Piss off out of it!' he shouted towards the bridge, waving a dismissive hand.

'Yes, SIR! At once, SIR!' 'Heil Hitler!' the band chorused back, saluting and gesturing, maintaining a fragile camaraderie with the factory hands, playing to their gallery.

'I'll bloody call Security in a minute...' The attempt to assert authority was lost under a fresh barrage of snowballs as he fussily pulled the windows closed.

Jon scooped a double handful of snow and quickly compacted and compressed it into a smooth, hard ball. He took aim and, using his schooldays' cricketing skills, threw with all his strength. The ice-ball smashed into the pane framing the foreman's head. Glass splintered and Jon snapped the man falling back, hands clutching a bloodied face, men rushing over to where he fell.

'Fuckin' hell, Jon. I'm outta here!' someone yelped, taking off, running for the end of the bridge and sanctuary. The rest followed, guffawing and cheering, waving arms in mock panic, play-acting a callous bravado.

Completely unmoved by what he had done, merely drunkenly curious to know what would happen next, Jon skidded to a stop as the footpath levelled out where it joined the road. The others dwindled up the hill, their raucous laughter fading in the dark. He peeked left along the road's right-angled sweep, down towards the factory's entrance.

'Wow! Amazing!'

The sterile industrial scene he hardly noticed as he passed daily on his way to college had been conjured into a vivid, incandescent film set. Spherical blizzards hovered around the floodlights illuminating the factory's facade; powdery whirlwinds pranced up and down the street. That night, within an hour, the snowstorm had deposited a foot of snow, surreptitiously softening angles, smoothing kerbs, plumping walls and sugaricing cars into king-size buns. Jon stared open-mouthed, the evening's marijuana and alcohol intake deranging perception, flattening perspective and intensifying contrast. He stood swaying, succumbing to the illusion of hurtling horizontally through a wall of suspended snowflakes.

A black, amoebic form emitting flashes of light swam into sight. He watched the shape pulsate and expand, slowly sliding across his visual field as though projected on a screen.

'What *is* that?' he wondered dreamily. Half a dozen uniformed security guards streamed from the factory gates, their flashlights bobbing as they ran towards him up the incline.

'Shit, it's the Gestapo.'

Galvanised, immediately fantasising he was starring in an escape movie, he turned and ran back towards the path. He vaulted a low, wooden fence, ran twenty yards, then prostrated himself in the snow covered long grass at the foot of the railway embankment, a little boy believing he couldn't be seen if he was unable to see them.

Torch beams zigzagged around him. Then a shout. 'There's one of 'em!'

Seized by a childlike frenzy, he scrambled to his feet and clambered up the snow-covered grass bank towards the railway lines, scrabbling for purchase on the steepening slope. He stretched for the top, nearly made it, slid back a few yards, started again, kicking toecaps into the bank like a mountaineer. Panting and sweating, he crawled over the embankment's crest, hauled himself up and ran in gawky panic along the railway lines away from the town, deep snow snagging his ankles, vision distorted by watering eyes. Looking over his shoulder he saw a blurred line of jigging lights cresting the embankment. The next second, he blundered into a cluster of drift-burrowing rails. The ground slammed at him, sharp-stoned ballast gashing a hand and grazing his knees. Pain and the shock of ice on bare flesh jolted him from the cinematic fantasy.

– What am I doing? These lines are electrified...!

Paralysed by waves of terror, he froze, down on hands and knees, not daring to move. As he stared inertly at the snow-covered ground, cries from the pursuing guards carried on the wind. A flush of panic immediately elbowed the fear of electrocution aside. He took off like a sprinter, running flat out, high-stepping over snow-buried sleepers – an animal fleeing before the hunt.

Rail-side stanchions, telegraph poles and junction boxes loomed from the darkness, mimicking out-flanking guards, generating fresh gouts of fear, spurring him on. As he came striding round a wide curve at full pelt, a gantry suspended in the cocoa-coloured sky tracked him with acid-green eyes. He passed under and an eye winked green as a clanking signal-arm dropped, bouncing out, 'Get him, get him, get him!' He lost control, whimpering as he ran.

Slapping through a blackly echoing, snowless tunnel, he heard them closing from all sides. He put on a spurt and exploded from the entrance sucking air with burning lungs. Three hundred yards more... His legs buckled and he staggered to an exhausted stop, bending forward, hands on knees, chest heaving.

Humiliated by their super-fitness, he turned reluctantly to face his captors, at once ready to plead for mercy and reprieve.

Nothing. Silence. It was so hushed he could hear only his own heavy breathing and the pounding of his heart – and then the pattering of snowflakes as they settled on his coat. A moment of clarity descended, and he laughed aloud.

'Shit – hallucinating. Thought they'd got me.' He closed his eyes for a moment too long and half-fell, stumbling awake as a current of sleep almost sucked him under. He began to shiver with cold and shock. For a second he felt exhilarated by his escape, then winced as pain from his injured knees gouged his body. He felt blood oozing from the throbbing gash in his hand and he held it up to catch the dim light, immediately sickened by the sticky, black mess.

Wrapping his shaking palm with a dirty handkerchief, holding it in place with folded fingers, he looked around, disoriented, attempting to take stock. He stood in the middle of a wide, steep-banked cutting, surrounded by ghostly tracks and rail-side paraphernalia – a gallery of abstract sculpture under the layering of snow.

– Think I live over there somewhere. Gotta get home. Need sleep. Knackered...

As he moved off, he sensed a rumbling in the air. He stopped and listened, confused. The grumbling grew louder and louder, becoming a howling growl as a lone locomotive burst from the tunnel, clanking and banging, bearing down on him at speed. Closing fast, it emitted a single, plaintive honk that reverberated along the cutting. The engine's sheer bulk and noise and velocity terrorised him. He stood paralysed, like a rabbit transfixed in headlights, and screamed involuntarily as the shrieking monster roared past on a parallel track a yard distant, belching hot electric fumes, churning a snowstorm in its wake. Displaced air and a cacophony of noise butted and slapped him around and he was forced to cower where he stood, hands over his head, eyes closed tight, breath held.

Then it was gone, rattling into the night.

Hurting anew and shaking with the fresh adrenaline rush, he turned and gingerly stepped across the tracks remembering to scan for the sly, live rail. After hoisting himself up an embankment and dragging his body over a fence, he shuffled in a head-whirling stupor down the length of a garden. Frozen fingers fumbling with a clinking gate-catch set a dog barking nearby. Nerves aquiver, he slipped hurriedly through. Drifting snow covered every surface – roofs, trees, pavement and road, eerily glistening under pale street lamps.

– *Where am I? Don't recognise a thing. Looks like some bloody ski resort...*

Staggering, tugging eyelids apart, he forced dead legs and frozen-chicken feet in the direction of the town's jaundiced glow, soaked through and shivering. Over and over he slid exhaustedly into sleep, seeing blood and splintering glass, hearing running footsteps, roaring engines – each time waking with a gasp.

After a perplexity of blurred turnings and intersecting roads, convinced by a growing panic that he was walking in circles, he finally recognised the London Road. Then with sweet relief, minutes later, the street where he lived. On its corner, lurking under a dull street lamp, stood a security guard.

– *Fuck! Keep calm. Act casual...*

Pulling himself together, pocketing his wrapped and still bleeding wound, he sauntered across. Light from a torch slapped his head aside and he raised a shielding hand.

'Where've you been, Sunshine?' the guard demanded.

'At my girlfriend's.'

'Where's that then?'

'Er...' – *Think, think...* 'Broadland Road?'

'Where you off to now?'

'Home. I live down there,' he indicated. 'Why? Is there a problem, officer?'

'Too bloody right. Some yobs have been chucking things at Courtney's windows. Injured one of our blokes. You seen a gang of yobbos? People running, anything odd?'

'No. Like I said...'

The hiss and crackle of a short wave radio interrupted the interrogation. The guard brought a handset to his face as though about to shave.

'Yeah...?' A metallic voice whah-whahed in the air. 'Right, be with you in five minutes.'

Jon watched him waddle off, back towards the factory, stiff-legged and lard-arsed, trailing puffs of white breath which hovered in the now still, frost-crackling air.

'Bloody brilliant, Sherlock. What a prat,' he muttered before following slowly down, careful not to let a suspicious distance grow between them, at last reaching the path to his front door.

As he groped in the dark for the lock with his key an ambulance crunched up the hill, its melancholy blue lights pirouetting on the snow…

And dancing in Jon's head…

A police car hee-hawed along the hard shoulder dragging him back to the present. The M25 angling in from his right was jammed in both directions, all six lanes festering in a miasma of fumes. Thousands of red and white, winking lights curved away, up and over the hill in the direction he was heading. Corpuscles stagnating in sclerotic arteries.

'Bollocks!'

Jon hit the steering wheel and cursed himself for not paying attention, not checking before he'd made the irrevocable turn onto the slip road.

'Now I'm gonna be bloody late again.' He reached for his carphone, unclipping it from its cradle. *No signal*, it smirked.

'Sod all I can do about it now.'

He imagined a newsvendor standing on a street corner hollering, 'Incumbent agency loses three-way pi-itch. Read all about it!'

– *Nah. The Press aren't into provincial agencies. Only interested in the big boys…*

– *P'raps that's why Mike's looking at other agencies, though; wants a big name to show he's coming up in the world. But they wouldn't wanna know about a two-fifty K spend, would they…?*

– *Nope. Still no idea why he's done it. Really thought we were doing a good enough job…* He shook his head and grunted aloud.

– *No loyalty, some people. God, I despise pitching. All that sodding work for nothing if you lose…*

The line of cars already on the slip road hurried forward five yards and stopped with a ripple of brake lights. He followed reflexively, recalling the last pitch they lost, the Marketing Director 'phoning to announce, 'Sorry, Jon. You came second.'

'Out of how many?' he'd asked brightly, masking the tidal wave of disappointment.

'Two,' the then ex-prospect had sniggered.

– *God, if we lose this one as well. So much hanging on it. Bastard bank's already threatening to pull the plug…*

A wave of self-reproach engulfed him.

– Should've talked to Mike more. Found out where he's coming from. Lost too many clients lately. My fault...

Then hope like a wink of sun on a drizzly, grey day.

– Did get his PA to call though – hasn't actually blown us out yet...

'He wants you here at five tonight.'

'Is it about the pitch?'

'He didn't say. Just get here. Try not to be late again,' and she'd hung up.

– Bitch. Nice looking, though. Wouldn't mind giving her...

The battered white van in front slipped across the broken line to merge with the metallic slug jamming the motorway. As Jon followed, a gaudily emblazoned ten-wheeler lurched forward, braking with a loud hiss a few feet from the van's rear, blocking him out.

'Wanker!' he spat up at the anonymous driver's cab, immediately angry, convinced the act was personal. He waited, feet competitively poised. As the van moved forward he accelerated into the space and slammed on the brakes, forcing the lorry to a bouncing stop. Its horn vented a long, sonorous note.

'Piss off,' he mouthed at his rear view mirror, raising a middle finger out into the damp air. He closed the window, activated the central lock-ing then reached for a cigarette, fumbling at the flip-top one-handed, while steering and slipping the clutch in the inching traffic. The van in front stopped sharply, its over-bright brake lights grating his eyes. He stamped on the brake pedal and the car jerked to a stop. The lorry climbed over his car's rear, snorting and hissing indignantly, its radiator grille filling his mirrors.

'Fuck off, will ya,' he shouted over his shoulder. He brought his lighter to the cigarette, sucking cross-eyed. As he inhaled a wracking coughing fit discharged in his rib cage.

'Jesus! Why the hell did I start smoking?' He recalled the fatal moment.

– Oh, God! At the fair, to impress Karen. My golden-haired goddess in school uniform...

Another drag and he was back in class, gazing doe-eyed across the desks at her, his adolescent adoration haemorrhaging in his chest, seem-ing to flood the room.

'If you could go out with anyone in the school, who'd it be?'

'Karen Wilson. She's really lovely,' he'd let slip, dreamy eyed. Suppressed giggles from his mates revealed it was a trap. Then they glee-fully gossiped the news, defiling and downgrading his youthfully pure love, turning it into an all-school snigger behind his back.

'Didja hear? Lucke fancies Karen Johnson...'

Then her friends had come with assurances that she liked him too and was longing to be asked out – and he'd felt an exultancy that had quashed innate caution.

Saturday morning. He dialled her number with nervy fingers, heart thumping.

'Can I speak to Karen, please? It's Jon Lucke from school.' He suffered a foreboding wait, muffled voices in his ear.

'Yes?'

'Karen? Hi, it's Jon. I was wondering if you'd like to go to...'

'I don't wanna go anywhere with you,' she snapped, clattering the handset down. He listened to the anguished whirr of the dialling tone, feeling her prepared curtness as a kick in the guts. He went up to his room, got into bed and stayed there darkly brooding all weekend.

On Monday it seemed the whole school knew, nudging and tittering as he passed by. Rejection and humiliation worked in concert to rip the wings off his fledgling self-respect...

The recall faded.

– Fell for that one, didn't I? Stupid cow. Didn't know what she was missing...

The show of arrogance was, he knew, a pretence. It worried him, though, that it still hurt after so many years, that rejection seemed to be a recurrent theme in his life.

The inching traffic came to a sudden stop, catching him unawares again. He braked hard and the shadowing lorry shrieked in his mirrors, inches from his rear bumper. He ignored it and took another drag. As the smoke scoured his lungs he squirmed, eyes shut.

– Christ! Twenty-odd years ago. Gotta give up. Lungs must be black as hell...

Into his mind came the horror-flick memory of visiting his once robust grandfather in hospital; seeing him propped up in bed, exhausted, an oxygen mask over his face, his breathing laboured, rasping: his frightened eyes darting to and fro as the lung cancer mouldered deep inside the grey, shrink-wrapped body.

'Oi, ar-sole!'

Jon flinched to one side in primordial recoil; a hulking gorilla was rapping on the window.

'Wotshore fack-in' game?' the shaven headed, ear-ringed simian demanded, bending down, glaring in, animal-red mouth gnawing the air.

Experience suggested submissiveness and perhaps a placatory gesture, but his pride ignored it.

'Piss off!' he sneered, presenting an air-prodding middle finger.

'Fack-in *cahnt*,' the lorry driver screamed, incensed. He tried to wrench open the locked door. Failing, he began to rock the car, kneeing the door panel, pounding on the roof with a fist. Jon felt it brush his scalp as it dented. The white van moved forward and Jon took tyre-yelping flight, squealing to a halt after thirty yards.

In his wing mirror he saw the lorry driver, starkly lit by headlights, leaning on a car gridlocked in the centre lane, amiably chatting with its passengers. He cringed seeing the man laugh, point in his direction, then swagger back to climb into his cab, king of the road.

– *What a moron. I should've...* His right leg began to jig involuntarily on the brake pedal.

The tight-knit traffic unravelled as it reached and passed a recent accident on the opposite carriageways. Jon stared in head-twisting fascination as the mangled metal slid by. Preoccupied, and desperate to leave the lorry behind, he pulled across two lanes. An old Vauxhall closing on him flashed its lights.

'Oh, for Chrissakes!'

Stabbing two fingers at his rear view mirror, he pressed on the throttle and the headlights dwindled. Seconds later, a black Mercedes casually sauntered into his path and he accelerated to make the offence seem worse, closing tight, impatiently flicking the flasher stalk, mouthing obscenities at the driver.

The one-mile-to-his-exit hoarding approached. Ahead, cars were bunching as a group of juggernauts battled it out side by side. He dropped a gear and wound the ageing BMW to a hundred, braking, accelerating, dodging from lane to lane. The half-mile sign blue-blurred across the lorries' roofs. He touched the brakes and deftly cut through a gap, angling across the convoy into the nearside lane as the demotion markers zipped by – sergeant, corporal, lance-corporal – and he was on the slip road travelling at a hundred and twenty, his anger mounting alongside his speed.

At the roundabout, he was forced to bring the car to a juddering stop as traffic crossed from his right. The costly smell of over-heated disk pads filled the cabin.

'Is the whole bloody world out to fuck me up?' he raged through clenched teeth, gripping the steering wheel with whitened knuckles, believing that somewhere a malevolent, Prospero-like figure was conjuring up traffic jams to thwart his every move. He lifted his carphone impatiently. It still read *No Service*. With an explosion of rage he smashed the handset down against the dashboard. The handset came apart in his hand.

CHANCE MEETING

Driving on auto-pilot on a mercifully clear road, he felt hollow now the anger storm had passed.

– *What's got into me? This time last year I was really happy; the business growing, doing really well. Suddenly, it's all slipping away and we're heading for the shit. And it's really getting me down...*

Desperate to avoid the depression he knew would follow from panic and self-pity's two-pronged attack, he leaned forwards to click on the radio.

'There are long delays on the M25 this evening due to an anti-clockwise accident near Junction...' The announcer's voice faded as an associated memory tuned in...

Jon awoke with a start from a dead sleep, disoriented, immediately jittery. He lay in bed staring up at the ceiling, wondering why it looked so eerie, so luminously white.

– *Of course. It's been snowing...*

His left hand began to throb. He pulled it from under the bedclothes and stared at his palm, startled by the raw-meat gash encrusted with dried blood.

Last night came flooding back, carried on a wave of fear. He threw off the covers and swung his legs over the side of the bed.

'Oh, shit! No!' He sat, head in hands, eyes squeezed shut attempting to stop the memories forming, praying last night wasn't real.

Skipping breakfast he went into college by the long route, avoiding the High Level Bridge. He had hoped immersion in work would induce amnesia, but a video-loop of the man falling back, oozing, then pouring, then spurting blood, played over and over as conflicting thoughts were shunted around his head.

– *What'll happen if they trace me...?*

– *Hope he's not hurt...*

– Could they trace me? Fuck it! Don't wanna go to court...
– Didn't mean to hurt him. An accident...
– Might send me to prison, though. Assault. Actual bodily harm...
– Hope he's okay. God! Feel terrible...
A leadened-stomach morning inched towards eleven o'clock.
– Can't take any more of this... He stood, tossing down a pencil.
– Got to find out... Walking briskly away from his workbench, he left the
building to find an untraceable callbox in the town centre.

'Courtneys,' said a remote voice. Jon pressed the coin-drop button.
'Can I have Personnel, please?' A pause, some clicks.
The Personnel Officer wearily picked up the telephone. His secretary
was off sick and he had last night's mess to sort out. 'Personnel,' he com-
plained into the mouthpiece.
'Uh, sorry to trouble you. I heard someone got injured at the factory
last night...'
'Who is this? How do you know about that? Do you work here?'
'A mate mentioned it this morning and...'
'Who are you?'
'Is he all right?'
'Who's this so-called friend?'
'Um. I think it's Jim...'
'What department does he work in?'
'Don't know him that well, but... Is the bloke alright?'
A charged silence hung between them. Jon gritted his teeth while the
Personnel officer conjured a picture of the caller – a skinhead wearing
tight jeans and Doc Marten boots, LOVE and HATE tattooed on his
knuckles.
'It was you, wasn't it?'
'No, no. Nothing to do with me. Like I said, a mate mentioned it and...
How is he?'
'He's dead.'
The floor of the kiosk wasn't there for a second. Jon steeled himself for
the adrenaline kick but it failed to land. Too much information to process
all at once.
'Died from a heart attack, thanks to you – you vicious thug...'
Jon stared at his face in the small square mirror, noticing a spot on his
nose. He prodded it exploratively.
'I don't suppose you're going to give me your name, are you?'

'Well, no, I...' Jon suppressed a giggle – emotion that had lost its way, been mistranslated.

'No. Your sort never do. Well, the police'll find you. I hope they beat the...'

As if not wanting to be heard, Jon gingerly replaced the receiver and tiptoed from the kiosk. After furtively glancing from left to right, he walked slowly back to college through the slushy, fast thawing snow, taking a roundabout route – his mind blanked and his emotions stilled by the awesome weight of events.

On cue, the recall ended as his client's building appeared ahead. He flicked the indicator stalk, changed realities with the gears, drove into the car park and slotted into a space. Stepping from the car he was immediately confronted by its dented roof.

– *That wanker...!* He turned and stamped towards the building imagining the lorry driver punched to his knees, begging for mercy.

Pausing only to peer into the interior of a brand new, metallic silver Porsche and to experience a gnat's whine of envy, he entered reception.

'Hi. Jon Lucke for Mike Fuller please, Love,' he said to the receptionist, a temp he didn't recognise.

She looked up at him as she reached for a telephone.

– *He's nice. Looks like that film star, whassisname...?*

Jon leant forward an inch to peek down her blouse glimpsing a soft swell cupped in black lace.

After a brief, one-sided conversation she told him, 'He's running late. He'll be with you as soon as he can. Take a seat please.' She pulled her shoulders back and pushed towards him in millimetres, projecting potential interest and availability. 'Can I get you anything? Tea or coffee?'

– *Nice tits. Fancies me...*

'I'm fine thanks.'

– *Wonder what she's like in bed? Nah. Not worth the hassle...*

Their prospective relationship having been evaluated and played out in second, he sauntered over to the seating area and collapsed into a wide, padded leather chair. From a low table he picked up a trade magazine entitled *Optics News* and began to riffle through its contents without reading. The reception walls were lined with exhibition panels produced by his company, all liveried with the logo he'd designed and originally won the business with some three years ago. He glanced up at them.

– *Funny. So important once; now they mean bugger all. Can't even remember working on them...*

Two employees, a tall, languid man in a dark suit and an attractive, short-skirted young woman walked through reception talking and laughing loudly. He watched them over the top of the magazine aware the man was making a play for the woman, walking crab-wise, claws hovering, ready to touch. The young woman's body language – serpentine, Jon decided – indicated she welcomed the attention as she gazed up into his face, over-laughing at a remark he had just made. The man irritated him.

– *What a tosser. Some blokes would do anything to get their leg over...*

Turning back to the magazine, his eyelids began to droop, lulled by the overheated reception area. His head slumped and he sank down into the chair, then the past, until he was back at his workspace in college again...

An elegantly tall, blond, blue-eyed and remarkably good-looking Fine Arts student swayed into the studio bringing a frisson of excitement. Jon had seen him around college and at parties, invariably at the heart of the action, one or more girls hanging on his arm.

All eyes were on him as he oozed around the room hugging and kissing, bantering and back-slapping, taking over, his public school accent charming the air. He slid onto a chair beside a vivacious young woman and slipped an arm around her waist. Her face lit up and she leaned into him, laying her head on his shoulder, smiling, coming alive. Jon observed their intimacy with nauseous jealousy – the girl was his latest secret infatuation.

Sensing Jon's gaze, the Fine Arts student looked up and Jon jerked his eyes aside.

'Just the guy I'm looking for.'

Taken aback, Jon half pointed to himself. 'Me?'

'You're Jon Lucke, aren't you?'

'Yeah...' he responded, surprised, flattered his name was known.

'I hear tell you're a guitarist.'

'Well, you know, I play a bit.'

'We're getting a blues band together. You interested?'

'I'm not sure I'm good enough.'

'Now, now, don't play modest – doesn't become you. We're auditioning in the function room, back of the Eight Bells, Wednesday night, about eight. Just bring your guitar, we've hired a PA system. I'm Simon, by the way...'

– Not Simon...

He fought to fend off the memory, half awake, shifting in his seat as a bats' cave of emotion was disturbed.

– Virtually fell in love with that bastard. Everything I wanted to be. Had it all – looks, personality. Filthy rich parents, too. What an idiot I was. Followed him round like a lapdog. Ran the band together – me doing all the donkey work, of course. Played all those college gigs. Great band, though. Then he got us that bloody record deal and it all went shit-shaped...

Humming to himself, Jon pushed through the door of the small, local recording studio they often used. Unexpectedly, the band was there, set up, running through a number, a long-haired thirty-something playing guitar in his place. The music dried as they became aware of him.

'What's going on?' he demanded.

'Ah, Jon. Most unfortunate. Meant to get in touch. Forgot. Won't beat about the bush – don't need you in the band any longer. You're out, I'm afraid.'

'What are you talking about, Simon? You can't kick me out just like that.'

'Can and have, old boy,' Simon replied, dragging on a joint, striking a typically majestic pose, microphone held sceptre-like in hand.

'Why? What's the problem all of a sudden?'

Simon pointed the microphone. 'Ask them.'

Jon turned and appealed to the others, frustration in his voice. 'Do you guys agree with this?'

They looked away embarrassed, shuffling sheet music, bending to adjust amplifiers.

'Yeah, we do,' the drummer spoke up. 'Simon's right. We need someone a bit more on the ball, like. Someone a bit sharper, you know?' He pointed. 'Dave here's sessioned with Bowie.'

Jon stared at the interloper. 'Who the fuck are you?'

'Nothing to do with me, mate,' he parried. 'Not my problem.' He looked away, disinterested, indifferent.

Jon swung back to plead, 'Si-mon...?'

Simon shrugged regret, amusement on his face. Jon's mouth tightened in fury.

'You – fucking – bastard!'

He swivelled on his heel and walked angrily to the door, slamming it shut after him.

The receptionist approached Jon nervously. She had not been trained to deal with people in reception rocking their heads from side to side, eyes screwed tight. She reached to shake his shoulder, then pulled back as though it might be contagious.

'Um... Excuse me,' she whispered. Then, more loudly, 'Excuse me!'

Startled, Jon opened his eyes and stared up at her, a manic look on his face. The suppressed emotion choked his throat, stung his eyes. The receptionist took a wary pace backwards. Embarrassment blossomed and Jon prayed he hadn't externalised his daydreams by whimpering or crying out.

'Sorry?'

'Er... Mr. Fuller's ready for you. Would you like to go up?'

'Great. Thanks.' He leapt to his feet, gathered his case and headed towards the stairs, overacting being normal like a secret drunk.

She watched him go, shook her head and wandered back to her desk muttering, 'Bloody nutter.'

Through the half open door of Mike Fuller's office Jon saw his client in typical pose. He was leaning over a seated young woman, one arm round her shoulder as he dictated a letter, his free hand twiddling locks of her long hair. She appeared rigid, uncomfortably perched on the edge of her chair, staring down at the notebook in her lap.

At Jon's token knock Mike straightened up and pulled away from the girl. His tie was loosened and his top shirt buttons undone, a crop of dark chest hairs poking through. He was jacketless and his gut hung heavily over his tight belt. Mike's flop of unruly hair and fleshy, moist lips reminded Jon of the debauched satyrs that leered from Renaissance paintings.

– *Or the stereotypical, hard-assed, womanising exec. Plus ça change, eh? What an arsehole...*

Mike noticed Jon's disapproving look. Ever since he'd known him, he'd sensed Jon was a prude at heart and enjoyed teasing.

'Come in, Jon, come in. Sit yourself down. Can I get you anything? Coffee? Tea? A woman?' Snickering at his own joke, he said to the girl, with lascivious emphasis and a wink at Jon, 'That's all for now, Janine. Come and *finish me off* later – know what I mean, darling?'

He patted her backside as she scuttled to the door, glancing sideways at Jon, raising her eyes to the ceiling and tutting audibly as she passed through.

'Delightful creature. Can't keep her hands off me,' Mike declared.

'Well, down to business, old bean. I've got good news and bad news. The good news is we really like your creative work for next year. We particularly like the contact lens cleaner positioning. What was it, now?' He sorted through a pile of visuals heaped on his desk. Jon's relief timidly poked out its head, sniffing the air, despite competitors' logos flashing into view.

'Here we are.' He pulled back the cover sheet. 'Yes. "Stop your patients seeing dirty films". Love it! Just love it! That'll cheer the stuffy buggers up down at the Institute,' he smirked, dropping the board back on his desk, rubbing his hands together.

'Now for the bad news. If you want the business for another year you're going to have to cut your prices by fifteen per cent.'

– You gotta be joking, you fat pillock…

'That's a tough one, Mike. Might just be able accommodate you, though. The price was pretty rock-bottom – but at least we've got the media spend to compensate.'

'Ah! Sorry, Jon. We're handling that ourselves. The journals are giving us a full ten per cent *and* series discount. They're either struggling like fuck or it's Christmas.'

'But they're not supposed to do that, it's unethical.'

'Unethical, schmethical, Jonny baby. It's a tough old world out there. Do you know how much product I've got to shift just to pay your fees alone?'

– No, but I bet you're going to tell me…

Jon sat trapped, forced to listen to Mike's catalogue of troubles followed by an honours list of his personal triumphs both at work and play. Unless he became a psychotherapist or a lawyer, Jon knew he could never charge for this service – and most clients expected it gratis, took it for granted, perks of the trade.

After an hour, Jon finally made his excuses and got away, plodding morosely into the dimly lit, almost deserted, car park. He knew that if he'd won the pitch straight out he'd be elated now, planning a holiday, thinking about a new car, relieved their money worries were over for a while. On the other hand, had he lost it, he could have perversely enjoyed wallowing in self-pity, giving himself an excuse to get drunk that night.

– Haven't won or lost. Mike bloody Fuller's won though – as usual. Got himself a shit-hot creative campaign for peanuts and saved himself over thirty grand on the media…

He climbed into his car and sat staring at the ochre husks of last summer's weeds still clinging forlornly to the chain-link periphery fence.

– Why do I take it all the time? Why can't I tell them all to get stuffed? Why don't I have any control over my life? Ah, sod it! I'm going to get smashed tonight whatever…

A loud, head-jerking crash shunted his car forward. He scrambled out, angrily throwing his seatbelt aside, running to look at the rear of his car. The bumper was crumpled, the boot-sill stoved in, shards of red and amber plastic dropping to the ground like spilt blood. The Porsche he'd admired earlier drove forward to disengage, its rear merely scratched. Jon stormed towards it, enraged.

'Can't you watch where you're going? Bloody *idiot!*'

'Terribly sorry about that,' a cultured voice wafted through the Porsche's open window. 'Completely my fault. In too much of a hurry, I'm afraid.'

The voice's readiness to take full blame was totally disarming and Jon's anger evaporated at once.

'Uh…That's OK. These things happen.' He looked down into a tanned, media-handsome face, a row of perfect teeth grinning up at him. The man was about forty, he guessed. Probably over six feet tall, wide-shoulders seeming to fill the car's cockpit, muscular legs jutting under the steering wheel.

'You're not hurt?' the driver enquired, swinging open the door, stepping out. He wore a beige Armani suit, a hint of Rolex protruding from under a gold cuff-linked shirt cuff.

Jon immediately sensed power. A man accustomed to being in charge; one who gave orders and got obeyed.

'No, no. I'm fine, thanks. No problem,' Jon hastened to reassure him, a note of deference already in his voice.

'Good. No documentation on me, I'm afraid. Don't even know the name of my insurance company. Leave all that to my PA.' The man leant diffidently against his car. 'I suggest we swap cards for now and we can sort this lot out when we have more time.'

Jon took the proffered card. He fished his own from his top pocket and begrudgingly handed it over feeling, as the sinned against, he had somehow surrendered rightful control of the situation.

Brancusi Art Investments. Offices in London, Rome and Zurich. Marco Brancusi, CEO… he read.

'I like this,' Marco Brancusi said, examining Jon's elaborate, designer card. 'Did you do it?'

'Uh, yeah. I'm in advertising and design. It's what I do.' Pleasure at being praised stroked Jon's feelings.

'That's very interesting. You know I may well be able to put some business your way. Assuming you're looking for work?'

'We have some capacity, yes,' Jon said, slipping into bullshit mode.

The man seemed to weigh something up, then added, 'Call me at my London office tomorrow, around lunchtime, and we'll arrange a meet – and get this mess sorted as well.' He looked at his watch. 'I really must dash.' He eased himself back into his car and called out before zipping up the window, 'Tomorrow. Don't forget. Ciao.'

With a rasping chord, the Porsche slalomed towards the exit. As it turned onto the main road, the car park lights went out.

Jon stood in the dark, clutching Marco Brancusi's card, staring after the receding tail-lights, listening to the engine's deepening rise and fall as it shifted up through the gears. When the sound was lost in the rush hour wash, he turned and walked slowly back to his car, shaking his head.

– How the fuck did I get manipulated into that...?

'Jon! Jon! Over here.' Across the crowded bar, Jon saw his friend Tony and made his way over. 'What you having, mate?'

'Pint of Benskins.'

'You alright? You look pissed off.'

'Yeah. Had a shit day. A client slashed his budget so we'll end up making sod all, and then some wanker drove into the back of my car. Dunno why I bother, sometimes. I'll come with you. Need a chaser or two, as well. Going to get rat-arsed tonight.'

'Did I tell you what happened to me?' Tony asked as they dodged their way to the bar. Jon shook his head.

'My motor failed its MOT, didn't it, 'cos some poxy side-flasher wasn't working. So, I mended it, but the day I was taking it back for the retest, I checked it and the fucker wasn't working again. So I took it to bits and cleaned it all up, and then, would you believe it, *none* of the indicators was working.'

'You'd blown a fuse, mate.'

'Yeah, that's what I thought. So, I checked it out and that was all okay, so I assumed it was a relay. Checked the handbook, pulled it out, took it over to the Lancia dealer, but they didn't have one, so they ordered it for me.'

'Bloody typical.'

'Yeah. Anyway, next day I collected it, put it back and the fuckers *still* didn't work. So I took the steering column to bits to check out the switch. Couldn't find anything. Then I took the fuse box to bits thinking some wires had shorted out. Nuffink!'

'Christ. Hope you put it all back together.'

'No problem, mate. But then it began to dawn on me... the fucking *handbook* was all wrong. The fuse marked sidelights had blown, but it was really the bloody indicators. Replaced that and everything was working again. So I had to pay for a retest and a relay I didn't fuckin' need, plus two trips to Chesham and back. Bloody cost me a fortune for bugger-all.'

Tony's self-deprecation and the need to release the day's tension, made Jon laugh more than the story. He'd known Tony for years. They'd grown up together a few doors apart, had gone to the same schools and been inseparable. Even after Jon went away to Art College, they'd remained friends, knocking around during vacations. By chance, they now both lived in the same town and continued their friendship regardless of the blue-collar/white-collar clash. Tony was 'one of the lads' – uncultured, uncouth, but warm-hearted, funny and sanguine by nature. He remained a bachelor, still full of life, stories and fun, and he always made Jon feel better.

'You going to sue Lancia for all that wasted time, then?' Jon asked.

'What's the fuckin' use? The car's fifteen years old. There's probably no one left there who even remembers the old Beta, let alone accepts responsibility for a dodgy handbook. Nah. Just fergetabouttit. Life's too short to get yer knickers in a twist. C'mon. Let's get 'em in. Then, me old china, we got some serious decisions to make. Do we go next door and watch the match, or do we chat up those two babes who've just walked in...?'

The question was encrypted in laddish code and merely required one of several variants of the correct answer.

'No contest, mate. We'll watch the footy...'

HONEY POT

Apprehension fluttered each time Jon caught sight of the business card taped to his monitor's frame. Preoccupied, hung over from the night before and jittery, he reached across his desk for a folder and toppled his half-empty tea mug. He leapt up cursing, pushing back his chair, tissue-dabbing at the creeping amber pool.

'Clumsy prat!' he admonished himself.

– Why is all this making me so nervous? It's only some rich geezer who reversed into my car…

He made the timorous call around lunchtime and, to his surprise, was put straight through to Marco.

'Jon, dear boy. How are you? I hope you got back safely?'

'Yeah, thanks. No problem…'

'Good, good. Now, as soon as you have the repair bill, email it to my office and my PA will post a cheque by return. And please – add fifty per cent for your troubles.'

'But…'

'I insist: no arguments.'

Jon's jitters vanished, sucked into a vortex of bonhomie.

'Now, I believe you said you're looking for work?'

'Well yes, we certainly could do with…'

'In that case, why don't you come to my home this weekend? Stay over Saturday night. We're throwing a bit of a party and there are people I'd like you to meet.'

'This weekend? Sorry, I can't…'

'Short notice, I know. Do you play golf, by the way?'

'Yes, but I'm not very…'

'You do? Excellent! Bring your clubs – we're having a tourney on Sunday morning, at my club.'

'I honestly don't think I can.'

'Come on. Do you good to get away.'

Jon sighed, feeling worn down. 'I'll see what I can do and let you know.'

'Saturday, then. About four. My PA will email over a map.'

He reluctantly half-accepted the invitation, resenting again the sense of being manhandled. Having replaced the receiver, he realised he felt both worried and excited.

– We're getting dragged into something here… the inner dialogue began.

– Well I don't give a shit – something good's happening, something I've been wanting, expecting, for a long time…

– Oh, yeah? Then why do I feel we're going to regret this…?

– Come on. What's the problem…?

Thus he prevaricated all week despite the growing certainty that nothing would prevent him from going.

Yvonne had become heavier, almost statuesque, since they met sixteen years ago; but her face still radiated the almost unbelievable sculptural perfection of an African beauty, with its sensual, large mouth, wide nose and huge eyes, the whites of which, when she was happy, seemed to grow even larger in the setting of her smooth, indigo-brown skin. She was tall, nearly six feet, and still moved with the loose-limbed lucidity of her youth.

Jon asked her once, while they were courting, lying side by side in bed, 'Don't you ever want to know where you came from in Africa? What tribe you belonged to? Stuff like that?'

Yvonne snorted with laughter. 'Tribe?'

'You know what I mean. Your roots, stuff like that.'

'Christ, no. It's all meaningless to me. I'm third generation British, that's my culture and that's where my heart is. Anyway, I'm Afro-Caribbean, not African.'

'Does that make a difference?'

'Course it does. The Caribbean's where my ancestors lived. Where my great grandparents came from, to England. There were no records kept when slaves were brought over in the eighteenth century, anyway, so it'd be pointless. Apart from that, Africa looks like a hell hole to me... no decent shops, no hairdressers, no rule of law, too many insects and diseases – and too bloody hot, for starters.'

'Well I'd love to know my origins. Especially if I was as racially pure as you.'

Yvonne hooted in disbelief. 'I don't believe you said that.'

'No. Seriously. I feel like I've no roots, no definable origin at all. Like I'm the result of centuries of European inbreeding, a mish-mash. I've got German, French, Irish, Anglo-Saxon blood. A right bloody mongrel.'

'Watch it. You're beginning to sound like a neo-Nazi.'

'Those idiots...'

'Nasty idiots, though. That's something that still pisses me off, you know. Blokes shouting "Get back to your own country" if you make a mistake driving. Then being ignored in shops, sometimes, or kept waiting for hours in restaurants. Stuff like that. Bloody institutional racism. It's everywhere still.'

'Really? I had no idea. You sure?'

'Next time you take me to a restaurant, you watch. The waiters will ignore us for as long as they can; and when they take my order, there's a faint sneer in the voice.'

'You're not being paranoid here?'

'No. But I am over the fact you haven't taken me out for some weeks.

There's more to a relationship than hours of passionate sex...'

'Is there?' Jon laughs, leaning over, kissing Yvonne's breasts one after the other.

'Mmm. Maybe not...'

'What you up to today?' Jon asked Yvonne over breakfast, putting his paper aside.

Yvonne was four months pregnant. She stood and arched her back. 'Christ, this one feels like it's going to be huge. Shopping. Then I'm going to put my feet up for the rest of the day while you take the girls bowling.'

'Er, I gotta problem taking the kids out.'

'Jon! What now? You promised...'

'Yeah, I know. I forgot to tell you, but you know that rich guy who reversed into my car...?' She nodded, eyes at the ceiling. 'Well, he's invited me over to his place for the weekend. He wants to introduce me to a bunch of people who apparently need a lot of work doing. Can't miss out. Not with the state of the business. Have to go. Sorry.'

'Well you'll have to tell the girls. I'm not doing your dirty work for you.'

'I'll make it up to them.'

'That's what you always say.'

Jon grunted. 'You don't happen to know where my evening suit is, do you, by the way?'

'At the cleaners, actually. Took it in earlier in the week.'

'Shit! Will it be ready today?'

'Yes. Probably.'

'You wouldn't collect it for me, would you?'

'Jon!' Yvonne warned.

'Okay, okay! I'll do it myself.'

A sign told him he was entering the village of Steeple Claydon.

'Through the village and take the second right. We're two hundred metres on the left – house called The Manor,' Marco's map instructed from the passenger seat.

Jon made the turn and drove parallel to a tall, ivy-covered red-brick wall atop a grass bank. He saw *The Manor* carved on ornamental pillars, steered through the opened, decorative metal gates and followed a sweeping curve, tyres scrunching on gravel. He full-locked around a central, low-walled flower bed brimming with late-flowering plants and parked.

At the bed's centre, a stone fountain spouted water that rose and fell in the golden, late afternoon sun, giving the illusion of honey gurgling from a subterranean well.

The house was large, Georgian, built foursquare from creamy sandstone and lovingly maintained. The precise flower beds, striped lawns, manicured trees and topiary incorporated into the vista stretching before him displayed that extreme order only achievable with a team of gardeners. He felt envious and impressed by turns as he struggled, bags in hand, between the items of car exotica haphazardly lining the drive – Aston Martins, Bentleys, Ferraris.

– *Jesus! There must be a few million quids' worth parked here...*

Stepping up to the entrance portico, he yanked on a wrought iron bell-pull. He heard jangling somewhere in the depths of the house. A bracketed video camera dipped and stared condescendingly. He grinned up at it, feeling foolish, as though caught trespassing.

In the kitchen, as he collected bottles from a wine chiller, Marco looked across to a colour monitor. 'Good. He's arrived. Duty calls, Lucia.'

His daughter cocked her head, appraising Jon on screen while continuing to crush ice in a bowl. 'He's rather dishy,' she commented, surprised.

'Glad you think so. Go let him in, then. Bring him through to the conservatory. And, Lucia... Be nice.'

A slender, black haired, olive skinned young woman opened the door to Jon.

'Hi,' he postured, 'Jon Lucke – to see Marco Brancusi?'

'Sure. Come in, then.' Her voice was as mellifluous as she appeared diffident. She turned and swayed into the hallway stopping to indicate where he should leave his bags.

'Put your stuff there. Someone'll take it to your room later.' She watched amused as he stood gawping, taking in his surroundings – antique furniture, objets d'art and Persian rugs. On the walls, Renaissance pieces hung alongside Impressionist and contemporary British works.

'This way.'

Jon dropped the bags and followed, eyes darting back and forth from the girl's swaying hips to the paintings. Passing one of Hockney's celebrated Royal College pictures, he felt a jag of jealousy remembering he hadn't been able to afford even a small Hockney etching he'd seen in a local gallery recently.

'These are all originals, I take it?' he asked of her back.

'They are,' she threw back over her shoulder. 'One of Dad's businesses. He loves collecting things.' She stopped, turned and added archly, 'And people. Are you one of Daddy's collectables?' She held him in a searching gaze until he was forced to look away.

'Wow, That's neat.' He walked over to a table on which an architect's model lay – a Frank Lloyd Wright-style design mitred into the side of a green-tinted, papier maché hill. 'What's it for?'

'Daddy's house he's having built near Sienna.'

Jon tore himself away hurrying to catch up. A signed photograph in a silver frame standing on an eighteenth century escritoire caught his eye.

'She looks familiar,' he ventured.

'That's my step-Mum in her heyday. She was quite famous once, in a cultish kind of way. Starred in some minor classic movies. Sonia Harvey. No? Well, she doesn't work now. Far too busy with her groups and clubs. And she doesn't really need the money any more.'

'No, I don't suppose she does.'

He followed her through a spacious, stuccoed drawing room. Tangerine light from the setting sun gushed in, parallelogramming the carpets, bouncing reflections off glass panelled cabinets and the black-lacquered surfaces of a Steinway. The complementary blue of a swimming pool, seen through the tall, mullioned windows, jived on Jon's retina.

They entered the conservatory. Some twenty people stood grouped among the hothouse plants or lounged on ornate, cushion-covered bamboo sofas. They chattered brightly, spraying laughter, ice clinking in glasses.

'Ah! Jon, dear boy, welcome, welcome. So glad you could make it.' Marco strode towards him holding out his hand. 'Good journey? Come, let me introduce you.' With his arm around Jon's shoulder, he steered him to the centre of the room. 'Andrew, someone I'd like you to meet.'

Jon was astonished to be shaking hands with a media-famous billionaire. A bearded, longhaired Australian of Jon's age, who owned High Street chains, publishing groups and a Premier League football club.

'Hi,' Andrew greeted, smiling warmly, enthusiastically pumping Jon's hand, flashing perfect teeth. After a round of pleasantries he asked, 'What line are you in, Jon?'

'Design and advertising. Run a small group in the sticks.'

'Hey! You don't happen to be looking for new clients, do you?'

Jon nodded affirmation, adding with a laugh, 'Yeah. Always.'

'Give me a bell sometime. We'll have a chat. The people I use in Town are getting a bit above themselves? Like I'm paying for their Ferraris and getting juniors doing my stuff nowadays?' He spoke with a flat, Australian accent, each end-of-sentence syllable lifted as though asking a question. 'I like it better when the guys working for me are the ones that roll up their sleeves?'

'Know exactly what you mean,' Jon concurred, acting the urbane equal.

'Andrew, mate. How's it hanging?'

Jon turned to see his all-time blues hero standing behind them, a guitarist with a meteoric, twenty-year career in popular music – and its pursuant wealth – to his credit.

'Rick! I'm good. Long time no see? Do you know Jon, by the way?'

'No, good to meet ya, man.' They shook hands and Jon and Rick were soon deep in conversation, swapping opinions of the blues greats. They had just reached the point where Jon was being invited to design Rick's next album cover, when an American accented voice interrupted.

'Ricardo, honey, introduce me to this *hunk*.'

'Yo, Kim, baby. Meet Jon Lucke, new kid on the block.'

The woman's aura of celebrity confounded Jon. He had seen her face, and virtually every inch of her body, magnified on cinema screens and posters; read in the press about her marriages and dalliances, her likes and dislikes and felt he already knew her intimately – yet she was a stranger – shorter than he'd imagined. Despite the preternatural sensation, he regained enough composure to offer, 'I really enjoyed your last film, Kim.'

'Aw! He's sweet, too,' she laughed, placing a hand on his arm.

After several hours of introductions and whirlwind conversations, Jon was again feeling both exultant and nervous. He had met a dozen blue-chip company directors, a handful of media and sports celebrities and an oil Sheikh. The businessmen and women had enthusiastically divulged the telephone numbers of various marketing executives in their employ and exhorted him to make contact and to ensure their names were mentioned. From bitter experience he knew if he'd tried to cold-call these people they'd've been so well defended, he wouldn't have got past reception.

– They'd blow me out on the spot. Just another groupie begging for scraps. Yet here, in their natural habitat, I'm accepted as one of their own, one of the pack, no questions asked. Why? Because they assume I'm Marco's buddy? The old pals act? Is this the way it really works…?

An innate distrust made him feel that at any moment he'd be rumbled as an impostor and asked to leave. Another self began to revel in the acceptance, convincing himself that he had always been a high-flier really. It had just taken a while – a long detour – to reach home.

'Dinner at eight,' Marco told him, closing the door after having amicably escorted Jon to his room.

Jon hurled himself onto the high, brass bed and bounced up and down, feeling extremely pleased with himself. Then he lay on his back, hands behind head savouring the five-star surroundings, noting his bags were already on a trestle at the end of his bed.

'Per-lush. That's the word. Yeah, I could get very, *very* used to this.' He noticed a familiar picture on the wall, got off the bed and went over to it.

'Bugger me! An original, signed Matisse.' He shook his head in disbelief, mentally comparing the almost unusable guest room at home, stuffed full with tatty old furniture, unwanted books and broken toys.

'How the other half live, eh? Or top one percent, more like.'

After showering and shaving in an exotically perfumed and marbled en suite bathroom, he began to dress for dinner. He hadn't worn his dinner suit for some time and was disconcerted to find he could only zip up and top-button the trousers if he sucked his stomach in. The jacket felt tight across his shoulders and the arms seemed a centimetre too short so he had to keep hitching up his shirtsleeves. The suit smelled faintly of dry cleaning fluid, too, and his ready-made bow tie wouldn't sit straight over the points of his shirt collar. He appraised his reflection in a full-length mirror.

– *Look ridiculous in this. Like an illegal immigrant moonlighting as a waiter...*

Staring back at him in a switch over copy of the room was a stranger verging on middle age. A man with a once athletic figure now covered in a layer of fat, double wrapped around the stomach.

– *What a state. To think I once had a trial for Arsenal...* The image took a fold of shirt-covered flesh between its fingers.

'If you can pinch more than an inch...' an old TV jingle played – written for a fat-free, chemical spread, he remembered. He and his reflection were pinching two. He felt irritated and, for the tenth time in a week, vowed he would start visiting the gym again.

Craning closer to the mirror, he peered at the face angling towards him, framed by lengthy, combed back hair; a face that tanned well in the summer, but turned sallow in winter. He didn't recognise it. The physiognomy was disjointed, somehow out of kilter in this affluent setting. A stranger's hazel eyes, set above an aquiline nose, large mouth and cleft chin, stared back quizzically. He turned his head from side to side, slowly acknowledging his re-emerging twin.

'People used to say we looked like a young Kirk Douglas,' he told it.

– More like an old Michael Douglas, nowadays… his doppelganger reflected back.

'Oh well…' They shrugged in unison.

– Just have to make do with what we've got, eh…?

'No choice, I suppose.' His reflection nodded agreement. 'We still get glances from girls in the street, though. And Kim said I was a hunk!'

– Not members of the old and ugly club just yet, then…?

'Nah. Still got what it takes, mate.'

They smiled knowingly at one another, re-brushed their hair and stepped back posing, hands in pockets, hips jutting. His double returned the appreciative, American style salute and went its separate way as Jon headed jauntily downstairs for dinner humming, 'Hey, good lookin', whatcha got cookin'?' under his breath.

The dining room was large and opulent, obviously conceived and crafted by professional interior designers. Three of the walls were rust-coloured, one featuring a Francis Bacon triptych housed in chunky gilt frames and displayed under spot-lights. The fourth was entirely covered by a huge, ancient looking tapestry depicting hunting scenes. A delicate glass chandelier of contemporary design floated at the apex of the coved ceiling. At the centre of the room, an ovoid, eight-legged, mahogany dining table hunkered, laid for twenty-four people. It was being fussed over by two serving maids dressed in black and white uniforms incorporating unusually short skirts. They toured the table, adjusting plates and glasses, tweaking silverware and lighting strategically placed candles.

– This is a first, being served by maidservants in a fucking palace… Jon chuckled to himself.

– And I can't even guess how much that Bacon would set you back. God, I love it! Feel so at home. Can't wait to tell the others about this…

Guests stood murmuring in small groups until the moment Mrs. Brancusi arrived – a focussed 'Ahh!' from around the room heralding her entry. Jon gulped her in. Accustomed to choosing models from catalogues, he recognised the look photographers kill for – the crimson, sen-

sual mouth; the blue, main beam eyes precisely placed in a symmetrical-
ly oval, perfectly tanned face. Late thirties, early forties he guessed. She
was tall, slim and honey-blonde; sexily curvaceous in a black, halter-
necked designer creation that was hardly there.

'Good evening, everyone,' she projected with a faint, mid-Atlantic
accent as beguiling as the minutest dab of expensive perfume. She made
eye contact around the room, smiling wide. 'I'm so *glad* you could all
come. Ah, Prince Rasjid, how are you?' She oozed across the room and
clasped the oil Sheikh's hand in both hers. 'And how are your *lovely*
wives?'

'Not as beautiful as you, regretfully' he flirted, kissing her hand, staring
at her cleavage.

She smiled her acknowledgement, dropped his hand and smoothly
engaged another guest.

'Kim, darling. You look *won*derful. Hollywood must be *so* good for you.'
She mimed kissing Kim on both cheeks. 'Mwaa, mwaa.'

'And you must be Jon Lucke. How do you do?'

He took the proffered hand. It felt pampered and he sensed a pulsing
vibrancy beneath the skin. 'Nice to meet you, Mrs. Brancusi.'

'Sonia, please,' she insisted, staring into his eyes, holding on to his
hand. 'Marco tells me you're a designer.' He nodded, rooted, inarticulate.
'You must come and show me your work. I adore designers and what they
do. So clever.'

– Is she offering...? She wouldn't. Would she...?

'Thank you,' he stammered. 'That'd be great. I'll...'

Sonia smiled and slipped seamlessly away to greet another guest. He
watched her glide from one acquaintance to another, ever ready with per-
tinent, individualised bon mots – the perfect hostess.

'Please sit. Dinner is served,' she announced, nodding to the sentinel
maids.

Jon was seated next to Rick's girlfriend with Lucia on his left.
Stimulated by the presence of two young women, he launched into an
overconfident, bantering conversation – a technique he'd developed as a
youth to disguise shyness and as an escape route from debilitating rejection.

As the dinner progressed, side conversations developed and he was
irresistibly drawn to Lucia. In addition to stunningly beautiful, he found
her amusing and interesting as shared tastes emerged despite their fifteen
years' age difference. In the candlelight, through his rosy wine-haze, Jon

had the illusion of her growing sexier and more desirable. She was wearing a sparkly, blue evening gown with a low cut front. His eyes became restless birds flitting from her face to her breasts. Through his absorption he heard her telling him she was studying fashion at The Royal College of Art.

'Elite, or what?' he semi-slurred, half in admiration, half as put down.

'Daddy's contacts helped,' she replied knowingly, 'but I wouldn't have got in if I hadn't been incredibly talented as well. I'm gonna be a star one day, you watch. And while we're on the subject of design, do you use computers in your studio?'

He stared at her, entranced.

– *Beautiful eyes. Delicious mouth. Perfect...*

'Uh, yeah. Of course. We've got a network of Macs. Why? Do you use them at college?'

'We're supposed to, but they're always busy, so I conned Daddy into getting me one at home. It's up in my room.'

'Useful to have a Daddy like that.' Again, a mixture of envy and admiration.

'Sure is. I'm working on a project at the moment and I'm a bit stuck. Got all these shots of models wearing my designs, but there's loads of tat in the background. I've uploaded all my photos, but I can't understand the bloody instruction manuals from then on. Can you tell me how to do things like cut-outs?' She leant animatedly towards him and their knees touched. He focused on the scalding contact point, aware she didn't pull away and a delicious current flowed to his groin.

– *God! I haven't felt like this since I was sixteen...*

'Yeah, they're pretty simple. I can show you if you like.'

'Tonight? After dinner?'

'No problem. If you've got PhotoShop and Quark I can show you the easy route.'

– *God! I want her. Gotta get her on her own. Ask her out...*

– *I don't want to go anywhere with you...* sneered a voice from the past. A minuscule frown and an inner flinching as the castrating memory reverberated in his head. He ducked out of the mental ambush and urgently re-entered their intimate cocoon, talking, explaining, his confidence alcohol fuelled.

Lucia stared at him, not listening to his technical talk.

– *He's okay. A bit yobby, but fun. I like him. P'raps this won't be so bad after all...*

Marco caught Sonia's eye and nodded almost imperceptibly. She responded with a trace of smile then unfolded from her chair to suggest they all took coffee in the games room. The guests rose from the table, full of food, wine and good humour and ambled out, arms round shoulders or waists, following their hosts. Lucia linked her arm in Jon's and pulled him away from the mainstream.

'Come and help me, please. I've got to get this project finished this weekend and I'm absolutely stuck.'

Jon emotionally puppy dogged at her side as they made their way upstairs. They passed room after room before finally reaching a door from which a small ceramic plaque announced, 'Lucia's Room. Keep Out'. It incorporated a Thelwell drawing of a horse and rider – a studied kitsch left over from pre-teen years and pony clubs. She led him in. The room was high, wide and chintzy; floral patterned cushions were scattered and heaped everywhere. It struck him as odd.

– *Strange. I expected ultra modern. Designer furniture...*

He breathed in; it smelt sweetly of perfume, female things, softly erotic. A latest Macintosh computer hummed on a desk; a monitor, scanner and printer stood by, tiny green eyes staring.

They sat side by side and he called up QuarkXpress and opened a new document at speed, showing off, feeling like a hero under her gaze.

'Where are your photos?'

'There, on the screen.' She pointed to a haphazard group of tiny rectangles.

'Desktop,' he corrected. 'TIFFs – well done. In future, give them file names. You know – Thesis one, two, three and so on; and keep them together in a folder,' he advised. 'Makes life easier. Right, call up a picture box. What sort of size do you want?' She told him. 'Okay. Now import a picture.'

An image of a whippet-thin girl swathed in scrap metal and diaphanous material flowered on screen.

– *Christ! Looks like a last minute fancy dress...*

Jon sharply reined in his habitual sarcasm, not wanting to blemish the nice-guy image he was projecting – the basis of a hazy seduction strategy.

'Okay; now use the magic keys, Alt, Option and Caps and the right pointing arrow key and enlarge the image as big as it will go. There. Now you see this tool here? Click on that; now click your cursor all around the edge like this, scrolling down as you go. You see? I hope you're taking notes. The more points you make, the more accurate the cut out. When you've got all the way round, click on the very first point you made and there's the shape you need. Now delete the old box, call up the piccy again and re-scale to fit...'

Jon did the work expertly and fast... 'There... Simple! There are more complex ways of doing it, but...'

'Oh, Jon, that's so neat,' she squealed in delight, interrupting. 'Thanks so much, that's brilliant!'

She leant towards him placing a hot hand on his thigh, inches from his groin, and kissed his cheek. He inhaled her body heat, sweat-tinged and perfumed, and his penis pulsed alive. He slid an arm around her back and pulled her closer, his fingers settling delicately on the smooth skin between her shoulder blades. She acquiesced and their mouths locked, tongues wetly wrestling, exploring the novelty of unfamiliar textures and tastes. With his free hand he gently cupped a breast – a deliciously warm weight hanging loose inside the cool material of her dress. As he sank deeper into his own sweet, elastic throb, she pulled away.

'No. Not here, Jon. Not now. Call me. I'll give you my number in Town. We'd better go down, they'll be wondering where we are.' She eased herself from his embrace and stood, her hands sliding suggestively over her gown as she smoothed it down.

Jon shook his head and breathed deeply, struggling to regain composure. He got slowly to his feet, awkwardly tumescent, aware one step would bring him to orgasm, tight trouser fabric rubbing.

'God! You really are beautiful,' he heard himself anguish as he deflated.

Lucia laughed, part flattered, mostly embarrassed by his evident gaucherie. 'C'mon. Let's go play snooker. I'm really good and I want to beat you.'

Jon followed her out, head swimming, not sure if he should be happy or depressed.

For the rest of the evening, down in the games room, he couldn't stop gazing at her, drinking her in, aware that she lapped up the attention, preening and performing for his benefit.

Reminders of his pregnant wife nipped his conscience. He deftly mind-swerved around them, thereby slowly and inexorably edging himself closer to that invisible fidelity/infidelity border, despite knowing once crossed, there could be no return.

Towards one o'clock Lucia bounced over to where her father sat chatting and laughing with a group of cronies. She bent and kissed him on the proffered cheek, walked to the door and turned to announce playfully, 'Night, everyone. See you tomorrow at dinner after your boring old golf.' As she exited, she turned again, seeking Jon's eyes, locking on, conspiratorially kissing the air once in his direction.

Over the next hour the guests slipped off to bed. Jon sat nursing a glass of twelve-year-old malt, keeping score while the last two finished their game. Lucia had been good at snooker. She'd beaten him easily and had stayed on the table for some time before being deposed by one of the guests, a pro-footballer with years of serious play under his belt.

Jon stared into his whisky glass, an emotional soup simmering in his feelings.

– She's perfect, wonderful, amazing – and I think I'm in lerve. *Well – in lust...*

The realisation both delighted and frightened him. Again, guilt cut into his self-absorption, reminding him he should have called Yvonne.

– Oh-oh! Forgot. I'm in trouble – with a cap T...

– Too late now. Do it in the morning...

– God, what would she say if she caught me snogging a nineteen year old girl...?

– Slice my balls off in my sleep, probably...

– After she'd forgiven me...

Closing his eyes, he surrendered to his teeming feelings and the engulfing leather armchair, lazily stretching his legs, very drunk.

'I'm pregnant.'

The background babble in the crowded café faded as Jon staggered under the weight of Yvonne's announcement.

'You sure?'

– Fuck. No...!

'I've been to the doctor's, Jon. The baby's due on the twentieth of July – no mistake.'

He leant forward, eyes shut, elbows finding the café table, and nervously rubbed his sweating forehead.

– Fuck. No! Fuck. No! Fuck. No...!

'What are we going to do, Jon?'

'Christ! I don't know, do I?' he snapped, opening his eyes, sitting upright again. 'Get an abor...'

'Don't even think about it, Jon.'

'Yeah. Sorry. You're right.'

– Commit fucking suicide, then? Run away…?

'I don't suppose we could get married?' she said, looking away, hands white knuckling in her lap, mouth tight, as though expecting a blow.

Teetering, inwardly struggling for balance, he wrestled with the problem.

– What am I gonna do? What am I gonna do…?

Then, with a sickening relief, a desperate solution.

– Go with it for now. Get married. Sort it later…

'Yeah,' he sighed, 'I guess we could…'

– What the fuck are you saying, man…?

Yvonne burst into tears. 'Oh, Jon, thank you, thank you. I love you so much.'

'I love you, too.'

– Oh, shit! What have you gone and done…?

Jon opened his eyes and stared ahead, focussing on nothing.

– Jesus! What a weak prick I was. Talk about naïve. Never occurred to me that real-live people might be involved. Like Yvonne and her parents and then our kids. They exert a sort of moral pressure, somehow, and it turns out you can't just walk after all…

He looks down on his tawny-tinted, miniaturised reflection at the bottom of his glass.

– Guess I hoped it would all sort of vanish one day. Stupid fuck…

Hope was Jon's enemy posing as friend. He allowed his life to be filled with it. Thus he was forever hopeful – always expecting what he desired or desiring what he expected. As a consequence, all aspects of his existence seemed temporary, in transit, as though forever waiting at a bus stop.

One day, he fantasised, an express coach would pull in and he'd climb aboard and be taken to his real life destination. Perhaps he'd discover he was, after all, a ground-breaking designer and would be headhunted and offered top design jobs in the States. Or maybe he'd win the lottery and could separate amicably from his family, leaving them wealthily cared for while he toured the world – an arrangement his wife would accept with alacrity nowadays, he was certain.

After, he'd buy the best teachers and become a world famous guitarist; or a Grand Prix driver; or a sought after artist living unfettered on the Pacific coast, painting great works, making love to long-haired, golden-skinned hippie girls on moon-silvered nights. His real-life-avoidance fantasies invariably ended with him meeting his dream woman.

– *Problem is, reality's too unpredictable for me. Too hard to understand; too difficult to control; too – well,* real, *I suppose…*

An alcoholically powered optimism welled up and he chuckled.

– *Yet here I am, somehow accepted into this rich guy's world. Perhaps something'll rub off on me this time, and I'll learn to be like them. Always in control, never doing anything I don't wanna do; never taking no for an answer…*

– *Not forgetting the promise of Lucia as well…*

– *Yeah. Things are definitely looking up, old mate…*

Finishing his whisky in one gulp, he stood on unsteady legs and mumbled goodnight to the remaining guests. He meandered off to his bed feeling drunkenly pleased with himself, already living in an almost graspable, ecstatic future.

STALKING

Early Sunday morning. Marco knocked and wandered into Lucia's room.

'You and Jon seemed to hit it off last night.'

'Yeah, he's okay,' she replied, reservation in her voice.

'Well, I want you to be especially nice to him. Get involved.'

'I'm not sure when I'll see him again. I've got to go back to London this afternoon.'

'Write him a note. Invite him to visit you in Town. Use your initiative, girl.'

'He's married, though.'

'Since when has that been an obstacle? I assure you he won't be able to resist your charms, my sweet, no matter what.'

'Well… What do the others think?'

'That he's perfect – just what we're looking for. Do this for me, Lucia. Indulge your father.'

'Okay, Dad. I'll do what I can.'

Down in the dining room the houseguests were drifting in, ready for breakfast. They lifted domed lids from silver salvers, spooned food onto plates and ate while browsing the Sunday papers. Talk was desultory and only of handicaps and who was paired with whom for the day's golf. Jon discovered he was drawn to play his first round with Marco, whose handicap was down as two. Jon's was an average to poor twenty. He never

47

practised any more, never made time. He approached each rarer new round hoping he'd been visited by the magic golf fairy in his sleep and all the practice and all the games played in the past had subliminally melded and he'd awoken as a scratch player.

– *Nah. Never works like that. How you play golf is how you play life...*

A pulsating hangover coupled with tiredness was making him morose.

After a good humoured scramble, fitting clubs into car boots and debating who was to be driver and who passenger, the party finally embarked, driving in convoy – Marco leading the way. Jon was cheered to be in the passenger seat of the Porsche, admiring the retro-styled knobs and dials.

'Beautifully designed. You happy with it?'

'It's not perfect. It was a squeeze getting our clubs in the trunk,' Marco reminded him.

'True. What's the name of the course we're playing, by the way?'

'Glenbourne – about twenty miles from here.'

'Not heard of that one.'

'It's a rather select club. The complex was built by an aristocrat turned entrepreneur. His father died ten years back leaving him enormous debts and an estate that annually costs the GNP of a small African nation to run.'

'How could he afford it, then?'

'The Duke's a smart cookie. Wielded his title like a weapon; seduced American money with his aristo charm, sucked up to the right people, did favours – all the usual. Simply unearthed the ancestral skills that bludgeoned out the estate in the first place.'

'You know him?'

'Yes. He's a great pal. We go back years.'

They arrived, parked and walked up the steps of the imposing clubhouse, passing through a pseudo-classical facade complete with fluted columns. They pushed into reception. Contemporary style oil portraits of the Duke and his ex-model wife hung side by side, dominating the mahogany lined foyer. The route to the changing area was lined with notice boards on which was pinned a mass of standard golf club trivia; posters advertising lessons, equipment for sale and social events; handicap lists, competition and league tables. As they passed the main bar, Jon glimpsed wooden panels hanging round the walls, the names of past cup winners and captains inscribed in gold lettering. Marco's name was prominent. He was the current captain and had won the club championship for the last two years.

– *Oh, great!* Jon moaned to himself, following the others through into the heated and carpeted changing rooms.

– *This is going to be a massacre...*

Jon and Marco, the first pair off, walked to the start tee together. Jon had hired a club trolley, which was cumbersome and badly designed – a perfect foil for his technically superseded, second-hand clubs.

The course they were to play, one of four of varying difficulty and design, nestled in a corner of what was once hunting woodland, preparing to entertain a fine, windless day. An autumnal sun peeked through the early morning mist to sparkle off the dew-strung spiders' webs lacing the hedgerows. The fairway stretching green to blue-grey ahead was speckled with fallen leaves. The scene was hushed, the feathery background melody of birdsong punctuated by the cooing of pigeons. Above a clump of trees to his right, Jon spotted a kestrel circling in a wide arc, wings extended, deltoid tail feathers twitching as it made minute adjustments on rising currents of air.

Used to queuing on public courses, Jon was surprised to find they could begin immediately, that there were no doddering pensioners or beginners' groups ahead of them holding up play. He remarked on this to Marco.

'Good heavens, no. We have the course to ourselves for the day. Captain's privilege.'

Marco won the toss and elected to start. Jon observed him standing muscularly tall on the tee, executing seamless practice swings. He was becoming fascinated by Marco and found it difficult to keep his eyes off the man's big-cat grace. Marco's first drive looked effortless – a smooth shoulder turn, sinuously arcing arms and a spine-flexing follow through. Marco sent his ball soaring then bouncing two hundred and fifty yards, straight down the middle of the fairway.

'Nice shot,' Jon called. An instant envy augmented nervousness and his own shot was a tetchy slice. It zinged noisily through the air, veering crazily haywire. The ball dropped dead a hundred yards ahead, buried in the right hand rough.

'Takes time to warm up, eh?' Marco grinned.

Jon grunted, feeling embarrassed by his inept start. He thrust his driver crossly into his golf bag, grabbed the handle of his trolley and dragged it impatiently in the direction of his ball.

He chipped out of the rough only to reach the opposite side of the fairway, the ball coming to rest against the half-mown grass. Feeling angry with himself, a prickle of sweat cousing between his shoulder blades, he tensed up and topped his next shot. The fluorescent orange ball surface skimmed, leaving a curving, dotted-line trail across the dewy fairway. With his fourth, a good connection at last, he finally reached the edge of the green. Marco calmly sent a well struck five iron to within twenty feet of the flag and putted out in two. Jon three putted and lost the hole despite his two strokes handicap allowance.

The next eight holes were variations on the same theme and at the turn Marco was seven up with two drawn.

'You're a good player, Marco,' Jon offered as they crossed a service road to join the second half of the course, spikes clacking on the wooden bridge. 'I hope I'm giving you an interesting enough game.'

'I'm enjoying your company, Jon, and the fresh air and exercise. Life has taught me to always enjoy the moment. Usually makes things a lot more satisfying.'

'Yeah, I know what you mean.'

'Do you, Jon?'

'Oh, yeah. When I was a student I used to read a lot of stuff about Zen Buddhism. You know, being in the here and now, not wanting anything, accepting whatever happens. Somehow, though, real life didn't turn out quite that simple,' Jon added ruefully.

'And why is that?'

'Well, there's always something nagging in the background, isn't there? Usually creditors and not enough money in my case.' Marco nodded and Jon inferred understanding.

They arrived at the raised tenth tee. The fairway was narrow, bordered by ancient, tall oaks, golden liveried in the autumn sun. The warming air smelt sweet – an olfactory cocktail of decaying vegetation and recently mown grass. As they mounted the steps, Jon felt a breeze of nausea noticing on the bank a scattering of grey feathers and the bloodied stump of a wing – a recent fox kill.

'Why money problems, though, Jon? You have talent and I assume you're not lazy.' Marco bent to place his tee into the ground. 'My honour, I believe,' he added, following etiquette for the ninth time.

'I dunno.' Jon gazed down the fairway. 'Sometimes, we're doing really well and it feels like we're going to make it big-time. Then it all slips away and we're struggling again. It's a kind of self-fulfilling prophecy, I guess –

like fate. All I know is, no matter how hard I try, how high I go, I always seem get knocked back down, and end up merely surviving. Relatively no better off than my Old Man...' He tailed off, sensing he was over-responding, becoming aware of Marco politely waiting to drive.

He watched mesmerised as Marco addressed his teed up ball. A swish and click sent the ball gliding with a well judged, curving draw. It touched down and bounced through a gaggle of strutting pigeons pecking for worms. They flapped off squawking in vexed alarm. The ball came to rest a few feet from the rough, just out of sight behind the copse, perfectly placed for the next shot down the dogleg.

'Nice one,' Jon congratulated, envious again. Marco retrieved his tee with a supple, one-legged stoop-and-gather motion. Jon set up and took his one-wood shot, connecting well. The ball rocketed straight down the middle but dropped short, leaving him blind of the green, stockpiling trouble. They sheathed their clubs and began strolling down the fairway in silence, side by side.

After fifty yards, Marco suddenly asked, 'Tell me, Jon. Do you know exactly what you want out of life?'

'Easy. What everyone wants, I suppose. Success, money, happiness. I don't know, the lot – what you've got.'

'And how do you think I achieved them?'

'Talent, hard work and a ton of luck?'

'You're right, to a degree. But you're missing the most important ingredient.'

'Which is...?'

'A very special kind of quality is required. One I sense you have in spades.' They reached where Jon's ball lay half concealed in a rabbit scrape. 'You can move your ball. Preferred lie – local rules.'

Jon replaced the ball some inches behind the small, brown furrow pock-marking the mown and rabbit-clipped grass. He selected a four iron, planning to make up distance, hoping to bend the ball around the copse shielding the green from his sight.

– *Proper golfers go for the percentage shot, chipping the ball into a better position...* common sense cautioned. He ignored the advice and swung hard at the ball, using all his shoulder strength as though demolishing a brick wall. The ball sliced cruelly, spinning in an anti-clockwise arc, burying itself deep into the rough a hundred yards ahead, at forty five degrees to where they stood.

'Fuck it!' he shouted, smacking his club into the ground. He turned to face Marco.

'What are you talking about? What special quality? I'm a second division adman with a piss-poor business and a none-too-happy marriage.' He turned away, biting his lip, embarrassed by this over-revealing, frustration-fuelled outburst. He felt he was as off track as his ball.

'That's because you try too hard, Jon.'

'What do you mean – try too hard?'

'You use your energies inappropriately – as your last shot proves.'

'Can you explain that, please?' Jon was still irritated with himself, but intrigued, unaware of slipping hungrily into disciple mode.

'Tell me,' Marco continued as they sauntered towards Jon's errant ball, 'how do you think people achieve power?'

'I don't know – I guess they're born that way, aren't they?' Jon offered with a shrug.

'All humans are born with the potential to be a Christ or a Hitler no matter what their background. Very few have the necessary passion to fulfil that kind of destiny, though. Most people are a mush of conflicting drives and emotions manifesting as neuroses through to full-fledged psychoses. They'll betray friends they love for gain or self-survival: swear loyalty to marriage partners then cheat on them: bay for the blood of criminals while robbing the tax man blind. It's all paranoia and inferiority complexes with them. They're emotionally unstable, Jon. Corn in the wind, blown this way and that by whatever affects them at any given moment. Consequently, all their plans and endeavours come to naught because they misuse their energies and are, in turn, used by all kinds of disparate forces. I rather despise them for that.'

– Is he talking about me...? Jon wondered, his brow furrowing.

'Yeah, you could be right. But you are what you are, so what the hell can anyone do about it?'

'You can summon up your genie, Jon.' Marco gently touched Jon's arm as they walked – the salesman's old trick implying an intimate relationship.

'Genie? Don't follow, sorry.'

'An innate power, Jon. Remember the Genie of the Lamp story? It's an analogy for the energy we all have locked inside. One that will grant your wishes, help you realise your dreams and ambitions – if you would but let it out.' Marco pointed. 'There's your ball.'

It sat proud on the lank, damp grass two yards into the rough. Jon drew a five iron from his bag and placed its face behind the ball. He looked up searching for the red flap of flag in the hazy distance.

'Before you take your shot,' Marco interrupted, holding up a hand, 'a word of advice. The secret of golf is relaxed tension.'

At that moment, a wave of energy passed through Jon, sensed as a cooling breeze, instantly altering his inner atmosphere. He was certain it emanated from Marco but couldn't be sure – the sensation was too new. A palpable wave of relaxation rippled through his torso. His arms loosened and his shoulders sagged, correcting his posture and realigning his weight. The club felt alive to his fingers and palms lying delicately comfortable along its grip. He looked up and visualised the perfect trajectory the ball would take, experiencing a self-assured conviction of success. His shoulders arced slowly through ninety degrees. A second's pause and his body spring uncoiled, unleashing the raised club head's mass. As his weight transferred from right side to left, he sensed his own athletic grace for the first time in years; a perfect and total physical harmony.

With a satisfying swish and click the ball soared as if on an invisible wire, singing on the air. It landed and continued bouncing down the hill, then rolled and stopped a few yards beyond the fringe of the green.

'Nice shot, my friend. There's a real golfer in there just waiting to be let out.'

'How the hell did you do that?' Jon demanded, astonished.

'All your own work, dear boy,' Marco assured him, smiling benignly.

– I'm certain he did something, but what? How? This is too weird...

They recommenced their ambling walk towards the green, Jon full of speculative thought, unable to rejoice in the perfect golf shot he had just executed. His mind connected with college days and the spurious student quest for a spontaneous creativity.

– That painter, Paul Klée. He wrote something about the artist being a tree – the sap being the creative juice and the leaves and fruit the final work. P'raps that's what Marco's talking about. Something free of thinking, involuntary; a pure energy...

He shook off perplexity to ask, 'You were talking about genies and some innate power.'

'Ah, yes. The Genie of the Lamp. As I was saying, only a handful of people ever wake to reality, attempting not to be corn in the wind. And they usually divide into two groups. The so-called Saints, who strive to be rid of all bodily desires...'

'Hey! What do they want to do that for?' Jon laughed.

'To return to what they call heaven. This world is anathema to them.

53

They are not at home here, believing it to be a testing ground. To them, all forms of worldly enjoyment are traps, temptations, and succumbing to them is what they term sinful.'

'But that's crazy.'

'Perhaps. But they genuinely believe the weight of their so-called sins will bind them to this earth when they die, that they'll have to spend aeons in Purgatory. You know, I rather despise this group too, yet respect them as one does a sworn enemy. They are at least single minded and, paradoxically, passionately desirous for reunion with their God.'

'And the others...?'

'We wish to remain in this world for as long as possible, enjoying absolutely everything it has to offer. Power, influence, wealth, personal success – and all the trappings they bring – the best healthcare money can buy; rare and exquisite possessions; country estates; world travel; first class wine and food; abundant sex – you name it.'

'And that's your group?'

'Yes Jon. The Crème de la Crème.'

 – *He really is an arrogant sod...* A frisson of distaste and Jon could not resist the childish desire to pinch.

'So, if you don't want to be saintly, you must want to be evil, then?'

'Don't be so black and white, Jon. In my book, evil is the absence of passion and therefore life – just as coldness is the absence of heat, and darkness the absence of light. We live passionate lives Jon, rejoicing in this best of possible worlds. Religion, on the other hand, spreads the life-denying concept of enjoyment as the hallmark of evil – the sins of the flesh and all that tosh.'

'I see that, but...'

'And there's worse,' Marco cut Jon short. 'In order to control the masses, religion propagates the idea of original sin in one form or another. The notion that we're all excrement awaiting redemption. It's spurious religious morality that's life-denyingly evil, Jon. Ask yourself, are two noble stags locking horns over territory evil? Is a hunting lioness evil? Or a couple making love, attending to each other's needs, achieving mutual climax? Would you call that evil?'

They stopped and turned to face one another, golf momentarily forgotten. Standing staring into Marco's eyes, embraced by his conviction, Jon felt himself surrender like a lover.

'Well, I hadn't thought of it like that.' He looked away, finding the unacknowledged sexual charge in their deepening intimacy too disconcerting for eye contact.

'It's not possible to get to the top by championing modesty, chastity, so-called 'decency' and so on – unless you're the Pope,' Marco laughed. 'To make it big-time in this world you need gut-passion and single-mindedness, allowing nothing – and nobody, repeat, *nobody* – to stand in your way. And that's not evil, Jon. It's evolution. Survival of the fittest. It's natural for a man to want to be the greatest hunter or the most successful gatherer.'

'But everyone can't be top dog, can they? I mean...'

'Of course they can't. For every top dog, every fat cat, every winner, there's a million also-rans. You could say we need the failures in order to be successful. Pawns, Jon. Pieces to be used and sacrificed so we can achieve our personal goals of success, wealth and power.'

'Talk about self-centred...'

'But I thought personal success and wealth were exactly what you want most out of life, Jon?'

'Well yes, I do. But I wouldn't tread on others to get it...'

'Would you not?' Marco arched an eyebrow and stared at Jon.

Jon immediately knew he would – if only he knew how. Another self denied the possibility and he felt stymied. He needed time to absorb this, to think it through.

They reached where Marco's ball lay. Jon stood by, lost in thought, while Marco effortlessly lofted his ball to the heart of the green with a nine iron. It backspun to a stop three feet from the hole. They continued walking downhill towards the flag now flapping sporadically in a stiffening breeze.

'I still don't think it's right to use people like that – as pieces, as you call them. It all sounds kind of self-centred and manipulative to me.'

'But you have choices, Jon, as does every one. You can remain a piece – even become a Saint if you so wish. Or...' a pause, 'you can become one of life's winners.'

'How? How could I possibly...?'

'By locating your genie, Jon.'

'I'm going in circles here. How the Hell do I do that?'

'I'm a very lucky man,' Marco continued, pulling back like a veteran seducer. 'Like you, I came from very humble beginnings. Actually grew up in the slums of Naples. As a child, I struggled; I survived – and not always on the right side of the law. My only route out of poverty was to become a priest and I managed to enter a seminary as a novice, when I was about sixteen. I was eventually expelled, though. They decided, when all was said and done, that I had no vocation after all.

'Oh, but Jon, I did. A passionate calling! What they meant was I didn't have the correct orientation. However, what I studied there – theology, languages and Italian art – were extremely useful. A gallery that specialised in pre- and early Renaissance pieces took me on. That meant travel and hob-nobbing with the wealthy – the international jet set. And being, if you'll excuse my arrogance, very sought after for my looks and charm, as well as my knowledge, I became a kind of cultural gigolo.'

Jon imagined him as a young man and for a moment the conjured image had Simon's face. Jon flinched and quickly re-tuned to Marco's monologue.

'But something was missing. I couldn't find that resolve, that requisite single-mindedness.' Marco clenched his fist to accentuate the point. 'Couldn't find my genie, in other words. I was aware of these qualities in virtually all of the rich and powerful I met – some of whom had inherited their wealth or position, but mostly those who had carved it out for themselves. I knew, as a certainty, that it was there, but something would come into play denying its expression. In truth, I was weak; too angry, too sentimental; all over the place emotionally.'

They had arrived at the edge of the green. Their golf balls sat invitingly on the smooth, manicured grass.

'Your putt, I believe.'

Marco tended the flag while Jon, whose ball was furthest from the hole, putted first. He judged the distance well but his ball rimmed the cup and ran two feet past. Marco laid the flagpole to one side and walked to his ball. He carefully positioned his putter, looked up at the hole and down at his ball again.

'Then I discovered...' He gently swung the putter – an audible click and the ball rolled and dropped into the cup with a hollow rattle. 'Doh-Nai-Zen.'

'Good putt.' Marco's theatricality passed unobserved and Jon asked, as he hunkered down, immersed in trying to read the subtle dips and slopes of the green, 'So what's this Do-Ra-Me thing?' .

'Doh-Nai-Zen, Jon. The name of an association of people who have found the way to release their genies. In short, those who have discovered the secret of worldly success.'

Jon tapped in his putt with relief, stooped to retrieve his ball and, feeling better, asked, 'Come on then. What's this secret?'

'I'll tell you all about it some time soon. It's a long and involved story. Let's concentrate and get this game finished. I have a gut-feeling you're going to start winning some holes.'

Jon shrugged, acquiescing, his eagerness to learn more tempered by scepticism and disappointment. Deep down, he had been hoping Marco had been on the verge of offering him an over-paid job, or perhaps a lucrative business deal.

They walked across to the next tee.

Jon was surprised to win the next three holes and later the sixteenth, the rest being drawn, leaving Marco the winner by four – not the total massacre he had feared earlier.

In the afternoon, he was paired with the pro footballer and they played against Rick and the oil Sheikh, finally beating them in a Texas Scramble. At tea, back in the clubhouse he discovered he had won the par three sixteenth 'nearest the hole' competition. He revelled in the applause as he stepped up to receive his prize – a crystal plate. He had never, ever won and collected a prize before.

Although Marco's team had triumphed marginally, Jon experienced, as they returned to The Manor, a sense of having contributed well to the day. He lapped up the 'well dones' and back pats, feeling unusually pleased with himself.

'We'll eat at eight,' Marco announced, and the guests wandered off to their rooms to relax and change.

Jon luxuriated in a deep bath, a self-satisfied smile on his face.

– All I need now to make the day perfect is some time alone with Lucia...

When he came down early from his room he was disappointed; she wasn't there. He drifted into the games room and the conservatory searching for her, then sneaked up to her bedroom, knocked and peered into the empty room, inhaling the newly familiar, heady scent. He went back to the drawing room where the guests were gathering, but was unable to fully engage in the small talk and analysis of the day's golf. He was feeling jittery and over preoccupied with thoughts of Lucia. Just as the party were filing out for dinner, Sonia beckoned to him.

'Lucia had to go back to London early. She asked me to give you this.'

Jon thanked her and hung back to open the letter in private. Lucia's handwriting was calligraphic – embellished serifs on ascenders, flourishes on descenders – a designer's hand. He found it enchanting.

Dear Jon,

Sorry to miss you, I have to get back to Town early to get ready for tomorrow (big assessment day). I so enjoyed our time together. Thanks for the little demo (on the computer, idiot). Call me in the week at the number below. Don't forget.

Lotsa Love, Lucia xxx

The 'Don't forget' was underlined four times, each line interpreted by Jon as a promise of promiscuity – a love cipher. Thrilled by the letter's girlish contents, his shoulders pulled back and he felt debonair, a man of the world again, despite the childlike, anticipatory excitement bubbling inside. Throughout supper he was at ease, laughing and joking, a temporary equal.

After coffee, as the tired and now subdued guests were preparing to leave, Marco asked him to come to his study.

'I hope you made some good contacts, Jon.'

'Yes, I did. Thanks. And I was wondering about what you were saying on the course...'

Marco glanced up at the grandfather clock lazily tick-tocking in the corner of the room. 'It's late.' He picked up a book lying on his desk. 'Here, take this. Read it and let me know what you think.'

Jon took the proffered book. It looked and smelt old and he experienced a trace of resentment, as though he had been fobbed off. Glancing at the cover, the words *Doh-Nai-Zen*, gold-blocked centrally onto a crimson, Moroccan leather cover, jumped at him provoking a trill of apprehension.

'Call my PA tomorrow,' Marco's voice interrupted. 'I want you to look at a few marketing jobs for one of my subsidiaries.'

Satisfied with the crumb Marco had thrown him, he went through the motions of saying goodbye, thanking everyone for an enjoyable weekend, daring to plant a kiss on Sonia's cheek, before finally sinking into his car and setting off for home.

It was near midnight and there was little traffic on the roads. Driving automatically and chain smoking (not one of the guests had smoked throughout the weekend, he'd observed), he constantly re-savoured the weekend's highlights, perceiving a fresh nuance here and a new perspective there, feeling elated.

Around one-thirty, he drew up outside his home and sat contemplating in the dark. His house was a forlorn suburban semi in need of a lick of paint and some tender loving care. The demarcating privet hedge was overgrown and unkempt, its base a litter trap. Bicycles and an old tent, just discernible in the amber glow of a street lamp, cluttered the front lawn, which hadn't been mown since late summer. Planks of wood and a rusty wheelbarrow leaned against the garage door, which would not quite close because of the junk crammed inside. The malodorous minutiae of his existence, newly perceived as overwhelmingly mundane, began seeping back into awareness. He remembered there was a broken gutter to mend, and a leaky tap that needed a washer and shelves to put up.

– *Shit! The Council Tax is overdue – and the electricity bill needs paying...*

Anti-climax flattened the weekend's peaks. He got out of the car and locked it, collected his bags from the boot and laboured to the front door, the crystal plate clutched under his arm.

At the same moment, Marco was making a long distance call.

'Put me through to Chi-Chi,' he ordered in Japanese. A short wait.

'Marco.'

'Good morning, Father. I trust you slept well?'

'I did.'

'Good. I think I have found our new guinea pig.'

'You have? Go on.'

'Yes, he has all the qualities we discussed. Mid-thirties, humble background, bright but not brilliant, very discontented. He's also talented, gullible and, most importantly, greedy for success.'

'Excellent.'

'I'm certain he's right. More potential than the others – I can feel a latent power in him. Definitely the top candidate. Moreover, my daughter has taken a shine to him. I know she won't let us down.'

'I need to meet him.'

'Of course. I'll endeavour to bring him to New York early next week for you to assess.'

'Good.'

'Thank you, Father.'

Marco bowed reflexively and replaced the receiver. He sat back in his chair, finger tips together, feeling extremely satisfied with his weekend's work...

BITING

One seminal evening, whilst serving in the Imperial Japanese Army on the islands of New Guinea during the Second World War, I was practising, as was my custom, the ancient meditative arts learned from my Shinto master. I had just attained the level called 'The Still Lake', when I experienced the sensation of leaving my body, of floating to the ceiling, then rising through the roof and above my quarters. I discovered that if I felt concern, my inner being descended, but if I submitted to the sensation, I rose higher and higher. I continued to levitate into the sky, soon leaving the material sphere of the Earth far behind.

Eventually, after what seemed hours of travel, but which proved later to be minutes, I became conscious of an indescribable apparition hovering before me. Greetings and welcome were projected into my mind in an unknown language that, miraculously, I could understand, and, at once, my feelings became calm.

The apparition communicated to me as follows:

– You have been summoned because you are of the purest lineage, a direct descendant of the great Samurai warriors. You are elect; the one destined to be our representative on Earth. Soon, you will receive into yourself an energy. A power which will purge your psyche in readiness for your destined role. You will experience inner pain and some years of struggle in order for the necessary psychic restructuring to be achieved. However, when the process is complete, you will be in command of great powers. Use them to amass wealth in order to gain a position of high rank. When accomplished, you will pass on the purging power to others world-wide, but only to those whom you perceive to be aristocratic and ready, thus assembling around you an association of noble warriors...

The apparition asked if I was willing to accept my destiny and I concurred that I was, expecting time for questions, preparation, study and tuition. However, at the very moment of concurrence there emitted a fiery ray of light which entered my body through my genitals. I felt an explosion of exquisite pain, sweeter than a thousand orgasms, and I lost consciousness.

When I awoke, I was in my body, back in my quarters and the being and its celestial home had disappeared.

Every night, for a thousand nights, I was visited by the energy source pouring down from above and made to undergo what we now refer to as the purging. Slowly, inexorably, painfully, my negative feelings, my physical and mental weaknesses were expunged – my emotionality, my sentimentality, my guilt, my superstitious beliefs.

As the purging continued, new powers and energies arose in me – physical, mental and psychic...

'Load of old bollocks!' Jon shook his head in disbelief and tossed the book aside, getting up and walking to the kitchen. Rummaging through cupboards, he found a half-bottle of cheap brandy and took it back to the sitting room.

It was four o'clock in the morning. He had gone to the spare room after he'd arrived home, made a space to lie down, but hadn't been able to sleep, churning over the weekend's events. He'd got up, watched an old film on TV, drank a bottle of wine and then, feeling bored, had eventually dipped into the book Marco had lent him, struggling with the overblown language, scoffing at the fairy tale events.

The book was obviously privately published, devoid of any publisher's imprints, printer's identity or publication date. He noted it was numbered ten of twenty four, but could glean no further information regarding its provenance; except that on the fly leaf it announced, 'For Doh-Nai-Zen and prospective members only'.

He picked it up again, skimming through the anonymous Foreword. He learned that the author was called Chi-Chi, an affectionate diminutive for father in Japanese.

– What is he? Some bloody giant panda...?

After having survived the war, Jon continued to read, *Chi-Chi returned home to become one of Japan's emergent millionaire entrepreneurs, specialising in motorcycles and electronics. Over the years, Chi-Chi attracted around him a devoted group of acolytes. Later he formed a covert and highly elect organisation, which he named Doh-Nai-Zen. Nowadays , Chi-Chi, or Father, spends his time travelling the world, with no permanent address, meeting with and advising his family of followers on the true path of Doh-Nai-Zen.*

The second section of the book was headed *Practical Guidelines* and read like a new-age, self-help manual written by a quasi-religious therapist. Jon continued to browse with an admix of distaste and curiosity. He held the book almost at arm's length, reminded of watching surgery on TV, wanting to pull back – the viscerality repugnant, too near the bone – yet unable to wrench his eyes away.

As the sky began to lighten, he fell into a troubled sleep.

The house began to stir around seven thirty. Jon awoke on the sofa, stiff and tired and hung over, aching everywhere and in a bitchy mood. After dressing and showering he traipsed back down to the kitchen. Yvonne nodded curtly at him. Her aloofness reminded him, as designed, that he'd forgotten his promise to call her. In turn, he felt annoyed that she didn't ask if he'd had a successful time. Thus a spiralling tit-for-tat sprang up, threatening mayhem like a looming tornado.

– *She's the one being emotional – I'm not going to be the first to speak…* He experienced a spasm of distaste at the way she looked – old dressing gown, unbrushed hair, no make up and as pregnant as the atmosphere.

– *He is so infuriating. Thinks only of himself all the time. And look at the state of him. Drinking again…*

– *Why isn't she interested? Doesn't she know how dodgy things are? That our only hope is for something to come out of the weekend…?*

They were both already in their corners, warming up self-righteous anger, preparing for the birth of the gestating fight.

Their more and more frequent clashes were the constant fruiting of a fecund collusion. Because Jon didn't get involved in family life, Yvonne was too angry to give of herself in their lovemaking. As a consequence, he felt unmanned, castrated and unconsciously punished her by being even less involved. This mutual withdrawal competently ensured a lack of intimacy. It was an habitual game played out between two equally matched Grand Masters.

Their daughters drifted into the kitchen in various states of readiness for school. Tina, the youngest, had her eyes glued to a Gameboy, feverishly manipulating buttons; she looked cuddly, impish to Jon. She had a bright, perky face, warm Latinate skin, her mother's jet black hair and Jon's cleft chin.

– *She's going to be very beautiful when she's a teenager…* he thought as a wave of affection threatened to engulf him.

Wendy, their middle child, had a Walkman in her hand, the headphones pulling back from a dark forehead the long, blond hair inherited through a fluke of genetics from her paternal grandmother.

Jon stared at her wistfully.

– *Alice in Wonderland…* She was his favourite – sturdy and athletic like Yvonne; not pretty, but handsome, with her wide brow, flat nose and stolidly oval, *café au lait* complexioned face. A pang of love burst inside. His children were successfully undermining his tight-lipped pique.

Behind them, Natalie, the eldest, entered surrounded by an aura of depression. She was having serious problems with the injustices of the world, boys, puppy fat and acne. She brooded deeply. Natalie was the clever, studious one, the one who had inherited Jon's familial tendency towards fleshiness, his generous brown hair, Yvonne's skin colouring and the best features from both her parents' good looks – but she didn't know that yet. Jon's vexation was artfully restoked as he remembered their recent history of arguments and the on-going battles of will.

Engrossed, ignoring their parents, all three collected cereal bowls, piled them high with corn flakes, shovelled on spoonfuls of sugar, followed by half a carton of milk each. Jon observed them like a policeman.

'Bloody Hell! You girls go worrying about your figures and spots and yet look at the crap you eat. All that white sugar. Shouldn't you be eating fruit and yogurt or something for breakfast?'

'You never do,' chirped the youngest.

'I'm not worried about my figure,' he retorted.

'You should be.' Natalie's remark caused the other two to burst into giggles.

Irritated, but not yet enough, he tried another approach. 'Have you all done your homework, then?'

'What do you care? You're never here, anyway,' Natalie sneered with that look of arrogant defiance only teenagers can conjure at will. She was still smarting because he hadn't taken them bowling as promised. And, because of a boy at school who would not – or could not – respond to her infatuated overtures; her father stood in as scapegoat for all males at that moment.

Her dart hit the mark and Jon erupted, banging his fist on the table, catching the edge of his cereal bowl. It flipped over, disgorging its soggy contents onto the table.

'Don't talk to me like that! Show some respect – I'm your father!' he screamed, spraying chewed muesli, rage distorting his voice. For a second he had the illusion that he was his own father raging at him some twenty-five years ago.

The three girls stared at him – in disdain he mistakenly thought. In reality they were terrified – spoons half raised to their mouths.

'Oh for Christ's sake, Jon, will you stop being such a bully!' his wife shouted from across the kitchen. 'Just leave the girls alone. Let them have their breakfast in *peace* for once, will you!' She slammed down the kettle she was filling, underlining the word 'peace'. The irony went unnoticed.

Their youngest's eyes brimmed with tears and her bottom lip wobbled. 'Please don't have an argument…'

'What do you mean, in peace, for once?' Jon threw back in a mock whining voice. 'You implying *I* cause all the aggro round here?'

'Well, you're the one with the short fuse: the one that expects everyone else to jump when you're in a mood.'

'Any other faults you'd care to drag out?'

'Yes, now you mention it. How come you're totally out of it when any of us need something doing? When we need help or support?'

'Right – let's have a slag off Jon session then, shall we?'

'Don't go all pathetic, Jon, for God's sake. You always do this!' Yvonne's anxiety was overridden by frustrated anger.

'Oh, I get it. I'm the problem. I'm the one who fucks up everyone's life. Everything's all my soddin' fault. I had no idea...'

'God, you're so bloody *infuriating*! It's all me, me, me with you. And you can't even be bothered to phone when you say you're going to. I sometimes think you don't give a shit about me and the kids. All you ever think of is yourself and your poxy business and...' She burst into tears. 'I can't take much more of this.'

Jon felt a pang of concern seeing her tears, but he was in full flight, unable to stop. 'So *that's* what all this is about. Just because I forgot to phone. Well, I was busy, okay? Busy trying to save my "poxy business", as you call it. The poxy business that pays the fucking mortgage and feeds your bloody kids! Shit! I work myself to death and all I get is grief. Christ! It's all so fucking unfair.'

– Hypocrite. Are you going to tell her about Lucia, then...? his guilt prodded.

'Oh, *poor Jon*,' Yvonne threw at him, unable to edit the sneer from her voice.

'That's it.'

The long running drama had reached its well-worn finale. On cue, playing the child tormented by an unfair world, he stood, grabbed his jacket and strode out, slamming the door noisily behind him, swearing he was never coming back.

He got into his car and thrust the ignition key into the lock, twisting it violently as if to transfer anger to the engine. The starter moaned and the engine grumbled. He yanked the car into first, revved until the tacho needle red-lined and dropped the clutch. With an angry screech, the car slewed down the street, a rubber-pungent cloud billowing from its rear wheels.

When he reached his work place, forty minutes later, his anger had transmuted into self pity.

Why won't anybody cut me some fucking slack...? his head whined.

An accusation of being at fault suddenly jumped him from behind.

– Oh, God. Perhaps it's not right to leave my wife and daughters crying...

A child's voice, desperate to dodge blame, countered with,

– *Not my fault. They're females. Emotional. It's their way of handling things. Doesn't mean anything...*

– *Oh, God!* – *What is* wrong *with me...?*

Self-absorbed, his feelings reverberating inside, he unlocked and entered the building. Neither of his partners were in yet, nor his PA.

'Pain in the Arse,' he mumbled aloud, remembering that he had to talk to her soon about her continual lateness. He scooped up mail from inside the door and flicked through the envelopes. He was hoping for cheques, but there were none, only invoices and junk mail and a letter from the bank, one he really didn't want to open. The recent meeting with their so-called Business Manager, requested to try to increase their overdraft, had not gone as planned.

'I'll have to take this up with my Regional Office,' the young man had said after Jon's presentation. 'I haven't the authority to increase your borrowing any further.'

'We could move the overdraft to a loan account,' Jon had suggested. 'And start again with a new one.'

'I don't think so,' the young man had shot back, elbows on chair arms, fingers together – aping his institutional superiors. 'You have little security left and, with these latest figures, I doubt you could service a loan of that size.'

'But we've got a pretty good record. We've been successful in the past. This is just a glitch. We'll get over it.'

'I'm sorry. It would be imprudent, to say the least...'

The manager had half-rotated his wrist, glancing down at his watch. Jon had inferred from this small gesture that he and his business had ceased being valued customers.

– *Fuck knows why, he thought, ruefully. They're only bloody barrow boys selling cash; and we've bought enough from them in the past – and at rip-off prices...*

He'd left the bank feeling humiliated, impotent.

Jon tore open the envelope and scanned the contents quickly.

With no more security available, the Bank must now take the view that a further increase in borrowing is not an option at this time. We would reiterate that employing a factoring agent to assist with debt collection and negative cash flow, a reduction in staff and other overheads, plus an increase in sales...

He crumpled the letter and slung it at a waste bin. It hit the rim and bounced onto the floor.

'Pompous arsehole.'

'Thanks a bunch,' said Rob, one of Jon's partners, as he walked into reception. Rob was short and overweight. He looked like a giant school-boy in his ill-fitting, scruffy clothes – a satchel over his shoulder, horn-rimmed glasses perched on a button nose pinched from a waxy-white face. The Greenpeace T-shirt under his donkey jacket caught Jon's eye.

– *Wanker. Save the lesbian, single parent whales, my arse...*

'The Bank's blown us out, Rob. We'd better have a meeting as soon as Brian comes in.'

'Shit. What are we going to do? Any ideas?'

Rob had five children and a six-figure mortgage to support and Jon knew exactly where to hurt.

'Well, you can either try bringing in some decent new clients for a change, me old mate, or we're all gonna be signing on.'

Madeleine, Jon's Personal Assistant, crept through the door. Although she often irritated him and her work could be infuriatingly slipshod, he felt a kind of affection for her – she had a stalwart attitude to life despite her wilting, cut flower aridity. She was in her late thirties and fast losing what looks she had; and there was something unfulfilled in her, as though she were going to waste. Jon empathised with her more than he was aware. Perhaps there was an echo of his mother – or himself. As she hung up her coat he sensed something was wrong.

'You okay, Mad?'

She turned to face him. Her mascara had run and her face looked puffy, clown-like, and he was forced to stifle a laugh.

'Yes. Fine, thanks.' Madelaine's lips began to tremble and her face col-lapsed. 'No. Toby's left me,' sobbed out in a voice that was so forlorn, Jon felt a rush of pity. Her shoulders shook and she began to wail uncontrol-lably, the keening emotion as thick as mucus.

Rob scurried embarrassed into the studio as Jon stepped forward to put a consoling arm around Madelaine's shoulders, leading her into his office. He sat her in a chair and perched on his desk with a hand lightly touching her arm. He waited, occasionally patting or stroking her curved back, staring down on the bowed head, noticing the dandruff flecking her parting. When the sobbing subsided, he tenderly teased out the story, patiently listening between the sobbing fits.

Toby, her live-in partner for the past two years had walked out, gone off with another woman. 'He's been two-timing me all along – using me. We were going to marry, have children. He was my last chance.' The words seemed to spew forth from a mouth made ugly by emotion.

'Why do I pick such bastards, Jon? What's going on? What have I done to deserve this?'

She burst into tears again and Jon resonated with her, feeling her pain mixed with his own rising anger. He was angry because he felt impotent; frustrated that there was nothing more he could do, that he had no skills or magic tricks to ease her – or anyone's – suffering.

When the wracking sobs gradually slowed again, then finally petered out, he suggested affably, 'Why don't you take a few days off. Go stay with a friend. Someone you can really talk to; someone who'll understand. We'll get by without you. Just come back when you're ready, yeah?'

She took his hand and kissed it. 'Oh, Jon, you're so kind. I think I will go home. I know I just couldn't concentrate on work, I'm sorry. God, you're good to me, you know,' and she threw her arms around his back and began to snuffle again, leaning forward, head pressed against his chest. Embarrassed, Jon gently disentangled himself, stood and lifted her to her feet.

'I'm so sorry...' she began, noticing the teary mascara stain on his shirt, attempting to wipe it off with a hand. Jon felt a frisson of sexuality from the intimate, caressive act. In a microsecond the possibilities were explored and the tacit understanding reached that it would never work between them.

'Don't worry about it, please.' He gently pulled the hand away, ushered her towards the door and into reception where he quickly helped her on with her coat. 'Off you go, and best of luck. I hope something works out for you. Keep in touch.'

He wandered back to his office; relieved she had gone, wondering what it must be like to be that much in love with someone, to be that vulnerable.

'A living hell,' he concluded.

Sitting at his desk he sighed, 'Why is life so...?' He searched for the most apt words. 'So fucking *tawdry*?'

Brian, the triumverate's third member, didn't show until eleven thirty.

'And where the bloody hell have you been?' Jon threw at him as he strolled in. Brian was as underweight as Rob was over. At six feet two and with a loping walk, he reminded Jon of a giraffe. A lanky, grey giraffe with an oversize Adam's apple, limpid brown eyes and an angular, jutting nose. Jon found him infuriatingly phlegmatic.

'Sorry, mate. Had to take my car in for a service. Didn't I tell you?'

'Yeah, yeah, whatever. Listen, bloody Bank's blown us out. We need to talk.' Jon was hoping to spark some reaction from him.

'Tell 'em we'll take our overdraft elsewhere,' Brian called over his shoulder as he sauntered off into his partitioned workspace.

It irritated him that Brian never took their situation seriously – and that Rob was so timid. He began to ask himself again how they'd ended up in business together, despite knowing exactly why.

– *Drifted into it, didn't I? Pretty much how I drift into every bloody thing in life...*

They'd met when he'd advertised for freelance help with a larger than usual project. Rob was an illustrator and visualiser, Brian a copywriter. After working on several more projects together with some success, it had seemed a sensible idea to formalise their relationship. They'd pooled their individual clients, created a company and moved into a studio together. Later came bigger clients, staff, a pension fund, the building they were buying – and then, notwithstanding the early successes, an exponentially expanding overdraft.

– *Sometimes, it's like being married all over again. Except there's no dinner or sex to come home to...*

Jon sat, elbows on desk, chin in hands, morosely staring into space.

– *Wish I could just walk away from the whole caboodle – business, debts, marriage. Travel the world, maybe – ideally with Lucia at my side. Fuck it! Got to get some of what Marco's got. I've got to do something for* me *for a change...*

The late morning meeting with his partners produced no immediate solutions as they talked in circles. Their pension fund had already been utilised and the building's equity siphoned off for essential alterations and repairs, leaving them with a hefty mortgage debt. They currently owed more than they'd recently earned – some creditors getting nervous, threatening court action – and there was very little new work going through the studio. Now that the Bank was on the verge of freezing their account, they knew it wouldn't be long before they called in the overdraft. That was when they'd be forced to sell the building for zero profit and to down-size all round – ending up with nothing. Things were pretty dire, the lowest ebb thus far.

'So, it's true. The higher you go, the harder you fall, eh?' Brian suggested affably.

'We can do without the aphorisms, thanks,' Jon snapped.

'Ooh!' Brian mocked. 'Touchy.'

Rob laughed nervously, looking from one to the other. 'Seriously, what we gonna do, guys?' he asked.

'Well, there's one bit of potentially good news, but I'm not sure it's a reality yet...'

Jon cagily hinted to them about the weekend, the contacts he had made and the work Marco might want them to do. Brian and Rob looked happier, relieved, and Jon realised that he would have to carry the can awhile yet.

The meeting broke up. As he wandered back to his office, responsibility bore down on him and, like an overextended weight lifter, he buckled under its weight, wriggled from under its crush and let it fall heavily to the floor.

– Looks like I'm the only one who's going to get us out of this mess...

'Bollocks. I'm not having this. It's action time.'

Shutting himself away he began to make a series of calls to the people he'd met over the weekend. At lunchtime he sent out for sandwiches, continuing to work at his desk. By mid afternoon, he had eight appointments set up and was beginning to feel like a whiz kid again, regenerating the enthusiasm and hunger he'd experienced when they'd started the business. He decided to risk his veneer of good feeling by telephoning Lucia.

'Jon, hi! How are you?' She sounded delighted to get his call.

'I'm good. How about you. Did the assessment go well?'

'Yeah. Brill. Listen, when am I going to see you again?'

Her question electrified him and he recklessly suggested, 'Tonight?'

'That'd be great. Come and pick me up at my place about eight. You got my address?'

'Yep. On your letter.'

'I know a neat little Italian restaurant – I hope you like Italian? You'd better, 'cos I love it.'

'Yeah, whatever. Look forward to it. See ya' later.'

Jon could not refrain from pumping the air with a fist and hissing, *'Yessss!'* through clenched teeth. Then, as pleasure exploded in his chest, he told his empty office, 'I'm over the moon, man; floating on cloud nine, in Seventh Heaven – a living, breathing, bloody romantic cliché.'

Calming down, he made two more calls. First, he telephoned Marco's secretary to set up a meeting for two o'clock the next day, and then rang his wife.

'Hi, Yvonne. Look – sorry about this morning – and for not calling over the weekend. It was pretty crass of me. I really am sorry. I'm just so worried about money and business – totally stressed out. I'm gonna try to be a bit cooler about things for a while, maybe take a break.'

She forgave him and he told her he'd be late that night, maybe not home at all.

– With a bit of luck... he thought, crossing his fingers.

'I've a meeting with some of the people I was introduced to over the weekend. They've got a lot of work for us, and frankly, I can't let this opportunity pass. Didn't go well with the Bank, and if it wasn't for this we'd be in deep shit. So, I really gotta go. Sorry, sweetheart.'

Jon had created a scenario that virtually convinced himself of its veracity and he cradled the handset convinced he had made a successful sale. Cock-a-hoop again, he decided to go shopping for some new clothes and forgive-me presents for his wife and daughters, knowing it would max out his credit cards.

He refused to acknowledge the guilt clamouring for attention – part conscience, suggesting duplicity was not a good thing, part anxiety in case he got found out.

– Piss off! I'm on a roll...

Yvonne clicked off the cordless, laid it on the worktop and arched her back, hands behind hips. This pregnancy was making her feel very tired most of the time and she ached all over.

– And now I'm getting varicose veins...

'Not easy having a kid at forty plus,' she told the kitchen.

Her brow furrowed as she re-sensed something was not quite right. Jon had been too gushy, too ready to admit he was in the wrong, particularly after such a long run of angry depression. She couldn't quite formulate the words.

– Seemed to be overselling himself, somehow...

She eased the worry aside. It was nearly four o'clock and the girls would be home from school soon.

She made herself a cup of tea and wearily sank onto a kitchen chair, lifting her legs up onto another. Sipping the hot tea, the cup cradled in both hands for warmth and comfort, she recalled the first time she'd seen him – when he was being shown round the agency on his first day.

– Mmm, he was so shy, so young and so good looking. And he had that forlorn air about him. Fell in love with him there and then. Invented excuses to go up to the studio to see him – questions about P45s and holiday entitlements...

Yvonne hadn't worked outside of the home for fifteen years and her memories of her book keeping duties were hazy.

– He was very witty and charming – when you got to know him...

She smiled to herself. *– And he made me laugh – so much...*

One day, a complete surprise, he'd asked her for a date and her world had turned into a Doris Day musical.

She'd been twenty-six, five or so years his senior. She'd always known he didn't love her the way she loved him, that she'd never possessed that white, US 'media look' he was culturally attracted to.

– But we got on so well, had such fun together...

And she'd taught him about sex. Had shown him how to enjoy the mutuality, the give and take, because she had been the more experienced. The overwhelming mothering feeling he'd aroused in her had added a piquancy to their lovemaking.

– God! how I mothered him. Suckled him back to normality, weaned him off his depression...

Yvonne had listened, sympathised and praised him; had made him feel better about himself and they'd became best friends; had gone everywhere together.

– We used to walk around for hours, just talking – sometimes through the night – well, he did most of the talking. He was so interesting, and so interested in everything. Sometimes, though, when he got onto art or philosophy, he seemed to spiral up and away. But I was always there, open armed and loving when he came back to the planet...

Her eyes closed and she sank into a warm cocoon of memories.

– Wanted him so much in those days. Ached for him, would have followed him anywhere, done anything for him...

The desire for a child by him had masqueraded as sexual wantonness, she recalled. And then she'd got pregnant – and he'd married her.

Finishing her tea, putting the cup on the table and staring at it unfocused, she sighed herself back to the present.

– Dunno what's happening any more. I can tolerate the constant arguments and the fighting – at least we're involved. It's his distancing himself I can't take. When he goes off into his dream worlds – usually pissed. I know the business isn't doing as well as it was and he never grieved properly over his Dad, but... Now he's suddenly all chipper... She furrowed her brow.

After nearly fifteen years, she was so sensitive to his moods, sensing subtle, impending changes with a hair-trigger barometer.

– Another woman? Can't see that. Not Jon. But you never know. Change in mood, staying away for the night. Better keep my eye on that...

The child growing in her womb kicked, sending an apprehensive thrill of pleasure through her body. She shook off the burgeoning anxiety and became stalwart again. She resolved to take more care of her family in future. Told herself that she was so lucky to be doing what she'd always wanted: being a mother and a wife, running a home and a family.

– *Not many people in this world get to do what they really love for a living...*

She heard the girls noisily bursting through the front door and got up stiffly, a smile of pleasure on her face.

Jon pressed the bell with trepidation. Lucia's apartment covered the top floor of a Georgian house tucked away in Eaton Terrace – one of those areas of London that, through an aura of run down refinement and an almost designed lack of ostentation, paradoxically screamed affluence and privilege.

When she opened the door he was taken aback – Lucia was dressed, ready to leave. She wore a tan-enhancing, light blue, tightly fitting suit with a pillbox hat perched jauntily on her head – a fishnet, white-sequinned veil half-covering her face. He appreciated the visual pun of an elderly woman's outfit on a young girl – regardless of the shortest skirt and the most exquisite legs he had ever seen.

They left his battered BMW parked in the street with her resident's permit propped in the windscreen and drove to the restaurant in her Lotus Elise. Sitting beside her, the aroma of leather and her expensive perfume teasing his nostrils, he succumbed to a rarely experienced sense of being blissfully alive. Looking around as they drove, he devoured the head-craning, envious stares from men walking the streets or sat in cars held by traffic lights – at the same time experiencing a prematurely proprietorial jealousy.

The restaurant was snug and warm, illuminated by low-level lighting. Tables intimately set in booths lent a deliciously louche ambience, as though only catering for trysting lovers.

'So,' he said, after they'd ordered, 'What are you up to?'

'Not a lot,' she laughed, 'Apart from college and projects. Although in a couple of weeks it's half term and I'm off to Minorca for a week with some friends – get some late sun. Then it's back for more college until skiing over Christmas. God, I hope Fergie and her gang aren't there again, taking the place over. Can't stand that crowd.'

He let her do all the talking, throwing an occasional question, relishing her youthful exuberance, just enjoying observing her every move.

Celebrities' names peppered her conversation, interspersed with fabled, jet-setting resorts – St. Tropez, Biarritz, Cannes. He assumed it was not an affectation, that she had merely forgotten he was not part of her world, or perhaps presumed he was.

As she talked, he recalled touring the States in his youth, visiting the legendary names of popular music, yearning for enchantment – Tulsa, Route 66, Tallahassee, San Francisco, Memphis, the list was long – but he'd found the reality banal and worn-looking, empty. Nevertheless, he envied her social melée, longing to immerse himself in the romantic sounding, star-studded locations in which she seemed so at home.

– *Perhaps this time some magic will rub off on me. Colour me rich…*

Their food arrived and, fascinated, he watched as she managed to talk while forking spaghetti, doing both with equal gusto.

– *She's so at ease, so herself. Kind of 'take it or leave it' confident…*

– *Wish I'd been like that at her age…*

– *Wish I was like that now…*

In case he was driving later, he had only one small glass of the Valpolicella he'd ordered. Lucia finished the bottle and seemed untouched by it, except for a slight pace-quickening of her non-stop chatter. She asked for a zabaglione. Jon declined a dessert – his daughters' remarks at breakfast had hit their target.

Over coffee he began to worry about the bill, unable to recall if there was enough credit on his cards.

– *Better get it over with…*

Catching the waiter's eye, he mimed writing on the palm of his hand. The waiter brought the bill folded on a silver salver held outstretched as though part of a religious ceremony. The total made Jon wince, but he casually placed his card on the tray and mentally crossed his fingers as it was whisked away. He re-focused on Lucia while trying not to notice the waiter and the owner on the periphery of his vision, in huddled conversation at the bar, by the till.

The restaurateur approached their table, Jon's card held by its edges between thumb and fingers.

– *Shit! It's been bounced…* he cringed.

The owner beamed at Lucia as he handed Jon's card back.

'This onna the house. Specially for you, Bellisima, an' a-your boyfriend.' Jon experienced surprise, then gratified relief – and a trill of pleasure at the word boyfriend.

Lucia and the owner began to converse in Italian – lots of laughing, gesticulating and touching, Jon realising she had more Italian blood than he had first appreciated.

'What was that all about?' he asked as they were walking back to her car after a deluge of effulgent handshakes, hugs and goodbyes.

'Friend of the family. Daddy put up the money for the restaurant. Gianfranco really adores me and usually does something nice like that. That's why I love the place so much.'

When they pulled up outside her apartment block, she told him that if he was coming up, they'd have to sort out their cars. He had to park some streets away and, as he paced apprehensively back to her flat, prayed there were no clamping patrols out at this time of night, or wardens handing out swingeing fines to the riffraff – non-residents with beaten up old cars and no parking permit.

He knocked tentatively on her half-opened door. She admitted him and, following her in, he immediately felt awkward. Should he sit by her on the sofa? Should he kiss her now, before coffee, during, after, or what? He stood in the middle of the room paralysed, out of touch with the sexual mores of her generation, terrified to put a foot wrong, thereby irrevocably damaging the cool-guy image he was still attempting to project. Like her father and mother, though, she was totally at ease, ever in control.

'I'm going to take a shower. D'you want join me?'

Jon swayed for a moment, incredulous, repressing a gasp. Again, he had the reality-bending sensation of starring in a movie.

She slipped out of her clothes, naturally, gracefully as she meandered towards the bathroom – totally unashamed of her nudity. Jon followed gauchely, clumsily undressing, hopping after her as he removed his shoes. Becoming acutely aware of his gut, he sucked it in, pulling himself as erect as his penis. He ogled her retreating rear with media acute eyes.

– *Sweet Jesus! She's a photographer's dream...*

They embraced in the shower. The hot water cascading down his back intensified a sense of dissolving. She slid a hand around the back of his neck and unceremoniously pulled his mouth to hers. The spectres of AIDS and unwanted pregnancy loomed and he vaguely wondered if he ought to be wearing a condom, but the recently bought pack was in his jacket.

– *Sod it. Just go with the flow...*

His hands fitted round her buttocks and he lifted her, his penis urgently seeking her out with a manic life of its own. She pulled her head away.

'Don't rush, Jon. We've plenty of time. Don't particularly like doing it in the shower.'

At her direction, they washed each other's body, caressing, exploring.

'Let's go to bed,' she whispered in his ear.

They towelled off and Lucia lead him by the hand to her bedroom. She laid languidly across the bed, hands linked above her head, Jon kneeling beside her, studying her perfection. His fingertips became alive as they traced her contours, slipping into hollows, gently rising on mounds, revelling in the changing tactile textures of her liquid smooth, warm skin – elastic over flesh, taut over muscle, tight over bone. He wanted this moment to last forever, but the dam holding back his lust was creaking and spurting. He leaned over and gently kissed her nipples. They stiffened under his tongue and he all but fainted with desire.

'Fuck me now,' she urged, pulling him down.

The dam split and lust came cascading and coursing through his veins. The ancient sensation of slipping into silken slime wiped his mind. Reality shrank away until there was nothing but the sweet suck on the heart of his being.

Lucia clamped her legs around his torso, arching her back, thrusting at him, eager as a man. He had never experienced another's sexual hunger this intense before, and it amplified his own. He grabbed her hands, intertwined fingers and pushed her arms up and away. He threw his head back, spine arched, mouth open, eyes closed – a wolf about to howl. He began the primal, rhythmic beat of copulation – her rising cries matching the in out, in out motion of his body.

It was too much. Within minutes he ejaculated, moaning in honeyed ecstacy as his sphincter muscles contracted and pumped, and pumped, and pumped.

His body limpened and he slumped forward, burying his face in her hair, the sweat on their bodies commingling as it trickled and cooled.

'Sorry.'

'It's okay,' she murmured, stroking his hair. 'We've lots of time. I'll get my orgasm later. And if not from you, then someone else.'

Jealousy mugged him and he tensed against the aggressive intrusion, hardly daring to breathe. Minutes passed. The insidious feeling began to subside.

'I'm going to clean up and have a pee,' she announced, easing herself from under him, pushing him aside. 'Roll a joint, will you. The makings are in my bedside cabinet.'

As she re-entered the bedroom, Jon lit the reefer he had inexpertly rolled. He hadn't smoked dope for years and the sickly bonfire smell filling the room combining with the first deep drag, began to pluck random memories from the time he smoked all day and every day.

Years of anxiety awoke, to be lived out over seconds. Memories of the incident on the bridge. The news of the man's death over the 'phone. Then the agonising trawl through local newspapers until the shock of the headline *Man Dies After Hooligan Attack*. And after – the gush of adrenaline every time he saw, or heard, a police car; the unexpected knock on the door; the paranoia that mushroomed from casual glances in the street; the cringeing relief at the Coroner's 'Accidental Death' verdict. And then, the guilt that never left his side, randomly ambushing him at will.

Staring hard at the floor, wrapped in the virtual reality of the narcotically reconjured world, he tried to reassure himself again.

– *Forget it, for fuck's sake! All over. Behind me now...*

As if slipping a gear, his mood changed, returning him to Lucia's room as suddenly as he had left. It seemed to have doubled in size, Lucia a mile away, sitting leaning against the head board, her voice echoing, her words unintelligible. His second drag re-kindled jealousy. He handed her the joint in slow motion.

'What did you mean by that – getting an orgasm by someone else, later?' His voice reverberated in his head and he wasn't even sure if he were the one speaking.

'I simply meant if you don't make me come tonight, especially after getting me so hot, I'll go and visit some friends.' She dragged on the joint, holding the smoke down, sucking air in a series of tiny gasps. 'I'm luckier than most,' she continued, exhaling noisily, head thrown back, 'I'm completely bisexual – AC/DC through and through. Happily, most men and an awful lot of women find me extremely desirable.'

Jealous, confused, annoyed by her matter-of-factness, he waved away the proffered joint, feeling spiteful, keen to hurt back.

'So you're the proverbial bitch-slut, then?'

'Don't look so shocked, Jonny baby. Anyway, I thought you were married or something?'

For a moment he teetered between anger and amusement, not sure if he would storm out or stay. He created a mental movie of her making love with a woman – a febrile collage of images culled from pornographic videos watched alone, in the dark. His erection pulsed alive again and the crisis passed.

'Touché,' he grinned. 'Can't be wasting your orgasm on a lesbian, though.' He leaned towards her and cupped her breast with one hand while roughly attempting to pry her legs apart with the other.

'Not like that,' she said abruptly, pushing his hand away.

She settled back on the bed, still holding the joint, and parted her legs, gently guiding his head with her free hand.

When she reached her climax, Jon observed she was completely wrapped in her own pleasure and he felt used – a mere sex toy. Then, when she let him into her again, insisting he took her from behind, she was completely passive and it seemed as though he, too, were masturbating, but he couldn't stop. Inflamed by her sleek back tapering to a narrow waist, the full roundness of her rump and the pendulous swing of breasts, he quickly experienced a second, wracking-sweet orgasm.

After, they lay side by side in the virtual darkness, an occasional flicker of car headlamps touring the walls, she smoking another joint and he a cigarette. His mind was stilled at last, his body humming with the fag end of the marihuana and his own natural chemicals. For a while, he was only aware of being – something not truly experienced since he was a child – and it seemed to him as though he were under a spell, one conjured by the witch lying beside him.

A thought floated into his mind, bursting like a bubble.

– *I want to be with this woman, here in this bed, forever and ever...*

'I think you'd better go,' she said suddenly, leaning out, switching on a bedside lamp, all in one unbroken motion.

'Why?' He propped himself up on one elbow, blinking.

'Because I hate sleeping with people. They snore and pull all the covers off.'

'When can I see you again?'

'How about same time, same place, next week?'

Disappointment. 'Can't I see you before?'

'Why so urgent?'

'Because I'm in... because I want to be with you.'

'Jon.' She was suddenly cross. 'We've only fucked. We haven't got engaged or anything.'

'But don't you want to be with me? Wasn't tonight good for you?' He hated the whine in his voice.

'Yes, darling, it was nice, and I do like to be with you, but I also like to be with my friends, my horses, my college people...'

'Nice? Is that it? *Nice?*'

'Oh, Jon. It was *wonderful*. And the earth moved and you're the greatest lover since Don Juan,' she teased, a note of exasperation in her voice. 'Now, please *go*. Call me when you get back from your travels.'

'Travels? I'm not going anywhere.'

'Oh yes you are. Daddy's got plans for you.'

'Plans? What are you talking about? How do you know?'

'I know everything. You'll find out. Now go, Jon, please. I want my beauty sleep.'

She gently, but insistently, pushed him from the bed using feet to demonstrate her seriousness. He did as he was told, got up and dressed, following the trail of his clothes back from the bathroom. He returned to the bedside and stood looking down at her. She lay on her side, a single sheet contouring a jutting hip, a naked arm across her eyes. He thought she was the most beautiful thing he had ever seen. He bent forward and tenderly kissed her shoulder. It was both cool and salty on his lips.

'Mmm! Turn off the lights and shut the door as you go,' she murmured, almost asleep.

As he drove home through the deserted streets, he wondered why he wasn't cock-a-hoop, experiencing anxiety instead.

– That's it. I've done it. Cheated on my wife. And I don't give a toss – as long as I don't get found out. It's what I want. I don't even care that she's a decadent little rich kid who's going to run me ragged. God, have I fallen for her – and there's sod all I can do about it now...

REELING IN

Jon had distributed his 'sorry' gifts and made it up with his wife and daughters. Over breakfast he had played the perfect loving father and husband. But he was so full of nervous guilt he had taken the morning off and spent several hours putting up shelves in the kitchen; shelves he had been promising for months.

'What's brought all this on?' Yvonne asked.

'I just feel good about last night and all the new work I'm pulling in. Things are really looking up.' He disliked himself for lying and was shocked at the newly discovered adroitness.

Yvonne didn't believe him. In reality, he was a poor liar, confirming her suspicions. She cocked her head to one side and looked hard at him. He appeared un-phased, measuring and marking wood. Inwardly he was panicking, wishing she would stop staring and go away. It felt as if the word 'adulterer' were tattooed on his forehead. Wiley by nature, Yvonne decided to hold fire and watch, knowing he would become complacent and give himself away. The time for confrontation would come when appropriate.

– *He's so bloody transparent...* she scoffed inwardly.

After lunch, he drove into London for his meeting with Marco, assuming he was leaving a happy, harmonious household behind him, surprised that they seemed to sense nothing different, that people in general base their reality on the mere gossamers of external impressions.

– *It's all so easy, really. What people don't know doesn't hurt them, I suppose...*

This seemed cold hearted, but he knew it to be a truism; knew, too, that he would continue to use their apparent gullibility for his own ends from then on as superciliously as any government. Marco's lecture, unconsciously consumed, had lit a fuse...

– *Oh, yes. Very apposite...*

Jon was walking towards Marco's office suite which was sited above the new Bentley showrooms in Park Lane. He entered the foyer and took the lift to the third floor. Stepping out, he was immediately struck by the reception's opulence – rare hardwood desks and lush carpeting. *Brancusi Art Investments*, in an elegant typeface illuminated from behind, arced round a curved wall of pale marble. The warmly lit space was still and hushed – an impression created by muted colour-ways and subtly positioned up-lighters. Nothing was out of place or strident. Renaissance style pictures were strategically hung, no wires indicating the proclaimed security system. Succulent looking plants and the powerful heating system gave a subtropical ambience to the whole. It reeked class and financial success precisely as designed.

An assistant escorted him to Marco's office. Jon decided she was succulent and classy, too – in a Bay Watch Babe kind of way – with breasts as imposingly large as her skirt was short; legs as smooth, long and brown as her hair.

She knocked perfunctorily on one of the panelled, mahogany double doors and opened it. Marco's office seemed cavernous to Jon, its wide windows overlooking Park Lane and across to Hyde Park. As he was ushered in, he heard no traffic noise whatsoever, despite the densely packed carriageways below. A fifteen feet long rosewood desk sat opposite the door, parallel with the windows. Marco had his back half to them, sitting in a grey, leather-upholstered office chair, Gucci-clad feet up on the windowsill. He was on the phone, left hand gesticulating as he spoke energetically in Italian. Ethnic carvings representing animals were the only artefacts in the room apart from an array of monitors displaying international finance figures. Marco swivelled round as he sensed their entry.

'Okay, I'll catch you later,' he announced, reverting to English. He indicated to Jon that he should come in and sit. 'Have to go now. My protégé's just arrived. Ciao!' He cradled the handset, stood and walked around the desk to shake hands.

Jon was again taken aback by Marco's sheer presence and was unable to keep his gaze off him.

– *Like being in a cage with a bloody tiger...*

Marco was wearing pinstriped trousers, part of a suit, white shirt and a loosened tie that matched bright red braces. The shirt looked as though it would burst if Marco flexed his muscles.

'Can we have some coffee, Julia?' Marco asked his secretary, who was collecting documents from tray marked 'out', resting on a table to the left of the door. She smiled and nodded assent then sashayed out. Marco sat languidly on the edge of the desk facing Jon, amused by his stare locked onto Julia's exiting rear.

Instinctively, unable to prevent his dominant male persona rearing up, he admonished, 'Now, now. Don't get ideas, Jon. Julia's no bimbo. She's an Oxford Graduate, speaks four languages fluently and is an invaluable asset to me and my business.'

'Sorry, I... she's very attractive.'

'She is. And what's more, she's so completely at ease with her self and her femininity that she really doesn't mind making coffee for mere men. Occasionally.' Marco had correctly divined Jon's conflict between his innate chauvinism and his recent, begrudgingly acquired, 'new man' stance.

'Now, did you read the book I gave you?'

'Most of it.'

'What do you think?'

'Dunno, really,' Jon shrugged. 'Weird. Interesting.'

'Good. We'll discuss it later. Now listen, I want you to come to New

York with me, this evening, all expenses paid.' He held up his hand, pre-empting the protests forming in Jon's mouth. 'It's only for a couple of days, so we'll have to fly Concorde. The MD of a subsidiary is on a US sales tour and I want you to meet him and take a full marketing brief. He needs advertising, new corporate, that sort of thing. We need fresh think-ing, new blood.'

'No problem.' Jon slipped into casual mode, masking the mounting excitement.

'Secondly, Chi-Chi – the man who wrote the book – is going to give a talk to a group of Doh-Nai-Zen members there. I'm translating for him, so I must go, and I'd really like you to come with me, if you would.'

'Yeah, I'll come. It'll be great. I'd better go and get packed.'

'No time, old bean. Too much to do before the seven o'clock flight.' He stood and, retrieving a wallet from a chair-draped jacket, handed Jon a credit card.

'Here, use this. Go and get yourself some expensive new shirts, a new suit, toilet stuff and a bag to put them in. Phone your wife and get her to find your passport and Julia will send a courier for it. I've laid on a bar-ber and a manicurist here in the building – got to have you looking your best. So let's get moving. Come on, chop, chop...'

'Why are you doing all this for me, Marco?' Jon asked, pausing in the doorway.

'Because you're a feather in my cap, dear boy. An investment.'

'Yes, but why me? And what do you mean – feather in your cap?'

'I'll see you back here in two hours. We'll go and have a bite to eat and I'll explain everything then. Now off you go.'

Marco firmly ended the conversation. Jon was so thrilled he did exactly as he'd been told, for once forgetting to feel manipulated and resentful.

Jon made a rash of calls as he was driven along Oxford street in the back of a cab. He rang his wife to tell her what was happening and where to find his passport; then called the company to tell Rob and Brian what was afoot. He asked them to cover for him and to make sure work was col-lected from printers and delivered on time; and to contact a couple of clients to rearrange appointments. Feeling as excited as a child on a sea-side trip, eagerly anticipating the sight of the sea and beach, he made one final call.

'Tony? It's Jon. Listen, mate. Won't be able to make the match tonight.

You won't believe this. I'm being flown bloody Concorde to New York in a few hours time. On business, all expenses paid. Going to be there for a few days.'

'You jammy bastard. How'd you wangle that?'

'It's for a new client. He seems to think I'm a genius. So...'

'Then he's either stupid or trying to get into your pants.'

'I'll send you a filthy postcard.'

'I'd rather have a New York babe.'

'I'll see what I can do. Ciao.'

'Fuck off, you pretentious prat!'

Within the two-hour time limit, Jon had managed to spend over a thousand pounds up and down Regent Street. Back in Marco's office suite, he had showered, changed clothes, had his haircut and a first ever manicure.

While he waited for Marco in reception, he watched Julia at work behind her desk.

'What's the cost of a return flight on Concorde these days?' he asked her, idly curious and hoping to imply that he has travelled Concorde in the past.

She looked up from the document she was studying, peered over the top of her glasses at a VDU and rapidly tapped some keys.

'About six and a half thousand Sterling. Each.'

'Thanks.'

– *Jesus! More than double what I pay myself a month...*

Marco strolled into reception asking, 'Ready?' Jon leaped to his feet, confirming that he was. Marco looked him up and down and nodded approval. 'Better. Much better. Right, let's grab a bite.'

At Marco's suggestion, they walked to a local sandwich bar, bought cellophane-wrapped baguettes and went for a stroll in Hyde Park.

'Such a glorious afternoon,' Marco pronounced. 'I do hate being caged in my office all day.'

It was a beautiful afternoon. The sky dome was an unmarked blue and the air felt pleasantly warm. Languishing in the late autumn sun, London appeared unusually soft and golden.

'Our Creator has certainly done a fine job,' Marco remarked, breathing deeply. 'The best of all possible worlds, just for us.'

'You don't believe in all that Creation and God stuff, do you?' Jon scoffed. 'An old, white bearded guy sitting on a throne in heaven – like in the Bible? Making the world in six days and meting out punishment to anyone who pisses him off? I'm a card carrying atheist, myself.'

He was feeling sharp and confident in his new clothes, enjoying being seen walking with this important looking man. The fact that he'd made love to Lucia last night and that he, too, was a father of daughters hazily connected in his mind, only to be immediately suppressed. Moral maze conundrums were not Jon's forté.

'God? Allah? Jehovah? Perish the thought, dear boy. No, the Creator I am referring to is an amoral energy that just is, always has been and always will be. And creation, the universe, call it what you will, merely mirrors its existence.'

'Okay, but if the universe isn't some massive accident, some sort of mad nuclear chain reaction, why was it created? And what are we for?'

'Our role is to revel in its creation – by simply enjoying ourselves.'

'Including getting diseases and dying hideously painful deaths?'

'You're referring to fate, Jon. In Doh-Nai-Zen we're only interested in destiny.'

'Is there a difference?'

'Fate is what happens to people – from winning the lottery to being burnt to a cinder in a plane crash. Destiny is fulfilling the Creator's, or Nature's, purpose. For example, the developing of one's animal nature to its full potential. Punishments such as diseases and unpleasant deaths are, in a sense, self-inflicted, reserved only for the dross.'

'Self-inlicted? I'm not with you... And what's all this animal nature business?'

'We're all animals, Jon. Nothing more, nothing less. Our species – good old homo sapiens – was created to be top of the heap; noble creatures, the gods of mythology. Yet, nowadays, even rats have more dignity than most humans.'

'You've lost me again.'

'Can you imagine creatures with the strength, speed and resilience of an animal coupled with the creative mind and physical dexterity of a human? Powerful animals with manual skills, language and logical thought? Imagine the potential, Jon. That was Nature's original plan. Unfortunately, mankind's brains grew out of control, invented verbal reasoning, then morality and finally, even worse, religion. All the stuff designed to stifle our instinctual energies.'

'You mean like zoo-born animals that don't know how to hunt if they're released back into the wild?'

'Worse than that, Jon. If such animals survive the first weeks, it all comes back. I'm referring to more than a generation or two's forgetfulness. I'm talking about having our animal natures castrated, repressed, shrunken for millennia. In today's world, most people only operate on the mineral or vegetable wavelengths, displaying just those qualities. They either perceive nothing, like a lump of clay, and allow others to mould them to whatever shape they wish, or are rooted to the spot, like plants, swaying in the breeze of whatever sentiment motivates them at any given moment. The animal energy within, however, needs to run, hunt, procreate, care for it's young, fight for dominance and live totally in the here and now, following only its instincts to satisfy its appetites. Animals have no room for sentiment, emotion or misplaced compassion.' Marco paused for effect and to take a bite from his baguette.

'How do you know all this stuff?' Jon asked, shaking his head, bemused yet intrigued.

'Because I am a Doh-Nai-Zen member and have experienced the reality, Jon, at first hand. Of course, I didn't always know, but Doh-Nai-Zen changed me from the inside out, gave me understanding.'

'How? How did it change you?'

'When I was young and serving those whom I perceived as the rich and mighty, I wanted desperately to be like them. I would imitate their style and their behaviour, but was constantly ineffectual. I'd invest and lose money, or I would set my will against another's and always come off worst. Then I met Chi-Chi. He made me realise that the same power existed within me, but was made impotent, as though incacerated in a dungeon, or languishing in an overgrown garden covered by weeds. Once initiated into Doh-Nai-Zen, its purging energy helped me to slough off my emotionalism and my weaknesses; revealed latent power beyond my imagination. Now, as you know, I am extremely wealthy with highly successful business interests globally. I own property and land all over the world and I and my family want for nothing. I'm an influential, sought after man, Jon, with friends in very high places. And all because a few times a week I practise kiyomeru.'

'What the hell's that?'

'The Japanese word for purgation.'

Marco noticed Jon's quizzical look and explained, 'It literally means cleaning out, right down to the foundations and often with a touch of violence. More sand blasting than dusting, I'd say. And that's a very apt analogy for the action at the heart of Doh-Nai-Zen.'

'Sounds a bit harsh – and painful.'

'Not physical pain. This is all psychic phenomena.'

'How do you do this kiyomeru stuff, anyway?'

'To practise kiyomeru, we stand in a room with other, experienced members, and simply allow the purging energy to do its work. We usually experience our own inner film show of the mistakes which keep us enslaved – admittedly, that can be extremely uncomfortable. Then we are made to perform physical acts – dancing, singing, shouting – all of which purge past wrong actions from our system. The Energy corrects old patterns and dispels fears that have been inherited from four thousand years of so-called, civilising culture, passed on to us through our parents – just as our genes were. The Energy simply breaks down the blockages that barricade the expression of out true animal natures. All that is required is to trust it totally and to go where it leads.'

'I don't understand how you're *made* to do things. How does that work?'

'The relationship is similar to the marionette and the puppet master.'

'So who's the puppeteer, then?' Jon asked, still thinking this was all a strange, sophisticated send up.

'The Creator. Nature. The animal force, call it what you will.'

'What happened to free will?' Jon scoffed.

'Delusion, Jon. The only freedom we have is to choose to be manipulated by low energies or higher ones.'

Feeling lost, Jon changed tack. 'But why join Doh-Nai-Zen to do all this? Couldn't you just learn all this stuff for yourself? Do it on your own? I don't see why you have to...'

'Impossible,' Marco barked, turning to face Jon who momentarily had the illusion of Marco towering above him. 'You have to be initiated: you must have the Energy passed on to you by someone that already has it developed within them.'

'Passed on? I still don't get it. How?'

'It's similar to conception, except it happens psychically, not physically.'

Jon conjured a mental image of spectral sperm entering his body and felt a frisson of revulsion.

Marco paused, apparently reflecting. 'You know, one has to be chosen to join Doh-Nai-Zen. Handpicked because one displays a particular potential. I see it in you, Jon, and I have personally selected you – for many reasons. And now, I am offering you the chance of a lifetime. This is your million-dollar jackpot. An epiphany – the most important moment in your life.'

'Oh yeah? Tell me more,' Jon laughed, both chilled and thrilled suddenly.

'Have you ever read Plato, Jon?'

'Can't say I have, no.'

'He wrote that most people live as though in a cave, turned away from the entrance, assuming the shadows cast on the wall to be reality. Doh-Nai-Zen takes us out of the cave and into the daylight. After your initiation, and a few years' practice, you will simply be purged of all your delusions.'

'Whoa! After my initiation? I'm not too sure about this,' Jon said with a nervous laugh. 'I don't like the sound of initiation for a start. Rolling up your trouser legs, and stuff.'

'No, nothing like that,' Marco chuckled. 'The initiate simply kneels in a room with a few experienced members. They begin their kiyomeru and the contact is made. Nobody will do anything to you and neither will they participate directly.'

'And that's it. No preparation? Nothing to study?'

'No. And no priests, no incense, no mumbo-jumbo and no dogma. Just a clean, uncluttered experience. All that's required is a willingness and a readiness. And that's it. So, it's up to you, Jon. Do you want to join? Do you truly want to take this opportunity to become one of life's winners? By definition, rich and powerful?'

'Yeah, of course I do. But there's got to be a downside. There ain't no free lunch – or is there?'

'No downside as you call it,' Marco answered. 'But neither is it easy. You'll have to work hard to fulfil your potential. And we do have enemies. Groups that would infiltrate and destroy our organisation if they could. We just have to be very, very careful. Covert, in fact. Nothing for you to worry about though.'

Jon had a sudden thought. 'They won't zap my goolies with a laser, will they, like in the book?'

Marco roared with laughter. 'No, Jon,' he said, still chucking. 'That level of initiation is reserved for the likes of Chi-Chi alone.'

Jon experienced pleasure at making Marco laugh. 'God, they made a mistake kicking you out of that seminary,' he said, shaking his head. 'You'd have made a great priest.' And then, he added eagerly, 'Okay. Why not? I'm sold. I want to join. When?'

'Why not this evening?' Marco insinuated, the slightest trace of triumph in his voice. 'In New York.'

'Sounds good.'

'Which reminds me.' Marco pulled a gold Half-Hunter from his waist-coat pocket. 'The New World beckons and Concorde's seven o'clock flight waits for no man. Time to go.'

Jon glanced at his wristwatch. It was after five o'clock. He wondered how they would get to Heathrow in time through rush hour traffic.

As if reading his mind, Marco announced, 'We're being picked up in half an hour and we're already cleared to board at Heathrow. There's no real panic.'

The helicopter was sitting on the roof at the centre of the landing circle, its blades idly chopping the air. They ran heads bowed and clambered aboard. The chopper climbed rapidly, turned through a hundred and eighty degrees and accelerated hard to the West, locating and following the Thames back towards its source.

Looking down over London's constellated sprawl, the river catching the last blazing reds of the setting sun, Jon took a deep breath, synchronising with a rising wave of euphoria.

– For the first time in my life, it feels like anything and everything's possible…

They were whisked the twenty miles from the VIP lounge at JFK to the Waldorf Astoria by limousine. It was a first visit to New York for Jon and he was disappointed that the busy schedule planned gave him little time to explore. He stared out through the limo's movie screen window for the whole hour-long journey, absorbing the city's sights with his old art student's hungry eyes.

Towering buildings slid by, diagonally cut by hard-edged shadows as the sun set for the second time in his day. The buildings grew in numbers, forming a deep fissure, the sides angling in perspective like out-crops of crystalline rock jutting irregularly into a darkening sky, facetted in acres of glass.

As they sped through, Jon imagined being a tiny creature submerged in a teeming rock pool. Things were happening throughout the layers above, but the concentration seemed to be at street level and below. Here it was shadowy, cold and dangerous. It was where predatory creatures lurked, cunningly camouflaged, awaiting their prey as it scuttled timidly from one hollow to the next. It seethed with activity, the atmosphere a mix of paranoid fear and excitement. And, he sensed, it was all about money.

The limo drew into the Waldorf's drop-off area in Park Avenue. Jon stared wide-eyed, craning vertiginously up at the towering Art Deco building. He followed behind Marco, through the swing doors and into reception.

– Wow! The extravagance, the glitz. This is so over the top...

After registering, a liveried bell-boy escorted him to his suite, ushering him in deferentially.

– *I love it! It's so big! Like being in an old Hollywood movie...*

He played out his fantasy – acting the cool habitué, not wanting to fluff his lines. He fished in his trouser pocket and withdrew a roll of dollar bills, courtesy of Marco. He peeled off a twenty and handed it to the bell-boy, holding it low as he had seen performed in countless movies.

The man's ingratiating, '*Thank* you, sir,' told him he'd got it right.

After unpacking and showering he ordered room service and spent a leisurely hour demolishing a huge serving of ham'n'eggs and waffles, drinking coffee and channel hopping.

– *God! American culture is unbelievable! They seem to churn out some of the very best, and the worst, in the world – like getting to the moon, yet creating the Vietnam war... But it's the amount of junk in between that takes the breath away.*

A knocking interrupted his contemplation. The door opened and Marco breezed in wearing what appeared to be a red Judo outfit. 'Slight change in plans, old boy. We're going to meet Chi-Chi now. He wants to initiate you personally. This is a great honour. You'll have to put this on, by the way.' He handed Jon a blood-red, silken suit similar to the one he was wearing.

'Do I have to? It's really not my colour,' Jon joked nervously.

'It *is* important.'

'But why? I thought you said there was no mumbo-jumbo...?'

'Even we have a few foibles. Indulge me for now – all will be revealed in time.'

Jon demurred and went to the bedroom to change. A while later, he accompanied Marco to the penthouse suite where Chi-Chi was in residence. He felt embarrassed in the flimsy pyjama-like suit; and apprehensive, as though being escorted to an operating theatre.

In the elevator, he confided to Marco, 'I feel really shaky and scared all of a sudden. Not sure I want to go through with this.'

'Don't worry, dear boy. Normal reaction. All those habitual low energies inhabiting and ruling your body don't want to be usurped. They'd do absolutely anything to stop this happening, so they act up. The fact that they're manifesting as fear is interesting. It tells me that what has held you back, stopped you developing your full potential, is just that, Jon. You've been a scaredy-cat most of your life, have you not?'

Jon recalled, in rapid sequence, a dozen incidents where this had been proved to be indubitably true before concurring meekly, 'Yeah. I suppose you're right.'

They arrived at the suite; Marco knocked, swung the door open and ushered Jon in. There were two men and two women in the heavily curtained, dimly lit room. They got to their feet flashing white-toothed smiles as Jon and Marco entered. Jon was introduced to each of them. All four were Americans, each wearing the red outfit. One of the women, Jon recognised, was a hot-property movie star. As he shook hands, he couldn't stop himself, despite his anxiety and discomfort, from gazing at her breasts, contoured by the silky suit, nipples in sharp relief.

After the introductions and sporadic small talk, a reverential quiet descended on the room. Twenty hushed minutes passed. The air seemed to gell with expectancy, the furniture solidifying, the drapes hanging tense. Jon sat breathing shallowly, eyes shut, hands clasped in his lap, clenching and unclenching them in unison with his grinding back teeth. Apprehension built as his heart rate increased. Time dragged... He jumped as an inner door opened.

He could never quite recall what happened next. It was as though five seconds were removed from his life, as though reality stopped, or a wormhole passed by and he fell through time.

A stocky, well built figure loomed in the doorway, silhouetted for a moment against the bright lights of the adjoining room. Then the others were standing again, heads bowed and Marco was at his side propelling him towards Chi-Chi. Jon became dizzy, unsteady on his legs. He heard Marco speaking in Japanese. Chi-Chi responded, his voice sonorous, guttural, a tape played backwards to Jon's ears.

'Inu-no Chi-Chi-oya welcomes you, Jon, and hopes you had a pleasant journey,' Marco translated.

At the back of his mind, Jon was aware that even Marco's dominant persona had wilted in this man's presence.

'Yes, thank you very much,' he stuttered, unable to stop himself bowing.

– *God, I hate that...*

Part of him giddily presumed he should lie on the floor, belly up, like an inferior, submissive dog. He shook the feeling off, lifted his head and looked directly into Chi-Chi's eyes. They were black, fathomless. He thought he would faint; the raw energy emanating from the man was overwhelming.

Chi-Chi extended his hand. Jon took it. All his attention was focused on where their hands met – his own being tightly gripped, not shaken as expected. Jon sensed an invasiveness, becoming aware of Chi-Chi probing his mind and feelings, staring hard into his eyes, somehow projecting his mind into Jon's heartland. He remembered a Cub Master trying to sexually assault him, the hot hand rummaging in his shorts, the saloon bar breath – that same sense of violation, of trespass into his most private space. He wanted to shout his objection, to protectively pull away, but was held prisoner.

After an agonising minute, Chi-Chi let go of Jon's hand and spoke to Marco in Japanese.

'You are correct, Marco. The animal force in him is strong. Very strong. I actually felt it leap in recognition. I'll initiate him now. After, take control of his development. Personally groom him. Let us see if you can turn him into a powerful and loyal work-dog.'

Marco translated for Jon *soto voce*. 'Inu-no Chi-Chi-oya pronounces you are very ready to be initiated, and we ought to start immediately.'

Marco ushered him to the centre of the room. Jon allowed it like a bullock taking the short, metal-walled walk to the slaughterer's stun gun and knife – despite stiff-legged reluctance, there was no way out, no way back.

'Kneel facing Chi-Chi.'

Jon did as asked. The others padded to the centre in concert, crouching, kneeling, making a semicircle behind him, heads bowed, each placing a hand on his body. Chi-Chi grasped Jon's head roughly between both hands and tilted it back, staring intently down into his eyes – and then began to chant.

An intense vibration emanated from Chi-Chi's palms. It pulsed through Jon in waves, peristaltic, almost sexual. His whole visual field was taken up with Chi-Chi's eyes and an intense sensation forced him to shut his own.

– *Fuck! It's like looking at the sun...*

Then a fierce twitching and fibrillation in the pit of his stomach; he heard noises and movement behind him – whoops, growls, barks, then thumps as people keeled to the floor. As if with a life of their own, his arms raised jerkily sideways, tingling with pins and needles energy. A schooldays' memory of a frog pinned outstretched on a tray of wax, twitching to the touch of an electrode – then his adrenaline glands detonated and, within a microsecond, a rose of fear bloomed.

Chi-Chi moved away and Jon was hauled to his feet. He opened his eyes, curious to know who was lifting. With a shock he realised there was no one near. Then pressure behind his knees, forcing him back down. A convulsing, blood red flash – and he tumbled forward onto all fours, aware of nothing but his own panting breath…

He was standing four-legged, long and low in brittle-gold grass, a remorseless sun beating down, hunger aching in his gut. His mind was thought-free in the dusty, stupefying heat; a dry breeze sporadically ruffled his fur. He could smell the pungent perfumes of the Serengeti; hear the monotonous murmur of flies around his ears. Through the rippling, hazy air he perceived the herd grazing a hundred yards ahead.

His ears pricked, distinguishing the sound of an abnormal gait beneath the snorting, shuffling din. He sniffed the air, smelled wounded gazelle and his heart leapt.

At the trot, he crept forward through the tall grass, keeping his head low. There, in front of him, at fifty yards, he saw the limping animal on the periphery of the nervously ruminating crush. The scent of hungry, hunting leopard rippled through the herd. It triggered a twitch of panic and an instant cacophony of clopping hooves. He kick-started his run, flexing his backbone convex to concave, muscular legs pumping with near maximum efficiency, his only focus the lone gazelle.

Despite the injury, she was fast, starting a darting sprint almost as he started his, running parallel with the thunderous stampede, trying to lose herself in the rising dust cloud. After fifty yards, sensing he was almost on her, she changed course, sacrificially veering sharply left, away from the herd. He ran wide on the turn, taken by surprise, losing ten yards, paw pads scrabbling for grip. He put on a gaining spurt and, as the gazelle prepared to manoeuvre again, clipped her rear legs, sending her tumbling. He pounced onto her hindquarters as she scrambled up; he flicked out claws, piercing through hide into flesh, hanging on, pushing her to the ground again, pressing down with his full weight. He locked expertly onto to her throat with his mouth, pulling the head to the earth, applying all his strength, gripping tight. An unconscious imperative demanded he held on regardless. The gazelle also instinctively understood that unless she could get to her feet and escape, she was meat.

Their wills and bodies battled. She kicked and writhed, hooves searching for solid ground, torso thrashing. He bore down on her heavily, gripping with his teeth and claws. The minutes passed.

Reaching exhaustion, she slowly surrendered the pointless struggle. He looked into her eyes; she stared back non-accusingly, dispassionately playing her part in the ritualistic *dance macabre*.

He took another fold of skin into his mouth, clamping off her breath completely, careful not to bite through the jugular, not to be blinded by spurting blood. He watched as her eyes clouded over then became opaque. The body slumped lifeless and he purred in pleasure at the well-earned meal to come.

The scene giddied and swirled. Immediately, Jon was back in the dimly lit room. He opened his eyes: the actress lay naked beneath him, her red suit a pool of blood spreading across the floor. A shockwave of terror...

'What the fuck... What is this? What have I done?' he shouted, desperate to flee, but immobilised by terror.

Another red flash reverberated inside his skull. He was on his feet. Around him, the others writhed together, naked on the floor, viscous patterned skin glistening. A wave of nausea... His eyes searched for the door but it had disappeared. He heard Chi-Chi howling, turned to the sound and saw a huge rabid dog standing on its hind legs.

A blink and the room was back to normal, its inhabitants fully clothed again, swaying and singing to their own inner rhythms. Relief – only hallucination – then a rising, breath-catching exultancy. Abruptly he was swatted to the ground as though flattened by a huge hand, and he lost consciousness.

He dreamed he was making love to Lucia and his orgasm went on and on and on...

His shoulder was being gently shaken, drawing him reluctantly back.

'Well done, Jon, well done.' Marco gently helped him to his feet. 'Welcome to Doh-Nai-Zen. You're now a fully paid up member.' He laughed, embracing Jon stiffly, patting his back.

Jon looked around dazed, noticing Chi-Chi had left the room.

'How long was I asleep?'

'Have you been asleep?'

Life energy was tingling throughout his body, everything in sharp relief, and he dimly recalled having felt the sweet sensation once before, when he was two or three years old.

– *Like Adam on the first day of creation. Where have I read that...?* He felt energised but could hardly stand.

– *I'm exhausted. Why? What happened...?* He was overwhelmed with the desire to slump back to the floor again, to curl up and surrender to the delicious sleep.

Marco's voice interrupted his thoughts. 'That was a great initiation, Jon, old boy. Now let's all go back to my suite for some tea. And after – we've a busy night ahead of us.'

The others ritually hugged Jon in turn, offering congratulations. They filed out of the room following Marco. Jon was wafted along with the group, immersed in their bonhomie, his weariness replaced by a rising euphoria.

After tea and changing into normal clothes, they all – except for Marco who had returned to Chi-Chi's suite – went down to one of the conference rooms in the hotel.

There were about sixty people in the hall seated facing a small raised platform on which three easy chairs were ranged behind a low table. The central chair was throne-like, crimson upholstery richly contrasting with dark, carved wood. Two elegantly designed microphones perched on the table. A buzz of anticipation filled the hall.

He found a vacant seat to one side near the front and idled away the time at first spotting famous faces in the audience, then mulling over recent events.

During tea he'd learned more about the movement he was now part of; membership was by invitation only; no proselytising or recruitment campaigns employed. Normally, a potential member would have to wait some months – even years – before being allowed to join, while the others observed them and debated their suitability. On hearing this – and after having received appreciative, knowing nods from the group while recounting his initiation experiences – he felt a rush of pride. He had convinced himself he really was a special case, a chosen one, as Marco had intimated.

'Be careful of that pride, Jon,' Marco had whispered. 'It's powerful.'

Jon had looked so startled, Marco added, 'You'll discover that kiyomeru develops the ability to tune into others' feelings, Jon. A very useful tool when needed. By the way, what you experienced *was* extraordinary, but it won't always be like that. Sometimes you'll think nothing's happening and may even find it intensely boring. Believe you me, it's always working away in there...'

'Is this seat taken?'

An aristocratic English voice intruded into Jon's daydream. He looked up to see a handsome, ruddy face, a shock of white hair and a friendly smile. The man's eyes were half closed, as though staring at the sun, creases radiating from the corners. An outdoor man Jon guessed. He was probably in his sixties, very regal in bearing, tall and well-built, and Jon sensed an openness, a warmth as though standing near an open log fire.

'No, help yourself,' he replied, indicating the vacant seat.

'You're English?'

'That's right. Live near London. Jon Lucke...' He held out his hand.

'Robin Buckingham. How do you do?' the man replied, shaking Jon's with a firm grip. 'How long have you been a member?'

'About two hours.'

'Well, congratulations,' Robin chuckled, taking his seat. 'Welcome aboard...' then, as movement was discerned behind the curtains, added quickly, 'I do hope we shall get to know one another back home,' before settling into reverential quietness.

Jon was certain he had met this man before. He was about to enquire when Marco entered the hall, pulling aside one half of the draped curtains, ushering in Chi-Chi followed by a young Japanese woman in a modern, split-to-the-thigh cheongsam. The audience's babble transmuted to a clatter of chairs as they stood. The party mounted the two steps to the platform in silence. Chi-Chi lowered himself into the sumptuous chair; Marco took stage right, the woman Chi-Chi's left. She crossed her legs, revealing a length of smooth thigh. Jon, who thought her stunningly beautiful, picked up her radiating sexuality as a tingle in his groin, his penis the antenna.

Two women fussed and fluttered, bird-like, from the wings to place a tray of refreshments on the low table. The people in the hall took their seats and a palpable hush descended, punctured by occasional coughs. Chi-Chi looked round the room, savouring the mood of his audience, his face devoid of expression. Jon took the opportunity to study the man.

– *Weird. He looks forty-fiveish at most – but if he was a high-up in the army back in 1940, he should be close to a hundred now. Bloody hell...*

He was about five eleven – tall for a Japanese – stocky, solidly built, with cropped, black hair and smooth, sallow skin. His almond-shaped eyes were alert, taking in every nuance and movement in the hall. He wore a sharp, well tailored, business suit, a white shirt and sombre tie. Jon found this odd, incongruous.

– *Expected more, somehow – flowing robes, a beard, something more eastern...?*

Chi-Chi leaned forward and gently tapped the microphone to see if it was working. The loud tocking declared it was, and he began to speak in Japanese. He talked non-stop for half an hour. The Japanese woman was taking what Jon assumed were shorthand notes and he wondered, already bored, if Japanese shorthand looked like written English.

To indicate he had finished, Chi-Chi sank back in his chair and Marco began to translate. He'd told Jon it was only possible to give a loose précis of what Chi-Chi had said – and that it took tremendous concentration on his part.

'Chi-Chi thanks you all for inviting him here tonight,' Marco began, 'and for making his short stay in the United States so pleasant.' A pause for applause and Chi-Chi nodded acceptance around the hall. 'Although he has done this many times before, Chi-Chi wishes to give you all some pointers, some guidance and advice, about the path of Doh-Nai-Zen. As you well know, Doh-Nai-Zen is a contraction of the Japanese words that mean total abandonment to and development of the pure animal energy within.

'You have all received into yourselves the force that purges you of your weaknesses, both inherited and self-created. If you do your kiyomeru diligently and pay attention to your experiencing, an external energy will unite with and augment your own innate force. An energy which can be likened to fresh-killed food for your inner animal. You will then discover a personal potency you could never have dreamt possible. To hone this power so that it is of benefit to you in your life, you must cease absolutely your old behaviour. And you must not only do your kiyomeru weekly, but must also train hard, keeping your body fit and supple...'

'Workout!' Chi-Chi interrupted in heavily accented English, leaning towards the microphone. His jibe elicited a gale of obsequious laughter from the audience.

'But your biggest enemy,' Marco continued as the laughter faded, 'your obstacle to achieving true Doh-Nai-Zen, is within your selves. It is your fear, your sentimentality and your morality. Whenever these...' Marco paused, leant back and looked left to the Japanese woman. She whispered some words and Marco nodded. 'Yes, spectres, parasites. Whenever these spectral parasites arise within you, you must be ruthless and side-step them, denying them control. Your biggest mistake is to act out such feelings. If you do that for a moment, you fall off the tightrope. You cease being a winner and become a mere also-ran again. You must allow the animal energy to develop within you – your material energy, your mind, as its servant. This is the true path, the royal road to health, wealth, success and power. It is the sluggishly emotional, vegetable energies that must be rooted out; cut back hard. Energies such as sloth, sentimentality, sympathy, pity, fear – to name but a handful – and, even more so, romantic love, jealousy and hatred. But all of this is well-documented in Chi-Chi's writings, which you must read daily and absorb...'

Jon's eyes began to close. His head drooped to his chest and bounced back with a start over and over until the weight of sleep finally pressed him down.

He dreamed his body was tangled in a lone bramble bush growing in a great, wide plain – thorns viciously spiking his limbs, pain shooting up his back, blood seeping from the wounds. He struggled, attempting to pull off the barbed tendrils with his hands – but they held firm, biting deeper, enmeshing him more. Chi-Chi stood before him, laughing at his futile attempts to break free.

'Help me, Chi-Chi! Help me. Please! *Please!*'

Chi-Chi threw a sharp looking knife into the ground, just within Jon's reach and laughed cruelly, 'Help yourself, help yourself...'

Jon awoke with a gasp, sweat prickling his body. He was still in the hall, in his chair, Robin sitting next to him, eyes closed, hands palm up in his lap. The dream had been unbelievably real, sharper than life, and he shuddered. He glanced at his watch. Over two hours had passed. His mouth was dry, foul tasting and he was craving for a cigarette. Chi-Chi had just finished and Marco took up translating again.

'...And so it is clear that if we are to achieve our aims to become members of the new, ruling élite, masters of our own destiny, you must all take responsibility for your own actions. You must surrender to the Energy one hundred per cent. In return, it will reward you with health, wealth, success and eventually power. Finally, Chi-Chi thanks you all for coming tonight, and wishes you all good hunting.'

Chi-Chi stood and the audience followed suit, applauding as he left the hall followed by his convoying entourage.

Around midnight, after dinner and a series of wearying but highly profitable business meetings, Jon decided to go out on the town. He had to see something of New York before being catapulted home the next day, hurtling towards the arcing sun at a closing speed of over two thousand miles per hour.

He collected a street map from reception and allowed the doorman to hail him a cab. He booked it for the night, telling the driver to take him to Fifth Avenue – echoes of his avid, film-going youth.

He spent an hour or more cruising the streets in the back of the yellow cab, being taken to one famous site after another – Times Square, Madison Gardens, The Empire State Building, Wall Street, Broadway – chalking up tourist attractions like a trainspotter.

As they toured, he slowly became aware of a burgeoning sexual lust. It rubbed gently against him at first, like a cat wanting food, then tugged at him, dog-like, becoming insistent, urgent. He allowed it to possess him and experienced the sweet rush of sensation to his groin. He decided to pick up a hooker. He had never done such a thing before, never been that hungry or driven. The craving pushed aside all vestiges of embarrassment and the nervous fear of breaking a long-instilled, cultural taboo.

With the driver's connivance, he was driven over to Forty Second Street. Arriving at the recommended red light district, they patrolled up and down until he spotted the prostitute he was intuitively seeking – one with all the qualities demanded by the psychopath now inhabiting his trousers. Jon told the cabbie to wait for him, got out and strolled towards the busty streetwalker standing at a junction, touting what was on offer, hands on hips, her coat open, despite the chill of the autumn night. She was black and tall, an inch or two over six feet, willowy and long legged. Her large breasts were clearly visible through the sheer blouse tucked into a black leather miniskirt.

'How much?' he enquired.

'A hunnerd bucks, with a rubber. Fifty for a blowjob,' she told him matter-of-factly, a gum-chewing, bored shop assistant longing for closing time.

'A hundred? Okay. Let's do it.'

'Where yo' wheels, honey?'

'I'm a visitor – came by cab.'

'Shit. Okay, follow me.' They walked in the direction she indicated. 'You Canadian?'

'English.'

'Wow, man. Ain't ever had no English before.' She seemed to perk up for a moment. The woman led him into an alleyway smelling of urine. A red and blue neon sign flashed Budweiser on and off, on and off across the street, its reflection fractured in the feet-disturbed puddles pooling the alley's length. Overflowing bins banked the walls, wetly spewing cartons, tins, bottles and sodden newspapers. A disturbed rat, its legs seemingly powered by clockwork, scurried along the gutter, adroitly dodging debris. The woman pulled him between two grossly dark wheelie-bins and leaned back against the damp brickwork.

'Okay, sweetheart. Gimme the dead presidents.'

'What...?' He realised she was referring to money. He handed the bills over. She counted them and stuffed the wad down her cleavage, fished in her handbag and produced a small silver, ridged packet.

'Put this on, honey. I don't wanna catch no English diseases.'

He did as requested – ripped open the packet, slipped the condom out, fitted it over and down, his throbbing tumescence facilitating the task.

'Okay, lover. No kissing and don't take for ever – I'm a busy working gal.'

She unceremoniously hoicked her skirt, grabbed his rubber-covered penis and roughly guided him home, half-heartedly curling a leg around his lower back, the other pushed hard to the ground, bracing them both against the wall – ever the consummate professional.

The sex was short, grunty and sickly sweet. Even before his climax ebbed away he wished he hadn't done it, the motivating force spent. They pulled apart hurriedly, adjusting their clothes, each contemptuous of the other. Jon held the used condom by finger and thumb in distaste, dropping it behind a bin as they briskly returned to the street.

'You come back and see me again, big boy.' Her parting shot was issued like a slogan, part of a marketing campaign.

'I'd rather cut my cock off first,' he mumbled under his breath. He gave her a false smile and a cheery wave.

As he approached the waiting cab, he realised it was the hunt he had craved, not the sex. He wondered if his initiation had anything to do with these strange, new appetites.

– *I'll ask Marco tomorrow. If I'm not too shy to admit to this little adventure...*

'You okay now, boss?'

'The Waldorf, fast as you can,' he told the grinning driver, ignoring his question as embarrassment bloomed.

Back in his hotel room, he felt dirty, tainted. The smell of the prostitute's cheap perfume pervaded his clothes, mingling with the odour of the alley. The combination invoked the foetid stench of a refuse tip. The olfactory connection stimulated a train of thought, then understanding. He saw the woman as a repository brimming with sloughed off rage and lust, dumped and discarded by countless men. He experienced disgust, shame, nausea; then an itchiness, feeling as though he had roiled in a dustcart. He spent over an hour in the shower, scrubbing and rinsing.

After, lying naked on his bed in the dark, the two diametrically opposed personalities that inhabited his mental world re-commenced their on-going battle with renewed zest.

– *Tut-tut-tut. Committing acts of adultery, consorting with women of the night. What ever next? How low do you want to sink...?* scolded a finger-wagging monk.

The other, a flippant roué revelling in the newly felt, pullulating power raised two jeering fingers.

– *Just get off my case, will ya! I know what I'm doing. I can handle it. I'm gonna do what I want from now on. Be somebody for a change...*

Around three thirty, he tried to call Lucia, but there was no answer from her apartment. He was immediately deflated and jealous. Then angry, disappointed, depressed. He thought he ought call his wife, but couldn't be bothered. Then he began to dial Tony's number but pressed delete – there was nothing to say – his back-home life suddenly registering as wan and lukewarm.

Before finally falling into a sleep of sheer exhaustion he bunched his fists, gritted his teeth and swore he would sort out all the loose ends when he got back to England – business, marriage, Lucia.

– *That's it! Thing's are going to be very, very different from now on..."*

* * *

'That's where we ended last time, David – and Juanita will be here in about ten minutes. Shall I stop now?'

'Yes. Thanks, Michelle. I've made some minor corrections on the pad. Would you tip them in for me?'

'Of course.'

Enjoying this fine-tuning more than writing, and not wanting to stop, he gets reluctantly to his feet and makes for the kitchen...

two

DAVID SETS THE dinner to reheat and quickly makes a salad dressing. Collecting plates, glasses and cutlery, he takes them onto verandah and lays a table for two. He looks up and stands gazing at a single cloud, tinted bright pink by the setting sun as it floats behind the summit of the dominant mountain peak silhouetted against a sky layered turquoise to magenta. The light level drops a notch and the air noticeably cools.

'Juanita's car is approaching the house, David.'

'Thanks, Michelle.'

After checking everything is in place, he goes back inside in time to hear Juanita's soft tap on the door. He crosses and opens it.

'Juanita, welcome. Come in.'

'Good evening, David. How are you?' Juanita's voice is mellow, her English near perfect.

She hands him a small, neat package. 'Chocolates. For after dinner.'

'Thanks.' He bends forward to kiss her on both cheeks and senses her rising body heat. It smells fresh, tinged with the minutest trace of an expensive, lemony perfume. She wears a simple, white off-the-shoulder blouse and a black, three-quarter length, straight skirt and on her feet, sandals. The outfit shows off her copper complexion, elegantly slender figure – despite her fifty years and five children – and girlish breasts to perfection . Her abundant dark hair, with its faint, grey stripes, cascades down her back and, as she flicks it back from her forehead, her large, hooped earrings flash reflected light. At that moment, she reminds him of an actress he once fell for, when he was a teenager.

– She was playing the heroine in a film about Spain, or Mexico. Such a sexy image still... he thinks.

'Go on though. Supper's nearly ready. Would you like a drink? Wine? Grape juice?'

'I'll have what you're having,' she decides, passing through, out onto the verandah. 'It has been very hot today, even for the Spanish. How have you coped?' she calls back.

'With difficulty, but I'm getting used to it,' he announces carrying the paella, salad and grape juice from the kitchen, one-handed, piled on a large tray.

'Let me help,' Juanita says, lifting bowls from the tray, placing them on the table.

He hands her her drink. 'Salud.'

'Cheers,' she replies, clinking her glass to his.

They make small talk throughout the meal and, when finished with cigarettes lit, he asks her what she would like to do for the rest of the evening.

'Go for a walk? Sit and talk? Drive into Orgiva, or just sit and watch TV?'

'I was hoping we could hear some more of your book.'

'Really?' He is surprised, but pleased.

'Yes. I found it so very interesting – and I really want to know what happens next. Not only that, but I feel I get to know you more.'

'I told you, though, it's only a story I made up. It's not autobiographical.'

'But novels are based on life experience, surely?'

'I suppose that's true, unless it's fantasy stuff.'

'But someone like Tolkein must have experienced conflict and power struggles in his life; otherwise how could he have written *Lord of the Rings?*'

'Good point. But it's not about his day to day life, per se.'

'No. But a novel's characters must be aspects of its author's personality, surely? The same way everything in a dream symbolises oneself and can therefore be read?'

'You're quite right. I hadn't thought of it that way.'

'And from the way you write I can intuit your attitudes to women, to race, to authority... I'm an art therapist, don't forget. I believe we leave a readable psychic snailtrail with everything we do, create, or say.'

'Do you really want to peer into my murky depths, though...?'

'I do; and it's also good for my English.'

'Okay, okay, you win,' he laughs. 'Let's go in and get comfortable. Leave everything, I'll clear away later.'

They re-enter the house and sit together on the sofa. Juanita kicks off her sandals, draws up her legs and rests her head on his shoulder.

'Could we turn the lights down? I like to sit in the semi-darkness.'
'Sure. Michelle, dim the lights and then read more of my manuscript. From where we left off earlier?'
'Certainly, David...'

LANDED

Jon aimed down the slip road and floored the throttle. He felt the silver sports car leap forward a nanosecond before the contoured seat collected his body, then his head – car and driver accelerating to sixty miles an hour in under five seconds. The wrap-around power still gave him a thrill. He'd bought the car a month earlier and hadn't quite lost the feeling that everyone was looking at him with envy. But he'd discovered the buzz of owning material things didn't last long; it slowly faded, and that's why people were always buying, buying, buying.

– A good thing to know when you're in advertising... he told himself.

The motorway was unusually empty, traffic intermittent, spaced out – apart from a ten-wheeler lorry on his immediate right fast closing the entry space. Accelerating harder, judging it finely, he hurtled in front of it at over eighty, joining the carriageway as the slip road tapered to a tyre width. He flicked the stubby lever into the next gear, flooring the throttle again and caught a finger wag of headlights in his mirror.

'Arseholes!' he jeered at the anonymous driver fast receding in his rear view mirror. He fingertipped the car into top and put his foot down hard again, straddling lanes. White road markings dashed like tracer bullets, bellying into the car's underside, and he pretended he was a fighter pilot on a low-level bomb run.

'Eat lead, suckers!' he shouted, clicking the flasher stalk like a gun trigger, weaving back and forth across the outside lanes. He was feeling good this morning, childlike, wanting to play. He stretched up in his seat, exhilarated.

– What a year. The most amazing year of my life – all thanks to Marco and Chi-Chi. Not forgetting the delightful Lucia...

Images of last night's lovemaking floated into his mind.

– God, that woman's insatiable – talk about the Kama Sutra... He shook his head not able to believe the sexual lexicon they were creating between them. She would still only see him once or twice week though, claiming that college, friends and Doh-Nai-Zen took up the rest of her time.

– I'll have to do something about that... he reassured himself, sidestepping the irritant of reality.

– Can't have a Doh-Nai-Zen member not getting his own way...

Jon was still practising the art of kiyomeru a year after his initiation. During that time, he had willingly allowed Marco to become his mentor and now hung on Marco's every word with reverential awe, storing advice, creating for himself a mental user-manual entitled *How to Become Rich and Powerful*.

Over the year, there had been subtle modifications to his personality and although he was aware of no longer being totally controlled by the slushy mawkishness, debilitating anger and depressions of old, he couldn't yet perceive the price he paid; the loss of affection, the withering of sympathy and the death of compassion. Nor would he care much if he could. He now construed every interaction as a challenge to his physical, mental and financial territory. Thus a will to win at all costs had begun to dominate his personality, his life.

An incident from a few weeks back drifted into his mind: playing squash with Marco, a conversation between shots, the smell of hot rubber and sweat tanging the air...

'By the way, Jon. I think it's high time you dispensed with those business partners of yours,' Marco announced, a propos of nothing.

'Yeah, I know. You're probably right, but they're nice guys basically and...'

'Quite honestly, you've shacked up with two losers and I'm afraid they're holding you back.'

'But it's complicated. We go back a long way and...'

'It's actually very *simple*, Jon. They're weak, and because you support them, you deny them any chance of ever standing on their own two feet. In turn, this makes them weaker still, so they hold you back more. A perfect example of a self-perpetuating, closed-loop system.'

'Nice one!' Jon called, masking frustration as Marco wrong-footed him again, gently lobbing the ball instead of the smash shot Jon had anticipated.

'A weak man keeps a bad situation in place with sentimentality, Jon.'

Thwack!

Marco had driven the ball to his left. Not concentrating and badly positioned, Jon was forced to run behind him, stretching for the ball, only able to make a weak backhand return.

'And sentimentality is, of course, a by-product of guilt.'

Thwack!

Again, Marco sent Jon the wrong way, this time with a disguise shot. In reply, Jon could only lob the ball back limp-wristedly to the wall.

'And guilt is the rope that binds us to our old behaviour.'

Thwock! Marco smashed the ball into the opposite corner. A rally began, Jon being pressed further to the back of the court, racing from left to right.

'And the worst possible behaviour, the greatest sin of all...' Thwack! 'is to not fulfil our potential.'

'I know you're right. What do you think should I do?' Jon gasped, breathless now.

Thwack!

'Get rid of them.' Thwack! 'Buy them out, or kick them out.'

Thwack!

'Do it,' Thwock! 'and do it soon!'

The latter was shouted as an imperative as the ball died in the corner, leaving Jon panting on all fours after a desperate lunge.

'Game, set and match, I think,' Marco stated, walking to the rear of the court to retrieve his towel.

'Uhh...'

After working for a week with Marco's accountant, Jon had at last felt well-enough prepared to arrange a meeting with his partners at the end of a working day. When all three were seated, he offered them two blunt choices.

'You leave the company tonight, both of you, each with a cheque for five grand, or I walk, taking my clients. If you choose the latter, you'll have to sort everything yourselves – buying the building back, staff, overdraft, the lot. So, take it or leave it.'

They both sat staring at him, not saying a word, Rob open-mouthed, Brian tight-lipped.

'What do you mean, "buying the building back"?' Rob stammered, his brow deeply creased.

'If you remember, when we borrowed to buy the building, the loan was in my name because my house was used as the guarantee. Well, I've paid off the mortgage and the building's mine now. So, when all the calculations are done, my accountant reckons I owe you both around five grand apiece – all that's left in your capital accounts. And that's being really generous – for old times' sake.'

'Old times' bollocks,' Brian muttered under his breath.

'This is a joke, right?' Rob suggested hopefully, beginning to realise that perhaps it was deadly serious. 'Come on, man, we've been partners for over six years. You can't just kick us out. There's gotta be a law against it.' His eyes began to brim with tears, his waxy face looking whiter than usual. 'We've been mates,' he whined, repeatedly poking his glasses back onto the bridge of his nose. 'Doesn't that mean anything to you?'

'Not in business terms, no.' Jon replied airily, unaware of aping Marco's insouciance.

'Fuck, man. What am I gonna tell my wife?'

'Tell her you're setting up on your own.'

Rob turned away, head bowed, nevously rubbing his temples with little circular movements of his fingers.

'Something tells me,' Brian spoke at last, 'that you've sussed all this out and it's legal and you're within your rights, yeah?'

'Totally. Got all the paper work here. If you decide to take the money and leave, just sign and hand everything over to me. If not, I sign the business over to you and walk. If you're smart, you'll take the money and go. There's no way you two could keep it running without me. Frankly, there is no business without me.'

'Aren't you the cold, heartless bastard, all of a sudden?'

'I thought we'd cleared the overdraft, though?' Rob cut in. 'And what about all the new work that's been coming through?'

'Most of the new stuff has been going through a company I set up months ago with a financier who wanted to finance me, not you guys. And, over the last six months, I've been lending this company money to pay everyone's salaries – including yours, don't forget – and the tax and VAT bills and so on. You've always left all the money stuff to me anyway, you lazy bastards, so it was easy. And we didn't pay off the overdraft, by the way. I did.' Jon pointed to himself. 'Paid it off with my own money to keep the company functioning.'

Brian and Rob sat silently, thoughts spinning, still wrapped in the shock of Jon's duplicity.

'So the company owes me now, not the bank. I *am* the bank. Simple as that,' Jon continued, increasing the pressure, keeping up the momentum as Marco had taught. 'We only ever had an informal partnership agreement, so we're not legally tied. If you refuse to sign I could close the building down tomorrow and have you and the company evicted. I don't want to do that – the office and staff set up here will be useful for a while. So... you've got two choices, only one of which is viable.'

'What about our pensions?' Brian asked.

'All sorted. I've topped up the fund, so you can take them with you and either keep paying in, or leave them as they are till you're fifty-five. So, what's it going to be, guys?'

'Where do I sign?' Brian asked, disdain in his voice and on his face. Jon pushed the agreement towards him. Brian scanned it briefly, sneered, signed and contemptuously tossed it back on the desk.

'Where's my cheque?' He stood and snatched the proffered piece of paper, staring hard at Jon, who, for a second, felt a spasm of regret as he tuned in to Brian's sense of betrayal. Immediately, Jon's resolve began to collapse.

'You're a cunt,' Brian spat venomously, turning and walking towards the door.

The word stung like a slap. An instantaneous anger brushed regret aside, forcing Jon to half rise in his seat. He pictured rushing after Brian's retreating back, spinning him round, screaming, 'Don't you ever call me that again,' then beating out an apology. He arrested the urge, reined himself in – and sagged back into his chair.

– *That was close. Must discuss that interesting little inner battle with Marco...*

He became aware again of Rob sitting open-mouthed, shaking his head, unable to comprehend what was going on, disoriented by the speed of change.

Jon found it easier to deal with Rob, who he'd always seen as an undisciplined slob, a do-gooder and a weakling. His whining and pleading had little effect, except to restore Jon's resolve.

Rob eventually signed. From the half opened door, he turned and said, strangely, Jon thought, but then shrugged it off, 'Keep in touch, man. I'm always there if you need me.' Then he, too, was gone to clear his desk.

Jon leant back in his chair, legs outstretched, hands behind head – a newly adopted, self-satisfied and cocksure pose. Phase one of creating his new life had, after all, been successfully completed. He was looking forward to giving Marco a blow by blow account, at the same time, as ever, longing for approval...

The action replay ended. Jon became aware he was driving at over a hundred and twenty and reduced speed slowly. When he reached the regulation limit, it seemed as though the car were crawling. He glanced in his mirror to make sure no police car was on his tail and reached for the cigarettes on the passenger seat before remembering he had quit.

– *Ouch! Those bad old bad habits sure die hard...*

He took to massaging his thighs, still sore from yesterday's training session. They were hard and firm when he tensed his leg and he felt pleased. His whole body, he knew, was trimmer, stronger, his beer belly long gone, a six-pack triple-ripple in its place. He had been working out and training hard in the gym at Marco's club.

'*My* club,' he corrected himself, having been accepted as a member a day or two earlier. That morning he had been surprised to discover he was a stone lighter and an inch taller than a year ago.

At the centre of his chest he re-experienced the pleasurable hum of being in love with himself; the sense of starring as hero in a self-directed, interactive movie. According to Marco, this inner thrill of pleasure was normal for Dai-Noh-Zen members, its intensity an ever-present guide to how well you were developing.

– *It's happening, just as Marco said it would...*

He was startled by his mobile's shrill trill. He picked it from the passenger seat, glancing at the illuminated screen.

'Shit!' He switched it off. Tony had been trying to reach him for some weeks.

– *Pub's so bloody boring. Same old stuff, week in week out. Might call him later...*

The half-mile to his exit sign flicked by. As he approached the three hundred metre sign, he half-registered ahead an old, battered estate indicating left, ladders tied its roof. If he tucked in genially behind, he knew he'd have to follow at its pace up the steep, one-lane slip road. He idly decided to cut in front and pressed the throttle, setting needles aquiver as the car craned forward, its engine barking, eager as a hunting pack on the scent.

Jon had misjudged both the distance and the other car's speed and as he overtook, was forced to pull more to the right than anticipated, just squeezing through the gap at the last second. His car lost grip as it danced over a drift-pile of detritus. He checked the slide with touches of opposite lock, then hit the accelerator hard. From under his low profile tyres, grit and dust sprayed, ricocheting off the overtaken estate's windscreen like shotgun pellets.

Glancing in his mirror at the fast receding scene, he saw the estate grey-ly emerging from a haze cloud, flashing its lights.

'Eat my dust, dudes,' he sniggered.

The roundabout was busy as he approached it at speed, cars pouring from his right, and he was forced to a stop, cadence braking like a racing driver. The estate pulled up behind him seconds later. The driver leaned out of an open window, waved a fist and shouted unintelligible abuse. Out of habit, Jon raised a stiff finger before accelerating into a gap in the oncoming traffic leaving a snarl of black rubber. He took the second exit at speed, tyres squealing, exhaust note howling – and then eased off, relaxing. The traffic was sporadic, grouped in small convoys, and he was in no real rush.

After some minutes, he became aware of the estate again. It had caught up and was tailgating him, flashing its lights. It closed then fell back as the traffic thickened and thinned. Jon realised his actions must have somehow insulted the driver's manhood, but shrugged it off.

– *He'll lose interest eventually. Ignore him…*

But their tailgating triggered an irritable anxiety. In his mirror, he noted there were two occupants, a heavy-set man driving and a younger passenger.

– *Driver looks like a builder, playing the hard man for his impressionable junior. Big blokes, though. Strong, violent, crude. Think they've got a poofter in a fancy car – no problem taking him. The old mucho-macho; good story down the pub…*

Then the car levelled with him, trying to overtake, the occupants gesticulating, miming 'wanker' signs, waving their fists and shouting. Jon looked to his right, sneered and mouthed 'Fuck off' before studiously ignoring them. A lorry hurtling round a bend in the opposite direction flashed at them, its horn blaring a Doppler effect *nee-yaaah* as it roared past. They were forced to drop back, the fresh loss of face and Jon's arrogance re-igniting animosity as effectively as petrol thrown on embers.

Jon signalled and made the left turn down a country lane leading to his destination. The estate followed.

– *Now this is trouble…*

From experience he knew that most aggressive flare ups on the road and in pubs and clubs are quickly over – passing dogs snarling, snapping, straining on their leashes. Usually – even if the protagonists stand off, continuing to hurl abuse – such incidents rarely go to physical violence without the catalyst of alcohol and a female presence.

– A couple of yobs up your arse for five miles implies they're looking for something a bit more meaty than a shouting match, though... he decided.

He glanced in his mirror again. They were still there.

– How did I get into this?

– More importantly, how do I get out of it...?

–Could outrun them... He imagined rounding a bend and ploughing into the back of a tractor or ponderous horse box.

– Too risky on these narrow lanes...

– How about driving to the nearest police station? Or just driving to Marco's and hope they go away?

– Too embarrassing...

– What, then...?

Jon started in surprise as a previously unheard voice began to speak inside his skull, as though he were wearing headphones.

'*In this sort of situation,*' the voice stated with professorial authority, '*When there is no escape, no reasoning, no charming your way out, you must act. Take the initiative. Go in committed and hard, finding the cold, animal ferocity in yourself. You have always known this. You discovered its truth, in the playground, on your first day at school...*'

A plan of action unfolded and Jon knew, but had no idea how he knew, exactly what he was going to do. The kiyomeru energy buzzing at his centre built to a roar... He slowed the car, half mounted the grass verge, and surreptitiously undid his seat belt. The occupants of the tailing estate took their opportunity, swung past and slammed on brakes, pulling into a gap marking the entrance to field.

As his car rolled to a halt, Jon opened the door and was out and sprinting towards them. The driver had already made the grave error Jon anticipated. A big man, running to fat and ponderous, he was swinging a leg out from the opened door space, ready to lever himself up. As he reached the car, Jon grabbed the open door and slammed it shut, using all his strength as though spinning the car on its axis like a top. Everything began to happen in slow motion. There was a sickening crunch as the door crushed the driver's shin and calf against the sill; the driver yelped, bending forward, his hands reaching for the source of agony; the door bounced lazily back open; Jon collected the recoiling door and rammed it shut again; a searing scream of heart-stopping pain echoed across the barren winter fields all around. Jon drove several punches from hip level into the contorted face. The half-conscious driver fell out of the car, rolling onto his side wheezing with pain, a dislocated knee agony-fused with broken fingers, his nose bleeding rivulets.

'Baftad,' he moaned, his mouth filled with blood and splintered teeth.

The young passenger was standing by his opened door, unmoving, rigid with fear, incredulous. Time abruptly jumped to its normal pace.

'All right?' Jon shouted at him across the car's roof with as much aggression as he could muster. 'All right? Don't move an inch or I'll fucking kill you. Just look after your mate when I'm gone. Okay?' The youth responded with a nod, staring down at the ground, paralysed, terror-struck, not daring to look up.

Jon walked back to his car feeling a vacuum inside, the kiyomeru buzz having switched off. His legs were made of jelly and he cursed his weakness. He climbed in, started the engine, declutched, snicked into gear and pulled away, not even glancing at the scene as he squeezed by. His right hand hurt, the knuckles beginning to swell and throb. The pain dragged him awake and he realised he had been holding his breath for the last minute.

A mass of emotion rushed to fill the interior emptiness.

'Oh shit. Feel terrible. Wish I hadn't done that.'

– *Bloody hell, Lucke. How did you pull that off? You're a genius...*

'What's happening to me? This is hell.'

– *Arseholes! He would have hurt you badly you if you hadn't done it first...*

He struck the steering wheel with his palm three times, each blow synchronised with a guttural scream of anger mixed with exhilaration. He tried to concentrate on the road. An image of the man lying bleeding elbowed its way into his mind.

– *Serves the fucker right...*

'No. I ought to go back, make sure he's okay.'

– *Don't. Weak. He'll survive...*

'I should call an ambulance.'

– *Forget it. It's over...*

As he drove, his old and new selves wrestled, releasing a gamut of conflicting emotion – contrition and jubilation; compassion and triumph; anxiety and pleasure.

'Jesus, I'm a living oxymoron.'

Sonia Brancusi, opened the door. Now like an old friend, she embraced him warmly, coming in a gnat's prick too close for propriety with a tiny push of her hips, Jon inferring that a deeper intimacy might one day be welcomed. He was not sure what to do about this. She was a very attractive woman but she was Marco's wife – and if he were mistaken... He put the dilemma to the back of his mind.

'Mwaa, mwaa,' she mouthed, kissing him on both cheeks. 'Nice to see you, Jon. Do come in.'

'You, too. Hey, you're looking really lovely today.'

She smiled, pleased, and touched his arm. 'Thank you, Jon. It's nice to be appreciated. Oh! Whatever have you done to your hand?'

'It's nothing. Got into a fight.'

She took his damaged hand in hers, gently exploring. Again, Jon felt a pulse of sexuality. 'You men. Come on through, let me put some salve on it.'

She led him by the hand into the kitchen, took a tube from a wall cabinet and gently applied the cooling ointment to his throbbing knuckles. He felt faint, watching this beautiful woman tend his wounds, the pain and her delicate massaging conspiring erotically with the sticky, white cream.

'There. All better...' She lifted his hand, turned it and lightly kissed the palm. 'Now off you go. The master's in the study. He's expecting you.' She smiled knowingly at a dumbfounded Jon, then turned to replace the tube.

Marco was sitting staring out of the open French windows. He swivelled round as Jon entered. 'Jon, dear boy, Good to see you. How are things?'

As ever, Jon experienced a purr of pleasure at the prospect of the imminent intimacy and attention. Over the next hour, he related how the meeting went with his partners and then told Marco about the fight, watching his face for the slightest hint of approval, or disapproval, choosing his words with care.

'This is excellent stuff, Jon. Things are really beginning to jump for you,' Marco enthused. 'Don't worry about the emotional reaction business too much. The animal in you is indubitably growing – your recent successes must tell you that. What you're feeling are simply old energies being sloughed off.'

'But why is it so difficult. I don't want them or need them any longer...'

'As I told you before, they don't give up easily. They fight to survive just as every living thing does. It's always a bit of a battle in the early days. Just keep doing your kiyomeru and it'll all work out. You've got four thousand years of very intense conditioning to overcome, don't forget.'

'Should I still be feeling things like remorse after a year, though?' Jon asked, basking in the sunshine of Marco's praise. 'And I was pretty frightened at first.'

'Don't be in such a hurry, Jon. Think of what you've achieved so far. The old you would never have been able to make such a stand. Look, next time you're doing kiyomeru, ask the Energy to show you how to keep these negative forces under control; where they stem from; how you feed them. They only take command because you allow it.'

Marco sat scrutinising Jon, devouring his eagerness. He took note of Jon's body language – the craning forward, hanging on every word, face bright with admiration.

– *He's so virginal; so ripe for this...* Marco mused before suggesting, 'Now you're a member at the gym, I suggest we get you signed up with the martial arts trainer. He's very good. And if you take to it, I'll let you come out with me some nights. There's nothing like prowling the streets looking for a scrap. Being predatory really hones up the old animal instincts. One of my little hobbies.'

Jon experienced a gout of excited fear. 'Thanks, Marco. I'll do that. It sounds... great.'

'Let's get down to business. I want to give you this.' Marco reached into a draw, retrieved and held out a slip of paper. Jon reached forward to collect it.

'What...?' was all he could say, staring at the cheque.

Marco was grinning. 'I could have had it transferred, but I wanted to see your face when I handed it over. Your reaction is priceless.'

'But, what's it for?'

In his hand he was holding a cheque for a half a million pounds, payable to Jon Lucke.

'Phase two, dear boy. And that's only a token – let's call it advance salary. There's another couple of million sitting in a bank account in our joint names. I want you to set up the newest, hottest, creative advertising agency in Town. You've got some real hard work on your hands, I can tell you – locating West One offices, fitting them out and hiring staff. Not forgetting a name, corporate ID, publicity – all that sort of thing. You have a year to do it in – in partnership with me, of course. What do you say?'

The anxious feeling that this was a set up, a cruel practical joke, began to vie with a rising celebration.

'But why me? I'm not sure I can handle it,' Jon stumbled out, almost panic stricken. 'And anyway, what do you know about running a full-blown advertising agency? And I've only worked in one for a while, after

I left college. Christ, this is scary, Marco.'

'It's all very simple, Jon. You leave running the business to me and the day to day agency work to your lieutenants, while you get on with the creative stuff. We have great faith in you, you know. We believe you have enormous talent – untapped depths. We want to use that potential – invest in it.'

'Why me?' Jon laughed, playing modest. At heart, he was arrogantly jubilant – feeling at last recognised.

'Simple. Doh-Nai-Zen needs to get more organised financially. Consequently, we'll need our own service companies – lawyers, accountants, insurance brokers and, of course, advertising and marketing groups. We have a few already, but as you know, an advertising agency can't have, say, two competing washing powder accounts on its books. Totally unethical – risks of collusion and all that – and we must always look kosher, even if we're not.'

'Not kosher? You mean we're going to do something illegal?'

'Let's just say it's a "creative grey area",' Marco answered, waving a hand, indicating the subject was not open for discussion.

'We have about ten clients lined up for you for starters; all blue chip, million pound plus accounts – over-the-counter pharmaceuticals, a supermarket chain, some kind of new, instant-noodle thing, a shampoo range, package holiday biz, all that sort of caper. They'll go out to tender in the normal way, inviting their own incumbents and the big boys – like Saatchis and Ogilveys – to pitch, as well as our good selves. And we'll win, of course – all set up beforehand because the companies are all controlled by Doh-Nai-Zen members. The work's got to be damn good, though, otherwise they couldn't swing it. So you'd better hire the top creative teams available. Get this right and you could end up as the Creative Supremo of the biggest agency in Britain – even Europe.'

Jon could only shake his head in disbelief. Marco stared dispassionately at him, a researcher observing a lab rat, then added, with a dry laugh, 'I know you'll rise to the occasion. You usually do, or so my daughter tells me.'

'Ah – I've been meaning to talk to you about that,' Jon mumbled, embarrassment mixed with a jag of anger at Lucia's discussing their intimacy with her father.

'It's quite all right, Jon. Don't look so worried. No need to be abashed. This new found amorality gives you Brownie points. Just don't go getting serious. She is earmarked for far greater things than you could possibly imagine.'

Jon felt a pang of resentment at Marco's last remark, but let it slip away.

'I still don't get it,' he said, evading the Lucia issue, holding the cheque in front of him by an edge, as though it might be poisonous. 'Why do we need all these companies?'

'For power, Jon, power,' Marco answered, leaning forward onto his elbows, bringing his hands together, as though in prayer. 'Enough to rule the world eventually – metaphorically speaking, of course. That's what every group wants when it comes down to the wire, be they political, religious or commercial.'

'I still don't get it. Sorry, Marco.'

Marco leaned back in his seat and continued as though delivering a lecture to a hall full of students. 'It cannot have escaped your attention that we have members at the helm of virtually every food and pharmaceutical multinational in the world, as well as globally in government, at the top of the armed forces and police, not forgetting most of the media worldwide.'

'No, I'm beginning to see that.'

'Yet, despite this, our power is nebulous, unharnessed. There's a loose symbiosis at the moment, of course. For example, our food people sell tons of over-farmed, nutrition-depleted crap, plus most of the sugar-based and fast foods on the market. Others produce alcohol and tobacco, and lately the artificial sweeteners used in soft drinks and, would you believe, chewing gum! All of which is heavily marketed, heavily consumed and is extremely deleterious to health. Regular usage drastically depletes peoples' immune systems; makes them violent, anxious, sick. The masses therefore develop all the twentieth century ills, such as migraines, obesity, asthma and all the heart-, digestive- and stress-related problems going. Then, and this is the masterstroke,' Marco laughed, 'our pharmaceutical boys move in with quack remedies designed to merely alleviate symptoms. And they make a *fortune* out of it.'

'Hold on a minute – what about the huge loss in man hours; the cost of hospitals, the police and so on?' Jon never actually argued with Marco. On the one hand he wanted to look intelligent and alert, on the other he enjoyed giving Marco feed lines like a comic's sidekick.

'Doesn't affect food and pharmaceuticals. They're such growth industries, they can afford massive wastage. They simply don't suffer from society's ills, but they surely prosper from them. Just like the arms trade, a pie in which we also have fingers. As long as there's a war somewhere, it's bouyant and prosperous and we don't give a shit about refugees and dead civilians.'

'Christ - that's hor... No, no: I think I see what you mean. Different kind of logic to what I'm used to, that's all.'

'It is, Jon, it is. And keeping that in mind, just consider what could be achieved if we pooled our resources and worked together as a cohesive unit instead of feathering our individual nests. The whole is always greater than the sum of its parts, is it not? Imagine the strength, Jon. A worldwide consortium of like-minded, top-ranking individuals – one great, covert, global multinational – all under the leadership of Chi-Chi. He masterminds all this, you know. And this is hardly scratching the surface of his genius. He has even more brilliant schemes cooking. His goal is for Doh-Nai-Zen members to be the new aristocracy, the future ruling élite. And I am offering you an in on the ground floor.'

'You're not going to tell me all those conspiracy theories are true, are you?' Jon scoffed.

'No, dammit, they're not. But they're surely going to be. The word conspire literally means to breathe together. And that's exactly what we in Doh-Nai-Zen intend to do, thanks to Chi-Chi.'

A look of reverence crept over Marco's face and he stared dreamily into the future, snapping back to continue, 'Do you realise that the combined wealth of all Doh-Nai-Zen members world wide is equal to the GNP of Britain? However, even that amount of money doesn't give us anywhere near the clout we need. By working together, though, we can, and will, achieve the goal.'

Jon detected a note of fanaticism in Marco's voice, not sure if he was serious or not, but didn't really care. He wasn't listening any more. He had real money now and began to realise what that meant. His feelings built to crescendo. If he'd been on his own, he would have danced around the room.

– *Bloody hell, Lucke! You've got five hundred grand in your sweaty hands and any day now, you're going to be a fucking millionaire...!*

'Well, enough of this. Let's have a round of golf,' Marco suggested. 'Then when we get back, we'll do kiyomeru before supper. I'd like to introduce a new technique to you. And Sonia would like very much to join us.'

As Marco quietly commanded, 'Commence,' Jon attuned to the now familiar kiyomeru surge, generated in the pit of his stomach, rising into his chest. He allowed the rush of energy free rein, feeling his hips swayed rhythmically from side to side.

After some minutes, Jon remembered Marco's suggestion to ask for direction regarding the myriad emotions that still plagued him. Even as the thought formed, an internal monologue began.

'First, feel your anger, Jon.' Unbidden, untriggered by external events, Jon's chest filled with hot rage. *'Now observe.'*

His awareness was shifted into to the core of the anger. As though watching a live performance, his body the stage, the kiyomeru energy slowly took the dense emotion apart. Jon was made to observe his layers of frustration and resentment being laid down – adult feelings interpreted and magnified by a child's mind. Then how they were compressed and annealed to become his lifelong sense of unfairness, of injustice.

'In time you will no longer experience febrile anger, Jon, one generated by childish weakness,' the voice continued. *'Soon, in its place will be pure, animal energy, to be used by you only when required as a driving ferocity – the will to win, to dominate.'*

In the same way, he was made to examine and unknot his guilt, his self-sabotage, his feelings of inferiority. Each time, understanding followed deconstruction, then the feelings subsided and were gone.

The incident on the road was re-enacted second by second, the sensations minutely analysed. After, he felt nothing for his victims. They became as pests, vermin needing to be controlled.

'Do you see now?' the voice persisted. *'It really was you or them. There is no moral issue. Merely animals coming face to face in the jungle, establishing who owns the territory, who is the highest in the pecking order. Natural. Animals feel no guilt or remorse, no shame or blame. Even the defeated accept their lot. If those men ever see you again, they will stand back, recognising a higher being. They'll despise you, but from now on, they'll fear and respect you. You're the one with the inherited morality problems, the one who has much to learn.'*

Then came the red flash heralding a shift of consciousness, a change of dimension.

The clacking of a stone on concrete and the cry, 'High School snob!' startled a thirteen year old Jon from his dream world. He looked over his shoulder to see a gang of be-jeaned and trainer clad lads from the local comprehensive chasing after him. He gave them a v-sign and stood on his bicycle pedals, treading hard to outrun them, tyres singing on asphalt. He prayed they would have forgotten him by that evening, when he'd be forced to cycle the same route home wearing his stripy school uniform, feeling as jittery as a cat traversing a dog pound.

'We'll get you tonight, you tosser!' they screamed after him, hurling stones and vitriol.

He cycled across the roadbridge that spanned the railway and entered the West Side of town. The scenery changed to avenues lush with mature trees and trim grass verges. Discretely opulent detached houses smugly lined the remainder of his route to the High School. The school where he suffered daily humiliation, being made to feel like an unwelcome foreigner by staff and pupils alike, because he literally lived the wrong side of the tracks – London overspill, a member of the detested New Town tribe.

His handlebars began to vibrate and jig to a rumbling from his front tyre.

'Oh, bollocks!' he spat, knowing the puncture would make him late yet again. He dismounted and made the futile gesture of feeling the flabby rubber. He began to jog, pushing the bicycle's useless weight alongside a growing panic.

– *Why does this always happen to me...?* he moaned, remembering he'd forgotten to write up his French translation last night – too interested in the big match on the telly – and the end-of-term exams were next week and he hadn't done a stroke of revision. He knew he was wallowing in a quicksand of trouble, already waist deep, and the more he struggled...

Arriving at the school gates in a sweat and panting heavily, he dumped his bicycle in the racks, ran down the side of the main building to the rear entrance and hurtled into the cloakrooms.

– *I'll hang around in here, sneak out and join my class coming out of assembly. I can tell Davies I missed registration because I got sent on an errand by the Head – or something like that. He won't check it out...*

The cloakroom door flew open, banging noisily, and Jon ducked behind a row of lockers.

'Who's there?' demanded an adult male voice.

'Me, sir,' Jon owned up, stepping from his pointless hiding place.

'Ah, Bad Lucke,' the Headmaster sneered, regurgitating the stale, old joke. 'What are you doing skulking there, boy, like a thief in the night?'

'Sorry sir, I had a puncture and it made me late.'

'*It* didn't make you late, boy. *You* made you late. Now, show me your hands.' He did as commanded. 'These hands are clean. You're lying to me, boy.'

'No, sir. I'm not, honest. I didn't have time to mend it... I pushed my bike... I...'

'DON'T answer back, you miserable wretch. Detention tonight. For lateness and for lying.'

'But, sir... that's not fair! Honestly, I...'

The Headmaster hammered Jon down with his voice. '*Another* night's detention, for insubordination and insolence – and because I don't *like* you, Lucke. You're trouble, and I don't want trouble in my school. You're scruffy, ill-disciplined, lazy and a bad influence. A hopeless case, Lucke. In future, leave your slovernly London habits at home and *do not* bring them into *my* school, if you please.'

He sighed histrionically before continuing, 'You know, the only things we can possibly hope to drill into the thick skulls of bad apples such as yourself before you leave this establishment, are self-discipline and respect for authority. Both sadly lacking in your case, Lucke. Now – get to your classroom and out of my sight.'

'Sir,' Jon demurred, choked with resentment...

He snapped back from the memory, reeling under the vivid impact of reliving the humiliation, the fear..

'*Jon. Jon,*' the inner voice called. '*Now see how you should have reacted. How you could have kept the upper hand.*'

The blood red flash again and he was back in the cloakroom, the Headmaster intoning, '*Another* nights' detention, for insubordination and insolence – and because I don't like you, Lucke. You're trouble, and I don't want trouble in my school...'

'Hold it right there, sir,' Jon interrupted, holding up a hand, feelings of relaxed confidence, of being in control, galvanising him. 'If you're going to take that attitude, you leave me no choice. I shall report that you sexually assaulted me, here in the cloakroom. You know the rumours have been flying for years about you and young boys.'

'You – you little bastard...' the Headmaster stuttered apoplectically. 'I'll...' He raised his hand and stepped towards Jon.

'Please hit me, sir. A bruise will make my story more convincing.'

The Headmaster stared at Jon in disbelief. He made lightning calculations and realised he could not take the risk; could not afford any prying whatsoever into his past. This wretched boy had somehow got the whip hand, just might carry out his threat and be believed.

– *He could well end up destroying my career, my life, my world...*

The Headmaster's hand dropped. 'Get out of my sight, Lucke, now!'

'Okay. Oh, one more thing, sir. I want to be made a Monitor. With all the usual privileges, of course.'

'Yes, yes. All right. Now go – and keep your disgusting mouth shut.'

'Say please.'

'*Please*,' the Headmaster spat through gritted teeth, shaking with suppressed rage.

'Thank you. Sir.' He brushed past the Head, who pulled back in alarm. 'By the way, I was on an errand for you, sir. That's why I'm late. Tell Mr. Davies if he asks. All right?'

Movement close by interrupted the spectral performance. The mirage dispersed and Jon was at once back in his thirty-six year old body. Sonia sidled up behind him and her arms encircled his chest. He stood rigid, not knowing what to do. Her hands caressed his nipples, his sides and she began to sway, pressing against him. He felt her breasts burning into his back through their thin kiyomeru suits. As she snake danced, hips grinding, her hands slid down to find his erection. Jon gasped in surprise. She stroked him expertly, teasingly, until he relaxed into the honeyed sensation. They began to sway in rhythm, as though dancing to a slow blues. Unable to stop himself, his hands went behind to clasp her buttocks, pulling their bodies tighter, their conjoined movements urgently coinciding with her gently kneading hand.

As he ejaculated, Sonia twisted away and slid from his grasp. Still dancing, she moved across the room. Jon fell to his knees hugging himself as the orgasm pulsed through his body.

The kiyomeru stopped and all three lay on the floor feeling the ancient energy glowing in their systems. Jon was totally bemused and confused, anxiously uncertain what to do next. He was embarrassed, too, sensing the cold wet patch against his skin.

Sonia sat up. 'I hope you're not shocked. Jon?'

'Well, I'm surprised, and... a little ashamed, actually,' he replied casting a wary look across at Marco.

'Well, there's no need. Marco knows as well as I do that it's important to always follow the movements, no matter what. You learn to trust them implicitly. There will be a reason for what I, what we, did,' she corrected herself. 'There's a lot of energy released during an orgasm. It could be to help purge either of us. Time will tell.'

'Was that the new technique you were talking about?' Jon asked, turning back, daring to face Marco.

'Not quite, old boy,' Marco replied with a grin, 'Nothing new about that. Don't look so worried – it's all right. I'm not about to pull the jealous husband stunt. I totally trust and believe in what we're doing, whatever happens. There are no wrongs, no mistakes, in the kiyomeru.'

'Yes... of course,' Jon nodded thoughtfully.

'No. The new technique is what we call authenticating. It's a way of asking questions of the Energy and allowing it to transmit the underlying reality through our bodies symbolically – avoiding our minds, of course. That way, we get a kind of objective overview of reality. So, on your feet. Relax and we'll do a demo. See what happens.'

They stood in a triangle facing one another.

'Let the Energy authenticate; how does Jon behave when he is in front of a rich and successful person?' Marco asked aloud.

A trembling force arose in Jon's body and he stepped backwards, contorting, twisting aside. The familiar feelings of fear, jealousy and deference activated. He began to bow obsequiously and a nasal whine emanated unbidden from his mouth.

'Stop, now,' Marco commanded, followed by, 'Now authenticate how Jon should feel as a member of the new élite.'

Jon was immediately pulled erect, feeling seven feet tall. A sense of superiority overwhelmed him, accompanied by a sneering desire for triumph, whatever the cost, whether threatened or not: a standing firm, not giving an inch, taking in every detail, every nuance, ready to manoeuvre for control, or attack, should a weakness manifest. The sensation faded...

'Did you observe the difference, Jon? Tell us what you experienced.'

He related what had happened, unable to believe the power of the psychic metaphors, yet excited by the wealth of possibilities on offer. Marco and Sonia appeared pleased with him, exchanging nods.

'Good, good,' Marco said, rubbing his hands together. 'You're making rapid progress. What a star! And now, I think there's a really important question to ask. Stand ready.' Jon had the fleeting thought that maybe they should discuss this first, but before he could object, Marco was already asking, 'How would it be for Jon's development if he remains married to his current wife?'

Jon staggered back, inwardly shrivelling, then crumpling to the ground. A sharp pain bit him in the chest; he couldn't breath and thought he might pass out.

'That's enough,' he heard Marco say.

'It doesn't bode well for the future, does it Jon?' Sonia asked.

'No, I guess not.' He got unsteadily to his feet, breathing heavily, stunned by what had been revealed.

'Now, again – authenticate. How would Jon grow if he were to divorce?'

Jon was immediately made to run round the room, arms outstretched. He imagined he was an eagle soaring giddily across a wide valley, sharp eyes seeking movement below; an aerodynamic body poised to swoop and snatch with sharp talons.

The sensation passed and he heard Marco pronounce, 'Up to you now Jon.'

'Especially now you know can afford the alimony payments,' Sonia chipped in, she and Marco laughing aloud at this. Jon perceived a callousness in them both, experienced a momentary distaste, but shrugged it off.

'And, it must be said, Jon,' Marco added, 'A mixed marriage is not exactly, ah, shall we say, appropriate for you at this juncture...' Marco had chosen his moment and his words with precision. Feeling beholden, Jon did not react to the racist comment at once, instead hiding behind incredulity.

'Why, for Chrissake? What's wrong with mixed marriages?'

'Nothing at all, Jon. Unless you're a Doh-Nai-Zen member, that is.'

'What? You're not telling me we're bloody Nazis? "Hitler was right" and all that white suprematist crap?'

Marco laughed. 'No, Jon. Doh-Nai-Zen is totally apolitical. And as for Hitler, we would never have accepted that superstitious, psychotic fool as a member, nor his cronies. We are not racists. Among our members you'll find Jews, Blacks, Indians, Chinese and of course, many Japanese. We're purists, Jon, like nature. We simply do not condone cross-species breeding.'

'Why ever not?' Jon asked, his hackles rising, uncomfortably aware of his children.

'If you take a moment to consider, you'll discover that in the animal kingdom interbreeding only happens between animals in servitude – domesticated and agricultural animals. Dogs, cats, cattle, horses – particularly mules. In fact, nature doesn't allow mules to breed. One has to go back to mating horses and donkeys if one requires more mules. In the raw, you'd never find, for example, a monkey mating with a deer, or an elephant with a rhinoceros, would you?'

'Don't know. Never really thought about it,' Jon answered, nonplussed, out of his depth.

'You should. It's fascinating stuff. Anyway, it is encumbent upon us to ensure the ruling élite remains racially pure – emulating, as far as possible, Chi-Chi's lineage. We simply do not wish to lose our élitist distinctions through interbreeding. We're white, red, black, yellow and brown supremists, if you like.' Noticing Jon's confused and worried look, Marco added, 'A lot to take on board, eh? You'll discover in time that each of Chi-Chi's premises leads to many surprising conclusions.'

Jon was confused and worried, his head awhirl with questions about his own origins, how he stood in relation to his children, what to do about his marriage – a maze of conundrums, enigmas and riddles. And because he was still deeply infatuated with Doh-Nai-Zen, ever hungry to learn and desperate to please, he did not see the flaws in Marco's argument. Failed to spot, for example, that the whole human race is a species per se.

'Let's authenticate around this, see if we can widen that somewhat narrow weltangschauung of yours,' Marco suggested. 'You're so very black and white, Jon. If you'll pardon the pun.'

Sonia giggled.

After the session, they changed into more relaxed clothes and sat down to an informal supper in the kitchen.

'Not much, I'm afraid,' Sonia said, piling food from a tray onto the kitchen table. 'All the staff are away tonight, so it's leftovers.'

'Except for this rather fine bottle of wine,' Marco announced, entering the kitchen, closing the cellar door behind him.

They dined well and after sat idly chatting about business and the intricacies of practising kiyomeru.

'One thing puzzles me,' Jon threw into the conversation as they prepared to retire for the night, 'I've re-experienced and been shown where a lot of my old emotions stemmed from, particularly today, but does that mean that's it? That I'll never experience them again? That I'm... cured?'

'Not necessarily, Jon. Chi-Chi has a saying; "You have experienced the state, but not yet arrived at "the station", the station here meaning a total personality change. Sometimes we get teasers, indications of what we will be like. It all has to happen at the pace one can take it But you, mon cher, are making remarkable progress. And now, bedtime. Goodnight and sleep well, my friend...'

Marco and Sonia had made Jon feel that he was their oldest, most intimate pal and was not, therefore, unduly surprised when, half an hour after the house had stilled for the night, Sonia knocked on his door, opened it and entered.

'Are you awake?' she whispered.

He sat up and switched on the bedside light. Sonia walked to his bedside.

'Make love to me,' she commanded.

'But what about...'

'Don't. Everything's fine.' She pressed two fingers to his lips as if conferring a blessing, then slipped her pale silk dressing gown from her shoulders and slid between the sheets. He saw she was beautiful naked and he could not refuse her – as she well knew. All the misty vestiges of embarrassment, morality and thoughts of Marco dissipated in the sunshine of overwhelming desire.

She was skilled and expert and Jon allowed her complete control. She preferred to straddle, using his erection to achieve her orgasm. He concentrated very hard, not wanting to disappoint.

Sonia's eyes were closed, her head pulled back as she centred on the intensity of feeling radiating through her body. When her facial expression and elegant sighs told Jon she was in the throes of her climax, he let himself go, exploding into her.

Sonia cried out, leaning back. She held the position for some moments and then relaxed, falling forward. She stayed bent over him, panting lightly, her hair covering his face. Jon felt emptied; completely satisfied – and tired, wishing she would leave now.

A minute later, she dismounted, picked up her dressing gown, draped it over her shoulders and stood looking down at him.

'Thank you, Jon.' She bent to kiss his cheek.

'My pleasure,' he replied distractedly. She left the room without another word.

Languishing in his bed, completely at ease, knowing there would be no recriminations, that Marco condoned this, Jon sleepily enjoyed the novel sensation of zero anxiety.

He thought of Lucia, of Sonia and Marco – his friends – and of the cheque pulsating kinetically in his wallet. An ecstatic future stretched ahead into a Disneyesque landscape as the delicious kiyomeru buzz danced in his chest.

– *I deserve all this...* he congratulated himself.

– *I'm a chosen one. A winner. A soon-to-be millionaire and member of the ruling élite...*

With these thoughts and feelings gambolling happily inside, he drifted into dreamless sleep.

INTO THE FAST LANE

'Hi, Yvonne. How you doing?'

'Tony! What a surprise.' She invited Tony in and offered him tea. In the kitchen and they chatted as she filled a kettle and took mugs from the rack.

'How's the new kid?'

'Exhausting, but lovely.'

'Must be weird, having something so small so dependent on you all the time.'

'You get used to it. Actually enjoy it – eventually.'

'Yeah, well. Family life... not for me.'

'The confirmed bachelor, eh?'

'Yeah. I guess.'

She handed him a mug of tea. 'So, have you called to see Jon? He's at work, won't be back till late.'

'I was just passing and... Truth is, I haven't seen Jon down the pub for a while, and he never returns my calls. Just wondered if everything was okay?'

'Haven't seen much of him myself lately. He's changed, Tony. Different bloke now. He's joined some cult. He doesn't say much about it. Very distant most of the time. And you know he's got another woman?'

Tony shifted uncomfortably in his seat, looking away. 'Well, I...'

'It's all right. Doesn't even bother to deny it any more. I forgive him though. Must be difficult for blokes – pregnancy, breast-feeding and all that. We're off it for a year at least...'

Noting Tony's acute embarrassment, Yvonne changed subject. 'We're moving in a couple of weeks. Did he tell you?'

'No! Where?'

'Other side of town. He's bought one of those new five-bedroomed monstrosities they're building. He says the business is doing well now...'

'Yeah, I guessed that from the motor he was driving last time I saw him.'

'He's coming up in the world, eh?'

'Yeah. And dropping his old mates, by the looks of it... Well, I'd better be off. Thanks for the tea. Tell him I called by.

'Oh, and if I can do anything for you, if you ever need anything, you know where to find me.'

'I do. Thanks, Tony. That's sweet of you.'

'Sure. See ya.'

Over the next months, Jon worked unstintingly alongside Marco. They located prime West End offices in Wigmore Street and Jon headhunted three award winning creative teams from the biggest agencies, luring them aboard with the simple technique of virtually doubling their current salaries.

'So when do the new boys start?' asked Marco.

'In about two weeks.'

They were sitting facing each other on office chairs, surrounded by new desks, cabinets, book shelves and other items of office paraphernalia – most still protectively wrapped. Between them was a large carton containing computer hardware. On it rested a half-finished bottle of wine, two plastic cups and the remains of a sandwich lunch. A jungle of coloured wires dangled from the ceiling, attended by snipping, wire-twisting electricians poised on stepladders, occasionally shouting technical instructions or invective at one another across the open space. At the far end, a group of painters in spattered overalls worked brushes rhythmically, turning walls from a dingy-looking, stained white to a delicate, pale turquoise. Through the frameworks of partitions that would eventually create offices and seal off the reception area, two men in pristine white dungarees and gloves could be seen carefully lifting into place a large, curved sheet of green-edged glass with the new company name – *Brancusi, Lucke & Harvey* – etched into its surface.

'I've a lot more staff to hire yet,' Jon added, picking up the wine bottle, refilling his cup. 'Media specialists, market researchers, computer guys, some dishy looking receptionists and a drop dead PA for me. I don't suppose yours is looking for a new career opportunity?'

'Hands off, old boy. She's mine. Oh, by the way, did I tell you we're now officially "Practitioners in Advertising" and members of the Institute?

'How the hell did you swing that so quickly?'

'Don't ask,' Marco laughed. 'Let's just say our legal team has all the right institutional connections.' Marco glanced at his watch. 'God, is that the time? I must dash. I've a meeting with our new accountants. Catch you later. Kiyomeru at my house at nine? Ciao.'

Jon raised his paper cup to Marco, downed its contents in one and stood ready to recommence organising his new empire.

Within two years, they had become the largest advertising agency in Britain, billing over two hundred and fifty million pounds. Marco had operated with a cosmetic surgeon's precision: no one noticed the sutured tucks, the folds and joins, or even questioned from whence the upstarts had sprung.

'We'd better slow down a little, mustn't go too fast,' Marco told Jon, over yet another celebratory meal at their club. 'We don't want to look too suspicious.'

Jon had a twenty-five percent stake in the company, sported the job title Creative Director and commanded an annual salary of two hundred thousand a year, excluding benefits. He also had several million pounds tucked away in various banks, thanks to having sold part of his initial share holding – on Marco's advice. He had also sold – at the height of a local property boom – his ex-company's building, banking a fat profit. And he'd finally leased the shiny black Mercedes that, to his mind, epitomized and reflected personal success.

In order to avoid weekday commuting, he had moved to a *pied à terre* from which he could see Marble Arch. The annual rent, paid for by the company, was treble what his father earned at the time of his death.

Sitting gloating over his fattening bank statements, Jon began to believe that he had really arrived. His life was at last sorted – except for a few minor irritants, namely his unfulfilled partnership with Lucia, thanks to her prevarications, and his bipolar relationship with his wife. He was still tormented over what to do about his marriage. Although he wanted out, feeling he was in a cloying trap, another part of him still held tenaciously to his marriage vows, despite Marco's disapproval. He tried to tell himself this was mere sentimentality, something to be rooted out at all costs, Doh-Nai-Zen style. He reminded himself often of the session with Sonia and Marco, but the harder he tried, the more the feeling of loyalty, of a promise made, persisted. The inner war paralysed him and, unable to decide, he let the situation drift.

The current stop-gap solution, to simply not be around much, only delayed the coup. When he went home at weekends, the strain between him and Yvonne was so intense they were forced to avoid one another, or sit watching television, separated by silence, every other interaction ending in an odious row. Consequently, they rarely made love. Yvonne usually went early to bed, tired out, leaving Jon downstairs pacing up and down like a fretting wild animal newly brought to a zoo...

'Morning,' Jon breezed, entering the kitchen.

'What do you want for breakfast?' Yvonne asked.

'No time. Big meeting this morning – presenting the new Sungrown campaign.'

'Oh, really.'

'You could show some interest. This is important.'

'I would if you showed a little more interest in your own family, Jon. Aren't we "important", too?'

'Ah! So your five-bedroomed, detached dream house, your brand new MPV and private education for our kids is not showing interest?'

'That's not what I meant,' she replied, frustration in her voice.

'What, then?' Jon sighed, casting his eyes to the ceiling.

'You bloody know. Being at home more, getting involved with the kids. You're away all week and asleep or out most of the weekend. You hardly ever see them. And you seem to actively avoid being with your son. He's two, Jon. He needs you.'

'Shit! I haven't got time for all this. I'll call you later. We'll talk.'

'Can't you come back early, just for tonight? I'll cook supper for us.'

'Er, no. Can't. Got a meeting at Marco's, in Town.'

Yvonne turned on her heel and walked out of the kitchen, not wanting Jon to witness her brimming tears.

'I'm off, then. I'll miss you, too,' Jon sneered sarcastically after her back, assuming she was merely pre-menstrual. He picked up his case, collected his car keys from the rack and left the kitchen, theatrically shaking his head.

Yvonne lay on her bed sobbing quietly, trying to puzzle out what had gone wrong. She was still operating under the delusion that she could, somehow, change things, get back to how they'd been.

'What's the point of all this wealth if it takes away what kept us together in the first place?' she asked no one. 'At least then we shared our problems, struggling to sort it for the sake of the kids.'

What she could not yet admit to herself was her intense dislike of the personality that had stolen her husband's body. He seemed so aloof, so cocksure, so cold and – worst of all – untouchable. She was dimly aware that she would welcome back, with open arms, the irascible, self-denigrating, cuddly pauper she'd married.

By being unpleasant for weeks, Jon had engineered Yvonne into the role of nagging drudge. Driving into work, grasping that perception tightly, he forced a decision.

– That's it. Next week I devote to finally reorganising my domestic arrangements... His real motivation surfaced.

– Then perhaps Lucia will see I'm serious...

'Don't they remind you of a pack of hyenas, Jon?' Marco asked. They were sitting in a hired, nondescript car, dressed in tracksuits, somewhere in Streatham, observing a gang of youths fooling around on a street corner.

Jon grunted in reply, feeling nervous. Marco had invited him on one of his predatory jaunts to help hone their martial arts skills. He was still not sure why he came, presuming he'd relented, forced by pride, when Marco had taunted, 'You're not *afraid* are you, Jon?'

There, on the street, Jon wasn't sure if he was unnerved by what Marco may have been dragging him into, or if he was irritated because he'd allowed himself to be led by the nose again.

– *Still doing things I don't want to do. Got to learn to say no...*

'This is perfect.' Marco enthused. 'No CCTV. No people on the streets; low light levels. And an easy escape route back to the car – and away, after our fun is over. Ah, look, they've spotted us.'

The young men were pointing and staring in their direction, curiosity aroused.

'Come on Jon. The game's afoot, as they say.'

They got out of the car and walked towards the gang. As they closed, Jon's mind raced. There were eight of them. All young, athletic looking men in their early twenties. They sported various hair styles, from swept-back, long hair to close cropped crew-cuts. They all wore slacks, white shirts and sunglasses even though night was falling.

– *Contemporary hoodlums*, Jon mused.

– *Basing their style on their heroes – cinematic, US gangsters...*

The group were petty criminals: the flotsam and jetsam of a sea of social injustice. All they cared about was entertainment, having a good time and drugs to intensify their experiencing – and the money to get both, usually obtained illegally to augment their Social Security handouts.

– They look so stereotypical. Just like those blokes accused of murdering that black guy...

Jon recalled watching, on the news one night, their swaggering, aggressively posturing, devil-may-care walk from the judicial enquiry through a frenzied, virtual lynch mob of a crowd. A tiny, but growing, part of himself actually admired their obstinate, defiant pride.

– They were scared shitless, but they weren't going to show it...

– Pride, my arse. They're cowards – always have go in mob handed. They're not fit to be alive... contradicted a second voice.

– Consider the life they had, though. Different family values to me, to most people. Low self esteem, the eternal victim... argued a third.

– They have an animal pride, almost a nobility... Jon's first voice insisted.

– Bullshit! They're hideous, fascist bastards. I'd stick 'em against a wall and machine gun the fuckers...

– Think like that and you're one of them... warned a fourth.

'Backs against the wall, lads. Here comes the queer brigade,' the group's obvious leader quipped as Jon and Marco approached.

'Evening, gentlemen,' Marco greeted amiably, a smile on his face, looking at each one in turn. They shuffled uneasily, uncertain of their ground, instinctively forming a threatening half-circle around the strangers. 'Where's all the action to be found in this God-forsaken hole?'

'Try the local bogs, faggot,' one of the men sneered, feeding on aggression and hatred, picking up on his leader's angle.

'You got any money on yer, then?' another demanded, taking a step closer, feeling secure within his pack. Jon was aware of several of the men inching to his rear, ready for an attack. Instinctively, he knew one of them had a knife. The plume of fear he experienced was suddenly quelled. With surprise, he sensed Marco's inner presence and received into his mind a cache of information.

– Stand shoulder to shoulder with me. The one on your left will strike first with the knife. Feel the moment, turn, go back to back with me, disarm and neutralise him then deal with the other. After, rejoin me and watch my back. Reach inside for the animal power, Jon, the strength...'

'Give us yer fuckin' money...' The gang leader moved closer to Marco. The others closed in, eager for the spark that would ignite fury; hungry for the kicking to begin. 'Now, cunt, or you're fucking dead.'

'Go screw yourself, you little turd,' Marco offered in a blasé voice redolent of the British Empire. The youth on Marco's right pushed him and Marco took a step the left to brace himself. The leader swung a kick at

Marco's knees and an exquisite explosion of violence erupted.

Marco grabbed the leg and twisted it violently, the plop of popping knee joint echoing wetly off the surrounding walls. Jon turned as the knife wielder lunged. He rode with the thrust, grabbing the arm with both hands, snapping it at the elbow. The man shrieked in pain and knife span through the air and clattered onto the road. As the other attempted to grab him, to bring him down, Jon straight–arm punched him on the bridge of the nose. The youth grunted once and sagged to the pavement, his shirt calligraphed with spurting blood, his nose and cheek bones splintered under the flesh.

Jon turned to see Marco delivering a whirlwind of punches and martial arts kicks – youths dropping to the ground. Marco jabbed his elbow into the face of a boy charging at him. The boy ricocheted to the ground, his head cracking the paving stones. He lay motionless. The last left standing turned to run. Marco grabbed him around the neck and dragged him down.

'Vermin,' Marco hissed into his face, then twist-jerked the boy's head, breaking his neck with an audible snap. He let the body slump to the pavement.

'Time to go,' Marco announced, standing, dusting his hands, looking round, surveying the eight bodies littering the scene. Some groaned or sobbed and bled, two were spread-eagled, unconscious, one was dead. 'Good, eh?' Marco beamed.

As they began to walk back to the car, Jon stepped over the knife-wielder, who was curled in foetal position, rocking to and fro, whimpering and clutching his elbow. Jon could not prevent himself from turning and kicking him in the ribs as hard as he could with a residual ferocity. The boy squealed in agony and fear.

'That's the spirit, Jon.'

They drove away in silence, Jon steeling himself for the inner battle he knew would come.

– *Jesus! Did you see the way he snapped that kid's neck…?*
– *The man's a nutter, an animal…*
– *Shit, that was exhilarating…*
– *God. I feel sick…*

Yvonne answered the phone, a tearful infant perched on a jutting hip.

'Hi, Hon, how ya doin?' he asked, forcing lightness into his voice.

'It's the stranger,' she replied, bitterness in hers. 'Where the bloody hell have you been? You haven't been home for weeks.'

'Ten days, actually. I've been busy-busy, I'm afraid. Look, things have quietened down for a while and I need to talk, so I'll be back this evening, okay?'

'Yeah. I'm not going anywhere, but if you're late, come in quietly. I don't want you waking Nicholas. He's not been well.'

It gave Jon a quiet satisfaction to see the neighbours' curtains twitch as he parked his brand new, top of the range Merc. It had cost more than they earned a year. He let himself in. The house smelled of recent cooking; brightly coloured plastic toys littered the floor; damp washing draped a radiator.

'Hi, it's me,' he called out, heading for the sitting room where he found Yvonne slumped on a sofa watching TV with the sound off. 'Where are the girls?' he asked out of habit, laying his coat over the back of an armchair.

'Out. Where do you think? Eagerly waiting in for Daddy?'

'They okay?" he enquired, ignoring her sarcasm. 'Not into drugs or anything?'

'No, not as far as I can tell. Just boys.'

'You okay? You look worn out.'

'Yeah, well, like I told you, Nicholas is poorly – tummy trouble. Keeps me awake at night. What with that and worrying about you – and us.'

'That's what I've come to talk about. You and me.' He didn't like to use the word 'us', putting them together as a couple again. He remained standing to convince himself he was on a visit. 'I'll be straight. You realise we're getting like those old Darby and Jones who stick together because all they know is bitching and arguing? And that's what their whole relationship is based on? In the end they just hold each other back.'

She didn't respond, not understanding, not wanting to understand.

'Couples like that neither have the nous to make it work nor the courage to finish it. They just end up despising one another,' Jon continued, feeling on song, as though presenting a new advertising campaign. 'I suspect you don't particularly like me much nowadays, and, to be honest, I don't feel a lot for you any more. Frankly I'm past trying to make this marriage work. I think it's time to end it – formally. So I want a divorce.'

To avoid the rushing, rising shock, she resorted to sardonic anger. 'That's a pretty speech. Who wrote that one for you? Whatsisname? Marco?'

132

'There you go again. You really dislike me, and everything I stand for, don't you?'

'I just don't know you any more, Jon,' she shouted plaintively. She was confused and hurt, terror clutching at her insides.

'I'll move out and give you the house – I've paid the mortgage off. I can also give you thirty grand a year alimony, plus I'll pay the medical insurance, school fees – all that kind of thing. That should cover all your and the kids' needs for now. You can always ask for a little more if you need it, my door's always open. And that's for life, by the way – except we'll renegotiate the alimony if you remarry. We'll go for irrevocable breakdown. I'll handle everything, including the solicitor's fees. You can have uncontested parental rights to the kids – I'd like to see them occasionally, of course, mutually agreeable times and all that. So it's all totally in your favour, really.'

Yvonne sat stunned, saying nothing. Jon misinterpreted her silence, assuming she was weighing his offer. 'I suggest you accept these terms. If you want to fight for more, I promise you'll not get it.'

He marvelled at how having money made everything so simple – he could easily make what appeared to be a generous settlement without having to share his newly acquired fortune. He knew he must keep her away from greedy divorce lawyers who would make her aware of her equipotent rights.

She stared up at him, not understanding how everything had come down to money and solicitors so quickly.

'Well, say something,' he said after several minutes had passed.

'I don't know what to say, Jon. Don't know anything any more. You've become hard, cruel, horrible.' She shook her head, tears forming in her eyes. The rush of emotion made it impossible to think or speak. All she wanted was for him to hug her until this madness had passed. She began silently weeping, head bowed, shaking with the effort of holding back the emotional explosion that threatened to rip her apart.

Jon saw a tear splash onto her hands lying tightly clenched in her lap. Sadness and remorse clutched at him jerking his body forward. He pulled back to an ice-cold centre.

– *Careful...*

Yvonne eventually looked up, temporarily back in control of herself.

'So, you're telling me that twenty years of being together, courting, making love, having kids, collecting a house full of treasures and memories – all that means absolutely nothing to you all of a sudden. Yeah?'

'Uh-huh,' Jon agreed, nodding his head. 'That just about sums it up.' The wavering moment had passed. He experienced only distaste now at her mawkish outburst – and was impatient to get away.

'And you're quite prepared to see your children grow up without a father around and everything that implies?'

'They're tough. They'll survive.'

'Twenty years, Jon!' she screamed, angry again. 'Twenty bloody years! And you're just gonna walk? As though it never even happened? Like trading in an old car?'

Jon shrugged. They sat staring, Jon into the far corner, Yvonne into her lap, both saying nothing.

Yvonne looked up at him. 'Are you going to her?'

'If she'll have me, yes.'

The affirmative seemed so final, she knew there was nothing more she could do.

'Well, go then. Fuck off!' She hurled a cushion at Jon. He swayed to one side and it thumped into the corner of the room. 'Let her wash your bloody underpants for you!' She had no idea what she was saying anymore.

He judged it was the moment to leave, picking up his jacket as he went. 'My solicitor will be in touch. He'll handle everything.'

'You've become fucking inhuman!' she screamed after him.

– *Yes. You could say that...* he laughed to himself.

As he gently shut the front door he heard her sobbing loudly, drowning in an ocean of emotion.

He walked with a light step to his car, congratulating himself on a job well done. He slipped into drive and he and the Mercedes purred away from the kerb and his past...

CRACKS

Over the next three years The Agency grew exponentially, opening offices across Europe – Paris, Munich, Milan. New business was apparently won competitively in the open marketplace, but the real deals were made with a handshake during Doh-Nai-Zen gatherings – in saunas, at clubs over dinner. Marco orchestrated it all to perfection, exploiting the financial media's poor memory and thus collusion was neither detected nor even suspected.

'Jon, we've done it,' Marco enthused over the phone. 'We're now officially the biggest advertising agency in Europe. Number One.'

'You're kidding,' Jon hooted, jubilation in his voice.

'Absolutely not, old boy. It's kosher. That puts us in the top twenty worldwide. We're now billing over five billion dollars, apparently. I've just come from a meeting with the board and I have some more very good news. I've just been ratified as the new, International Chairman.'

'Congratulations.'

'And guess who's the new pan-European Creative Director?'

'Who?'

'You, dear boy, you. Well done! Unanimous vote. I'll fill you in when I get back.'

'Where are you now?' Jon enquired.

'Somewhere over the Atlantic. Meeting Chi-Chi in Washington later, then we're off to do a spot of fishing. Talk to you when I get back. Ciao.'

Jon sat back in his chair, a self-loving warmth stealing over his body.

– *I always knew you had it in you, old mate. Always knew you'd be a star one day...*

He toasted himself with his coffee cup, forgetting the rejections and depressions of five years ago, totally unaware of the ironic delusion.

Creatively, Jon was rarely stretched. He had discovered that kiyomeru had given him an extraordinary ability to probe into others' inner worlds, accurately sensing clients' needs and even buying-public trends, almost reading minds and feeling moods.

'Don't mistake it for telepathy,' Marco had warned him. 'It's an ability all animals possess but humans have lost, thanks to overdeveloping their minds. It's the same sense that facilitates a bird's migration, enables animals to know when a volcano is about to erupt, or whether other creatures mean them harm.

'It's a mixture of body language, auras, psychic perception, intuition and common sense. Use it in conjunction with your professional knowledge and linguistic skills and you'll be most surprised, and highly gratified, by the results.'

After re-interpreting his inner gleanings as a creative brief – and making sure the market research concurred – all that was required of him was to cajole the creative geniuses working under him into a demonstrably correct solution, then to sit back and collect the awards and accolades. This way he had built an enviable reputation as the hottest creative in

Town. For this he was paid a total package worth over a million pounds a year.

'We're in the advertising game and in today's world, advertising is its culture. It's what gives society its tonality and its colour,' he remembered lecturing the creative directors under his command, attempting to inspire. 'That's why I want wit and passion from you guys. Clever, make you think stuff. I don't want boring, conventional. I want alive, street cred, here and now campaigns. I want at speed, in depth solutions; and I want them yesterday! Don't want slackers, dilettantes, prima donnas. I take no fucking prisoners. Any one that can't hack the pace is out.' And he meant it. Hire and fire was now his style. He would no longer tolerate passengers or space and time wasters.

'You wouldn't recognise him now, Father,' Marco was telling Chi-Chi as they sat strapped into their seats, side by side, facing out to sea, high at the bow of a bobbing, ocean-going motor launch. They were fishing for marlin somewhere off the Bermudan coast and had passed an excellent morning's sport together, landing several three-hundred pounders.

'He looks fit and powerful and very well groomed – every inch a Doh-Nai-Zen member. He's even developing an authority; beginning to use it, too – commanding respect. He can be quite ruthless. It's a joy to watch. Basically, he has taken to it like a fish to water. And so willing to learn and so keen to advance. I'd say success is definitely on the cards. We can start bringing others on stream soon.'

'Mmmm,' Chi-Chi responded, weighing Marco's words. 'We should still err on the side of caution. It is a well-documented phenomenon in the animal kingdom that when a low caste creature is raised in the pecking order it will subjugate those newly below it more ferociously than is necessary. This is how its innate instincts train and ready itself for a challenge to the group leader. This invariably fails and the upstart has to be excluded. Let him learn his lessons well before advancing him further. We would not want an out of control experiment on our hands – our own Chernobyl – particularly at this delicate juncture. First he must come to understand his precise place in the food chain.'

'Yes, Father. But I can't see any kind of challenge coming from him. He's still a pup in some respects. Very full of himself, though...' Marco was interrupted by an urgent, arm-wrenching tug on his line, his rod dipping down into the boat's wake.

'Jesus! This is a big one – a fighter,' he yelled rapturously.

'Good morning, Sir. Breakfast is served,' Jon heard bizarrely reverberating through a waking dream. He sensed the tray placed over his legs, then heard his butler swishing the curtains back, aware of the rush of light. He opened his eyes and reconnected with the conscious world.

'Morning, Henry. What time is it?' he asked, sitting up in bed, stretching like a cat.

'Seven thirty, Sir. And it is a beautiful day. What time are you due at the office, Sir?'

'Uh, I've a board meeting at ten thirty. So I guess about ten.'

Jon had discovered with relief that being a world class player was no more onerous than choosing a new car, or what colour to decorate the bath room. The business decisions he was called upon to make were already toothless by the time they reached up to him, requiring merely a signature, or a raised, complying hand around a board room table, despite involving millions of pounds.

'And what will you wear, Sir? The Armani or the Gautier?'

'Surprise me, Henry. Surprise me.'

'Very good, Sir. And will you be dining at home tonight?'

'No. I've another wretched Awards dinner to attend. Don't wait up.'

Henry left the room, turning to give a curt bow as he pulled the double doors closed. Jon sat upright in bed sipping a freshly squeezed orange juice. He flicked quickly through his mail. There was little of interest apart from invitations to an aristocratic ball and dinner at a Cabinet Minister's house.

– *Mmm. Friends in high places, now, eh...?* he self-mocked. It was true. Nowadays, he hung out, dined and holidayed with politicians, celebrities and tycoons, discovering they were just like him, really. All they wanted, outside of their individual daily power struggles, was a good night out, lots of laughs, titillation, admiration and sex. His haunts had become the trendy nightclubs and restaurants, the society events and country house weekends that once he only read about in glossy magazines. Apart from the journalists constantly in evidence, hyenas hanging around a lion kill, he'd discovered they were, after all, little different to his old local pub. There was that same tribal sense of belonging and inherent hierarchies, the same stupid pranks and in-jokes, gossip and banal conversations full of sexual innuendo – except the gang all wore celebrity masks. Jon would have been just as bored as before but for the self-congratulatory atmosphere that hung in the air and the delicious, heart warmingly addictive taste of éliteness.

Glancing at the *Times*' headline, it told him Concorde had crashed – the first time in nearly thirty years' of flying – and they'd all been withdrawn from service, 'until further notice'.

'Damn!' he cursed aloud, knowing that meant reverting to six-hour, gruelling flights across the Atlantic on sheduled flights, or in the company's private jet.

He picked up *Campaign* and riffled through it. His photograph dominated the feature spread, covering ten columns. The article was headlined *Jon Lucke – Europe's hottest creative property*. Out of habit, he clamped down on the rising surge of pride and recalled being asked by the interviewer, 'To what do you contribute your phenomenal rise to success?'

'I simply employ people that are cleverer than me,' he replied, mock-modest, urbane.

– In other words, he told himself, I've finally begun to grasp the inner nature of power...

Jon had observed to Marco, over dinner one night, 'You know, I get paid a fortune for rubber stamping other people's ideas, and win awards for it. It's like my word is law, nowadays. Like they seek me out, assuming I have all the answers. Yet, what – five, six years ago? – I got paid peanuts for slogging my guts out overnight, only to have the client change everything the next day as though I never existed. Creatively, I'm still the old me, yet they respond differently. So what's changed? It's all very odd.'

'Not really, Jon,' Marco had replied, slipping into the guru mode Jon had implicitly begged. 'The reality is, you *have* changed – dramatically. You now radiate an animal energy that simply coerces people into instinctively performing for you. They're not even aware of what has transpired. Observe others' reactions to you more closely. Learn how to shape this unconscious effect, and to use it to your own advantage. The truth is, you are experiencing high rank. You're now a member of the élite, at the top of life's pecking order, front echelon – a leader. A very small percentage of humans experience this. In the past it was the domain of kings and emperors, princes and generals. Thanks to Doh-Nai-Zen, poor boys from the wrong side of the tracks, like us, can experience it now. So, just accept it, dear boy. Enjoy! Play up and play the game, as they once said – on the playing fields of Eton, I believe.'

– Yeah. And I've quite a few of those old Etonian arseholes fawning over me now...

The thought was pleasurable and energising. Jon jumped out of bed and headed for the shower. He stood in front of the full-length mirror and appraised his body. He looked and felt ten years younger and, because he worked out religiously every day, and continued with his martial arts training, he was taller, stronger and fitter, a rippling of muscle all over his body. His diet had changed, too. He was constantly ravenous for rare steaks and red meats, discovering all other members developed this propensity, needing to feed their ever-hungry, inner animal.

Before leaving for the office, he walked through the apartment enjoying a proprietorial satisfaction. He had, over the last few years, become an expert on antiques, collecting nothing in particular, just things that he liked, artefacts he snapped up on his world travels; Persian rugs, African sculpture, old silver, period furniture – they all graced his various homes. He now boasted, apart from the London flat, an apartment in Milan and houses in Paris and Spain – all purchased since his divorce from Yvonne.

Catching sight of his collection of seventeenth century, lead-crystal drinking glasses – Champagne flutes and sherry schooners, wine goblets and whisky tumblers, liqueur and brandy glasses – tastefully arranged behind the glass doors of an antique French cabinet, it occurred to him that being rich was not only about money. Being rich meant order. It meant the minutiae of his life was taken care of. No more shopping for razor blades; no more standing in bank queues. It gave him a sense of completeness, of control, to return home at night to find everything was in its place, exactly as he had left it, or put back to how it had been. So different from being poor and married, living with a bunch of kids and the ensuing chaos. Being rich also meant never being ignored, fobbed off or let down. He didn't even have to shop for clothes. His lifestyle con-sultant organised his casual wear, while Jon merely visited his tailor and his shirt and shoe makers annually for a fitting, then ordered ten of this, a dozen of that every month. He spent thousands on clothes without giv-ing it a thought, often wearing items only once.

– *Yep, being rich means life is hassle free...* he smiled to himself.

Most of the time his inner feeling sang with an existential exhilaration and, at those moments, it seemed as though he were acting in a thickly clichéd movie, the star of which was a forty year old tycoon and hunk called Jon Lucke. A man who travelled first class, stayed in penthouse suites at five star hotels while being smarmed over by deferential staff and obsequious lackeys.

As well as his manservant and lifestyle consultant, Jon employed a social secretary, a cook and a personal trainer cum dietician, all of whom attended to the banalities of life. Apart from Lucia, Jon now had everything, and more, than he had ever dreamed possible.

– *The only problem is, my life is so boring, really...* He was shocked again by the thought, his brow furrowing, his world darkening. It puzzled him that, with increasing frequency, he was being assailed by doubts and anxieties.

– *With all I've got and everything I now am, how come I can still feel empty, discontented, kind of wretched...?*

Jon fought the twitching Maserati around the bend. The kick of adrenaline told him he'd nearly overcooked it this time. He slowed a little and looked right down the mountainside catching sight of his destination nestling in the valley. Several helicopters were parked on the lawns and he saw another descending.

'Good, I'm on time for a change.'

Ten minutes later he arrived at the gates. Security guards stepped to the car, checked his invitation, discussing his arrival on two-way radios. Getting clearance, they waved him through deferentially. He parked in front of the château's imposing facade. A be-wigged flunky, costumed in a red, eighteenth century long-coat and white breeches, opened the car door and bowed. Jon handed him the keys without acknowledgement or eye contact, presuming his car would be parked and his luggage placed in his rooms.

Jon entered the hall, picked a brimming glass from the proffered tray and scanned the gathered crowd. He spotted Marco laughing with the US ambassador and walked across.

'Marco, Stephen. How are you?'

'Welcome, Jon. Good journey?'

'Yeah. Five hours flat, door to door. What's the programme?'

Marco checked his watch. 'Kiyomero in half an hour or so. Then dinner, then the first meetings. Fun later.'

In this august company, Jon knew he was still a junior. After dinner, the top members – chairmen of multi-nationals, government ministers, diplomats and media barons – would retire to confer behind closed doors. Jon harboured the ambition to be one of them, one day – soon, he hoped.

He could only trawl glimpses of what they discussed, but knew it was about dividing future power, about who would rule what, when Chi-Chi's plans fructified. Through hints from Marco, conversations with other members and a little private research, he knew Chi-Chi was cultivating alliances with arms manufacturers and oil producers. He was aware, too, that Western governments were deeply into destabilisation, supplying arms to carefully selected 'rebel' groups – usually residents of oil-producing countries – thereby fuelling their own arms industry and, in turn, economies. The resultant trouble-shooting military incursions, masquerading as the policing of democracy, had a hidden purpose – simply to protect the dollar. The West's economy would collapse if ever the dollar oil debt was called in. It was brute imperialism in sheep's clothing. Power and control; hegemony. It all seemed so transparent to Jon, and he was bemused that the public at large bought the cunningly wrought scenarios created by spin doctors and sold through the very media owned by the protagonists.

Personally, he had no particular interest in global power games, but driven by blind ambition, linked to his longing for Lucia, he feigned interest and a willing eagerness.

'Tough news about the *Cole*. Many hurt?' he asked the Ambassador.

'Seventeen dead and forty injured, I believe.'

'Any idea who was responsible?'

'Our arch enemy, Osama, no doubt masterminded it.'

'Surely not. Wasn't he 'Our Man in Afghanistan' once? The man we trained and armed against the Russians?' Jon asked, archly naïve. 'And I remember reading somewhere that his father and George Bush had been business partners once. What's he got to do with us?'

The Ambassador and Marco caught one another's eye and laughed.

'You've no need to worry your pretty head about world politics, Jon,' Marco mocked. 'Just concentrate on that agency and making us a fortune.' Jon experienced a frisson of anger at Marco's patronisation – something else he had noticed happening more and more.

'Let's just say the Cole was a precursor,' the Ambassador added. 'Nothing to what's going to happen next, and that things are… on schedule.' The Ambassador turned back to Marco. 'How's that beautiful wife of yours these days?'

Jon took his cue. He'd had his wrist slapped, been fed a tit-bit and clearly told that's all he was getting.

– *A useful tit-bit, though. Two and two sometimes make five with the right information…* he told himself smugly.

– *Bide your time, mate, bide your time…*

He noticed one of the creative heads from the agency group across the

141

room, a svelte, raven-haired woman in her thirties, a rising star.

'Catch you guys later,' he said nonchalantly and moved away.

'Maria!'

'Hi, Jon. You look tanned! Enjoying your holiday?'

'Yeah, great. How are things back at the ranch?'

'Busy. We need you.'

'I'll be back next week sometime.'

'You going to the dance tonight? There's a scratch band of old sixties rock stars. Could be fun.'

'Is there an alternative?'

'You could come up to my room for an evening of passionate, unbridled sex,' she suggested, leaning into Jon.

'Sounds interesting. I'd prefer 'bridled', though, if you know what I mean...'

'I just happen to have my S and M kit in the car,' Maria laughed, flashing white teeth.

'Ladies and gentlemen,' a voice shouted. 'Would you please change for kiyomeru and afterwards, meet in the main hall.'

At once, the gathered herd began to shuffle to their rooms as one.

As Jon pulled his apartment's front door closed with a satisfying clunk and walked the luxurious yards to the lift, it occurred to him that the richer he became, the wider were his options.

–Yeah. And the opposite must the definition of poverty. When your options run out, you're as poor as fuck...

He was pleased with this insight, but experienced a familiar bite of irritation as he stepped into the lift. The final sticking point, the one area where his options were narrowed, where he couldn't buy or get his own way, was in his so far unresolved relationship with Lucia. He had continued to pursue her ardently, still bewitched, but she would only see him once or twice a week at most. He knew he could have virtually any other woman he wanted – and he did have women in droves, as many as he could handle – but was bored with vacuous starlets and models, society girls and hungry career women. The sex was like a Kentucky fried; readily available, reliably the same, quick and clean – and left you satiated for now, yet ever hungry.

'Isn't it about time you found yourself a Doh-Nai-Zen wife, Jon? We need you young bucks to swell our numbers with pedigree kids, you know,' Marco had prodded him recently.

'I'm working on it. I'm so busy I just haven't found the right one yet,' he'd prevaricated.

It was Lucia he wanted: he yearned for her despite knowing things were never done this way in Doh-Nai-Zen. Marriages were arranged, for convenience, for power, for self-promotion and aggrandisement. But, in this area, he could not help himself and neither did he dare discuss the truth with Marco. It would be a cardinal mistake to reveal to his mentor such a serious weakness as being romantically besotted by a woman.

On days of clarity, he was sometimes aware that he was not besotted by Lucia herself. He often found, after sex with her, that she too could be vacuous and he has been surprised to discover he could be bored in her company. At those moments, he felt empty, drained. Felt that there was nothing left in him, nothing left in the world.

– *No, it's not her, but the way she makes love. That's what I want, what I'm addicted to. What is it...?* he asked himself, closing his eyes, concentrating hard.

– *It's the way she lies there, more naked than naked; totally open. No barriers, no hang ups – offering a direct line from her sexual centre to mine. And it's like she totally loves herself and her body, too. Yes... and the way she gets off on my getting off on her. The more I want her, the more she loves it. And the more she loves it the more I want her. So it spirals up and up. Then it's like she's saying "the more you take, the more I get". And then she's demanding I take more and more and more – to increase her pleasure. Anything and everything goes... Nothing fazes her... Reminds me of that sculpture, The Passion of St Theresa... That's it. There's something religious, something mystical in the way she wants to be fucked stupid. Like she wants God Himself to screw her...*

He was amazed to find he had an erection, and it hurt.

– *I've never found a vestige of this quality in any other woman. There's always a barrier, a holding back. And that's why I can't let her go. She's rare, precious...*

– *Fuck! What am I going to do...?*

'You've got to crack it, someday...' he told himself ruefully.

– *One way or the other...*

'Can't have a top player involved in a game he can't win... All very un-Doh-Nai Zen...'

Pushing through the restaurant doors, Jon inhaled the dark-rich tang of coffee permeating the warm atmosphere.

'Good *evening*, Monsieur Lucke,' the maitre d' greeted him, bowing unctuously.

'Evening, Pierre.'

'Madame is already at your usual table, sir.'

Jon followed his escort into the subdued dining area. His eyes immediately settled on Lucia. She was talking with a young waiter and flirting outrageously, leaning back on her chair, her short-skirted legs stretched out either side of the waiter's feet, holding him in her orbit. Jon felt a fly-whine of jealousy. But she looked so beautiful, so desirable, he swatted the feeling, regained control and approached the table smiling.

'Hi, Lucia,' he greeted, acting casually as he slid into the seat pulled out for him, taking and acknowledging with a nod the menu handed to him by the maitre d'.

'Dry Martini,' he snapped imperiously at the waiter, observing him pull reluctantly out of Lucia's spell before scuttling off to do his bidding.

'God, Marcel's a hunk,' she groaned, staring after the waiter. 'Beautiful arse.'

He sensed she was in combative mood tonight and refused to take the bait. 'How are things going for your show?' he asked attempting to restore the intimacy he craved.

'Great,' she enthused. 'I'm a star. Love the new haircut by the way.' She leaned forward and ruffled his hair.

'I'm thinking of taking a few weeks off. Maybe a trip to Bali. Fancy coming with me?'

'Can't, Jon. Too busy.'

'Well, how about going away together somewhere for the weekend? You choose where.'

'No. Told you, I'm busy. Really tied up with the show.'

'Christ, Lucia. You're always too bloody busy to... ' With an effort, he managed to dampen the rising heat, knowing from experience if he pushed her too far she'd walk out in a huff. 'Never mind...'

He relaxed and throughout dinner – she wolfing a rare steak, he a dish of Steak Tartarre – managed to make himself amiable.

In response, Lucia was almost loving until she suddenly asked, 'Are you still sleeping with my step-mum, by the way?'

Hesitation. He became nervous of her reaction, knowing to lie was pointless. She and Sonia no doubt confided in one another and anyway, she would, like any Doh-Nai-Zen member, immediately sense his being untruthful. And Jon's affair with Sonia had continued apace, albeit sporadically. They met, made expert, technically perfect love – and that was it. They had little to say, little interest in each other and the arrangement suited them both perfectly, he role playing Benjamin Braddock to her Mrs. Robinson.

– *Why is my whole bloody life a continuous homage to films...?* he wondered often.

Through Sonia he had come to understand that women in Doh-Nai-Zen either battled in business alongside the men as equals, or took a back seat from choice, but never as victims. The latter reared families and zealously supported their husbands – gladly supplying sexual favours to high-ranking males if required; or happily being shared like female apes in a close-knit, simian community. These women let the males do the foraging, chest beating and fighting. Their power was of a more subtle, behind the throne and cradle rocking kind.

'Occasionally,' he shrugged, answering her question, looking away.

She stared at him, then nodded acceptance and looked round the room for Marcel.

While waiting for coffee and dessert, both sitting wrapped in their own thoughts, she started to rub Jon's leg idly with her bare foot, then suddenly lifted it into his lap, massaging his crotch.

'Christ, that waiter has made me feel randy,' she whispered, leaning forward conspiratorially. 'I'm going to go into the loo. Follow me after a few minutes. I've got to have sex, right now, Jon.'

The heavily marbled and mirrored washrooms were empty and she grabbed him as he walked in. She kissed him feverishly, backing, pulling him with her, hoisting herself up onto the washbasin surrounds, her skirt riding high as she wrapped her legs round his back. Jon was swept into the passion of the moment, furiously scrabbling at his fly. He managed to enter her and began the rhythmic thrusting. She suddenly became rigid and pushed him away.

'It's no good, Jon. I've got to have Marcel.'

He couldn't move, paralysed by the contradictory emotions storming inside. He wanted her, wanted to hit her: he loved her, he hated her. He was enraged, on the verge of screaming, yet longed to hold and caress her.

'Put it away, Jon. You look ridiculous. Someone might come in.' She turned to study herself in a mirror, re-arranging her hair as though nothing had happened.

'You bitch.' He zipped himself up and strode angrily towards the door, propelled by crushed pride and the fearful, animal desire to rip her apart.

– *I'm like her bloody lap dog...* he agonised, driving home disconsolate, all passion dissipated.

– *She calls, I come running...*

– *Better than nothing, though...*

– *Yeah. At least we get to be with her...*

– *And make love when she wants...*

– *God, why won't she come and live with me...*

He'd asked her to move in with him many times. She invariably reacted angrily, quickly changing the subject, refusing to discuss their situation, sometimes walking out. And Marco continued to drop dark hints that she was destined, in some mysterious way, for a bigger, brighter future than being the next Mrs. Lucke.

– *Why do I want her so much...?* He remembered at once his revelation that she was an addiction, a unique drug. Not one commonly available, in bars or on street corners, but one that was as though distilled from a plant found only at the heart of the Amazon Rain Forest; one that flowered once in every ten years; a coveted rarity, only available to the most decadent afficionados.

– *And, like all junkies colluding with their drug of choice, the price of a short-lived heaven is an eternal, power-sapped hell...*

Threading his way through the dense, London traffic, he recalled how different he could be when the narcotic of their relationship was not coursing through his veins.

– *If only I could forget about her. Just concentrate on doing what I want, what I do best...*

The idea of building himself an ultra-modern designer home close to Marco's country house in North Bucks had come as a whim. A brief search had unearthed an ideal four-acre plot, bordered on two sides by a small trout-beck river. The site was being run as a successful garden centre by a wheelchair bound ex-serviceman. The lease had been about to expire, and, because the owner had recently and suddenly died, the estate's solicitors had a fiduciary duty to sell through a closed-bid auction in order to obtain the highest price.

The story became a cause célèbre as first the local press got wind of it, dressing it up, exploiting the full emotive potential of the situation – *Property developers to push wheelchair bound hero from home* one headline ran.

'Nauseating sentimentality,' Jon sneered, tossing the paper aside, snickering at the headline's unfortunate ambiguity.

The lessee had village allies, people of compassion and those with their own 'Not in my backyard because it'll affect the price of my house' agenda, and thus a consortium was formed, setting up a fund which quickly grew to the estimated asking price: a cheesy, Christmas card concept of a cosy, pseudo-Victorian, village co-operative had been the driving force.

The local radio station became involved and a neighbourhood pressure group convened, organising a petition. The local MP's support was enlisted and the District Council members individually lobbied to not grant planning permission for a new dwelling, or change of use, using the 'thin end of the wedge' argument. The two other interested parties, both local builders, withdrew, knowing victory would be Pyrrhic and not good for business reputations. Thus, the result appeared to be a foregone conclusion as only Jon and the alliance were left in the running.

A desire to win this one at all costs obsessed Jon, and he decided to use his own devious tactics to take them all on.

A word in a Doh-Nai-Zen Cabinet Minister's ear made sure that the local MP was off the case, a message on his bleeper making it clear he should quietly remove himself; take an all expenses paid, fact finding tour of the Bahamas for the duration.

Jon next made absolutely certain that the council would grant planning permission by making a generous, ostensibly anonymous, donation towards the new village community centre. He also arranged – with its Doh-Nai-Zen owner – for several leading councillors to be allowed to join an exclusive golf club with a long waiting list. Finally, he called the estate agents handling the auction, asking for an informal meeting.

'How can I help?' the agent enquired after Jon had taken a seat in his office. Jon immediately sensed the chubby, bespectacled man was weak – a low caste animal.

'I want to know what the opposition will offer so I can outbid them.'

'Really! I couldn't *possibly* discuss the other party's affairs with you. I can only refer you to the guide price. You will have to make your own judgement,' he replied pompously. He was a covert supporter of the consortium, allying himself strategically, with one eye on future business opportunities lurking within the village's wealthy community. Consequently, he found it difficult to hide his aggression towards the outsider.

Jon probed the man's inner. He sensed he was in parlous financial difficulties, struggling to survive – and therefore had his price.

'I'll make it worth your while. Let's say fifty grand if you help me find out what the others will bid,' Jon leant forward in his seat, projecting inner pressure. The man looked startled, picked up a pen and began to toy with it nervously.

'I shouldn't even be talking to you about this,' the man blurted out, disconcerted, 'but, supposing I were to agree – just supposing...' He produced a white handkerchief, removed his spectacles and pretended to clean them. 'How could it be done? Hypothetically, you understand. They'll be sealed, typewritten bids, delivered to this office on a specified date and opened together at an agreed time in front of all parties' representatives.'

'It's very simple. First, you'll find out everything you can about their solicitors' office set up, computer codes, security staff, the lot...'

'And how could anyone possibly achieve that?'

'I don't know. Use your initiative. Chat up one of the secretaries, or an office boy – whatever turns you on.'

'And what then?'

'We'll break into their offices the night before.'

'We?'

'Yes, I'll need help.' Jon drew an envelope from his case and laid it on the desk.

'There's twenty-five grand there. The balance after I've won.'

The man stared at the package as though it were a bomb, seeming to press back in his seat. He began to sweat, rubbing his waxy looking forehead, revealing his inner turmoil – greed battling with the fear of getting caught; professional ethics merely objecting from the sidelines.

Ten seconds elapsed. The agent swooped, quickly placing the envelope in a drawer.

'How do I contact you?'

'Here's my mobile number. Plumb it into yours and call me when you're ready. I really want this place,' Jon emphasised, rising from the chair, striding for the door.

'This conversation never happened, you understand?' the agent called after him. 'If one single thing goes wrong, I'll deny everything.'

'Yeah, yeah. Just do it. And don't let me down.'

Jon had related the story so far to Marco one evening and had been taken aback by his reaction.

'Jon, I think you're being very stupid. Why take risks? If you were found out, or the story leaked, it could ruin your reputation and reflect badly on

Doh-Nai-Zen.'

'Oh, come on, Marco,' Jon retorted, irritated. 'Nobody even knows about Doh-Nai-Zen outside of the organisation – we're a secret society, aren't we? Anyway, I'm not going to get found out. It's just sport, for Chrissake. The whole thing's a game. One that I intend to win, that's all. What's your problem?'

'It's foolish, Jon. You could have just bid fifty thou over the reserve price. Or bought land anywhere. There was no need for all this cloak and dagger stuff. I think you have been extremely rash. Take my advice, drop the whole thing now – especially as it's on my patch.'

'Bollocks!' Jon shouted, standing, feeling outrage as months of frustration boiled over. 'Who the fuck are you to tell me what to do?'

Marco leapt immediately to his feet. 'Be very careful how you speak to me, Jon.'

They glared at one another, inwardly beating their chests and snarling, teeth bared – Jon the upstart ape, challenging the group leader for supremacy.

Spontaneously, they charged one another as fury burst through the veneer of civility. Although Jon was the younger, more agile and fitter, Marco was taller, heavier and stronger. Jon felt as though he'd smashed into a cliff face.

They grappled for a few moments, trying to find a hold, a weakness in balance, each trying to topple the other. Marco turned Jon hard in one direction; Jon used all his strength to oppose the move. Marco suddenly switched directions, unbalancing Jon, sweeping his legs from the ground with a judo kick. They toppled to the floor. Jon was pinned under Marco's weight, unable to roll him off. Marco drew back a clenched karate fist, ready to drive it into Jon's face. He checked himself and leant back panting, sitting astride a winded and now submissive adversary.

'Please don't get too cocky. You have so much to learn, you know,' Marco said quietly, placatory. He heaved himself up, adding, 'Let's end this now, before it goes too far. Jon, I beseech you – drop this charade. It's too risky by half.'

Deepening humiliation informed Jon he was beaten and that he should back off for now. His instincts assured him there would be another time.

'I'll think about it...'

'Good.'

Marco offered a hand and helped pull Jon to his feet. They both began to grin as they brushed themselves down, feeling slightly foolish, relieved that it was over. But something had changed in their relationship, Jon realising fully, for the first time, that he disliked Marco, that the feeling had been building over the months.

They stared at each other through smiling masks, their minds racing.

– *That's the last time Marco gets the better of me. It's time to break away, become my own man. And fuck him! I'm going to pull this off regardless...*

– *If he doesn't drop the whole stupid affair played out, of all places, on my home territory, he's finished. And he's damned well outmanœuvered me. There's no way I can get involved now; far too risky if it all goes pear-shaped...* Marco inwardly fumed.

– *And then there's this business with Lucia. It's all getting a bit too hot. Maybe Chi-Chi was right. Something must be done, and soon...*

'I think we both need a drink after that,' Marco suggested affably.

Jon switched off the ignition and rolled into the car park, drawing alongside the only other car as its driver scrambled urgently out. Jon closed his door quietly, turned and asked the estate agent, 'All set?'

The man shut his eyes as though making one last desperate supplication for the nightmare to end, then squeeked assent.

Observing, with a snort of laughter, the agent's attire – black jumper and trousers and a Balaclava helmet – Jon could not resist a jibe. 'Christ, man. You look like Batman – apart from the gut.'

'Let's just get this over with, please.'

Jon noticed the agent was shaking. 'You scared?'

The agent nodded and Jon laughed again. He felt only as tensely excited as a fox prowling the perimeter of a chicken coop.

They walked in silence to the rear entrance of the office block. The agent let them in with a key.

'Lock it,' Jon whispered. 'Just in case security decides to have a wander.' He flicked on his torch, pointing the beam up the stairs. 'Now, where to?'

'It's up on the third floor.'

They located the office; it had been left unlocked as arranged. The agent took a folded drawing from his pocket, studying it under the light of his torch. 'Third desk on the left.'

Jon sat in font of the VDU and switched on. Blue grey light filled the room. 'What's the password?'

'RobbieW.' Jon looked askance. 'She's a fan,' the agent replied with a shrug.

'And. I hear, your bit of tottie, now.' Jon began to search through files. 'I hope you've been discreet.'

'That's it.' The agent whispered, pointing. 'Wroxborough Park.'

Clicking on the folder, Jon quickly found "Bid letter final.doc" and opened it. 'You greedy bastard. You've got them bidding five thousand over the price I told you I'd go to. You blokes love your commission, don't you.' The estate agent simpered, embarrassed, and Jon made a note of the figure. 'You're absolutely certain this is the final one?'

'Got to be. Yesterday's date, at five p.m.; they wouldn't have time to redo it for nine this morning. And I can't see any other files or documents. That's it, just as Lisa said.'

'Lisa, eh? You dog. Right, let's go.'

As the computer blinked off, the corridor lights flickered on.

'Shit! Oh, God! Security! They'll catch us! What are we going to do?' the agent stage-whispered in Jon's ear, gripping his arm.

'Keep fucking quiet for a start,' Jon hissed back at him. 'Just get under a desk and stay there until he's gone. Don't panic, for Chrissake.' He pushed him down. 'Get under there. Now!'

A silhouette loomed in the glass panelled door. Jon ducked down, gently eased an office chair aside and slipped under a desk just as the handle dipped and the door swung open.

The security man stood in the opening, swinging his torch around the room. Seeing nothing unusual, assuming the door had beeen left unlocked by incompetent staff, he switched off his torch and began to close the door, reaching for his pocketed keys. The agent, shaking with fear, gave an audible sob.

'Who's there?' the startled guard shouted, edging back into the room, nervously groping for the light switch. Fluorescent tubes blinked awake. 'I know you're there, I can see you. Come out, now!'

From his hiding place Jon could see the agent's legs protruding from under the desk and the guard heading straight for them. He reacted instinctively as the man rushed past his hiding place, grabbing at the guard's legs, tripping him. The man dived forward, falling heavily, striking his head on a desk as he crashed to the floor, scattering papers, sending an office chair scooting and clattering. Jon scrambled out and leapt on the man's back. He raised his torch, prepared to knock the man senseless – anything to avoid being seen and later recognised. The man lay inert, blood oozing from a gash in his head. Jon felt for a pulse in the guard's neck and was relieved to feel a delicate, elastic throb.

'Get out from there, idiot,' he called to his inept accomplice. 'Now listen. We've got to make them think this prat interrupted a robbery, or some yobs on the rampage. Start smashing the place up. Empty all the draws, chuck stuff around. I'll wipe any surfaces we may've touched. I hope you didn't take your gloves off. I know I didn't...'

After five minutes of frenzied activity, Jon assessed it was enough. 'Come on, let's go.' The guard lay still, breathing shallowly. The agent was hardly able to walk, wanting only to curl up on the floor.

'You sure he's alright? You haven't killed him? Oh, God!' he wailed. 'Why did I get involved...'

'For fuck's sake, man. He's fine. He'll feel a bit sick when he comes round, that's all. Come on!'

Jon manhandled him to the door. Having a sudden thought, he ran back to the prostrate guard, turned him over, unclipped his short wave radio and smashed it repeatedly against a desk until it shattered. As a precaution, he wiped its plastic case before tossing it to the floor.

They made their way downstairs, Jon supporting and half dragging the trembling agent until they arrived at the locked, rear-entrance door.

'Give me the key. Quickly, man.'

The agent began slapping at his pockets as if he was on fire. 'I can't find it, I can't find it!' he gibbered in panic.

Jon grabbed the man by the lapels and slapped him hard across the face. 'Calm down. Go through your pockets one by one.'

Slowly, he tried each pocket with agonising slowness, softly sobbing like a reprimanded child.

'For fuck's sake, come *on*! He might wake up any second.'

With a look of triumph, the agent produced the key from a back pocket.

'Open it!' Jon demanded. The agent fumbled at the lock, hands shaking.

Once outside Jon ordered it locked again. 'Now go home as fast as you can and don't have an accident on the way. I'll sort things here. And lose that key... No, better give it to me. I'll do it.' The agent scuttled away, Jon relieved to be rid of him.

'What a tosser!'

Jon collected a jemmy from his car and ran back to the door. Using all his strength he wrenched it off its hinges, splintering the wooden frame. He stepped back to inspect his work.

– *Shit. That'll have to do. I hope that looks like a break-in and not a bit of industrial espionage. I'll find out tomorrow...*

The next morning Jon strode into the estate agent's office where the others were already assembled.

'Morning, Gentlemen.'

They ignored him. He handed in his bid, exactly on time. The agent, looking pale and jittery, accepted it, unable to look Jon in the face.

The bids were opened and it was revealed that Jon had topped the village consortium's price by two hundred pounds – his little joke. Thwarted and fuming, the consortium's solicitors walked out, refusing to shake hands, glaring at the estate agent who could only shrug his shoulders as if to say, 'I don't know how he did it, either.'

One of the reps turned at the door and sneered at Jon, 'How funny we had a break-in last night...'

'I'll pretend I didn't hear that,' Jon replied affably. 'What is it? Libel? Defamation of character? False accusation?'

The man snorted and left to face his soon-to-be disappointed clients waiting outside.

Jon turned to the agent. 'Everything alright?' The agent nodded. He looked weary, washed out, a frightened man. Jon opened his case and cavalierly tossed a fat envelope on to the agent's desk. 'You'd better check it.'

The agent whimpered in terror, grabbing at the envelope, stuffing it in a draw. 'Please go away. I don't want anything more to do with this, or you, ever. You're an evil...' the agent couldn't bring himself to say it.

'Give it back then?' Jon laughed, amused by the man's emotionality. He walked to the door. 'My solicitors will handle everything from now on. You'll never see me again.'

As he left the office, Jon was forced to run a gauntlet of several hundred hissing and booing villagers. He felt no emotion. The other's loss of home and livelihood and the villagers' outrage meant nothing to him. One by one the baying locals averted their eyes and went quiet as Jon stared from side to side, walking to his car.

Driving away he felt very pleased with himself – he had, after all, triumphed resoundingly.

'Fuck you, Marco,' was all he cared.

He never did build the house. He simply lost interest and sold the land on to a developer – and made a thirty-percent profit.

'You dog in the manger,' he mock-admonished himself, glancing through his solicitor's final account letter.

'Father...? It's Marco. Everything is in place for the presentation and your visit to London next week... Yes, you'll be staying with us and I'll be collecting you as scheduled... No. No problems. Jon Lucke is getting a little carried away with himself. Nothing I can't handle. You were absolutely right about him, as usual. He needs taking down a peg or two. Needs his wings clipped, that's all... Good idea. I think he'll concur. He wouldn't risk losing all he's achieved over a job title and a little sideways promotion...

'You've heard Lucia's news...? Yes of course, Lucke must stop seeing her immediately... Yes, I'll get him to come over for the weekend after the presentation and tell him then... Thank you, Father.'

Marco replaced the receiver. 'Right, Mr Jon Lucke. Time to teach you a lesson in leadership.' He relished the moment, feeling power rush like a drug. This was not the first challenge to his authority he has had to deal with, neither would it be the last.

Jon was at the gym, lying face down on a massage table when Marco called.

'Jon, dear boy! Got you at last. Listen, I'm bringing our monthly board meeting forward. Chi-Chi has something very important he wants to announce and I'm preparing a presentation. How are you fixed for next Tuesday morning? All of the rest of the pack are up for it. How about you?'

Jon stretched to switch on his palmtop. He noted he had arranged to meet with Sonia that afternoon at his house in Paris. 'Nothing I can't cancel.'

'Good, see you there, usual time.'

Jon concurred and switched off his mobile. He altered his dairy and then called Sonia to postpone their session.

'When duty calls,' she responded, no trace of disappointment in her voice.

His morning's work completed, he re-surrendered to the pleasant muscle kneading supplied by the masseuse.

The soi-disant pack was already assembled when Jon arrived late on the appointed day. The group made up the board of Global Brand Marketing (Europe), now the tenth largest advertising agency in the world. He moved amongst them shaking hands, joking and laughing, very much at home.

The gathered glitterati stood with heads respectfully bowed as Chi-Chi entered the room and was seated at the head of the boardroom table, Marco standing by his side.

'Sit, everyone' Marco ordered and they took their places. Jon looked round the table. The élite of the European advertising and marketing world was gathered, each hunted out and seduced aboard for their track-records and brilliance. And they were all Doh-Nai-Zen members.

Marco tapped a glass with a pencil, bringing quiet to the room. 'Chi-Chi has asked me to make a rather special announcement. We are, he judges, ready to commence the next phase of our, ah, global business plan, and you are all to play important roles. Lights, please.'

The lights dimmed. A wall at the far end rose swiftly and silently into the ceiling revealing a hundred-inch plasma screen. It flickered to life and an image formed, depicting their new corporate logo – the letters GBM sitting centrally in a three-dimensional, diamond-facetted lozenge. The logo span slowly on its axis. Jon's team had designed it, and he enjoyed again the subtlety of the computer-generated reflections, highlights and shadows travelling across the revolving logo's surface in a surrealistic chiaroscuro. The twenty-four board members had swivelled in their seats as one to stare expectantly.

'As you all know,' Marco began, 'GBM is already one of the largest advertising groups in the world billing over fifteen billion dollars. We are now ready for the most significant step in our short history – a global campaign.'

Marco pressed a laptop button, bringing up the next screen image. It was the Doh-Nai-Zen symbol – a tiger's paw, claws extended, dragging down leaving jagged, red gashes in its wake, the same blood red as a kiyomeru suit. Jon disliked it; called it 'the World Wildlife Fund with attitude' logo. He had mentioned this once to Marco, suggesting it be redesigned.

'Impossible. Chi-Chi personally authenticated it,' Marco had responded curtly, indignant.

Jon re-engaged with Marco's voice as it continued, 'The next project is our biggest challenge yet, and will help make Doh-Nai-Zen's business arm the largest commercial conglomerate on the planet.' Marco paused for effect, and clicked up an image of the world turning in space.

'Our newest client is to be the recently formed, world wide consortium of Doh-Nai-Zen food growers, distributors and retailers namely, Global Foods Incorporated.'

A series of images of young people eating in fast food outlets appeared onscreen, followed by a rapid succession of dissolve shots – pastured cattle, wheat fields, orchards, market gardens and supermarkets.

'They have commissioned us as their sole marketing and advertising agents to launch a new product in Europe. Our American and Australasian equivalents will be handling things their end, each working in their own cultural climate, all of us in close collaboration.'

A buzz of excitement from the audience.

'Now, as you are aware, the environmentalist lobbies ranged against our new client's fast food divisions have achieved a notable level of success recently, particularly in Europe with the assistance of BSE scares – and worldwide with ill-founded fears over GM crops, nutrition values and so on. Luckily, they have made little impression on the concept of fast food per se, which is, I'm glad to report, still a lifestyle choice for millions and a growth industry.'

Marco paused for a moment, before stating portentously, 'Our task is to successfully promote, on a global scale, our client's latest innovation – a food product which has been designed, tested and produced painstakingly in their own laboratories over the last decade.'

Marco paused again to allow a murmuring hum, team members looking from one to the other in puzzlement under the bright, reflected screen light of white-coated scientists working in a laboratory.

'In essence, our underlying marketing brief is to radically alter the eating habits of the First and Second Worlds. In creative terms, your task is to conjure a stunning brand image, initially launching, then positioning our new product as a generic global brand, leap-frogging its way to the top – a feat never achieved before. This campaign is to be on a scale that will make the Coca-Cola Company and Unilever look like market stall traders.'

Knowing chuckles from the audience bubbled around the room.

'The new product is a highly refined food composite, as yet unnamed. A facet of your brief will be to create a brand name. One that works in all target-country languages.'

On screen there appeared a photo of a stack of uniformly oblong, brightly coloured blocks with wooden sticks extending from their centres.

'The prototype product shown here is coded for reference purposes as DNZ. Each of these blocks contains all the vitamins and nutrients you would find in regular food, representing a snack through to a typical, western main meal – with regional and cultural variations. The ingredients are completely natural, the only additives being colourings and flavour enhancements – sweet, fruit, fish, meat, whatever is found, through intensive market research, to be the most marketable combinations. The product is infinitely flexibile. Thus we can modify it to create, or react to, buying trends, all of which, of course, we will eventually manipulate.

'Our aim is to covertly undermine all the old traditions, habits and values around food preparation and dining, both at home and in restaurants, in order to establish this product as the trendiest, most 'now' alternative – a ground breaking, time and labour saving concept-product for the twenty first century. It is to be positioned as the young, fun loving, nightclubbing lifestyle consumable. Hence the similarity to an ice-lolly. It's to be a meal on a stick. Chic, ultra-modern, designed to dovetail with an on-the-run, urban lifestyle – food with real street cred. Food that is faster than a MacDonalds, sexier than a Håagen Dazs, more desirable than a pair of Levi's and inured in a culture more pervasive than Nike.'

Apposite images presented on screen at the mention of each brand.

'Are you beginning to imagine the commercial possibilities?' Marco asked his audience. Shadowy heads muttered and nodded. 'Once established, a billion units will be sold every day...'

Chi-Chi touched Marco's arm and said something in Japanese. Marco nodded and said, 'Chi-Chi asks me to remind you of the personal wealth that would accrue to each of you if we are successful.' An appreciative laugh rippled around the table.

Marco paused, waiting for quiet. 'Now, before proceeding, let me give you a microcosmic example or two, as part of your brief, of how you will need to approach this project.'

The audience shuffled their feet and altered their positions, sensing this was going to be a longer than normal session.

'In the early fifties, when Doh-Nai-Zen was still small, a group of members pooled resources and invested heavily in palm oil, hoping to corner the futures market.'

An image of palm trees flowered onto the screen.

'Unfortunately, the following years brought market gluts and we risked losing a great deal of our hard won revenue – a serious blow in those days. We looked hard at how we could unload the millions of tons of palm oil on an already oversubscribed and depressed market. We decided that a particular product, which in those days depended heavily on palm oil, had never been exploited to its full potential. Namely, ice cream.'

Marco clicked up a series of pictures before continuing, 'We used cinema and the new, embryonic TV advertising, plus press coverage and PR to persuade people to change their endemic buying habits, weaning them off milk based sauces – such as custard – with their Sunday lunch dessert. Using proven advertising concepts emerging from the US, appealing to peoples' unconscious desires instead of reason – a concept you now take for granted – we sold them the idea of ice cream as the chic, modern, time and labour saving, luxury alternative. The strategy cashed in on the contemporary sound bite "You've never had it so good", reflecting the emergent political zeitgeist of that grey, moribund, post-war era.

'We redesigned the packaging and the way the product was sold, actually creating the 'carveable' family block – in its day as revolutionary an innovation as sliced bread, toothpaste in a tube, a single spoon of instant coffee per cup and the tea bag.'

A series of archived advertisements flicked on screen. Jon stared at a dated looking newspaper ad consisting of rigid, letterpress typography and a grey-looking photo of a gingham table cloth spread under hooped Cornish-ware, each bowl filled with crusty pie and thick slices of ice cream. The overall image looked naive to Jon's professional eye, yet managed to conjure nostalgia. He knew that it couldn't be ice cream under the studio lights. It would melt. It would have to be a look-alike, thermoplastic substitute – such is the cynical alchemy of advertising.

'And it all worked beyond our wildest speculations,' Marco continued. 'Within two years, eighty percent of the West's population swapped from custard to ice cream with their Sunday lunch dessert. Sales boomed and the ice cream industry took off.' A succession of animated, exponential-growth sales charts appeared.

'New products and ice cream concepts followed. Palm oil prices soared and we finally cornered the market, recouping our losses tenfold. Within two years, Ladies and Gentlemen, we covertly changed the eating pattern of the entire industrialised West. And no one questioned the lack of nutritional value, or the fact that we were selling a lesser quality product at a more expensive price. Or even that they were buying a product that's over fifty percent plain air.'

Marco paused for the expected laughter, then continued, 'A more recent sleight of hand, using rather more sophisticated techniques, was created by this very agency for a Doh-Nai-Zen owned product, namely Sungrown. To be frank, this was a rather unpleasant concoction of fruit flavourings, sugar – about a cupful a litre, I believe – and an oil additive that gave the mixture the kind of gloopy texture modern kids apparently love. To children we advertised an energy boosting drink, but we had to convince those who bought the product, too – their mothers. The stroke of genius was getting supermarkets to place the product in their freezer cabinets, thus implying a short-life, organic product with no added preservatives. And it worked, as you know, toppling Pepsi and Coke from the number one spots within weeks.'

Marco paused to take a sip of water before continuing, 'We now need a world-wide campaign to do similar things for product DNZ – thereby revitalising the fast food market, then spreading into supermarket family shopping and street corner kiosk sales. The aim is to totally transform traditional eating habits on a global scale.'

A ripple of applause and Marco held his hand up for quiet.

'We need concepts and brilliantly creative ideas for TV, film, poster and press advertising campaigns, all backed by multi-media spectaculars, competitions and coupon collecting promotions. Packaging, point-of-sale, dispenser and kiosk design will sing out "Must have! Buy me!". There's tough competition out there, and we have to knock it dead.

'We also need references to be insinuated into television soap operas, reality TV and radio shows, pop songs and blockbuster movies; we want websites, discussion and focus groups, fan clubs, a furore created in the press and so on and so forth – you name it, we'll do it. I want you to particularly look at the Euro-youth culture phenomenon of text messaging and the burgeoning new social media sites like Facebook and YouTube, I believe they're called. We must come up with a way of cashing in on all of these new phenomena. Every conceivable aspect of mass, popular culture is to be trawled, mined and utilised. A total brain and feelings washing, if you like, of the entire food consuming population of the industrialised world. No expense will be spared. This will be the first ever billion-dollar campaign. Lights, please.'

The room gradually brightened and the audience again burst into spontaneous applause.

'I take it from that, Colleagues,' Marco said with a boyish grin, 'That you are willing to accept this exciting challenge?' Nods, yesses and absoluteleys from around the table and hands were raised.

'No questions until you've all read the discussion and briefing packs, which will be handed out now. I am your international project co-ordinator and responsible for client liaison. You'll see that we've divided you up into six action groups relating to your own specialist area of expertise, each with a team leader. Eloise will head up Market Research and Dominic Strategic Planning. Media will be handled by Edward, and Creative by Maria, including liaison with the overseas creative chiefs. Mansur heads up PR and finally, Retail and Below-the-Line – which won't come on-stream for some months – will be Jon's baby.'

Jon became rigid, a fixed, stupified grin on his face, humiliation storming below the surface.

– I should be creative head, not Maria. What's he playing at...? He knew immediately this was a choreographed, public demotion, a pointed insult.

A sudden painful, migraine-like surge of images strode through his mind. He saw himself entering the recording studio, another guitarist in his place: then Simon's callous nonchalance, the band turning their backs on him. The power of the long-buried emotion made him reel.

'Everything you need to know is in these briefing packs,' Marco continued, apparently wrapped in his presentation, but keenly tuning in to and enjoying Jon's inner turbulence.

– Let's see how you handle this, Lucke... he was thinking, highly amused.

'Product is already available for study and assessment. We want test marketing in six months and product launch, world wide, in twelve. I want to see initial focus group reports, preliminary drafts and ideas one month from now. From then on, we'll meet fortnightly. Go to it, and good hunting.'

Chi-Chi's voice cut through the excited chatter, immediately gaining silence. He made a short statement in Japanese and when finished gestured towards Marco.

'Chi-Chi wants to remind you that now, more than ever, is the time for diligence in performing your kiyomeru, and that confidentiality is the watchword. An unscheduled, unofficial leak to the press at this, or any, stage would be disastrous. And you all know the penalty for breaking ranks. That is all, and he also wishes you good hunting.'

Chi-Chi rose, nodded curtly, turned and left the room followed by Marco.

The others turned to one another, some standing and crossing the room to shake hands and congratulate, all talking excitedly. Jon sat where he was, staring into space, stunned.

Rising anger urged him to storm after Marco, to demand an explanation and his rightful role back, or to vent itself by screaming abuse and after, to walk away, two fingers raised in contempt. Fighting for control, he fended off the compulsions, realising it would be disastrous to act out his feelings there and then amongst his peers, each of whom was aware of his fate, relishing the *schaudenfreude*, but none of whom was prepared to comment to his face.

– *I won't let him get away with this...* he resolved. He turned to Maria sat on his right.

'Congratulations. Well done!' he feigned, touching her arm.

'Thank you,' she smiled giving a minuscule bow, at the same time thinking, – *That's the last time, Jon. I'm your senior now and don't you forget it...*

After a sullen lunch on his own, brooding deeply, he received a blow upon a bruise on discovering he had not been invited to the preliminary meeting of the action group heads. Cold with fury, he made his way up to Marco's office intent on bearding Marco at the first opportunity, desperate for justice – or retribution.

The meeting was already underway when he arrived, and he was forced to wait. He sat, then stood and paced the anteroom, two doors away from where Marco was chairing the briefing session.

'I've gathered you together to give you a more in depth brief,' Marco opened with. 'You are the most trusted, the generals, so to speak, and a lot of what I am going to tell you this afternoon is on a need to know basis only. Then I'll take questions. In a sense, the creative process is now underway. So, open minds please, everyone. First, anyone know anything about genetically modified, or transgenic foods?'

A silence. Maria tentatively raised a hand. She had a dark, Italianate beauty – her face framed by long, black hair. She kept her muscled, mannish figure trim by taking intense, daily workouts and by wearing expensive, tailored clothes.

'I believe transgenics can be...' she ticked off the points on her fingers, 'one: designed to either not need pesticides and herbicides to facilitate growth, or will not be affected by their usage. Two: especially created to be high yield, disease free, drought or frost resistant – depending on where needed geographically. Three: they can be made to have have shorter planting to harvest cycles, allowing two or three harvests a year. Four: they may have "built-in" extended transport and storage times before ripening, and five: useful innate qualities can be cross bio-engineered. For example, cacti genes spliced into wheat to facilitate desert growth and so on. In theory, even addictive qualities could be engineered into innocuous food plants – if one were cynical enough, that is. All, of course, with major commercial implications.'

'Clever girl. Someone's been doing their homework,' Marco praised. Despite the fact Marco had advised her to mug up on transgenics as they laid side by side in bed one night, she still felt gratified by his compliment.

'What has this to do with DNZ, though?' Maria asked.

'Good question. We've had transgenic and genetic engineering research programmes running for some years now, and out of that has come the formula for the highly refined, vegetable and animal foodstuffs that are, in fact, the basic ingredients of DNZ. A raw material ingredient that affords growers, wholesalers and retailers actual warehousing and shelf-life times quadruple that of normal foods, while continuing to retain nutritional integrity. This product will be manna to warehouse, transport and supermarket managers. But we've taken the concept a stage further.'

'In what way?' Edward asked.

'Cultures, dear boy! Cultures! Great, self-regenerating vats of meat, fish, vegetables and sugar, all growing and bubbling away like yogurt, helping us to make a fortune!'

A babble as people asked questions all at once. Marco held up a hand and continued into the ensuing silence.

'With a projected thousand million people in the world by 2020, governments are aware that current farming methods could never sustain such a level of food production. Consequently, they have been funding and helping GM research – and Global Foods have made the definitive breakthrough. Eventually, we foresee that most conventional, indigenous vegetable and cereal crop foods, and in time animal products – fish, fowl and dairy – will be replaced by transgenics in the form of genetically engineered food cultures incorporating only the attributes we require. These will be marketed in the West as DNZ consumables and derivatives on a huge scale. Can you imagine the commercial possibilities of replacing inefficient, old-style crops with culture-growing facilities? No more archaic farming techniques, where only a small percentage of the animal or plant is utilised – and no more subsidised farmers, agricultural diseases, vets, abattoirs and tied land?

'More importantly, never again seasonal famines or gluts. And if that scenario were applied across the whole spectrum of food production, can you even begin to conceive the potential market and its profit margins for us?'

Marco looked around the room at the stunned faces and continued, 'We have already the tacit backing of governments worldwide. Our strongest ally, as ever, is greed. All they see is inexhaustible supplies of cheaper food, vast economic savings and large tax windfalls for their treasuries. They are, consequently, either blinkered to the possibilities of more sinister scenarios, or blatantly cynical. Any questions so far?'

A babble of questions and raised hands. Marco pointed to Edward.

'You say governments are blinkered to more sinister scenarios. From that, am I to infer that there *are* more sinister scenarios?' he asked, his concern deepening the worried expression he habitually wore. Edward was small and dapper, sharply dressed despite his rotund figure with its small feet and hands – often the sign of a punctilious nature. He was sallow complexioned, sported dark, wavy hair, and was considered brilliant at his job.

'It's possible, but unlikely,' Marco replied with a shrug. 'The following is highly classified stuff, by the way, for the ears of those present only. Now I won't go into all the technical details – don't understand most of them myself. Basically, our research scientists have no doubt that even small experimental sites growing GM plants could introduce mutating, rogue genes into food chains – thanks to untold quadrillions of pollinating insects and seed eating birds which we, as yet, have no control over until we get the vats up and running in sealed production units. The process will accelerate, no doubt, when genetically engineered animals begin to be reared. They estimate that, based on merely today's low level GM farming, within five years there will not be a human being on this planet that doesn't have a synthetically mutated gene in its system somewhere – they do tend to replicate remarkably quickly. Rogue genes that are, in fact, more robust and more dynamic than our natural, congruently developed ones. What this means in evolutionary terms, no one has any idea whatsoever at this juncture. I guess we'll just have to cross that bridge when we come to it.'

Hubbub erupted, everyone in the room asking questions simultaneously. Marco raised his hand and pointed again to Edward, sensing a problem.

'Let me get this straight, Marco. Are you telling us that you actually know there's a risk that these man made genes could go out of control?'

'There's always an x factor in every new venture, so, possibly, yes,'

Marco answered, 'But as I said earlier, highly unlikely.'

'Well, has any research been done to find out?'

'Some, but nothing conclusive either way.'

'I'm sorry to labour the point, but as we're dealing with my children's futures here, I'd like to be clear,' Edward continued sardonically. 'It appears that you're preparing to unleash these self-replicating and mutating rogue genes on the world – genes that may well have their own agenda and could possibly interfere with current evolutionary trends...'

'That's a little over-dramatised, Edward,' Marco interrupted. 'You've been reading too much science fiction, I'm afraid. The risks are very small indeed, and a long way off.'

'But you admit there are risks and you're willing for us to take them?' Edward demanded to know, irritation over the put down straining his voice.

'It's a very, very tiny risk,' Marco insisted, smiling, slowly shaking his head. 'Not in the same league as the kind of risk that, say, Marie Curie took when she first experimented with radium. Now, of course, the world reaps the benefits – from medicine to nuclear energy.' Marco was obviously becoming irritated. Edward was made temporarily speechless by Marco's convoluted argument.

'What about us?' Maria interjected. 'Are we to be contaminated too? Isn't that like shooting ourselves in the foot?'

Marco pulled from staring at Edward in antagonistic disbelief and turned to Maria. 'My dear girl, you don't have to eat the stuff. One of the joys of having wealth is that one does not have to live like the hoi-polloi. The rich rarely suffer, even during war. Going without, or accepting second best is merely a function of a lack of money – and social standing. As I pointed out during the presentation, fast foods have been getting a bad press just lately and, although our enemies are successfully knocking our products, they are failing to make inroads into the lifestyle concept. The public simply want faster food with guarantees of cleanliness. And that's exactly what we'll be supplying, which is our job. We're not paid to be moral guardians of the planet. And anyway, there'll always be people like Edward, whose hobby, as you know, is farming.'

'Hardly farming,' Edward replied. 'I have a modest five-hundred acre site in Sussex, to which I retire for the weekends.'

'I'm sure you'd supply all your friends with traditional foodstuffs if asked,' Marco smiled sweetly at Edward, 'And no doubt healthy and organically grown?'

'Well, of course...'

Certain he had contained any dissention, Marco continued, 'Although this all has government support, confidentiality is still the watchword. But now I need to disclose an aspect of Chi-Chi's plan that does not have overt government support, and must not go beyond this room. Frankly, the conventional way forward will take far too long for our purposes and will be extremely arduous. What we intend to do, using GM skills learnt by our own technicians, is to splice an addictive gene, apparently cloned from tobacco, into the DNZ raw material. This is, as far as we can foresee, a relatively harmless additive, one that mimics endorphins, our naturally produced euphoric and analgesic drug. Apparently, once the body senses endorphin look-alikes in the blood, it ceases to make its own. If the substitute is then removed, the body takes weeks to reinstate production and we experience what are called withdrawal symptoms – mild pain and depression in short – and that's what's called "a habit".'

'I hope we are at liberty in this meeting to say exactly what we feel, off the record?' Edward asked, his voice restrained, anger focussed.

'But of course, dear boy,' Marco responded affably, thinking he had Edward's measure now. 'Fire away.'

'Frankly, I'm totally stupefied by what I am hearing. I pride myself on my amorality, and as you well know, under normal circumstances, I would do anything for Chi-Chi. But this is not amoral: it's totally immoral and completely insane! I'm sorry, this whole...' Edward was lost for words. 'This whole stupid... farrago has a ring of utter madness. Millions upon millions of addicted zombies fed on drugged pap by a ruling élite...? It's, it's – *preposterous!* We're all as wealthy as we need, so what's the point? I just can't go along with any of this, I'm sorry.'

'Oh, come on, man. That is somewhat over-egging the pudding. And anyway, power groups have been doing this for millennia. What's the difference between stuffing the populace with lies, mass entertainment, tobacco, alcohol and feeding them DNZ?' Marco responded, irritated again, not expecting or welcoming yet more discord. 'If you think about it, in reality we're actually giving them freedom from hunger, at last. What do they care where their food comes from as long as it's cheap, readily available and they and their kids have full bellies? Bread and circuses, old boy. Bread and circuses.'

'Well I still happen to believe in freedom of choice,' Edward replied scornfully. 'I have no problem regarding the use of advertising to attempt to manipulate people into making certain choices – if it still allows choice and a semblance of freedom. But to cynically remove those alternatives so there is no choice whatsoever... It's tantamount to spiking a woman's drink with an opiate so you can... It's rape, technically. Every human, no matter how lowly, should be allowed choice – some kind of free will. I cannot condone rape, Marco, for any amount of wealth!'

'Come off that high horse, Edward. How the hell can anyone have free will if motivated solely by childhood traumas, religious and class indoctrination, jingoism and the like? Think bigger. This is why you joined Doh-Nai-Zen if you remember, or has your newly-found wealth diluted your will? Spare me the bleeding heart platitudes, if you will.' Marco spat out the words as if they were ill-tasting, profane.

'I joined to create a secure future for myself and my family – admittedly as part of a covertly ruling élite – but not to – to revert back to some kind of dark-ages tribalism. This whole scheme has a ring of Nazism to it and, being Jewish, I cannot tolerate, let alone subscribe to, no matter how obliquely, such a philosophy,' Edward spluttered, apoplectic now.

The argument wore on, acrimoniously fermenting in the crucible of Marco's office. Like a catalyst, Marco remained unmoved by Edward's acidic attack. He had long suspected Edward's equivocation and had seized on the opportunity to test his theory.

'So, where exactly do you stand, Edward?' Marco eventually slotted in. 'Are you with us or against us?'

'As you narrow the options, you leave me no choice – ironically. I resign here and now. And I shall pull my companies from the group, cease to be a member and, if this preposterous scheme goes ahead, I promise you I shall alert both the non-Doh-Nai-Zen establishment and the alternative media.'

'If that is your wish I can do nothing to prevent you,' Marco added, shrugging. 'But I would seriously consider the consequences of shooting your mouth off, if I were you.'

'I do have standing and clout without Doh-Nai-Zen, Marco.'

He stood and left the office without another word, passing Jon still waiting in the anteroom.

'Protect your back, Jon. The shit is about to hit the fan.'

'Sorry?' Jon asked, taken aback.

'You'll find out soon enough.'

In the office, Marco got to his feet to announce, 'Damage limitation time, I'm afraid, Ladies and Gentlemen. Time to go. Keep this little incident to yourselves and we'll meet again in two weeks as scheduled.' They filed out subdued, deep in thought.

Jon impatiently pushed through them. 'Marco, I need to talk.'

'Make it brief, I've some calls to make,' Marco snapped imperiously, his mobile already in his hand.

'How come I'm not heading up creative on this one? What's the problem?' he demanded aggressively.

Marco stared at him for a few seconds, eventually responding with a measured sigh. 'Jon, Jon. Frankly, we don't think you're up to it. Your mind hasn't been on the job just lately, so we decided to take the pressure off for a while. We're sure you'll do a fine job on the below the line stuff. It's still a major responsibility.'

'Well, you could have bloody well discussed it with me first. We're supposed to be partners,' Jon spat, unmollified.

'We chose not to discuss it with you, Jon,' Marco replied sharply. 'We are not a Social Services department. We're a business. You hack it or you're out, simple as that. You know the way we operate – performance related, you're only as good as your last project. This applies to directors and office boys alike. However, do a good job on the retail stuff and maybe you'll win back your Numero Uno slot.'

'Is this personal? Is it because I went against you over the house?' Jon demanded.

Marco stared coldly. 'Let's just say we feel you've been getting above yourself just lately and a short, sharp lesson in humility is required.'

'Humility? What the fuck are you talking about? I thought the bloody aim was to be the opposite, to get more powerful...'

'These are Chi-Chi's orders, Jon,' Marco barked. 'He has asked me to remind you that it is a well-documented phenomenon in Doh-Nai-Zen that one can feel powerful without actually being powerful. One is only truly so when one has judgement and constraint. If you are wise, you will go away and reflect on this and ask the Energy for guidance. Now, if you don't mind...?' Marco pointed an open hand at the door.

Jon turned on his heel and without another word stamped out, smouldering with humiliation, only just holding back from attempting to rip the door off its hinges.

'Father, we have a problem...'

'Serious?'

'Very. As we suspected, something has changed in Edward and, sadly, he's going to leave us. I sense he has been looking for an excuse and DNZ appears to be it. More worryingly, he's threatening to talk to the Press...'

'He must be prevented. No loose cannons, Marco.'

'Understood. Do I have your permission to implement the solution we discussed if ever this scenario became a reality?'

'Of course.'

'Good. Consider it done...'

'What about Lucke?'

'Angry – and feeling a little humiliated, but he'll get over it. That gives me an idea... May I suggest we kill two birds with one stone? Let's use him to solve the Edward problem, at the same time testing his commitment. I'm certain he's ready.'

'Try it, but be subtle. And bring him down at the weekend for me to assess his state of mind, no matter what the outcome.'

'I will. My driver will collect you from Heathrow tomorrow as arranged. And thank you, Father.'

REALISATION

Jon stormed back to his apartment and immediately dismissed his manservant for the evening, needing to fume and curse in private. He symbolically drew the curtains and paced around his apartment fretting, occasionally kicking a chair or the wall. His body felt distorted by a pent up, internal pressure he could not release. He began to long for a confidante, a close friend.

– Need someone to talk to... He thought nostalgically of Tony and his ex-wife.

– No, they wouldn't get it. I'm on my own now...

Then he began to yearn for Lucia. He had not seen her for weeks. She was currently touring the States trying out her independence, seeking backing for her own fashion house – and causing a media stir wherever she went. The photographs appearing in newspaper and magazine gossip columns portrayed her socialising, ever on the arms of celebrities and America's wealthiest and most influential.

Driven by a melancholic jealousy, he tore a full colour page from a glossy magazine and placed it under his scanner. He enlarged the image onscreen and sat and stared at Lucia's life-size head. He idly took a picture clipping of her face and searched for porn on the internet, downloading an image of a naked woman in a suggestive pose, then expertly grafted on Lucia's face. He sat ogling the image, hoping it would ignite sexual desire and a vicarious intimacy. It failed to touch him and he felt suddenly childish, the deft operation having merely reinforced the ache.

He dialled her hotel in Washington again.

'May we enquire who is calling, sir?' He gave his name and was told she was out and they had no idea where, or when she would return. For the third time he left a message asking her to call him. He next dialled her mobile, got the familiar recorded voice again and sank back into depression feeling thwarted, sidelined, somehow impoverished.

'This is turning into a very bad day,' he announced morosely to the silent room. He reviewed what had transpired, trying to make sense, to see if there was a pattern, but groped blindly, falteringly, finding nothing.

– *I thought Doh-Nai-Zen was supposed to make me eternally happy. Instead, I've lost my job; Marco treats me like shit; Sonia bores the pants off me and Lucia plays me for a fool. I think I want out of this...*

– *But what does it all matter? I'm a wealthy man with everything I could possibly want. Why rock the boat...?*

'Because I despise fucking, manipulative, controlling Marco,' he screamed aloud, punching the sofa. The sudden explosion of anger pinpointed the truth, bringing temporary respite.

– *That's it. I have to find a way to hit back. Show him he can't treat me like this, that I'm bigger than he realises...*

Feeling better, the debilitating anger acquiescent, he grabbed his coat and went out on the town for the rest of the night.

The following day, Jon was sitting at his desk when Marco walked in unexpectedly. They exchanged pleasantries and discussed the DNZ project, both circling around their personal agendas, each awaiting the opening for their individual game plan.

'Sorry about yesterday,' Jon eventually injected. 'Point taken.'

'Glad to hear it. You won't regret it in the long run. By the way, there's something I want to ask you. Would you say you were one hundred per cent committed to Doh-Nai-Zen, Jon?'

'Of course.'

'Committed enough to take an enormous, personal risk? But one that would render the greatest possible service to us?'

'Yes. Probably. Depends...'

'If you were successful in this undertaking, you could virtually name your reward.'

Jon immediately thought of Lucia, then judged it would not be wise to reveal his true feelings at this juncture.

– *Marco may not have that level of control over her and she might not go along with it...* He pulled from thinking to ask, 'How about heading up the creative on the DNZ project?'

'If you're successful, that could be arranged. No problem.'

'So, what do you want me to do?'

'Eliminate somebody, Jon.'

'Eliminate...? What do you mean? Not kill someone, I hope?'

'Yes. Someone who is an enormous threat to Doh-Nai-Zen's integrity, Jon.'

In the stunned seconds that follow, Jon's feelings ran amok, unable to believe what he had heard.

'Tell me you're joking.'

'Deadly serious, Jon. We would like you to arrange an accidental death. We'll back you with all the necessary resources. Obviously, if you were to get found out, you'd be on your own; this conversation never happened; Doh-Nai-Zen doesn't exist... And if you refuse – which, of course, you are perfectly entitled to do – there'll be no ramifications whatsoever. On the other hand, pull this off successfully and you automatically become one of the Doh-Nai-Zen élite.'

'You must be out of your fucking mind,' Jon blurted, unable to control the rising revulsion, surprised at his own vehemence. 'I wouldn't do that for anyone, or anything...'

'You're quite sure, Jon?'

'Totally. What do you think I am?'

'In that case, Jon, forget I asked.' Marco changed gear as smoothly as a Roller. 'Why don't you come and see us at the weekend? Chi-Chi and Lucia will be joining us Saturday evening. I can promise you a very quiet, relaxed time. We could knock ideas around about the project – and a few golf balls. Do you good to relax.'

'Yeah, sure. That'll be great,' Jon replied, still shellshocked.

'Good.' Marco stood. 'I'd better be off – work to catch up on. I'll see you at the weekend – around lunchtime Saturday. Ciao.'

Marco's proposition had lifted a veil, revealing something murky; something Jon could not quite make out, yet which left him feeling deeply discomforted. He could no longer concentrate on his work and left the office for the afternoon, going home to sit and brood again. A dread that he was into something deeper than he was prepared to handle manifested. He could not fully admit to himself the horror of his situation. The thoughts and feelings winged and stung like angry wasps defending their disturbed nest until he was exhausted. He decided to do kiyomeru, to ask the Energy for guidance, not considering whether this would enmesh him deeper or not. Like the alcoholic who drinks to forget the abysmal life he has created because of his drinking, he was oblivious to the irony. He stood, inwardly directing his awareness as he had done once or twice a week for the past six years.

The moment arrived when the sluice gates were lifted and the Energy came fluming and coursing through the canals and furrows of the black-domed cave of consciousness. Like twirling the dial on an old radio, different tonalities, foreign dialects, alien sensibilities faded in and out of white noise until the tuner locked on to the station broadcasting the programme he sought.

'What the fuck's going on?' he demanded, dispensing with formality. A scurry of static and sparks hissed in his head.

'Trials and tribulations are sent as gifts. They are growth points, handholds up and out of your enslavement. You are feeling growing pains. Learn from the experiences. Rejoice in them. The Energy is growing in you and around you. Those who surrender to it are guaranteed the most glorious of futures, but only if you follow without question...'

'Shit and bollocks!'

The disappointments, the humiliations, the sadness, the hunger for Lucia, the truth about Marco and the so-called élite all swamped him in a tidal wave of revulsion. He fell to the floor raging and sobbing. A firestorm erupted inside and he ranted and kicked, his body thrashing and bucking with paroxysms of rage, gouts of fear and loathing. His eyes turned up into his head and frothing foam flecked his mouth as the fit reached its climax. With one last spasm, his torso bucked into the air and crashed back, spent and motionless.

His body lay cataplectic on the floor, curled in foetal position.

Several hours passed. His awareness awoke, conscious of a long forgotten tranquillity pervading his system. He felt cavernous and quiet; fresh and stilled. His awareness began to float through his inner world, exploring, observing. It arrived at a place it had never visited before. There it hovered, perceiving for the first time the source of his animal energy.

Movement. Something alive below him, inside him. He was looking down, observing his inner animal as if in a dream, symbolically, metaphorically, but understanding it was a reality – a different kind of reality; one keener and more intense than the mirage created daily by his overt senses.

Freed from its routine dilution of sensory perception – the filters of a lifetime – his consciousness registered the Energy's presence as a sentient being dwelling in a cave. It had a form; that of a ghoulish dust mite seen through an electron microscope. It was big, grey, six-legged and covered in a leathery carapace. The creature looked prehistoric – jaws, mandibles, antennae, bulbous eyes, coarse hair – a nightmarish mix of insect, fish and lizard-like animal.

He sensed its nature was vicious, red in tooth and claw; that it was avaricious, cruel and predatory. Its virtual nest, the place where it resided in his inner world, was hot and humid, the walls glistening with excrement, the stench of the reptile house pervading the atmosphere.

Quietly grunting and snuffling to itself, unaware of being observed, the tightly knit energies, masquerading in animal form, ruminated and rummaged among the artery-like tubes that pulsed and glowed along the cavern's walls, ferrying energy to all parts of Jon's psychic body.

Absorbed, humming contentedly, it buried its proboscis deep into a tube and proceeded to suck up the vital flow. The young and ravenous animal visibly grew larger as it engorged, resembling a semi-transparent tic sucking blood.

Jon experienced a shock of connectivity; loose ends were tied; things slotted into place; then illumination and realisation. It was one of those seminal moments of clarity that changed perception for ever.

– *It's parasitic – and I'm its host. It's feeding on me, usurping my energy, transforming my humanity into itself…*

With revulsion, he severed the association with the foreign, hostile force, attacking, ripping out the proboscis from where it was sunk, snapping it at its base. The animal emitted an air-renting bellow and ran amok, yelping like an injured dog.

Jarring pains like a series of high-voltage electric shocks reverberated and ricocheted through Jon's body. He snapped from the coma back into everyday consciousness, gasping for air, eyes wide, stupefied. He sat up, hugging his knees, shaking with shock and panting for breath.

He sensed the animal prowling, separate now, but caged inside; wounded, unable to feed. Disgust and horror overwhelmed him and he sat, rocking to and fro, head in hands, forced to experience the nauseous welling of the deepest shame and revulsion.

For over an hour, Jon had paced the room, pondering, analysing, attempting to think things through. Finally a plan of action had emerged.
– *First off*, he told himself, *no more kiyomeru. I have to kill this bloody thing inside me, stop it feeding on me...* He shut his eyes and shuddered.
– *Secondly, I've done pretty well out of the whole mess financially and that means I can do anything I want now. So, tomorrow I'll start to separate my personal money from the business, sell my shares, hand in my resignation and take a long holiday. Then I'll start something of my own. Design, the movies, whatever, as long as it's creative. Maybe Lucia and I could start something together. I'll give her an ultimatum. Live with me, or that's it. And if she won't – well fuck the lot of them. I'm never going to be in thrall to anyone or anything ever again...*

'You were correct again, Father. Lucke would not play ball, even to get his old position back. Frankly, I'm bemused. I would have thought by now...'
'It's only an experiment, Marco. He may have needed more time, or some harsh discipline, or we may have misjudged. Whatever the outcome, he is dispensable. Do not blame yourself. More importantly, how is the project proceeding?'
'The agency is humming. They're all very excited.'
'Good. And the legalities, the mergers?'
'The legal teams and accountants are redrafting contracts, sorting shareholdings and all the peripherals. Global Foods will be a legit corporation within days. That'll mean another fifty or so billionaires in the world.'
'As long as my generals are content and loyal.'
'After this, Father, you'll be their god.'
'For just as long as long as they are well fed, hmm? And Edward?'
'Arrangements have been made. Consider the matter closed.'
'Good. And you'll bring Lucke to your home at the weekend?'
'Yes, Father. In a specimen jar.'
Chi Chi chuckled and switched off his mobile. Marco walked from his office feeling inordinately pleased with himself.

By noon the next day Jon had cleaned out his bank accounts and had over a million pounds in low denomination notes stashed away in safety deposit boxes across London. Another two million had been electronically dispatched to a Swiss bank account. His stockbroker had already left for the weekend, so he would have to leave instructing the sale of his his shares until Monday. He started to enjoy mentally crafting his letter of resignation as he drove to the office. Once there, he pottered around – acting normally, reading the DNZ project briefing documents – then decided to have a late lunch on his own.

Outside, he tried to hail a cab. It was drizzling and vacant cabs were as rare as happy looking people so he was forced to walk. In passing, a newsvendor's billboard caught his eye.

'TOP AGENCY DIRECTOR DIES IN FREAK ACCIDENT' it shouted. Mild shock and curiosity welled up. It was probably someone he knew. He bought a copy and pored over it as he walked.

Edward Scott, 45 year old Managing Director of Scott Media, a subsidiary of the worldwide advertising giant GBM, died early today when his Aston Martin plunged eighty feet down the car-lift shaft of his company's multi-storey car park adjacent to Scott House in Holborn, the article ran. *The safety barriers had been switched off prior to a maintenance programme. The forty-six year old Director ignored warning signs and drove into the lift space, plunging to his death. Colleagues hinted that he was under a great deal of stress due to the pressure of new business. He leaves a wife and three children,* it concluded.

Jon felt no emotion about the death. He had never really liked Edward that much. But to Jon, it appeared glaringly obvious what had transpired.

– *Or could it have? Am I being paranoid...?* he questioned. He dialled Marco's number, locating him at their club, and asked for a few minutes of his time. Marco agreed affably, and Jon headed for St. James Street.

He found Marco alone, sitting reading a newspaper among the hushed leather chairs, surrounded by oak panelled walls and dense bookshelves. When they had signed for their drinks, and he was sure they couldn't be overheard, Jon broached the subject, observing Marco's minutest reaction.

'You've heard about Edward?'

'Yes, I have. Shocking.' Marco shook his head.

'I must verify something with you. Edward's demise – was it an accident? Or was it orchestrated?'

'Orchestrated. What a colourful term.'

'You know what I mean. Was it connected with what you and I discussed yesterday?'

'Jon, my dear boy, I'm really very surprised you don't know the answer to that question,' Marco prevaricated, looking over the top of his half-moon glasses – a recent affectation.

'Yeah, yeah. I know,' Jon demurred nodding sagely as his mind slowly worked it out.

    – *Edward displayed a lack of commitment, somehow...*

    – *And he was taken out...*

    – *He must have been a liability, a risk...*

    – *Must've done something real bad...*

    – *Once involved at this level, there's no escape...*

    – *Yeah. It's for life...*

After confirming he would be at Marco's for the weekend and making his excuses, he left the building, relief clambering over anxiety.

    – *Thank fuck I haven't delivered my resignation letter yet. Could well have been my death warrant...*

    – *Have to play it very carefully from now on...*

    – *And now there's this weekend to worry about....*

    – *Must make sure I'm well defended. Don't want them discovering I want out just yet...*

Jon returned to his apartment to prepare for the weekend away.

'Pack me a weekend case, Henry, including golfing clothes. And you might as well take the weekend off. I probably won't be back till Monday morning.'

'Thank you, sir. Oh, by the way, this came for you this morning, just after you had left.'

Henry handed Jon a stuffed A4 envelope with *JON LUCKE – BY HAND* written in capital letters.

'Any idea who it's from?'

'None, sir. It was delivered by a motor cycle messenger.'

'Okay, thanks.'

Jon went to his study and slit the envelope. Inside was a report marked *Highly Confidential. For Departmental Heads Only. DNZ AND ADDICTIVE GENE STRAINS.* Attached was a handwritten note.

Jon,

If you get this, it will mean I am dead – probably from some 'accident' or other. I know we were never exactly bosom pals in the past, so you're probably wondering why I have sent this to you. I have often sensed, through kiyomeru,

that you are not – how shall I put it? – one hundred percent committed to the cause; that you are more like me, not born to this, but have been brought in, recruited from outside. Your recent demotion hints to me that you are currently out of favour with the hierarchy. The enclosed may be extremely useful to you in the future. Please read and do with it what you will. And if I have misjudged you and the situation, well then – I guess Chi Chi, Marco and gang will have had the last laugh...
    Regards
    Edward.

The weekend proved to be as informal and laid back as promised – no other house guests, just Jon, Chi-Chi and Mikho, his assistant, being entertained by Mr and Mrs Marco Brancusi at home. Jon was delighted to hear that Lucia had returned to England and would arrive later that afternoon. He was aquiver with anticipation; it had been weeks since he'd seen her last.

She arrived late on Saturday and Jon fell for her all over again. She seemed to have matured, lost her girlishness. He was jealously aware that the media and celebrity attention she'd received in the US had played its part. Her clothes, hair, make up – everything about her – displayed a new quality, one of languid potency. He got little chance to be alone with her. She felt distanced, bored, and he sensed no warmth, despite the display of pleasure at seeing him.

At supper, Chi-Chi told stories about his past, talked about the future and asked them all to describe their kiyomeru experiences. Jon made certain his barriers were strongly in place and sensed no probing into his private space. He was satisfied they suspected nothing of his true feelings, and that they knew nothing of Edward's contacting him 'from beyond the grave', and he confidently acted out being the exemplary Doh-Nai-Zen member in the presence of both his mentor and his Master.

When Sonia came to his room that night, he was disappointed it was not Lucia, but he didn't show it, and neither did he let Sonia down. The time would come when he could dismiss her from his life completely.

– Just doing my duty – and being careful not to rock the boat... he excused himself, enjoying the physicality nonetheless, aware that this would probably be the last time they would have sex together.

On Sunday morning, he was on the golf course with Marco. It was a warm and sunny day. At the highest point, the North Bucks, farming countryside spread out before them – a crazy paving of ochres and golds, edged by dark, rich greens fading to subtle blue-greys in the misty distance. Marco was a member and master practitioner of the 'Not In My Backyard' lobby. Big cash crop farming – rape seed and sugar beet monocultures had, therefore, not yet come to this part of the world. The small, irregular-shaped fields growing wheat, barley and oats had not been widened out – reshaped for the combine harvester's ease of manœuvre. The old hedgerows and copses were still in place, following the contours of the land, offering a range of habitats that supported myriad wildlife. It had a medieval feel, an ancient beauty redolent of human activity working in harmony with nature – a plenitude; a fulsome bounty. The air was feathery soft and full of the fragrant aromas of wild flowers after the overnight rain. Jon felt as physically lithe and supple as a frisky, young dog. Only the hidden secret and repressed anxiety nestling like black cancers threatened to spoil the pleasure of the moment.

– *What do they want to go and ruin all this for...?* he wondered, surprised, but gratified such a sentiment still survived.

– *They are totally crazy...*

Revulsion rose again, wafting through him like a sickness.

'What are you thinking so deeply about?'

Marco had ambled across to where Jon stood gazing down over the valley. He was immediately uncertain as to whether Marco was being darkly ironic, the question loaded with implication, or merely making small talk. Jon opted for the former and immediately went on the defensive. He thought he sensed the subtlest probe from Marco and decided he would take no more chances, would rein in his thoughts and feelings more tightly.

'Just wondering if there was any mileage in linking this kind of old world, English landscape with DNZ. Maybe saying we're conserving it by taking the pressure off,' he said, thinking fast. 'You know – a pre-planned reassurance before the environmentalists put their oar in? Might draw the teeth of their arguments.'

'Not on your life!' Marco retorted, a deadly serious note underlying the jocularity. 'Well off-target. I'd prefer to keep the great, unwashed masses away from my patch. So no cameras within a hundred miles, if you please. Come on. Enough of this. We're supposed to be playing golf, remember? Learn to prioritise old boy. Relax. You feel pretty tense to me.'

This tacit skirmish convinced Jon that he was somehow on trial this weekend. A little quiet digging and office gossip had already informed him of Edward's antagonism, his threat to leave.

– Edward must have really rattled the branches, unsettled the group. No won-
der they wanted him bumped off. And now I know what I know…

Jon's refusal to do Marco's bidding, his inability to get involved, had put him in a dangerous situation, he realised. And he fully understood now what to expect if his true feelings were unearthed.

– I mustn't be careless, or over relaxed; but neither must I appear too con-
trolled. A fine balance. Marco has obviously picked up my anxiety with that
subtle probe and I'm sure he's already suspicious… He recalled Marco's oxy-moronic advice from years ago – relaxed tension – and immediately felt his body respond.

– But that document Edward sent me. It's dynamite. I might well be able to
blast myself out of this hole with that…

After supper that evening, Marco asked Jon to come to his study for a chat, and he went nervously, not sure what to expect.

'Jon, I won't beat about the bush,' Marco stated when they were seat-ed, whiskies in hand, 'Sonia and I want to you to stop seeing Lucia. Now, full stop.'

'Well… What does Lucia have to say about this?' Jon demanded, irrita-tion rising.

Marco delivered the expert coup de grace. 'You do realise that she is to announce her engagement imminently?'

'No! I-I had no idea. She hasn't said a word to me,' Jon stammered out, stupefied.

'She'll be married in about six months' time. To Morgan Langton. You know who is?'

'Bloody hell! The Governor of California.'

'That's right, and certain to be the next Republican presidential candi-date. He is one of the richest men in the world, about number twenty, I recall, and a good Doh-Nai-Zen member, like most of his family. They made their money from oil and armaments and are highly respected pil-lars of the community. Morgan's very smart: a Harvard man and an ath-lete in his youth – college football and all that. And extremely good look-ing, apparently. I think Lucia's quite genuinely fond of him, not that that matters one jot.'

The effort of repressing the rising tide of emotion was beginning to make Jon sweat.

'So you can see how important this is to us, to Doh-Nai-Zen. Lucia will, in all probability, be married to the next President of the United

States. She'll be the First Lady – the single most powerful woman in the world. Think what that means, Jon, and you'll see why we can't have her little peccadillo on show for the world media to get their teeth into. Annoyingly, there are pockets of the media we don't control. Hacks who love to drag little rich girls through the pig swill – especially those who are talented and ambitious.

'Now, as far as they're concerned, you will check out to be merely a youthful fling and the world will admire her for it. However, should you go on seeing her during her engagement, we risk too much. The great, prudish American Public would never tolerate infidelity during a betrothal from a potential First Lady. Even Presidents can't get away with it if they get caught nowadays – unless they lie through their teeth and have the charm of the Devil, as we well know. And secondly, their marriage must never actually *appear* to be a sham, one arranged for power, whether it is or not.'

He could hardly hear Marco's voice over his pounding heart and the rushing of blood.

'So, attempt to see her after she's married, and you become not only a ticking time-bomb for us, but a national security risk – a very bad man indeed, classified as a public enemy, in all probability. And we can't have any rogue reporters delving into any of our private lives, can we? For obvious reasons. So you must stop, now, tonight. Finished, kaput. Do you understand?' Marco was not asking, he was telling, growling out a last warning like an aggressive guard dog.

With enormous effort Jon pulled his fragmenting self together. 'Yeah, yeah. I hear what you're saying. It's tough, but I understand. Doh-Nai-Zen comes first with me – you know that. It's a shock, but I'll get over it,' he contrived.

'Good. Make sure you do. And you know you should never have got into this situation in the first place, and neither should Lucia. Such naivete.' Marco paused and shook his head, acting like an aggrieved headmaster. 'And now, there's another matter. You've been a very bad boy Jon. Yet more black marks, I'm afraid.'

Jon flinched inwardly as though expecting another blow after a beating.

'It's also time to stop sleeping with my wife, for similar reasons. Need to present as squeaky clean to the press from here on in. You understand?' Marco said this coldly as though settling an old score, staring full of enmity at Jon.

'Agreed,' Jon replied, feigning meekness.

Marco continued to stare hard at Jon, then, seemingly satisfied, nodded acceptance and looked at his watch. 'Chi-Chi would like us all to do kiyomeru together in about an hour's time. I suggest you go and get ready.' Jon stood and left the room looking suitably hangdog.

– Fuck! Fuck! Fuck…! Rage scoured like caustic soda. *– Why didn't she tell me? The fucking manipulative cow…!*
He went straight to Lucia's room and burst in without knocking. She was sitting on the bed in her dressing gown, hair towel-wrapped, painting her nails and talking animatedly into a mobile tucked under her chin. Grabbing it from her, screaming, 'Bitch!' he threw it into the corner of the room.

Startled by his unannounced entrance and violent actions, she leapt to her feet, galvanised by fury.

'You bastard!' she yelled, swinging a fist.

Jon grabbed her wrist before she made contact, but was not quick enough for the other hand, which raked his face with long fingernails. He snatched it and twisted both arms down, forcing her to her knees. She yelped in pain, continuing to struggle.

'Why didn't you tell me? Why didn't you tell me?' he brayed at her. She stopped fighting and sagged to the floor.

'Jon, I'm sorry. I was going to, honestly. I've been so busy. You *know* what it's like. Please don't hurt me.'

His anger immediately subsided. He dropped her arms and slumped on the bed in despair. 'I thought we really had something going between us…'

'We did, Jon. Raw sex – and that's all. I thought you knew that.' She glared at him, standing, rubbing her wrists.

'But I love you,' he whined and her mood changed abruptly to anger.

'For Christ's sake, Jon. We're Doh-Nai-Zen members. We don't go in for all that cheap love and romance crap.'

'You've used me, haven't you?' he snarled at her. 'I've just been a diversion for you while you've been getting ready to rule the fucking world.'

She laughed. 'Of course I was using you – weren't you using me? That's what people are for, for fuck's sake. Grow up, Jon – get real. I've been in Doh-Nai-Zen since I was fourteen, I'm a superstar with a fantastic future ahead of me – I wouldn't let a good screw get in the way of that. They're ten a penny if you know where to look. There are, strangely, more interesting and exciting things in life than sex.'

There was a pause until he looked up and asked limply, 'Do you even like this Langton guy?'

'Yeah, he's okay.' She shrugged. 'He's solid, a real go-getter.'

'Is he better in bed than me?'

'Different.'

'How different?' he asked, looking like a little boy.

'God, Jon! I don't know. Just different,' she responded, irritated again. She was tired of this and seized the opportunity to kick him now he was down, her animal self rearing up, fight replacing earlier flight. 'You know, the only thing I'm going to miss while I'm in the public eye are my girl-friends. Men are okay, but women are *so* much better.' She had Jon's measure now and used her words like talons. She sensed the crisis had passed, that he was manageable again, predictable. Jon sensed it, too.

'So, we'll never see each other again after this?' he added abjectly.

'Not in the same way.' Lucia retrieved her mobile from the corner of the room. As she stooped, revealing her perfect form, a wave of yearning engulfed him and he suddenly knew there was nothing more he could do or say. With a trace of compassion, something not felt for years, he suddenly understood how his wife and his former PA had felt – betrayed, their emotional world caved in, the raw wound open wide and weeping.

'We'll probably bump into one another occasionally,' Lucia added. 'There are big plans for you, too, I hear. You're heading to be one of top brass, now. Although, the way you're behaving, that surprises me, to be honest.'

Her words fast rewound him back to reality. As if waking from a dream, he became aware of being free of his addiction, as though it had all been illusion. There followed a cold understanding – in order to survive, he must take control of himself again.

'No, I'm fine. Now I know the truth I can handle it. Just a blip. Won't happen again.'

'Glad to hear it. Now, come on Jon. Go, please. I have to get changed for kiyomeru. They'll all be waiting.'

He left her room with a cheery wave and smile, but underneath he was suddenly a frightened man. He could feel his own lurking doubts and fears, enmeshed with hatred and revulsion for them all.

– Christ, if they find out what I really think and feel – and know... He considered if he should leave this minute.

– And go where...?

It would be too obvious, he calculated. He needed time to think before he acted.

– *Let's just get this over with first…*

All weekend he'd been dreading the prospect of doing kiyomeru with Marco and Chi-Chi, notwithstanding this latest bombshell.

– *Now it's going to be much worse than I thought. Talk about going into the lion's den…* He wondered if he'd have the inner strength to conceal his altered attitudes.

– *You're about to find out, mate…* he told himself, dabbing his raked and oozing cheek with a handkerchief.

Kiyomeru began in the darkened room. Jon felt the accustomed energy all around him, stronger than usual due to Chi-Chi's presence, but it failed to connect with his estranged and moribund animal. He acted out performing kiyomeru, hoping none of them would notice. Within minutes, he felt subtle probing and checked that his inner doors were secured and bolted.

When the full onslaught came, its power made him gasp. Tentacles of animal energy ripped into him. He tried to stand firm but was brushed aside – an ageing matador too slow for a young bull. He sweated as the tentacles battled with his mental striving to keep how he felt, what he knew, what he planned locked away. The doors were wrenched open, one by one; the spaces behind punctiliously explored. Jon experienced the Energy's grief then venomous rage upon encountering its mortally wounded offspring: sensed it vowing revenge as it withdrew.

– *That's it. Now they know everything…*

With no warning, he snapped into a trance. He was standing in a clinically white, empty room. Marco, Sonia, Lucia and Mikho advanced on him. Catching him unawares, they pinioned his arms and legs and carried him, bucking and writhing, towards Chi-Chi. His head was roughly pressed to Chi-Chi's bared breast, his mouth forced onto the nipple. A milky energy spurted forth.

'Feed, feed!' Chi-Chi insisted, pressing Jon's jaws apart with one hand, pulling his head down with the other. 'Feed your dying animal!'

Jon gagged and choked as he fought, wrenching his head from side to side, refusing to swallow. Chi-Chi eventually gave up the struggle and flung Jon aside. He crashed into the wall and passed out.

He was standing in a huge, domed hall among thousands of blood-red-suited members grouped in serried ranks, facing an ornate podium. The Doh-Nai-Zen symbol was emblazoned all around on flags and banners, the scene reminiscent of a Nazi Party convocation. Chi-Chi entered to an audible gasp. He was twenty, thirty feet tall. He had the body of a man, walking on two legs, but with the head of a Doberman. His teeth were bared in a snarl, canines glinting, pink tongue lolling, drooling saliva.

'Pups, dogs, bitches,' he howled. 'I am your Dogfather. Your progenitor. I have spawned you. I have given you contact with the Energy – the pure power that has grown your inner animal, which in turn, has brought you a life of plenitude; a life of riches and power beyond the paucity of your dreams. Now the Energy will use you. It is time to show your gratitude.'

The crowd cheered ecstatically. Chi-Chi raised his arms and the hubbub ceased.

'The runts of my litters, the weaklings, the flawed and the deformed will be culled. Only the committed, the iron willed, the faithful and the strong will accompany me on the journey to where I lead. To power! To liberty! Freedom to live the life of the animal spirit both inwardly and outwardly. Masters of the world and our own destiny.'

The audience began to chant ecstatically, punching the air in unison with each syllable.

'Fa-ther! Fa-ther! Fa-ther!'

Those near Jon turned and advanced on him, chanting and slavering. A paroxysm of fear corkscrewed his guts. He turned to run, but was surrounded...

The image faded and Jon pulled from the trance. He was back in the kiyomeru room, everyone sitting relaxing after the exercise. He felt wretched, in a cold sweat. He realised he was panting shallowly, at the same time experiencing both fear and relief. The illusions had beeen so real, so tangible and yet...

They returned to the lounge to watch television or read. On the surface, everything seemed normal. He sensed they were all playing a game, waiting, watching for the next move.

'Nasty graze on your cheek, Jon,' Marco mentioned.

'Yeah. Caught it on an overhanging rose bush in the garden.'

'Really? Have to get the gardener to see to that in the morning.'

When Jon was in bed, he lay in the dark, dreading the door would open, that they would burst in... and what? But no one came and, as the hours passed, he began to calm down, relieved. Unable to sleep, thoughts Dervish danced in his head, freed from their recent constraints.

– What am I going to do? They know everything now – what I'm thinking,

how I'm feeling, what I know. I can either risk begging to bow out gracefully, saying I'll be a good boy and keep my mouth shut, or make a run for it and go into hiding. But if I throw myself on their mercy and they don't buy it, I'm dog food. At least I'll live if I just disappear – assuming they can't find me. So, no choice. I'll take the money and run – fast and a long way away. Tomorrow if I have any sense. Where to go? South America? Australia…?

Unobserved, his mind slipped into the nattering, synaptic screenplay that is the precursor of sleep.

'What did you discover, Father?' Marco asked Chi-Chi as they sat conspiratorially in Marco's study in the early hours.

'A great deal, Marco. A great deal. He is certainly no longer one of us, no longer sympathetic. I felt his antagonism, particularly towards you, and his debilitating difficulties regarding your daughter. He obviously knows more about DNZ than he should. I sensed he has somehow been in contact with Edward, that there was collusion between them before the accident.'

'Not good,' Marco replied. 'What should we do, Father?'

'Obviously, the experiment has failed and must be terminated as soon as possible.'

'That's a pity,' Marco said, more to himself. 'Despite everything, I have a kind of affection for him.' He pulled himself together. 'So, do I have your permission to…?'

'As a matter of urgency. He knows we are on to him and is running scared and I sense he may be planning to go into hiding. Out of the fold, there's no knowing what he might do. And worse, there's a real risk of his being won over to the other side. That would be intolerable with the insider knowledge he now has – and *very* dangerous.'

DISPOSABLE

Jon awoke feeling nervously clear one minute, depressingly confused the next. He talked himself into keeping calm and managed to take a leisurely breakfast, small talking and trying to sound enthusiastic about the project. Inwardly, he felt as if he were in the jaws of a trap, sensing a single *faux pas* could set off the hair-trigger. Appearing unhurried, he took his leave on the pretext of a pressing workload and drove away, back to London. En route he considered a modified plan of action.

– Just carry on as though nothing has happened. Go into the office as usual. Keep up appearances. I'll call my travel agent and ostensibly book a short break somewhere – the States, maybe – then, after a few days, slip away casually under my own steam – go South, perhaps – Mexico, Panama…

Arriving at his apartment, he showered and changed clothes ready for work. He returned a few calls and consulted with his manservant over various domestic items including dinner that night, then threw in casually, 'Pack a travelling case for me, would you, Henry. I have to go to the States for a few days, leaving this evening.'

'Certainly, sir.'

Projecting normality, he wandered down to the underground car park. Although he only lived a stone's throw from the office, he preferred to drive. It still gave him a rush of pleasure swishing in his jet black Mercedes from one personal parking space to another.

– I'm gonna miss all this… he told himself ruefully, already experiencing pangs of regret.

– Am I doing the right thing, or being over-hasty? Should I discuss things with Marco first…?

– No! They know everything. I'm in danger. Stick to the plan; remember Edward; get away…

Fast drawing like a gunslinger, he unlocked the car from twenty paces with the ultrasonic key. The car reacted with a satisfying clunk and a flashing of lights. At the same moment, his mobile trilled.

'Jon Lucke.'

'Jon? It's Marco. Listen – a very unpleasant situation has arisen. Threats have been made against the lives of all Global directors – an offshoot of the Anti-Globalisation mob, we believe. God knows how the Global Foods story got out. Anyway, I'm gathering the team outside of London this morning to discuss and plan our personal security. Down by your car there should be two men waiting. They'll act as bodyguards and will escort you to the meeting – they have the address. They are totally trustworthy, Jon, and, please, follow their instructions to the letter. Do not, under any circumstances, attempt to contact me or any of the others, just in case. Total security blanket until we're all gathered and this unfortunate mess is sorted. It's all very irritating, I know. The price we have to pay, eh? I'll see you there. Safe journey.'

As Jon reached his car, two large men in dark suits materialised from behind a concrete pillar.

'Mr Lucke? Mr. Brancusi sent us – sir. We're your body guards. Mr.

Brancusi asked me to give you this letter. Sir.' The minuscule pause before the word 'sir' betrayed a total indifference hiding contempt.

Jon opened the envelope. Marco's personal letterhead and handwriting – an address near Cambridge where they should meet. He settled in the driver's seat, swinging his seatbelt across as the two clambered in, one in the rear and one beside him and he was forced to suppress both the affronted vexation at having his personal territory invaded and the irritation of having his day, and his plans, disturbed. He couldn't yet address the just discernible fear growing on the periphery of awareness.

– *Are they telling the truth, or are they kidnappers...?*

– *Or assassins...?*

'I'm Mike and this is Terry, sir. We're qualified bodyguards, both ex-Army and we're armed, fully trained and licensed. Sir.'

'Nice to meet you, Mike, Terry,' Jon replied, nodding over his shoulder to the man in the rear seat, noticing the bulge under his left lapel. 'Okay. We'd better get moving. Seat belts, please, gentlemen.'

He headed the Mercedes North through the glutinous London traffic to pick up the M25, then stop-started clockwise to the M11. He kept up a jolly bantering en route, attempting to put the men at ease, trying to elicit more information, but they seemed to know as little as he did. When they were on the motorway his carphone trilled. 'Can I answer that?' he asked, playing along with the game.

'I expect so, sir. Better make it brief, though,' Mike replied, casting a look over his shoulder at Terry.

He picked the handset from its cradle. 'Jon Lucke.'

To his surprise, he heard Lucia's voice. She sounded frightened. 'Jon – listen. You've got to get out of the country; go into hiding. Something bad's going to happen to you.'

'What? When?'

'Very soon. You're to be removed. That's all I know.'

'How do you know?'

'I overheard... Doesn't matter. Just be careful, and go. Now.'

'This is a surprise, coming from you. Have things changed by any chance?'

'No – nothing's changed. I'm fond of you, that's all. I gotta go.'

'Well, thanks. I'll be in touch.'

'No. Don't, ever...'

The phone went dead, and Jon added, talking into cyberspace, playing the game, 'I'll call by the office when I can. I'm a little tied up at the moment. Take care now. Ciao,' and replaced the handset.

'Sorry about that. Problems at the office.' Mike nodded, saying nothing.

– *Jesus, fucking Christ...!* Jon was screaming inside, struggling to keep the car pointing in a straight line, feeling as if he'd been plunged into an ice-pool.

– *What am I going to do now...?* It all made terrifying sense. Marco couldn't risk another accidental death to another director.

– *Too suspicious. But if I were to disappear, or rather be disappeared, they'd just tell my staff I'd cracked up, burned out; or simply been seconded to Hong Kong or Sydney. Who'd bother to investigate, or care, or even remember me after a few weeks...?*

Jon was fast sliding into flight mode. He commanded himself to keep calm, to make space inwardly to assess, plan, act. These men were almost certainly his killers.

– *If they are, I must try to fool them into thinking this'll be a walkover; get them to drop their guard so I can escape at the first opportunity...*

He sized them up, taking what he hoped were innocuous looks, half turning in his seat as he drove, attempting to engage Terry in bantering conversation.

They were both big and bulky under their black, cheap overcoats and, he guessed, super fit and fast. Probably ex-SAS; crack shots with a special skill like judo or karate. They were emotionless hardmen, used to killing. Knives, guns, the garrote, it was all the same to them. Just get the mission over with as cleanly and quickly as possible – using the right tools for the job. After, it's down the pub for a pint, then home to play with the kids and shag the wife. All so matter of fact. People, except perhaps their nearest and dearest, were just pieces of furniture to them. Removing someone from life was just a trade, no different to being in the furniture removal business.

– *I'm in deep shit here. I've no plan and no time to think...* he evaluated during a lull in the conversation.

– *What to do? Drive at a hundred and fifty and get stopped by the police? Crash the car, jump out while it was moving. Just stop dead in the outside lane? See what happens...?*

He imagined himself doing so. A shot, his body being bundled into the back, Mike driving the car away. A local disturbance seen by only a few people. Even if someone reported it to the police and they tracked them down, he'd still be dead. Anyway, how many of the police top brass were members? A cover up would be unproblematic.

– No. My only hope is to keep alert for an opportunity to escape. And if all else fails, I'm going to go down fighting...

'Fancy a cup of tea? My treat?'

Mike looked quizzically back at Terry, who nodded approval.

'Okay, sir. A quick one. We don't want to be late and get the boss in a flap.'

Jon pulled off into the service area and parked. When they were seated with their drinks and snacks, he stood, at the same time noticing Mike and Terry make minute, instinctive jerks forward in unison.

– Gave yourselves away there, didn't you...? he smirked to himself.

'Need a leak. Back in a minute.' He walked casually towards the washroom, entered and hid to one side. After a minute, certain they hadn't followed, he walked from the cafeteria, then sprinted across the car park. He leapt into the car, fumbling at the ignition with his keys. Mike and Terry casually lowered themselves in and closed the doors.

'Tut, tut. You really shouldn't put yourself at risk like that, sir,' Mike scolded, waving a playful finger. 'That was very naughty.'

'I was just getting a map. Wanted to see if there's a quicker route.'

'Well, take your time, sir. No rush.'

– They must be on an hourly rate... Jon decided ruefully, opening and reaching into the glove compartment for the map, keeping up the pretence, but angry his ruse hadn't worked.

– Round one to them. Right. Next time we stop, I've just got to go for it. Take them by surprise and...

Suddenly, a sharp pain in his thigh. He looked down to see a hypodermic syringe jutting, Mike pressing home the plunger.

'You fucker!' he screamed, pulling his fist back in the confines of the cabin, attempting to strike at Mike. His limbs lost all control and the raised arm flopped by his side as the narcotic rushed.

Body sleep overwhelmed him. He couldn't move, yet was fully conscious. Mike pushed and pulled and shook him, then bent Jon's middle finger back until it nearly snapped. Jon felt no pain, shouted no objection and could do nothing to stop him; he was slumped in his seat, mouth hung open, eyelids drooping, totally immobile, yet fully awake.

'Good old curare. Never fails,' Mike remarked to Terry. He turned back to Jon and punched him on the arm, shouting, 'It's your own fault for playing silly buggers and trying to escape, you fuckin' arsehole,' no longer pretending deference. 'Let's get him in the back, Tel. I'll have to bloody drive now. Why can't these rich pricks do anything right?'

Jon was seat-belted upright in the back, still unable to move his arms and legs, as the car sped along the M11. He was filled with a laissez faire inertia as though stupendously drunk. He remembered years back, wearily trying to lift his sleeping children from the car after a late night journey, their strange, double dead weight being re-experienced in his own limbs.

His unaffected mind maelstromed random thoughts and images: flies trussed by spiders; insects paralysed by wasps – stored with larvae on their backs munching into live food; then images of executions, hangings, shootings; axes swinging, the guillotine blade plummeting. He recalled once wondering why Jews had walked docilely into the gas chambers; why condemned men strolled to the electric chair, the gallows, the lethal injection room; why people facing firing squads just stood there, politely immobilised – all without screaming their protests. A memory of watching a programme about Kosovo on TV swam into consciousness. A Moslem survivor recounting how several hundred of them had sat awaiting their turn as the coach loads in front were taken out and shot by the roadside, under their gaze.

'How in the name of Hell could they just sit there?' he'd demanded of the TV screen, shifting in his seat, agitated. 'Why didn't they try to escape?'

Then he knew why. Because you didn't have the training and were unable to conceive the unfolding of events, a cocktail of hormones, fused with incredulity and hope, induced a lethargy that gripped your entire system.

'They'll stop before they get to me. They'll take pity on me. They'll run out of ammunition. Superman will swoop down from the sky and whisk me away. No! It ain't gonna happen. Impossible. Not to me!' you believed. Right up to the millisecond the bullet took to rip through your brain.

– *So, unless a solution presents itself within the next five minutes,* he reasoned, quite unemotionally, – *All I can do is helpfully sit here and be driven to a rendezvous with my very own death...*

They were driving alongside a chain link fence surrounding what appeared to be a disused airfield. The late morning sun flicked fence post shadows across Jon's eyes. The stroboscopic effect and the sun's warmth lulled him into a dreamy doze. He imagined he was cycling, freewheeling downhill at full speed, trees flashing by in the early morning sunshine. He felt untroubled, irresponsible free, gloriously young and healthy...

An entrance loomed into view, Mike slowed, turned in and jerked the car to a stop and Jon started awake. Terry got out to pull the gates open one by one. As they drove through, Jon noticed, through half-opened eyes, that the padlock chain had been cut.

– They've been here before, then, or someone has...

'Where to, Tel?' Mike asked, 'Any ideas?'

'Yeah, head over to that big hangar on the other side of the airfield,' Terry answered, pointing, confirming Jon's thought. Terry hadn't said much on the journey. He was as much the strong, silent type as Mike was the garrulous one. It had begun to emerge that Tel was in charge, probably of senior rank.

'Drive inside, mate,' he instructed.

Jon detected a note of tension in Terry's voice, amazed at how calm he himself felt, expecting to have had shaking legs, pounding heart, adrenaline pumping fear. All he experienced was lethargy. He couldn't really give a toss. He was so tired – and strangely at peace.

– Like that drug they give you before an operation. I was about thirteen, had appendicitis. What was it? Pethedrine or something; felt hilarious being wheeled to the operating theatre. No fear whatsoever...

They drove into a cathedral hangar. Mike stopped the car in the centre and cut the engine. Terry jumped out, opened and stood by the rear passenger door.

'Get out,' he spat at Jon.

'Mush warmer here,' Jon slurred, smiling like a sleepy drunk, the effects of the curare wearing off. 'Stay'n'wait, fu don mine.'

'Out of the car, NOW!' Terry screamed, reaching in, releasing Jon's safety belt. He unceremoniously dragged Jon sideways out of the door by the collar, half down onto the ground. Mike joined in and they heaved him away, each with a hand under an armpit, Jon's toe caps scraping on the ground, his head lolling.

The men hauled him some yards beyond the car and simultaneously let him go. He slumped onto all fours and stared fascinated at the patterns made by the oil-stained ridges making up the concrete floor.

'BACK ON YOUR KNEES – NOW, ARSEHOLE!' shouted Mike.

'HANDS BEHIND YOUR HEAD, YOU FUCKING PRICK!' screamed Terry.

'Why're you shouting,' Jon asked, mildly irritated, yet doing exactly as they commanded, instantly understanding that yelling confused; gave the target no time to think. Mike and Terry were as efficient as a medical team. Kneeling submissively, he knew he had played into their hands.

– *What else could I have done? They're far too experienced, and I've been the most perfect and the most stupid of victims...*

Thoughts sprinted through his mind, but were perceived at dawdling pace. His parents, brothers, Yvonne and his children all paraded across his mental stage. He smiled to himself as he saw their tearful faces, a yearning love brimming in his chest. Then anger rose as spectres of Marco and Sonia, Chi-Chi and Lucia appeared, one after the other, from the wings, to stand pointing and jeering.

– *So, it's all true*, he told himself dreamily.

– *Your whole life does go before your eyes when...*

'I'll do this one,' he heard Terry say, matter-of-factly.

He felt the hard, cold barrel of a gun in contact with the base of his skull. A sudden, cruel realisation; spurting adrenalin; a gush of fear transmuting to terror; an impulse to flee towards the white rectangle of light at the end of the hangar... His mind desperately sought the muscle controls, trying to galvanise his body but he was paralysed. He winced against the impending gouge of the bullet through his skull and brain. He remembered reading that bullets ricocheted around inside the body, slicing through arteries, rupturing vital organs, splintering bone.

– *Get on with it, for Christ sake! Get on with it...!*

– *This isn't happening! This can't happen...!*

His head sagged to his chest and he sobbed out, 'No, *please*. I don't want to die. I don't want to die...'

High velocity metal double-thwacked into flesh as two gunshots synchronously fractured the air, punching his eardrums, echoing around the cavernous hangar. Terry crumpled over him, a dead weight. Out of the corner of his eye, as he was pressed to the ground, he saw Mike leap backwards into the air, arms and legs flailing, flopping heavily to the concrete.

He lay under Terry's weight for thirty seconds, eyes screwed, teeth clenched, breath held, fists tight, waiting for a shot, a blow, someone or something. All he could hear was the distant, plaintive cawing of startled crows.

Nothing happened. His shirt suddenly felt cold, wet and sticky. He heaved and struggled to push off Terry's inert weight, drowning in panic – and experienced a heart stopping moment seeing his own shirt covered in blood. He scrambled to his feet and gingerly explored his torso, relieved to discover he was unharmed, that it wasn't his blood. He walked on shaking legs over to Mike's body which was lying on its side, flopped like a scruffy rag doll, his head lying in a pooling crimson puddle. There was a neat red hole in the centre of his forehead. Walking round the body, he retched as he caught sight of the pulpy, red and pink crater that once had been the back of Mike's head.

When he'd finished heaving, long after there was nothing left in his stomach, he went over to look at Terry. Thickening blood trickled through a hole in his white shirt precisely above the heart. The shirt had completely turned a bright, lacquered red as though freshly spray painted, and Jon experienced another gust of nausea as he caught the warm, butcher's shop smell of recently shed blood. Mike and Terry remained motionless, except for a reflexive twitching in Terry's leg, which soon petered out then stopped after one last spasm. Then they seemed at peace – and very dead.

'Jesus! Jesus! Jesus!' Jon repeated, talking to himself, shaking his head. He was giddy with adrenalin and shock, feeling faint, yet manic and physically ill at the same time. He began to quiver uncontrollably. He wanted to laugh, too; laugh out loud with the over-the-top drama of it all. Then relief overwhelmed him.

'Thank you, thank you, thank you...' he was gibbering over and again to the God he didn't believe in, trembling with emotion, tears of happiness coursing down his face. Then he felt drained and exhausted, his throat painful after the retching.

Pulling himself together, he walked cautiously to the entrance of the hangar and scoured the airfield but could see nobody. Whoever saved him had disappeared without trace.

'Well, thanks anyway – wherever you are now.' He returned and surveyed the scene.

– *But who the hell saved me? How? Why? What the fuck's going on....?* As his mind whirled, his body became suddenly desperate for a cigarette. He remembered that Mike had lit up while they were at the service area. Keeping his eyes away from the gory mess and feeling like a vulture, he searched through Mike's pockets. There was nothing except a mobile phone, the empty hypodermic with a trace of Jon's blood still visible inside the needle cover, a piece of paper with a biroed cellphone number, some loose change and the cigarettes and lighter. He lit up and inhaled deeply and nearly toppled over with dizziness. It had been many years since he last smoked. His body welcomed the nicotine, embracing it like a long lost friend.

'What do I do now, after *this*?' he asked himself, talking aloud, still disoriented by tobacco, trauma and relief.

Feeling his shirt crackle with Terry's dried blood, he realised he first needed a change of clothes. He rummaged in the boot of his car and found a creased golfing shirt and trousers. He put them on and stuffed the blood stained clothes into the spare tyre well.

'More in control now, bit shaky, though. Gotta watch I don't suffer delayed shock and lose rationality,' he warned himself. 'Must stay on top, weigh every action, every move. Can't afford a single mistake. Don't wanna go through this again. Might not be so lucky next time.'

He lit another cigarette, sat on the front passenger seat, legs out of the car, and considered. He calculated that first he must somehow let them think everything had gone to plan, that he was dead. That would give him a head start. Then he must get away and go into hiding as Lucia had suggested.

– *Could she have...?* He shook his head and changed subject.

'Thank God I've money stashed away. I must've had a premonition, or something. I'll get some cash to Yvonne and then find somewhere to hole up for a while. Passport's at the flat, so can't leave the country. Won't bother to go back there for clothes and stuff. I want them to think I'm dead. Dead's a good way to hide.' He rubbed his hands together, galvanising himself. 'I'll sort all that later. First things first.'

Retrieving his mobile from his jacket, he dialled the number written on the scrap of paper, knowing he was taking a risk. Suddenly alert, he cancelled the call.

'No, not on mine, you prat. On Mike's. That's exactly the kind of error I must avoid... Or would they have used mine so there was no trace of their being here...? Shit. What to do? I'm such an amateur at this game.' He made a decision, picked up Mike's mobile and dialled again. It was answered after the third ring.

'Yes?' said a gruff voice he didn't recognise.

'Mission accomplished,' he announced in his best Home Counties accent, holding his breath.

'Understood.' The phone went dead. He waited five minutes and redialled.

'The Vodaphone you are calling is temporarily switched off,' stated a familiar, recorded voice.

Relief. His ploy had worked and he felt pleased with himself, certain he had guessed right, giving the signal the hit men would have given – and that the mobile he'd just called was probably now in the Thames or an incinerator.

'That gives me twenty-four to forty-eight hours head start, not much more, I guess. Assuming I'm right,' he added, talking to himself, using his own voice as a talisman to ward off the threat of losing it, of insanity. He was suddenly glad that he knew what to do by some mysterious, vicarious process.

'Must be because I've watched so many movies. Is this life imitating art, or what?' he enquired of the corpses.

After emptying the dead men's pockets – nothing more but small change and, he noticed, no labels on any of their clothes – 'The professional touch, eh?' – he dragged the bodies into a far corner and covered them with an old tarpaulin.

– *Toting a gun is not a good idea,*' he decided. – *If the police stopped me, they'd ask awkward questions – and then almost certainly place me back into Marco's hands...* Not only that, the guns were big and bulky, and anyway, they frightened him with their explosive power, their cruel, cold potential. He found and lifted a drain cover, dropping both into the black water with a shudder of distaste.

After, he made a small fire of his bloodied clothes, the syringe, Mike's mobile and the biroed number, let it burn out, then crushed and scattered the ashes. As he prepared to leave, he had a sudden thought.

– *Shit. The Merc's got an anti-theft tracking device. I've got to disable it somehow.*

He remembered the salesman had explained how it worked and even showed him where it was, when he was buying the car.

'But where the fuck is it?' he began to panic. He focussed hard, remembered and managed to trace some wires, which he yanked until they disconnected. Trying the ignition, he was again swamped with relief as the engine fired.

After driving hard back down the motorway, he pulled into a service area, ravenously hungry now, needing comfort food. He bought sweet tea, bacon, eggs, beans and fried bread, wolfing it down. After, he lit another of Mike's cigarettes and relaxed back into the plastic chair.

– *It's only two o'clock. Collect the money first, sort out Yvonne and the kids; then go North – lay a false trail – dump the car, find somewhere for the night. Then work out where to spend the rest of my life...*

Driving back into London, he felt exhausted as anxiety and exhilaration, loathing and terror battled for control...

* * *

'It's two a.m., David. Shall I continue?'

'Good Heavens! I'd better go,' Juanita says, standing, stretching, looking for her shoes.

'Yes.. Stop there, Michelle. Low lights, please, then close and re-file.'

'Do you have any corrections or modifications, David?'

'In the morning, thanks.' David turns to Juanita. 'Will you be okay driving back on your own?'

'I think so, David. Can I come and hear the rest tomorrow? I'm really enjoying it. And I really want to know what happens next.'

'Of course, delighted. I've some paper work to do and calls to make during the day. Do you want to come to dinner? Risk my cooking again?'

'That would be lovely. Same time?'

'Why not?'

three

IT IS THE next evening. David and Juanita have finished supper and are settling on the sofa again.

'I am so looking forward to this, David. It's called the dénoument, isn't it?'

'Er, yes, I think so.'

'Did you work in advertising?'

'Yeah. For a while.'

'What did you do?'

'Oh, copywriting mostly.'

'So you're drawing on your experience of that time?'

'I guess. Well, to a degree...'

'Hmm. I seem to remember there was a product like your DNZ, about ten years ago, but it wasn't a success. "Never took off", I believe is the English colloquialism.'

'Uh-huh.'

'And wasn't GM experimentation banned a few years ago?'

'Something like that'

'Yes, I remember a lot of fuss, then it all died down... So, your story is based on real events?'

'Very loosely... It's all source material... found online, in the media.'

'So, you weren't involved?'

'No, I wasn't. Not at all,' David replies, a little testily. 'Right. You comfortable?' David asks, changing subject.

'Very,' Juanita confirms.

'Okay, Michelle, dim the lights and let's have the final part.'

'With pleasure, David.'

And Michelle begins to read again...

HIDING PLACE

The busy M4 mirrored Jon's teeming mind as he motored west, outrage and slippery-gut anxiety as garrulous passengers.

– Evil bastards! Callous indifference to peoples' lives...

– Supposing they're following me...?

– They can't be. How?...

– What if they hurt Yvonne and the kids...?

– Or take them hostage...?

– Use them as bait...?

It occurred to him that kidnapping his family was not an option.

– How would they get a ransom demand to me? They could hardly put an ad in the nationals. No. They can't do a thing unless I give myself away...

The thought offered momentary respite and he remembered he still had a march on them – and someone on his side, somewhere.

– Can't be Lucia. She may have warned me, but surely she couldn't have organised my escape? Who then? And why...?

He chipped at the problem from all angles, realising that with so little information he was wasting time and energy.

– Just keep on track. Do only what's necessary...

After having successfully collected his money the day before, he'd driven to Yvonne's house knowing she would be at work, the girls at college, his son at school. He left a cryptic note hinting that he was in trouble and would have to disappear for a time. He alluded to the danger they might all be in and suggested that she took the children away to safety for a while. Then he scored that sentence out, deciding it would be more sensible if they acted normally; making it appear he had not made contact.

There'll be problems with the alimony payments, too (look in the shed). Please – don't put it in the bank, hide it; destroy this note, say nothing to anyone; anyone asks, I haven't contacted you for months and take REAL CARE. I'm sorry for the melodrama. I'll be in touch to explain everything as soon as I can.

Love to you and the kids. Jon.

He stuffed the note through the letterbox and left a case containing half a million pounds tucked in the garden shed.

After – while motoring north – he reasoned that acting randomly was the only way to avoid detection.

– Musn't leave footprints in the snow...

From art school days he knew – as does anyone attempting to conjure winning lottery ticket numbers – just how difficult it is to manufacture true randomness, but it had to attempted. He pulled off the motorway, found a quiet country lane and parked across the entrance to a field. He waited, nervously poised, checking there was no one following, self-mocking his pernickety paranoia.

– Am I being a bit over the top here…?

– Yes. But it's going to keep me vigilant – and alive…

After twenty tense minutes, he finally relaxed.

– Right, time to find a bolthole… He took a leather bound road atlas from the glove compartment.

– Heads for even, tails for odds… He spun a coin. The Queen's raffishly crowned, disembodied head announced evens.

– Now, heads for pages one to seventy two, tails for the rest…

Continuing to split the remaining groups, he finally arrived at page twenty-eight. Without looking, he brought his finger down. It rested on Bristol.

– That'll do. Big enough to go anonymous in. And I know it a little, but have no real connections. Now that's pretty random. Marcel Duchamp eat yer heart out…

– Now I need a new name… He flicked through the index, jabbing his finger down again.

– Bradford. I'll be John Bradford from now on, but Jon with an aitch. Better keep my first name – I'm used to responding to that…

Later, he decided, he would buy a false passport and driving license. Get himself abroad – New Zealand, maybe. Once there, he'd organise a bank account, apply for credit and charge cards – all the accoutrements of a financial life-support system.

– Could even have cosmetic surgery. If I'm brave enough…

Making sure there was no one around, he left the car and crossed the lane into a copse. He made a small fire and burnt his cards, license, wallet, brief case – everything that might identify him.

– Better destroy my mobile, as well. Calls are too easy to trace if you know what you're doing. Get an anonymous, pay-as-you-go later…

– I'm going to keep Edward's DNZ notes. They're going to be a valuable resource and, perhaps, a bargaining tool someday…

As he watched the grey-black billows curl and rise, simulating smoke signals, it occurred to him how difficult it would be to survive off the land nowadays, like a Native American of the past.

– Too many people in the West. All natural resources under the control of the government, or landowners. No common land for grazing, growing, coppicing.

You have to get your daily bread from the food overlords. And so the ordinary bloke's somehow got himself in thrall, no better off than a Russian serf. Christ. I'm sounding like a Marxist...!

It then occurred to him that to become dis-enthralled, to become anonymous, to drop out of society, was virtually impossible. Today, who you are, where you live and go, what you do and buy are all recorded and reduced to digital data – a shunted stream of binary code – offs and ons, flow and no-flow – representing the whole pattern of your life. And, once digitised, your world becomes a purchasable resource to anyone in the market, enslaving you deeper.

– Unless you keep changing identity... He kicked over the embers satisfying himself nothing of his past remained.

– That's it. Jon Lucke doesn't exist any more and I'm on the road to freedom at last...

Returning to the car he re-consulted the road atlas. If he continued north, abandoned the car in a big city multi-storey car park, it might lead them to think he'd gone in that general direction. He had an idea. He rummaged in the glove compartment and found a fold-up map of England. He marked it with a pen, tracing a route to a small, working airfield that he knew of, near Newcastle. One with twin engine planes and pilots for hire – a jumping off point for unorthodox trips to Europe.

– Leave that in the car. A bit crude and they'll know it. But it'll have to be checked out. Slow 'em down...

After dumping the car, he'd get a train back to London, tube out to Heathrow avoiding CCTV cameras, find a large, anonymous hotel for the night – pay cash.

– I need to buy new clothes, toiletries and another case. Not all from the same shop, though. That's what gave the Lockerbie bomber away...

– Shit, I'm going to miss this motor. Not mine anyway. Leased by the company; so they can have it back – but without me...

After, he'd buy a local paper, pick up a nondescript car for cash – one already taxed – then head for Bristol.

– Reckon I'd have made a good spy in another life...

He was beginning to enjoy the game, realising he had a knack for subterfuge and duplicity, that it was not unlike playing chess, each move affecting and dictating the next and subsequent moves.

– Got enough dosh to last me a long, long time, thank God, and I'm certain none of the notes can be traced...

Mentally crossing his fingers, praying he'd thought of everything, he started the engine.

He breathed a sigh of relief as he spotted the 'M32 one-mile' sign as it grew larger then flicked past. Forty minutes later he was parking a five-year old Ford in the underground car park of a Bristolian, one-star hotel.

The room was bland, but clean and well appointed. Not quite the luxury he was used to, but satisfyingly anonymous. He stashed the suitcases, one containing his new clothes, the others money, in the closet, deciding he'd transfer most of it – and the DNZ documents – to different locations the next day.

– *Left luggage at the rail station and airport should do – just in case they trace me and I have to make another fast exit. Now, with a place to hide, I've got time to think and plan...*

It was late afternoon when the sun emerged, at the same time preparing to set. Feeling cheered, he decided he'd risk eating out and left the hotel furtively, checking he wasn't being followed, and headed into the town centre. While walking, it occurred to him that, as everything around him appeared so normal, perhaps he was having some kind of psychotic interlude.

– *Or early Alzheimer's...?* He vividly recalled the previous day's events and snatched himself back to certainty.

– *As long as I remember what happened and hold on to the fact my life is under threat, I'll stop doubting my sanity and reality. Then I won't become complacent. That's the only way to keep us all safe. And it's essential I don't draw attention to myself in any way. Got to be scrupulously careful and totally anonymous...*

The city offered plenty of scope for anonymity. As shops and offices closed for the day, a mass of humanity thronged the pavements, last minute shopping, catching commuter buses and trains for home, dropping into bars, calling friends, making plans for the evening's entertainment – informing, arguing, wheedling. A bustling, rushing herd, each individual life wrapped in its own drama, totally unaware of Jon playing out his.

Walking and observing, he re-acquainted himself with the city. He'd be there some time, he presumed, while he worked out the next move.

– *Next move? That's a joke. I haven't got the faintest idea what to do, don't know what they're up to, or even what the bloody game is. Not going to panic, though and end up making an unforced error. That's exactly what they'll be hoping for – once they discover I'm alive and kicking…*

Some nights later, stepping from a restaurant into the cooling night air, he saw the number of people on the street had noticeably thinned. Immediately feeling exposed, Jon decided to return directly to the hotel. Striding for sanctuary, he rounded a corner to be confronted with a bizarre *tableau vivant*.

In an otherwise empty, brightly lit square, a woman was seated on the ground hanging on to a handbag with both hands. She was seesawing backwards and forwards in unison with a young man, who had hold of the shoulder straps and was apparently attempting to wrench the bag from her grasp. Another youth stood behind her, methodically kicking her rear. Jon stared for a full three seconds before realising he was witnessing a mugging. Instinctively, he sprinted towards the scene flat out, forgetting to consider any consequences of involvement.

As he closed, he heard the mugger pulling at the bag shouting, 'Let go, you fuckin' cow!'

The man became aware of Jon's imminent arrival and only had time to brace himself for the unavoidable collision, half turning, stepping back, thrusting out a warding hand.

Using his old foot-balling skills, Jon body swerved and kicked at the hand still gripping the bag. A yelp as Jon's foot connected hard and the mugger flipped forward, letting go, clutching his wrist below dislocated fingers. Jon connected with a right hook. The mugger grunted and spun to the ground.

Jon felt an explosive crack behind his right ear and lights flashed in his head. The other youth had caught him with an off-target haymaker. Reflexively raising his right arm, blocking the next blow, Jon span on the ball of his right foot, swinging his left leg up hard. The youth grunted and doubled over clutching his crotch, slowly sinking to his knees as the nauseous ache expanded gutwards. The other scrambled to his feet and ran away bent low, still holding his wrist, his hand bunched into an agonised claw.

Certain the man kneeling was no longer a threat, Jon turned back to the woman, still sitting, completely dazed, hugging her handbag tight to her chest. He offered her a hand and pulled her to her feet.

'C'mon. Let's get out of here before their mates turn up. Can you walk?'

'Yes. Yes, I think so. Thank you,' she replied, brushing herself down, rearranging her skirt. 'I'm fine now. My bum hurts a bit, but I'll be all right.' The woman leaned on Jon's arm and hobbled painfully as they walked across the empty square to the sound of strangled curses hurled after them.

'Can I get you a taxi, or escort you home?' he asked, glancing sideways down at her. Jon found her attractive, but not in a media, hackneyed kind of way. She was in her mid-to-late forties, he guessed. Short and stocky, but well-proportioned – curvy: and conservatively dressed – dark business suit, a single gold chain around her neck. Her hair was straight, mid-brown, cut short. It smelled fragrantly clean. He noticed she didn't wear a wedding ring.

'No thanks, I'll be fine,' she answered, cutting through his mental appraisal, 'but I would love a cup of tea. Would you let me buy you one? To thank you for rescuing me from a fate worse than death?'

'Hardly. It wasn't that bad.'

'Losing my handbag wasn't that bad? I can tell you don't know much about women, young man,' she laughed, mock indignantly. 'Now come on, what about that tea?'

– Why not? I have nothing better to do. And I'm drawn to this woman. I've no idea why – it's not sexual, either. God, she reminds me of someone. Who…?

'Yeah, sure. Where?'

'I know a café just round the corner.'

They found a table and ordered tea.

'I really must thank you for what you did. It was very brave. I'm so grateful.' Jon shrugged, but felt pleased. She extended a hand and continued, 'My name's Emma. Emma Nagel.'

'John,' he told her, taking the proffered hand shaking it across the table. 'With an aitch.' Her hand felt soft, surprisingly warm.

'Well – John,' she said, sensitive to the fact he hadn't given his surname. 'And what do you do? Apart from rescuing damsels in distress?'

'Business mainly. Currently between projects. How about you?'

'I'm a psychotherapist. I have a consultancy not far from where you found me. I was on my way home when those two came up and demanded money. When I refused, they tried to grab my handbag. Something in me felt so outraged I just couldn't let go, even when they were kicking me. Stupid really; resisting is the sure fire way to get hurt. I should know better – I've counselled enough crime victims – and criminals – in my time.' He smiled, appreciating her knowing toughness.

Their tea arrived and they sat sipping in silence. Jon was still trying to pinpoint who she reminded him of, the answer becoming more elusive the harder he tried.

'Jon, forgive me for intruding, but you seem very preoccupied. Almost – unhappy?'

'Yeah, well... Going through a tough patch right now. Bit of a mid-life crisis I guess you'd call it. It'll pass.'

'Mmm. Mid-life crises can be difficult. If I can be of help...' She fished in her bag, produced a card and handed it across. Jon cast a designer's eye over it. Boring, like a million cards he'd seen before. *Ms Emma Nagel* it stated, with a string of letters after the name. *Psychotherapist.* No address, only a cellphone number.

'That's my mobile. Call me, any time, but you'll have to leave a message if I'm with a client.'

'Yeah, thanks.' He pushed the card into his top pocket.

'I've suddenly realised this must appear as if I'm touting for business.'

He half smiled and gestured it wasn't a problem.

'Well, a girl's gotta eat, you know,' she laughed. 'Seriously though, when I sense a need, I can't turn away. And perhaps it's the only way I know of paying back a debt of gratitude.'

She looked at her watch. 'Good Heavens. I really must fly. I have an evening class to lecture to. The poor dears will be floundering like beached whales if I don't turn up.'

'Are you sure you're okay?' he asked, concerned.

'Nothing a hot bath and some Arnica cream won't remedy,' she assured him, standing. 'And I have plenty of colleagues who can help me with any post-trauma symptoms.' She laughed again. 'Well, goodbye, Jon, it has been lovely meeting you and thanks again for your bravery. Please come and see me if that mid-life crisis gets too hot to handle.'

They shook hands. She picked up the bill, saying she'd pay it on the way out. Jon remained seated, still pondering.

– Got it! Auntie Jenny! When I was really young... He was jubilant at having hit the target.

– God, she was the perfect aunt. Always took an interest, never forgot my birthday, I really loved her...

When he looked up from the warm-sweet recollection, Emma had gone. He noticed that she had only drunk half her tea. He finished his and exhaled a drawn out sigh, wondering how he was going to pass the rest of the evening...

'You bring bad news.'

'Yes, Father. I'm afraid I do.'

Marco was approaching the sun-lounger on which Chi-Chi lay resting. He walked round to face Chi-Chi and bowed.

'Lucke has completely disappeared. Somehow, he got the better of our hirelings, who we found dead, shot by a high power rifle. He must have been helped – we don't know how. He has been more astute than we thought possible and for the moment his trail has run cold. No activity on any credit cards or his mobile. No contact with anyone and no sightings. He apparently cleaned out his bank accounts a week or so ago.'

'I warned you, Marco. You should have acted earlier. Continue.'

'Yes, Father. You're right – as ever. But we have all his old and current haunts under observation – clubs and homes. And we have twenty-four hour surveillance and telephone taps on his ex-wife, family and friends. We're also checking hotel registers, air and sea ports – although we have his passport. Just in case, all known forgers and false document suppliers have been discretely alerted and a large reward offered. We're doing absolutely everything we can – I'm sure it's only a matter of time before…'

'It is imperative that he is found,' Chi-Chi snapped, cutting Marco short. 'On the loose, he is more dangerous than you realise. Especially now he knows we want him dead. And, thanks to Edward passing on that document, he knows too much. You must double your efforts, Marco.'

'We could use his family against him, Father. I'm sure it's a weakness we can exploit.'

'No. Nothing blatantly illegal yet. Just concentrate all resources on surveillance and information gathering. Keep everything under wraps. He is bound to give himself away eventually. Just make sure you find him, Marco – and soon. Now leave me.' Chi-Chi flicked his hand and Marco backed away bowing.

As he walked back to the house, Marco clenched his teeth, anger and hatred battling for expression. Jon had made him appear inept in Chi-Chi's eyes.

'When I find you, Lucke, I'm going to personally rip you from limb to limb.'

A fortnight had passed. Jon had made no calls, written no letters, contacted no one. He had done little but watch TV, eat, walk, think and worry and the isolation was beginning to grind into him. He suffered seizures of boredom, leading to ever worsening anxiety attacks over the lurking threat of death and what might be happening to his children.

– *Can't phone. They're bound to have taps on… Shit! If only I knew my kids' e-mail addresses. I could buy a laptop, or use an internet café…*

Desperation trawled his brain, searching for a way to contact them without giving himself away.

– *Try their colleges…?*

– *Their friends…?*

– *No, whatever I do, once I pop my head over the parapet, in the flesh or electronically, they'll trace me. Got to hold on…*

He also missed sex. At night, aggravated by watching soft porn on TV, lust nagged and pulled at him like a spoilt toddler demanding the toys seen in commercials. Masturbation, in turn, merely keened guilt, so he denied himself the release. Although his thoughts bounced between love and hatred for Lucia, all the time he yearned for her and worried about her.

– *Is she all right…?*

– *Did they find out she warned me…?*

– *God, if only she were here now…*

Late one afternoon, as the depression deepened, an emotional photo album opened in his mind. He tried to force it shut, pushing it down into a dark, mental drawer, but it continually sprang back opened. Then, lying on the bed, he squirmed, forced to re-live the incidents he wanted to forget. Leaving his family without explanations or goodbyes, for the first time wondering how hurt they'd been; then the times he had broken promises to his children; the day he struck his wife, rage raping his insides, his daughters screaming in the background. There was no escape from the look of shock and betrayal in his wife's eyes.

– *Oh, God. I must've hurt them all so much. I was a fuck awful husband and an even worse father. And then I went and got myself involved with a bunch of narcissistic, Fascist wankers…*

Shame and self-loathing hung on him like a sickness. He begged for mercy, but his inner judge deemed he had not yet suffered enough and sentenced him to indefinite incarceration – relentless self-reproach for a cellmate. He came to the conclusion that contrition with no foreseeable possibility of forgiveness, or of making reparation, was the Purgatory described in the Bible.

After a while, he began to feel frightened. He questioned how much longer he could stand being cooped up with himself like this before the light went out; before all hope died and he was engulfed by despair. He felt so lost and alone that he began to believe he had made a stupid mistake, that he should give himself up, ask Chi-Chi for forgiveness, beg for his old life back. He tossed and turned on his bed, wracked with anguish.

Then, a momentary pardon; a sudden acquittal bringing a flood of relief as he intuited correctly that he wasn't going crazy; he was suffering Doh-Nai-Zen withdrawal symptoms. The parasitic animal within, now cut from its source, was clawing into his feelings, using them against him, as it panicked, slowly dying with dry-mouthed fear. He clutched at the thought like a drowning man.

– *Yes! That's it! The bloody thing's sabotaging me. Must get on top of it; keep my nerve until it's dead.*

– *Need something to do; have to find something to stop myself from cracking up…*

– *From being cracked up…*

Turning restlessly on his side, he caught sight of Emma Nagel's card propped on the bedside table. He picked it up, bending it between his thumb and middle finger, pondering.

On an impulse he reached for his new, pay-as-you-go mobile, pressed out her number and listened to the ringing tone's plaintive call.

'Emma Nagel,' answered a familiar voice.

'Uh, yeah. It's John here.' There was a pause. 'The guy who saved you from the muggers?'

'Oh, John – my knight in shining armour. How are you?'

'Not too good, actually. I was wondering if I could take you up on your offer. I need to talk to somebody. Anybody, really.'

'Well, that's flattering, John,' she laughed in his ear. 'Oddly enough, I've just had a cancellation for tomorrow afternoon. Could you come over at three?'

'Yeah, that'll be fine. What's it going to cost me?'

'The first session's always free, John, to find out if we can work together. There are no guarantees, you know.'

'Yeah, tell me about it.'

'Got a pen handy? I'll give you the address.'

As the next day wore on, he discovered he was filled with a schoolboyish anticipation. Arriving early, he hovered outside the building, then paced up and down, pretending to window shop, continually glancing at his watch. Finally, he climbed the stairs and knocked on her door at precisely three o'clock.

Emma opened it. 'John, good to see you again, do come in.'

She was wearing a white blouse, buttoned to the neck, a gold butterfly brooch pinned to it. Her skirt was straight and dark, part of a pinstriped suit. He liked the way her full figure filled it. Her office was small and tastefully decorated with reproduction landscapes and framed diplomas on the walls. Emma indicated a pair of facing easy chairs where they were to sit.

'No couch, then?' he asked, sinking into one of the chairs.

'No, never liked that idea – doctor and patient, analyst and analysand. Too divisive. I like to feel we're equals; in this together on a mutually supportive journey.'

'You're not a Freudian, then?'

'Certainly not,' she laughed. 'Totally eclectic, me. Jung, Adler, Klein, Rogers, Gestalt, you name it, I do it.' She laughed again, sitting, crossing her legs, Jon's gaze snatched by the curve of revealed thigh. His eyes snapped back to her face.

'So, where do we start?'

'Some routine questions first.' She opened a notepad and donned a pair of wire framed spectacles. He answered her questions regarding his medical history and his past honestly, blurring the truth around the time of joining Doh-Nai-Zen, revealing little after. He didn't give her his full name, real or otherwise, or an address, only his mobile number. Seemingly satisfied, she turned to a fresh page stating, 'Formalities over – let's begin. Do you have any questions for me?'

'No, none.'

'Okay. Can I ask why you've come to see me?'

Jon closed his eyes and thought about this, leaning back into the chair.

– *Yes. Good question. Why, indeed...?* A desire to unburden himself, to pour it all out overwhelmed him, immediately checked by caution. He locked on to what he presumed was an innocuous line.

'Because I'm lonely, I suppose. Need to talk.'

'Lonely. Why?'

'Probably because I've abandoned my old life. Friends, family, career. Everything.'

'Why have you abandoned your old life, John?'

'I guess because it all turned sour.'

'Sour? In what way?'

'I got all the things I thought I wanted out of life – you know, success, money, power, but...' Jon paused, concerned he had already gone too far.

'But...?' Emma looked at him over the top of her glasses.

'Well, none of it brought happiness or contentment after all. Looking back, it seems to have taken away what happiness I had. God! What a cliché.' It occurred to him that Doh-Nai-Zen was like fitness; it was quicker to undo results than it was to build them.

'So, you got everything you thought you wanted, but it didn't make you happy?'

'Well, not quite everything. I didn't get the girl I wanted.'

'Would getting the girl have made you contented?'

'Yeah, I guess... No. There's more to it than that.'

'What more?'

'I don't know. Self respect. Something like that'

'Would you have self-respect with all you had *and* the girl?'

A pause. 'No, I don't think I would.'

'So, you can't respect yourself?'

'I guess not. In fact, I think I rather despise myself.'

'And why do you despise yourself, John?'

'God! How long you got? Millions of reasons.' He paused again, lost somewhere between his head and his feelings.

After a minute's silence, he suddenly spat out, 'Because I'm so fucking gullible. I trust people and they always bloody let me down.'

'Who has let you down, John?'

'Everyone. Simon, Mar... ' he checked himself in time, and continued, 'Lucia, My Dad... Oh, shit. Now you're going to tell me it's all down to my relationship with my father.'

'Is it?'

'I don't know. You tell me, you're the shrink.'

'Sorry. I've only questions, John. You're the one with all the answers.'

Jon grunted, losing himself in thought again, eyes closed. Minutes passed.

'Describe to me an incident from your childhood. Anything under seven years old.'

'Funny you should ask that.' He opened his eyes and stared out of the window, into the distance. 'There's one I never forget. Don't know why. Must've been about five... my Dad said he'd take me fishing with him in the morning. I remember him describing what fun it would be – he made it sound really exciting. That night, I could hardly sleep. I was so hyped up, yearning to be there with him, like mates, fishing together – in bloody heaven, it seemed. Next morning, we set off, but it was cold and raining and I remember feeling so bloody bored. And he kept getting cross with me because I was doing it all wrong and getting in his way. Then I snagged my line on a bush and got it into a mess, you know, all knotted up, and he was really mad at me. Freaked out. And he smacked me, and I remember crying and crying, inconsolably, and in the end he had to take me home. He was furious; said I'd spoiled the whole day and that he'd he never take me fishing again.'

After a pause, Emma asked, 'How did that make you feel?'

'Useless. Stupid. Like it was all my bloody fault.' He turned his head aside to hide wiping a moist eye. 'Bit sad, isn't it?' a sarcastic self added.

Emma smiled gently and nodded. 'Everybody's sad in one way or another. We've all got similar stories to tell from childhood. What I find so intriguing is that these, apparently minor, childhood events actually symbolise the patterns that govern our adult lives.'

'I don't follow.'

'Well, out of all the millions of things that happened to you as a child, why do you remember that particular one above all?'

Jon shrugged. 'I dunno.' He mumbled the words like a petulant child.

Emma looked quizzically at Jon for a moment before continuing, 'It's because your unconscious chooses it as a metaphor for how you live your life now. It's you, the adult, that's doing the remembering, don't forget.'

'Hmm.' Jon was sceptical, but sensed she had a point.

'If you could take a photograph of any part of the memory you've just related, and give it a title, what would it be?'

'It'd be Dad telling me I'd ruined the day. And the title.... how about "Everything taken away"?'

'Could it be that's how you see life now? That everything is eventually taken away?'

Jon closed his eyes, nodding agreement. His chin sank to his chest as he retreated into himself.

– *My God! Everything taken away... It's true. Why does that happen to me all the time...?*

'Did you abandon your old life, as you put it, or was it taken away?'

Jon was startled by the question. Barriers dropped sharply into place. 'I really don't want to talk about the present,' he snapped, then added, 'Sorry.'

'It's not a problem.'

'Anyway, I thought psychotherapy was all stuff from the past.

Childhood traumas and – you know – abuse.'

'Some therapists work that way. I'm more interested in why we maintain "stuff from the past" as you put it; what's its purpose, its goal? If I were drowning, I'd be more concerned with staying afloat than who pushed me in.'

'That's interesting. What's this about goals? Give me an example.'

'How about striving to make certain things are always taken away?'

'Why would that be a goal?'

'As a child, we tend to feel inadequate in a world of apparently super-competent giants, so we desperately search for something that will make us feel equal, adequate, or even superior. Being very creative beings, we're usually successful, even if it's by being "the best worst". And from then on it becomes our mistaken goal, despite most often being a distorted way of seeing life.'

'Don't get it.'

'I would hazard a guess that as the eldest child you felt you'd been dethroned by the birth of a younger brother. It may have given you the sense of things being taken away.'

'How would that make me feel equal or superior, though? Doesn't make sense.'

'Some eldests may become achievers, others rebellious or difficult, either way getting all the attention – and their throne back. They may then feel highly superior through their manipulative behaviour – and will take that strategy into adulthood. Some may feel depressed, becoming aware of how the parents worry and fuss over them, again getting the attention and their throne back. Others may just feel deeply depressed, but feel superior because no one could understand how they suffer, how strong, how special, how superior they are to take all this pressure and misery, and so on – the best worst again.'

'That last one – it's me, isn't it?'

'What do you think?'

'I don't know.' Jon paused, thinking, then asked,

'But why keep such a strategy in place when you grow up? What's the benefit?'

'Unfortunately, we do tend to take such behaviours into adult life, still with the goal of feeling adequate, inferior, or superior. They might work when you're a kid, but they're not so useful in adulthood, because then the behaviour becomes neurotic. We always find people we can manipulate, people who allow it for their own reasons – so, if the strategy's working according to our view of the world, we keep it in place. When it stops working is the time we usually visit a psychotherapist.'

Again, Jon sank back into himself contemplating her words, knowing somehow she was right. Another part of himself was looking for flaws, for a way out.

Several minutes passed, until Jon said, almost to himself, 'I don't remember anything about my brother being born, but there were stories of me biting him and stuff...'

Another long pause.

'How are you feeling right now, John?'

He opened his eyes and looked up at her. 'Kind of split open. Confused. Sad. And yet happy somewhere, strangely...'

They sat, Jon staring across the room, Emma observing, head cocked. Yet more minutes passed. Emma glanced at a clock on her desk.

'Well, time's up,' she announced softly, adding, 'If any more memories crop up, or if you have any dreams, try to remember them for our next session – assuming you'd like to come again...?'

'Yes, I would. Very much.'

'Ms. Stapleton?'

'Yes. What can I do for you?' Yvonne asked the young, besuited stranger standing on her doorstep.

'I represent the Personnel Department at GBM, your ex-husband's company, and I was wondering if I could have a word...?' He produced an identity card.

Yvonne ushered him into the sitting room and offered a chair. He ignored it and wandered around the room.

'What a lovely house. Are these your children?' he asked unctuously, picking up and examining a framed family photograph. 'Delightful. I con-gratulate you on successfully raising them in such a dangerous world.'

'So, what's this all about?' She frowned, remembering the warning in Jon's note.

'May I ask, when you last saw, or heard from your ex-husband, Ms. Stapleton?'

'God, I don't know. At least three, four months ago,' she lied. 'Why?'

'I see. And do you have any idea where he might be?'

'Abroad? At his club? Shacked up with some woman? You tell me.'

'I wish we could. We're sorry to have to inform you that your husband has completely disappeared. Cleared out and closed his bank accounts, abandoned his position, the company, everything; simply walked away without a word to anybody. I don't suppose you have any idea why he did this, or where he could have gone?'

'None whatsoever. Like I say, I haven't seen or heard from him for months.'

'Well, if you do hear from him, perhaps you could give me a call on this number?' He handed her a business card. 'It's very important. His disappearance has seriously jeopardised certain sensitive projects and deeply compromised Global's integrity. The financial implications are gi-nor-mous. Legally, of course, he is in breach of contract and, unless he returns soon, will find himself in serious trouble with the law. And, of course, I needn't remind you that if you are withholding information you could be charged as an accessory. What would happen to your children if both their parents were serving prison sentences, Ms. Stapleton?'

'Is that some kind of threat?' Yvonne sneered, protective instincts firing her courage. His wandering round the room, touching and examining, put her in mind of an oil slick sliming a beach.

'Certainly not. I am merely acquainting you with the facts – and giving you good advice. I must also warn you that, as you can well understand, the powers that be are a little miffed at his irresponsibility. Consequently, in accordance with the terms of his contract, they will stop all salary payments and benefits forthwith. Therefore, any alimony or other monetary arrangements you have between you will cease automatically. And of course, since your divorce settlement, you have no claim on the company. We sincerely hope none of this will cause you financial stress, but we have no choice. Our hands are tied.'

'Nice friends he's got. Well if that's all, Mr...?'

EMMA NAGEL, PSYCHOTHERAPIST.
First Session Meeting Notes
DATE: 02. 08. 2002
CLIENT: John (surname withheld)
ADDRESS: Withheld
TELEPHONE: (Mobile) 07762 251105
OCCUPATION: Businessman 'between projects'
MARITAL STATUS: Divorced after 18 year marriage (4 children; three girls, one boy).
FIRST IMPRESSIONS: An attractive, athletically built, well-dressed man in his early forties. Intelligent, well read. Haunted, distracted look.

MEDICAL HISTORY: *Apart from the usual childhood ailments and an appendicitis operation aged 13, J has had no serious illness.*

CURRENT HEALTH: *J seems to be in remarkably good physical shape. More concerned with his state of mind (depression?). He briefly alluded to a 'fear of death' episode while at college, but put this down to experimenting with psychedelics (anxiety depression?). This will need further investigation when the time is right (inadequate death coping strategy as child?).*

BIOGRAPHICAL NOTES: *J was born in 1959 in Letchworth, Hertfordshire. His father (died 1993) was a blue collar worker (factory foreman); his mother (still alive) a housewife. Eldest child with two brothers, two and a half and four years younger. Has no contact with them now and very little with his mother. Attended local primary, then Grammar school – very unhappy at the latter, apparently. Average academically, but was outstanding in both art and football. Was asked to leave school after the fifth form; pro-football apprenticeship did not materialise as promised (nota bene); studied art at evening classes, passed A level and did a Foundation course at a local college, 1977 – 78.*

Took a degree course in Graphic Design at the University of Kent, (1978) leaving with a BA Degree (2.1) in '81. Seemed to enjoy his time there, playing in a band mostly (Note: 'kicked out' of band in his words). Worked for various advertising agencies and design groups in London. Met his ex-wife at work, became freelance after marrying. Eventually went into partnership with two other designers. This company now disbanded. Ran various businesses after this, with, I infer, considerable success, but J is reluctant to discuss or give further information about the recent past (Note: This reticence needs further exploration).

PRESENTING PROBLEM: *Lonely. Feels deep-seated guilt at having walked out on a marriage and children. Has abandoned his 'old life' as he put it (Note: paradox of 'abandonment' and 'taken away'). Deeply felt sense of 'lack of self respect'. Very reticent about his current situation (will not give a surname, for example), but garrulous about his past up to leaving his wife and children. Problems with unrequited love and a girl named Lucia hinted at, but he will not elucidate further. Relationship problems with father indicated.*

Adlerian Early Recollection technique threw up a life theme of 'It's all taken away from me' (client's words). This private logic, the abandoning of friends, family and business, or the setting up of rejection/abandonment scenarios, allied to his reluctance to discuss recent events, implies deep-seated inferiority complex. Am intrigued to know more about this man, but must be circumspect and patient. Observe the transference keenly. Don't want him to abandon our ses-

We have negotiated a preliminary month of twice weekly sessions, with assessment and review at the end of this period.

'I was parading through the shopping centre of my old hometown, the place where me and my mates frittered our time when we were broke teenagers. You know – eyeing up the girls, swapping dirty jokes and generally fooling around?'

Emma nodded understanding. 'Go on.'

'Anyway, I walked past a group of teenagers wearing American style sportswear, all festooned in logos like roaming point-of-sale displays. I was peering at them, hoping to unearth old friends. The kids circled me, scooting on skateboards, jeering at me and talking noisily into mobile phones. I felt confused, then I realised, with a pang of real sadness, that I should have been looking among the middle-aged fathers passing by. All these old blokes, thickening around the middle, thinning on top; bored out of their minds, carrying shopping bags for morose, pushchair-wheeling wives. I walked away urgently, gazing into shop after shop. Their windows displayed either package holidays, computers and games, or shelves of alcohol.

'Where are all the greengrocers and hardware stores? The newsagents and cobblers? I demanded of a white-bearded old man sitting begging cross-legged on the pavement.

"Run out of town by High Street chains and profit-gobbling rates," the old man shouted back, getting up, gesticulating aggressively. I backed away in alarm and then rose into the air...'

Jon paused to reflect.

'Is that it?' Emma asked.

'No. There's more... Then I seemed to fly across the mall and was somehow immediately browsing in an antique supermarket, discovering valuable piece after valuable piece, placing each one gingerly in a wire shopping trolley. When it was full, I proceeded to checkout.

"This card has the wrong name and it's over its limit," the woman tending the till said in a bored voice. Unsurprised, I realised the woman was you...'

Jon waited, searching Emma's face for a hint of reaction.

'Carry on,' she responded impassively.

'Well, then I asked you, "What can I get for this," and dumped a pocketful of pennies on the counter.

'Then you told me, "Only what's on the shelf behind you," and I turned and began to gather armfuls of CDs, videos and computer games. As I did, they crumbled to sticky, cobwebbed dust in my hands. Then I woke up so forlorn, and now I can't shake the feeling off. What does it mean, Emma?'

'Nice dream. The best way to understand it is to assume everything in the dream is a part of yourself – all conjured up by you. Then ask, what part of yourself is symbolised by the shops, the antiques, the credit cards, small change and so on.'

He sat, chin on hands, pondering. 'You'll have to give me more to go on than that.'

'Well, how would you define antiques, for example?'

'Erm. Beautiful things things from the past...? Ah! I see what you mean. Antiques could be beautiful things from *my* past...'

'That's it.'

'Yes! And although I collect them – or remember them – they can't belong to me because I don't have any credit. And I suppose the arcade and the shops are my self and going into them is like delving into my unconscious.'

Emma nodded encouragement.

'Not sure about the rest, though,' he prevaricated, immediately associating aspects of his current situation.

'Keep working on it.' Emma suggested, adding, 'Dreams usually supply the emotional energy to carry out something we've previously decided cognitively.'

'What would that be?'

'You must address that question to yourself. How do you feel about the dream, now?'

'Angry with myself. Like I've been stupid – destroyed something very valuable.'

'Or had it taken away?'

'Mmm. Both...'

CLOSE RUN THING

'Give me a progress report, Marco,' Chi-Chi demanded as they undid their seat belts. The Lear jet was levelling at thirty thousand feet over the Italian Alps, the sugar-glazed summits stained bright orange by the late afternoon sun.

'The DNZ project is on target. Formal government approval and licensing imminent. Production is gearing up, ready to roll; advertising space and air time booked. Concepts provisionally approved; design and advertising ready for test marketing – results in a month. When everything's analysed, we'll finalise the promotional material, and we should be ready to launch bang on schedule.'

'Good. And Jon Lucke?'

'Some progress. We are convinced he's still in England. There is early video footage of him at rail stations in Manchester and London. We eventually located his abandoned car. He'd disconnected the tracking device – clever bastard. The car surrendered no clues, however – apart from minute traces of blood in the boot. Unfortunately, it matches that of one of our hired hands, neither of whom has been traced yet. Lucke is certainly full of surprises. We also know he stayed in a hotel near Heathrow for a night. Thereafter, the trail peters out. No car hire firms have any record of him, no car is registered in his name, and we are still checking out used car lots and local paper car ads to see if he bought another, but it's a huge task.'

'And his family?' asked Chi-Chi, taking a drink from the tray proffered by a hovering hostess.

'So far he hasn't called or been near them – our surveillance teams are positive. We contacted his ex-wife, acting the concerned colleagues, then making a few veiled threats, but she knows nothing – or has been forewarned and is still irrationally loyal. We are observing no financial difficulties, despite her no longer receiving alimony, so he may well have got money to her before we moved on that one. Yet her bank account reveals no sudden influx of funds and a covert search of the house uncovered no cache. We do know he withdrew over a million in cash – which probably accounts for the lack of credit card transactions. Unfortunately, there is no record of serial numbers. We also know some two million is in a Swiss bank account and we're working to gain access to set a trap, but the protocol, even with a Doh-Nai-Zen member at the helm, is amazingly impermeable. I'm beginning to think that perhaps he's so scared, he won't ever dare to be a problem. Would it be wise to just forget about him? Assume he's had his teeth pulled and...?'

'No, Marco,' Chi-Chi interrupted, holding up a hand. 'What concerns me is that disappearing like this takes a lot of resources and know-how. He must have been aided. Keep looking. Concentrate on good hotels in the UK, I sense that's where he will go to ground. He is too used to the good life to slum it.'

'Yes, we're doing that. It is extraordinary how many lone men there are living in hotels and lodging houses answering his description – sales reps, people on courses – or on the run. It will take time to check them all, there are literally thousands – and I doubt he's using his own name. We need just one small breakthrough, one tiny error from Mr. Lucke...'

'It will happen, Marco. The Energy cannot locate him because he has stopped practising kiyomeru. However, I am assured the longer he hides from us, the more confused and disoriented his animal, and therefore he, will become. He will crack and reveal his hand eventually. He must. Then you can finish the job, Marco. It is essential – before they can use him, and what he knows, against us.'

Jon added a row of Xs to the bottom of the letter before reading it through once more. Satisfied he had given nothing away, yet communicated what he wanted Yvonne to know, he folded it and inserted it into a matching envelope. The plan was to drive to his Mother's house, ask her to telephone Yvonne, casually inviting her over, then to pass on the letter.

He sat staring at the envelope uncertain again over what he intended to do.

– *If only I had someone to discuss it with...*

How he missed the intimacy of a close, well-worn relationship. The nearest he had was the thrice weekly session with Emma, but she was away that weekend.

– *Daren't use the post and telephoning's definitely out. So, if I'm to enlist my Mum's help, I've got to sneak in and explain it to her, face to face. No alternative...*

Common sense counselled caution.

– *Don't go. Foolish...*

– *But, I haven't seen her for over a year...* guilt countered, supported by an unconscious concern for his mother's wellbeing. Then, because he was bored, recklessness overwhelmed him – a desire to take risks, to challenge Marco, just to see what would happen. He was a child again, prodding a wasps' nest, teasing a sleeping dog.

'Bollocks. I'm going.'

Heading east, he felt free and elated, until motorway tedium gummed his brain. Two hours later, as he entered his old hometown, weaving between parked cars cluttering streets redolent of his past, the old ghosts loomed. Forgotten friends, endless summer evenings, Bonfire Nights, Christmasses and snow... A cloying nostalgia descended like a mournful autumn mist.

– *How I wish I was twenty again – but knowing what I know now...* The wistful thought's blatant impossibility intensified melancholia.

His mother's street slummed it at the heart of the euphemistic New Town – a jerry built council estate seeded with anti-social design elements, now maturely fruiting, evidenced by graffiti, abandoned and wrecked cars, litter strewn all over. He parked some distance away, walked to her house and knocked on the weather-faded, paint-peeling door.

She half opened it croaking, 'Yes?' in an old woman's voice, cigarette in mouth, eyes screwed against the rising smoke and daylight.

'Hello, Mum.' There was a pause, a lack of immediate recognition.

'Jon! Nice to see you, Ducks – after all this time. Come in.' The deftly slipped reproach reminded him that he never could and never would get anything right in her eyes.

His mother looked even older than he remembered. Her hair was permed yellow-grey with lilac highlights. She was as lean and hard as a greyhound, dressed in a dirty, floral housecoat. Her false teeth were ill fitting, her cheeks sunken, her face heavily made-up. He pecked his mother on the proffered cheek, not having hugged, or even embraced her, since he was a child. Her wrinkled skin felt cool, rubbery under his lips. The cloying smell of face powder irritated the lining of his nose.

'Nice to see you, too, Mum. Here, I brought you some flowers.'

'Tut. You shouldn't have. What am I going to *do* with them?' she wanted to know, frowning, almost talking to herself.

'Put them in the sink for now,' he suggested.

'Would you like a cup of tea, dear?' she ritually asked, creaking towards the kitchen, smelling the flowers as she walked.

'Yeah. Love one,' he said, following her inside. The changeless interior greeted him with derision, as if to say, 'Ooh! Look who's back, then...'

'Sit yerself down. Tea won't be a minute,' she called back into the living area, ever designated 'the front room'. An acrid smell of dust hung in the air. He lowered himself wearily onto the old sofa and looked around. Surrounded by the same old tatty furniture, the TV blaring by the fireplace, mismatched wallpapers peeling in the corners of the room, copies of the Sun and the Daily Mirror on the battered pouffé, he was immediately overwhelmed by a familiar lassitude; one born of nostalgia and a prevailing sense of futility. The contrast between his origins and the life he had been living was as marked as between a pebble and a cut diamond. It struck him that he was essentially the worst of both.

– A rough diamond, or a cut and polished pebble? No wonder I'm so fucking screwed...

His eyes wandered to the cheap cabinet. Its shelves were packed with baubles and trinkets, knick-knacks and gewgaws. They were mostly mementoes from coastal resort holidays – ashtrays and plates, a glass lighthouse with striated layers of coloured sand, *A Present from Margate* scrawled in a crude hand on a badly painted, plaster base straining to represent rocks and sea. And more recent souvenirs from Spain – fans and drinking bottles, castanets and tambourines and a plastic Catholic crucifix. Everything was as flounced and fandangled as a fairground booth.

'How are you, Mum?' he called, knowing this would trigger a medically detailed catalogue of her ailments, followed by a litany of gossip about the neighbours. Then, as ever, she'd wind up with the inveterate list of his father's shortcomings and failures, as if she were talking to a social worker or the local vicar, still not sure who he was. She had become as self-centred as a child in her old age.

'Can't complain, dear,' she opened with, then, 'That milkman only left one pint again this morning. I keep telling him, but he don't listen. He's a darkie, so what can you expect...?'

Ignoring her remark, needing to avoid the ritual polemic laced with her dyed-in-the-wool racism, he called teasingly, 'C'mon, Mum. Where's that tea?'

'Hold yer horses, it's coming.' She re-entered carrying a tray. 'There you go, love.' She handed him his tea, her hand shaking, the cup rattling on its saucer. He sipped the over-strong, Burnt Sienna coloured brew, staring at the stained and chipped cup in his hand while she continued to prattle. The cup was part of the best china set, floral patterned, gold rimmed and badly designed. The cups were too wide at the top so the tea grew cold; too narrow at the bottom and therefore unstable. The handle's unnecessary embellishments – almost Rococo – trapped unwary fingers. The set was older than he was, having been bought from Woolworth's over fifty years ago.

'This new young doctor, he don't know nothing...' he heard as she warmed to her subject. Jon had tried several times since being wealthy to organise medical insurance for her, his feelings fuelled by an anxious guilt.

'...And you have to make an appointment to see him. They don't do visits anymore, unless yer dying, then they come running 'cos they gets a bonus...'

He'd also offered to buy her a new a house and furniture, or set her up in the best of nursing homes. But she always refused. Not only was she too proud – 'I don't want no charity,' she'd said, the double negative signifying a deeply felt rebuttal – but she really didn't want him interfering in her life.

'Work shy, they are, if y'ask me...'

She was as contented as she knew how with her cronies, both real – in the street, at her local church and bingo club – and those inhabiting the world of TV soap operas.

''E'd come runnin' soon enough if I was some dolled-up, young floozie...' she rolled on, well into her stride now...

After an hour or so, his impatience brimming, squirming for release, he couldn't take any more. He cut across her monologue and asked if she would call and invite Yvonne, and pass on the letter, grudgingly accepting the lecture on the iniquity of divorce, rich in clichés.

'I always liked that girl. Didn't matter to me she was coloured. It was a shock at first, mind, but I got used to her. Lovely girl. You was a fool to let her go. Me and your Father didn't always get on, but we stuck it out together. For you and your brothers' sakes. I don't know – you young people today, spoilt something rotten. Only think of yourselves. No thought for the future...'

When he took his urgent leave, he saw she was relieved, too. She had no fond memories, no beautiful antiques from the past. Now there were no exasperating children and a heavily depressed husband leaning on her; and no more financial struggling. She was free, relatively well-off and living in a childlike present. To her mind, she'd never had it so good.

The trip back in time left him desolate. He drove back to Bristol feeling he had made no contact and, apart from the letter, the visit had been futile, a wasted effort.

– It's like I've no foundations. No past I want to remember, no future I can conceive of and an intensely dissatisfying present...

– Perhaps I'm dead, he suggested to himself, aware of self-pity creeping over him like a mournful fog.

– Perhaps the hit men killed me and I just think I'm alive – a ghost going through the motions...

Emma sensed the desolation in his voice as he related the story of his abortive trip and the feelings it had engendered, suggesting, 'Let me try an experiment with you.' She got to her feet. 'Come and sit in my chair.'

Jon did as requested, not sure what was coming, sinking down, folding his arms defensively, feeling both reluctant and submissive.

'I want you to imagine your father is sitting opposite you. Can you see or feel him?'

He stared at the chair he had just vacated and grudgingly nodded that he thought he probably could.

'Good. Now talk to him. Tell him all the things you couldn't say to him when you were young, while he was alive...'

His eyes closed. Then, slowly at first, like an engine long left unused, coughing and chugging to life, he began... And then it felt as though he could never stop as he outpoured the accumulation of petty hurts and resentments that had built over his formative years.

'You never showed me how to shave. You never came to watch me play football: you never asked how I was getting on at school or if I had any problems. You never listened. You were always asleep or wrapped up in yourself. And you had no ambition, let them walk all over you at that fucking factory, content to be a sodding foreman for the rest of your life. You let me down. You always let me down and somehow, you made me feel it was all my fucking fault, always, always, always...'

When the accusational tirade finally spluttered to a stop, Emma gently placed a hand under his elbow, eased him to his feet, guiding him over to the other chair. 'Be your father, now Jon,' she whispered. 'Let him respond. In his own time.'

In a trance, Jon experienced his dead Dad's personality. It descended like fatigue engulfing the body after prolonged exertion. In his father's hacking Cockney accent, he groaned out the vicarious, borrowed words.

'Sorry, son. Yer right. Lousy farver. Couldn't 'elp it. So bloody tired all the time; fuckin' job killing me. But you made me proud. You was the clever one. Me first born; me 'eir. Loved yer so much. Didn't know how to say it. Didn't know how to talk to yer. So proud...'

The communion faded and images began to flash through Jon's mind. The factory, the snowball, the smashing glass and blood; the foreman with his father's face...

The newly realised paternal love, at last embodied, irradiated the marble-hard ball of ice lodged in his heart and, as it melted, the densely packed resentments transmuted to tears. Emotion overflowed, thick and green, and he wept, unchecked, ashamedly, yet unashamed of his shame – welcoming it masochistically. For ten minutes he wailed and sobbed for something missed, something lost and now agonisingly regained. For the first time in his life he acknowledged that he was, perhaps, lovable, acceptable – to the world, to himself – for who and what he was.

URGENT e-MAIL TO M. BRANCUSI.
The target has been sited and a car type and registration number reported. DVLC has no current owner recorded. A search revealed the previous keeper. He informed us he sold the car cash to a Mr. J. Bradford some months ago. The description he gave matches that of the target; the address given proved false. However, the car has been seen in the Home Counties and again recently in the Bristol area. Local police force informants have been activated and a full search is in operation (streets, car parks, hotel carparks, lock-ups etc) therefore, location imminent. Hotel registers in Home Counties, Bristol and environs are being checked for guests registering under the surname Bradford. Will keep you informed.

Two days after his catharsis, following a late afternoon session with Emma, Jon was dawdling back to his hotel. Although he felt lighter this evening, as usual, once away from Emma's womb-like office, he recommenced worrying about his real-life situation and next step. Despite their deep involvement, he still could not fully trust Emma enough and had not yet taken her totally into his confidence.
– *Is my hiding my dual existence fair on her...?*
– *Shouldn't she work that out herself...?*
– *Maybe she has already...*
– *I ought to confide in her – perhaps next time...*
– *But will she think I'm totally crazy, though...?*
– *Does she already...?*
A braying motorcycle rudely ripped through the chain of thought. He came to, suddenly aware of walking, of shops, milling people.
– *Christ! All these people. And if Emma's theory is right, somehow the sum of their consciousness is all focussed in the wrong place. They're all trapped, too...*
Slowly, his mind drifted back to the afternoon's session, the recall as real as being there...

'Why do I keep making the same mistakes, over and over, Emma?' he had

223

asked. 'Why is life so bloody difficult?'

'Have you ever heard the story of the monkey trap?'

'Can't say I have.'

'Well, once, in Africa, an old monkey was terrorising a village, stealing things and attacking children, so the villagers decided to catch it and kill it. They fixed a jar with a narrow neck to the ground, and placed a banana inside. The monkey came down from the tree, sniffed the jar, realised there was a banana inside and reached in for it. He could just get his hand into the neck, but when he grabbed the banana and tried to draw it out, he couldn't. His clenched fist was too big for the hole. Being a monkey, and very greedy by nature, he couldn't let go. It was impossible for him, so he was trapped. All he had to do to be free was to let go of that banana, but there's no way he could do it. His essence, the core of his being, wouldn't let him, even when they came to kill him.'

'You're telling me I trap myself because I won't let go of my... banana?'

'We all do.'

'What's *my* banana, then, Emma? What does it symbolise?'

'Your belief system about yourself, John. The way you decided life was to be when you were a child. Precisely what you're trying to uncover here.'

'And what is that?'

'As I told you before, only you can answer that. All I can tell you is, at some point in our early years, we decide we are unacceptable to our family – our whole world at that time – as we are. So we decide to base ourselves on someone we believe would be acceptable. Someone bigger, smarter, more good looking, better at sport, whatever. We then spend the rest of our lives trying to be that personality. That's the source of all our trials and tribulations because we're always going against our own essential grains. And it gets harder and harder to revert back to being our real, authentic self the older we get.'

'Why?'

'Because the status quo, no matter how unpleasant, is so much safer than the unknown. You had an amazing breakthrough the other day, but you still can't quite let go of that banana...'

As he walked, his mind chattered like an old telex machine receiving a message.

– It's true. I've always adopted some personality or other. I must've wanted to be like some three year old Simon or Marco at bloody nursery school. Always successful; never making a mistake, never putting a foot wrong. Mister Cool, or

so it bloody seemed at the time...
With his mind still churning, he walked into the hotel foyer...

Something was wrong. There was a man seated reading a newspaper, and out of the corner of his eye, Jon thought he caught a nod from the receptionist, saw the man reach for a mobile phone. Jon became immediately on guard. He approached the desk to ask for his key. The receptionist avoided eye contact. He felt her tension – jittery and nervous, not her usual smiling self.

The moment she turned back with the key, Jon made a decision and dashed for the entrance, hearing the man shout at his mobile, 'Shit! He's made a run for it. Get down here, fast!'

Jon hurtled from the hotel taking rights and lefts plunging deeper into back streets, knowing from weeks of walking the best areas to get lost in. He ran until he could push himself no further, slipped into a narrow alleyway between two old buildings, pressed into an unlit doorway and waited, panting, terrified.

Minutes later he heard running footsteps. Two men jogged past, legs in perfect synchronisation.

– Military types. So, they've tracked me down, at last. How? The trip to my Mum's? The neighbours? I knew I shouldn't have gone...

He pressed himself into the dark doorway deciding the wisest strategy was to stay where he was for as long as he could bear it, despite fear creeping over his body like a sickness.

– Funny, he thought *– how in films, the one hiding always makes a break for it after the bad guys have gone past. And they always get caught. I suppose it would make a boring film if they just stayed there for hours...* He wondered how it was possible to be so flippant yet terrified at the same time.

– Hysteria, perhaps...?

Several hours elapsed. His fear began to wane as night fell. No more people passed by. The old docklands area was dead asleep. Out of desperation, he decided to call Emma.

– She's the only person I know. Maybe she can help. Shit! Could she have shopped me...? He doubted it, but the worm of paranoia gnawed through logic.

– No choice... He scrolled for her number and pressed the send button, glad he'd brought his mobile with him. He prayed she was still at her office. When she answered he felt a surge of relief.

Disguising his voice, he told her, 'Good evening. I have Mr Brancusi of

225

Global Marketing on the line for you.'

'I'm sorry? Who did you say?'

'Mr Marco Brancusi,' he repeated.

'I don't know any Brancusis. Are you sure you have the right number?' she asked politely.

'It's all right, Emma, it's me – John.'

'John? Didn't recognise your voice.'

'Listen, Emma. I'm in trouble. I need help and somewhere to hide. There are some guys after me and – I know this sounds crazy – but they want to kill me. Can I come to your place for a while – not the office, your home? They probably know where you work, may have seen me there. I'm desperate, Emma.'

'This all sounds extremely bizarre. What's going on?'

'I'll explain later. What's your address?'

'I don't give my home address to clients, John.'

'Come on! This isn't professional – it's personal. I'm scared, Emma, and in bad trouble. Just need practical help from a friend and you're the only one I've got right now – so, please, please... I really am desperate.'

She sensed the urgency and the tinge of fear in his voice, but reluctantly gave him the address, adding, 'I'm still at the office. I've a few things to finish, so it'll be an hour before I'm home. Come over then. And, John – you'd better be on the level,' she warned.

'Thanks. See you in an hour.' He thumbed off off the mobile before she could change her mind.

Despite the night chill, he removed his jacket and stuffed it into a near-by bin. He found a puddle of murky water, mixed some mud and finger-painted a crude moustache on his upper lip. Thrusting his hands in his pockets, bowing his head he set off in the direction of Emma's home, intent on not drawing attention to himself by either skulking or rushing.

She lived in a block of smart apartments on the west side of town and it took him a long time to walk there by a meandering, back street route. Hovering in shadows, making certain he hadn't been followed, he darted to the entrance and pressed her bell. A crackly facsimile of her voice erupted from the door speaker.

'It's me,' he whispered. She told him to come up, electronically releasing the lock. When she opened the door to her apartment he pushed past her.

'Draw the curtains, quickly,' he commanded.

She did as he asked and turned back to him. 'Just what is all this about? And why have you got mud on your face? You look like a tramp. And you're shivering...'

While washing in the bathroom, he decided he'd have to tell her everything. He needed a confidante, somewhere to stay and someone to help him get the rest of his money – the net was closing tight. He had no choice. He had to take a chance and trust her.

Sitting nursing a cup of coffee, feeling warmer and calmer, he announced portentously, 'You're going to be pretty amazed by what I'm going to tell you, and it's going to stretch your credulity to the limit.'

Over the next hour he revealed everything – rambling, but omitting few details...

'So, there you have it,' he concluded. 'It sounds weird, I know, but I promise you it's all true. Do you believe me – or do you think I'm some kind of raving schizoid?'

She sat thinking for a few moments, weighing something up.

'I could show you the DNZ document, if you like,' he added, worried by her silence.

'No, I do believe you, Jon, without an aitch – just about. But, shouldn't you go to the authorities or the press with this? Secret societies, assassinations, attempted murder, international plots to have half the world addicted to some junk-food product – it's very heavy stuff.'

'I've thought about it, long and hard. Trouble is, I don't know who to go to – anyone in government, the police, the press, or even the alternative media could be one of them. Anyway, what proof do I have beyond Edward's documents? He's dead. It would end up my word against theirs. It'd be, "Poor bloke. Stress got to him. Cracked up. Better get him into a psycho ward." And, anyway, once exposed, how would I get guaranteed protection for myself – and my kids?'

'Assuming you could talk to the right people and could get a cast iron guarantee of protection, would you be willing to reveal what you know? To go public?'

'I don't know. It's all so risky. I don't think I could take the pressure...' He bowed his head to consider, rubbing his temples. 'I might, if I could be one hundred percent certain about my kids' safety. And I suppose they've got to be stopped, haven't they? But how? They're so powerful. And everywhere. No. I'd be better off getting out of the country.'

'In my experience, there's usually a counterweight to every political and socio-economic force. You've never come across any kind of anti-Doh-Nai-Zen group you could contact? Nothing subversive on the internet, or the dark net, for example?'

'No. As far as I know, nobody outside has ever heard of them. They're too clever – totally underground, élitist, well defended, always cover their tracks. Marco did once tell me that we had to be wary of what he called Saints, or some group attempting to thwart them. Apparently, they can negate our – their – power, or something. But I've never come across anyone like that.'

Emma shifted in her seat, crossing her legs. Jon caught sight of a curving thigh. It had been months since he'd had a sexual relationship, or had even been intimate with a women. A sudden thought pushed the rising pang aside.

'You're taking this all very calmly. You haven't called the guys in the white coats already, have you?'

'No, Jon,' she laughed. 'I haven't, not yet, anyway.'

Satisfied, he yawned. 'God, Emma, I'm so tired.'

'Let's talk more in the morning. You're welcome to stay the night. I think you'll be safe here for the time being.'

'Thanks.' He looked relieved. 'Where do I sleep?'

'On the couch. I'll get you a duvet.'

Jon was organising his makeshift bed when Emma re-entered wearing a fluffy, white dressing gown. She brought more pillows and as she leaned forward to place them on the couch, Jon stared down her revealed cleavage. The sexual yearning became suddenly overpowering and he reached out a hand to stroke her hair.

'I was really hoping I could sleep with you, you know.'

She stood upright, pulling back, stating flatly, 'No, Jon, you can't.'

'Why not? I'm really attracted to you. Don't you find me attractive?'

'Maybe, but I can't, Jon. And that's final.' She emphasised the last word by brushing Jon's hand aside.

'Aw, come on. No one'll know. It'll be great. The perfect way to cement our relationship...' He pulled her gently towards him by her dressing gown sash. As she resisted, twisting aside, the bow slipped and the gown fell open...

He emitted a choking scream as he fainted away, shock resonating, blood draining. For a moment, it seemed there was no body under the gown. Instead he saw a giddying infinite space filled with pulsing, filigreed light, opalescence spilling into the room.

'Jon, I'm so sorry. Don't be afraid,' she begged, seeing him stagger back, blood draining from his face as he fought for breath. She refolded and tied the sash and took a step towards him. He leapt back in alarm.

'I won't harm you, Jon. I can't harm you. I don't know what you saw, but whatever it is, I can explain...'

He continued to back away in fear and total disbelief, hands held defensively in front as his endocrine system red-lined, injecting massive doses of adrenaline into his bloodstream.

'Keep away from me! You're not human! *You're a fucking freak!*'

'Father, we have Lucke running loose within our net. We just have to haul him in. Any moment now...'

'Marco – I sense our enemies have made contact with him. You must find and destroy him as quickly as possible. If they win him to their side, the ramifications could be disastrous for us. Put all resources to it. Spare nothing. I cannot stress strongly enough the importance of your succeeding.'

'I will, Father. Trust me,' Marco grovelled, but the line had already gone dead.

The panic attack had passed, rumbling in the distance like a recent storm. Jon felt as if he had been struck by lightning. He was still shivering and his legs seemed boneless. He sat breathing shallowly, eyes shut.

'Feeling better, now?' Emma asked, handing him a cup of hot, sweet tea. 'I'm really sorry about all this. Something must have triggered a sort of protective mechanism I have. It's happened before, but I have no idea what transpires, it's all in the person I'm interacting with – a kind of momentary transcendence, I guess. The nature of the experience depends entirely on them. Not flattered you saw me as a freak, though.'

'Sorry. I was a bit freaked myself, at the time. But you look so normal again. And yet... God, this is weird.' He shook his head and shuddered. 'I thought I could take anything after Doh-Nai-Zen, but I guess that's all internal stuff. It's when things happen out there, seemingly against the laws of physics... Christ, that frightened me, Emma.' Nervous of her response, he tentatively asked, 'What the hell are you? Some kind of angel, or an alien, or what?'

She laughed. 'Just human. I was born with a special gift, though.'

'Special gift? What? Don't understand. Don't understand anything anymore.'

229

'There are maybe ten thousand people like me in the world, currently. We discover what we are little by little, as we grow up. Things happen – dreams, coincidences, psychic experiences, revelations. Then one day we are contacted. At first inwardly, and then outwardly by others, and all is revealed. It's a shock at first. Lots of soul searching, then it all falls into place. We're given a choice, of course. Very few turn down the opportunity to make a difference.'

'Make a difference? To what?'

'Our role is to protect the human race from people like your erstwhile friends. You see, I knew all about Doh-Nai-Zen long before I met you. And Chi-Chi certainly knows about us. I couldn't reveal the truth until we were certain you're a fugitive and not still one of them – some kind of infiltrator.'

'Christ! Are you the Saints Marco was always going on about?'

'No, Jon, she laughed, ' There's nothing saintly about us.'

'This 'us', your group, who runs it? You're obviously organised. Who do you work for?'

'We don't work for anyone as such. We're autonomous, individually guided by a power way beyond this realm, but we have a common agenda.'

'What power? You don't mean God!' he scoffs.

'Possibly,' she gestured.

'Possibly? Don't you know?'

'All I know is the source of our energy, and what it directs us to accomplish, is benign – full of love for humanity.'

'Still can't get my head round this God stuff...'

'Belief in God is merely a question of personal conviction. My God is nothing like the personified, Biblical one. I just know, from my own experience, that this physical world is only the tip of an iceberg of reality. Our universe was born out of nothing – the reverse of a black hole – yet precise, immutable laws govern its existence, so some intelligent, ordering principle is at work – and on many levels of consciousness. Therefore, I am certain there is an 'orderer', a Creator – an Omnipotence. I also know I could never comprehend what that is. How could a car know its driver, or a painting its painter?'

'Well, they can't think, can they? Don't have self-awareness...'

'And how exactly would you explain the phenomenon of self-awareness?'

He shrugged. 'Evolution over billions of years? I don't know. More interested in how you work, how you make a difference as you call it.'

'We work in loose groups, each knowing only a handful of others, although we do recognise one another should our paths cross – call it sixth sense. Information and instructions are delivered telepathically, or intuitively. Not a million miles from what you called authoring in Doh-Nai-Zen, but the sources are poles apart. Our role is to make life difficult for groups like Doh-Nai-Zen. Stop them gaining the power they need to upset the balance of nature, or slow the evolutionary process, which is their true aim.'

'Don't get it. What can they achieve by that?'

'Their own supremacy, freedom to do their own thing without restraint. A planet that's eternally at war... That would be their ideal. Civilisation is anathema to groups like Doh-Nai-Zen.'

'So there are others at it as well?'

'Of course. Collectively, they represent the sinister forces – darkness, chaos, destruction, atrophy and so on. We represent the opposite. Every positive must have a balancing negative – that's one of those immutable laws.'

'How come you know about Chi-Chi?'

'People like us have been doing this kind of work for centuries, so it's easy to recognise the symptoms.'

'Which are?'

'As a rule of thumb, anything where an individual, or group, or nation improves its lot to the detriment of another. Such as the arms trade fuelling sectarian and civil wars for profit; ethnic cleansing to gain power; ignorant fundamentalism; international commerce putting shareholders' interests before people and the planet... And it goes right down to ordinary people having their weaknesses exploited – handing over their birthright in exchange for an apparent freedom, while privileged minorities make a fortune. In short, anything that has an animal-like, predatory nature where one being or group dominates or enslaves another. Remember the monkey trap I told you about? They exploit that phenomenon knowing the same principle works for whole social goupings as well as individuals.'

'Well, that all certainly sounds like Doh-Nai-Zen...'

'Yes, But Doh-Nai-Zen is so frighteningly different because it's the first time in history that a group has become so organised on a global scale.'

'So if you know who they are, and what they do, why don't you just stop them? Blow the gaff, wipe them out?'

'We wouldn't, even if we could. Their presence is preordained – another of those immutable laws. Paradoxically, without them, civilisation couldn't progress. Evolution would stagnate. All we can do is to make sure the balance never tips totally in their favour.'

'How?'

'Various techniques from using our spirituality, our intuition, to direct action and...' Emma noticed Jon's eyes drooping. 'You look tired, Jon. We'll talk more tomorrow. Come and lay on the sofa next to me, if you dare; there is something I *can* do for you.'

Jon went to her, nervously obedient. He lay on the couch, gingerly placing his head in her lap. Within seconds he fell into a deep sleep.

He dreamed he floated cosily in his mother's womb, soothed by soft music, lapped by waves of contentment...

NEW JOB

'You're pensive,' Sonia told Marco, walking into his study. 'Something on your mind?'

'What?' He swivelled to face her. 'Yes, I suppose... Can't stop thinking about Lucke. Despite his rejection, I rather miss the silly bugger.'

'This is unlike you, Marco. Are you sure you're alright?'

'Yes. Just getting old.'

'And maudlin. Chi-Chi would not approve.'

'He wouldn't, would he?' Marco smiled. 'No, it's not that. He was just pleasant company. Always good for a laugh. Simply enjoyed him being around, I suppose.'

'Yes. Me, too. He had such passion. I used to feel so energised after our sessions.' They stared past one another each wrapped in their own reminiscence.

'Would there be a way back for him, if he were to rethink?' Sonia asked.

'Doubt it. Too late now. He's left us no choice. It all got out of hand. Very sad.'

'I do believe you're showing a little humanity...' Sonia teased, feeding Marco the line.

'Nobody's perfect.'

Sonia laughed, then asked, 'No Julia or Maria tonight?'

'I'm a little bored with Julia, and Maria's too busy on the project,' Marco sighed. 'God, I wish I could shake off this sense of foreboding.

That's what's getting me down. I failed with Lucke, and now I'm failing to find him. I don't like failure, it only breeds more of the same...'

'Come on. Let's go to bed.' She took him by the hands and pulled him to his feet. 'Perhaps we can rekindle the old magic and you can throw off your forebodings in a night of sensuality and passion.'

Marco snorted and allowed Sonia to lead him out.

Jon awoke on the couch alone and refreshed and stretched languidly. He inhaled the delicious aroma of fresh-baked bread. Feeling hungry, he wrapped a borrowed dressing gown and walked to the kitchen.

'Morning. That smells good,' he greeted Emma, who was laying the table. Everything looked so normal.

– *Perhaps it was all a dream...* The knot of worry nestling in his gut pulsed and reality reaffirmed itself.

'You look much better, Jon. Sit down and I'll get you some breakfast.'

He ate ravenously, and when finished told Emma, 'I've decided to make a stand, but I need you and your people to help. Can you? Will you?'

'Yes, of course. It's what we were hoping for.'

'But before I put my trust in you all, I must know your plans.'

'No problem. First, we must get you hidden away safely. We don't want you killed right now. You're important to us and that was a close call last time.' Her answer triggered a new wave of anxiety.

'I was going to ask you about that. I assume you guys saved me?'

'Yes, Jon. We did.'

'How though? Some kind of spiritual technique? Time warps? Psychic intervention? What?'

'No,' she laughed. 'Rather prosaic, I'm afraid. We'd targetted you, so to speak, and had been monitoring the situation for some time. We can be subversive, too, you know. We actually have moles in the organisation, so we knew exactly what they were going to do, and precisely when and where. So we set it all up in advance. We hired one of their colleagues to, what do they call it? "Take them out"?'

'Christ! That was risky. Supposing it hadn't worked?'

'We had contingency plans. Nothing could have gone awry.'

Jon shook his head in disbelief, then wondered, 'How come you're okay with killing?'

'We're not, but occasionally the end justifies the means. And anyway, we didn't actually pull the trigger. We just short-circuited the 'live by the sword' syndrome for them. As Krishna says in the Bhagavadgita, "The truly wise mourn neither for the dead, nor the living".' Noting Jon's bemused look, she added, 'It'll all become crystal clear soon, Jon. Have patience.'

Finding her philosophy incomprehensible he changed tack. 'You think they'll still want to kill me? No chance they'll just give up now?'

'Definitely not. You know too much. And now they're aware of our involvement you're even more of a threat.' She paused, deliberating, then came to a decision. 'Did it never occur to you how odd it was that you met Marco and within what, a year, you were a member of his inner circle?'

'Just chance, I suppose. And Marco seemed to think I had a marketable talent. Guess I was in the right place at the right time. Or the wrong place at the wrong time,' he added ruefully.

'Sorry to disillusion you, Jon. Everything was arranged, from the moment Marco reversed into your car, right up until you started to have second thoughts.'

Jon sat and stared in stunned disbelief.

'They gave you very special treatment, wined and dined you, softened you up, worked on your flaws and weaknesses. I'm sorry to have to tell you all this, Jon. Don't look so pained. It's better you know the truth.'

'Oh yeah? But why me? Why am I so special to them, for Chrissake?' Jon asked, shutting his eyes in humiliation, pulling to one side as though expecting a blow.

'Marco wasn't born a poor boy, as he led you to believe. He's descended from aristocratic Italian stock; his ancestors go back to the Roman emperors. Their kind are dying out – inbred, incestuous, exhausted. They need fresh blood, so they tried make the kiyomeru energy work on outsiders, people from the wrong side of the tracks, so to speak, but with potential – like you. They groomed you and a few others; made you think you were top men – and, had it worked, they'd have taken more, creating a band of lieutenants to do all their dirty, heavy work. Somehow, the transformation process didn't quite work on you. Perhaps it was to do with your feelings for Lucia, or some inborn quality – who can fathom our destinies? Now, because you've dangerous insider knowledge, they simply want you out of the way. You're an embarrassment, a failed experiment.'

Jon slowly nodded his head, eyes shut, mouth pursed, teeth clenched.

'However, lucky for you, *we* need you very much alive. You've somehow become pivotal in this latest battle.'

'Oh, come on! Pivotal,' he spat. 'Are you serious? Jesus! This is crazy! I don't believe a fucking word of it!' He leapt to his feet and a kitchen stool crashed to the floor. He paced back and forth until frustrated anger overwhelmed him and he punched the door shut.

'Fucking bastards!'

'I understand how you feel, Jon. It's difficult, I know.'

He picked up and replaced the stool, sitting again, head in hands.

'Try not to dwell on it for now,' Emma suggested, doctor-like. 'What's done is done. More importantly, will you still help us fight them? If you do, we can guarantee protection for both you and your family.'

Jon felt bereft, unable to respond. He didn't dare contemplate the implications in relation to Sonia and Lucia and he cursed himself for being such a dupe.

'I feel so used, so small, stupid, pathetic – a bloody victim again.' Then detestation of Marco and Chi-Chi bubbled to the surface.

'It's like I've been their prey...'

A desire to pay them back for their insidious manipulation flared.

'And I want *revenge*...' He looked up at Emma.

'Yeah, I'll do it,' he asserted, a cold determination in his voice. 'I'm going to fix those aristo bastards for good.' Emma smiled. 'Anyway, I don't have a choice, do I?' She nodded agreement. 'How are we going to fight, though? They're bloody powerful... So much control.'

'We'll use the internet. You're going to set up a website for us – a kind of truth site – and you're going to broadcast to the world – make people aware of what's going on. Get that new product of theirs a bad name for a start – make certain it fails. Later, we'll go for the really big stuff – the conspiracy theories.'

'I haven't got the faintest idea how to do that,' he protested. 'And as an ex-marketing guru, I don't see how that could possibly work – it would cost a fucking *fortune* – and that's just an estimate.'

'Not your concern. We do have unlimited resources, but we'll be using guerrilla marketing techniques; young people are our target. The whole process will take time, though, but with your insider knowledge allied to our global network, we can build impetus until the whole world is sharing in the debate. That's the objective, anyway.'

'Why a website, though? Wouldn't a full frontal assault in the media be more effective, particularly if you've unlimited funds?'

'No. You said yourself that they control a lot of the media. The one area where we can be absolutely certain of keeping control, where what we broadcast can't be sabotaged or corrupted, is our own website. The dark forces use the medium pretty effectively – paedophilia and porno sites, anarchic and terrorist networks, multi-national propaganda and so on, but because they can never control it totally, it's also a thorn in their side. To my mind, the world wide web actually reflects the transitional state humanity is in – symbolises our yearning for unity.'

'Don't see much evidence of that in the world.'

'Not yet, I know, but you will. We actually introduced the idea of the internet, by the way. To the people at CERF credited with the concept.'

'You introduced the idea...?'

'Yes. In certain situations, we can force low energies to relinquish their hold temporarily so that human minds can work as they're supposed to, tapping into the vast reservoir of creativity and knowledge that's just waiting to be downloaded. Most breakthroughs in knowledge happen that way. When they were led to the Internet idea, I hoped they'd shout "Eureka!" – but they didn't.'

'You're crazy!'

'I'm joking, Jon. Don't look so serious. We're allowed to joke, you know.'

'Sorry. It's like reality keeps slipping away from me the more of this stuff you tell me. I feel like I'm on the verge of a nervous breakdown.'

'I feel for you, Jon. But it's imperative you see the whole picture. Then we can leave you to get on with it.'

'But I know bugger all about websites, Emma. Not my forté.'

'Don't worry. We'll supply you with a team of technicians and support journalists. Creating the site's the easy bit. The hard work is getting people to visit! Your brief is to get the site established and to start denouncing the whole Global Foods affair. We've got some convincing proof of how threatening the whole GM issue is to life on earth. The ramifications are truly horrific and would be evident within only a few years. People think AIDS and BSE are scary enough. Manipulating food genes, especially allied to opiates, would be a million times worse, and there'd be no going back, no cure. And I'm only talking about the physical effects. The inner mutations would be even more catastrophic, but people, in general, are not ready for that.'

He grunted, shaking his head, unable to accept. 'I don't know. Feel so out of my depth.'

'It's simple, really. What we have to do is constantly undermine and chip away at their negative disseminations. We major on global injustice, the effects of globalisation, GM products, genetic engineering, especially addictions, the destruction of farming and so on. We needn't even mention Doh-Nai-Zen and mad schemes to rule the world. We'd just be perceived as another bunch of conspiracy theory loonies or doom merchants if we did – playing into Chi-Chi's hands. There are just too many zany theories around nowadays and they make a very effective smoke screen for what's really going on – but I think you know about all that, having been part of it.'

'Still not convinced, Emma, but I guess I'll just have to trust you. Right now, I'm more concerned about retrieving my money – and the DNZ documents. Got them stashed all over town. And I need to buy clothes and stuff – everything. We'd better get moving.' He jumped up, suddenly jittery, yet paralysed, not knowing where to start.

'Calm down, Jon. We'll organise all that. First, we have to get you to safety as quickly as possible. Before we go, though, there's something you must understand.'

'What now?'

'From this moment on, you're going to be virtually under house arrest. It'll be a long time before you'll be free to walk the streets again. We *can* protect you, but only if you follow our instructions to the letter. Slip out of our protection, and you're dead. Is that clear?

Jon nodded understanding as resignation settled in. 'How long do you think it will all take?'

'Four or five years, perhaps? It's hard to say. Things will get more difficult and dangerous the further our project advances and theirs falters. They won't just sit back and let us thwart them. They will fight. We foresee the Middle East and Africa exploding, the problems in Eastern Europe flaring up again and the Israel/Palestine conflict deepening dangerously. And there'll be a proliferation of global terrorist attacks and race riots. They'll do anything to destabilise civilisation, while ostensibly hanging on to the moral high ground – and all to make sure the dollar is the world trading currency. You know the sort of thing. On the one hand, "We believe in God and democracy, so we're coming to liberate you and to look after your oil..." And on the other, "Allah has instructed us through the Koran to destroy the infidel and look after our own oil..." Diametric opposition is never pretty.'

'Conspiracy theories again.'

'Maybe. But there's something else, Jon...'

'Go on.'

237

'To work with us, you must undergo the psychic equivalent of a detox-ification programme.'

'Why? What am I supposed to be on?'

'Doh-Nai-Zen, of course. We must wean you off it – slowly. Your psy-chic, neural and endocrine systems couldn't sustain such dramatic rever-sals if done all at once. Frankly, you'd go crazy.'

'Yeah... I nearly did. Tell me, are you really a therapist, Emma? Can I trust you?'

'Yes I am, Jon,' she laughed. 'Fully trained and accredited.'

'So, why would closing down the Doh-Nai-Zen contact make me crazy?'

'Well... there's a concept buried in the mystical traditions of all major religions that existence is hierarchic...'

'Bloody hell! That's what Marco always said.'

'Marco's beliefs are distortions of the truth, Jon. Always remember that. As I was saying, the material world is the lowest, then the vegetable, the animal, the human, the angelic and many layers above. Each force relates to, and incorporates, an area of the body. The material with the brain and thinking; the vegetable with the emotions; the animal with the passions; the human with knowledge and finer feelings and the angelic with the unconscious, or soul. A perfect human being would have the forces balanced evenly within, acting as servants, the soul in charge. If a lower force becomes dominant, a human can only act according to that force's characteristics. Am I making sense?'

'No. But go on.'

'Driven solely by the material, amassing wealth will be paramount, and other people will be seen and used as objects – you'd have a heart of stone, metaphorically speaking.'

'Yes. I've met a few like that...'

'If driven solely by the vegetable forces, one's own comfort and good feeling would always come first. Ever noticed how a plant will grow at the expense of another? Cutting off it's supply of water and sun if necessary? The animal force is about dominance, sex and power, as you well know. The human force believes only in itself, "Man is he measure of all things." The higher energies are...'

'Wait a minute, wait a minute. How do you know all this stuff is true?'

'It's been known for centuries, Jon. You only have to read the Kaballah, or listen to the Sufis. And it's all encrypted in the the Koran, the Bhagavadgita, the Bible.'

'Where?'Jon scoffed. 'I used to go to church when I was a kid. Don't ever remember hearing anything like that.'

'No? How about the Christmas story? Jesus, the highest power, can't be born in the inn, too busy – a good metaphor for the head. So he's born in a stable, the heart, and the animal and human forces worship him in the form of oxes, asses and shepherds; then come the wise men with gifts representing the richness of life and its bitter-sweet nature. And, as a therapist, being crucified in order to rise again rings bells for me. Also...'

Emma broke off suddenly, closing her eyes. She remained in this position for twenty seconds, then announced urgently, 'Jon, I'm told it's time to go. They've located my office. It won't take them long to find this place.'

'Who's "they"? And *where* are we going?' Jon asked, bewildered. 'And how? I can't go back for my car...'

'Go and get dressed. We're being picked up in fifteen minutes. I'll tell you who, what, why and where, en route.'

Julia handed Marco an e-mail printout. He grunted his thanks and began to read.

FIELD REPORT:

We have located the target's whereabouts. He has been living in a hotel in Bristol under the alias Bradford, but gave our operatives the slip. We made an immediate search of the room and discovered a suitcase containing approximately £25K sterling. A range of new clothes was found in the wardrobe, the usual toiletries in the bathroom. Tests revealed nothing out of the ordinary. We discovered a business card relating to a Ms Emma Nagel, a psychotherapist, with only a mobile number. We located the address of her office within an hour. The space had been cleared and vacated by the time we arrived and a thorough search revealed nothing. Later in the day, we tracked down the landlords and they gave us the home address of Ms Nagel – an apartment on the west side of Bristol. When we arrived, it had also been cleared and vacated. A meticulous search unearthed no clues.

Neighbours interviewed at both locations had no knowledge of the occupant(s) and had been unaware of any comings or goings or recent removal personnel, except an elderly female who claimed she saw a man and a woman getting into a white van early this morning. CCTV cameras covering all routes out of Bristol are being checked.

Our assumption is that the target is being helped by a highly efficient, professional team with vast resources on a par with Mossad or the CIA.

We have no further leads at this time and await further instructions.
Marco finished reading and bowed his head, rubbing his temples with
a forefinger and thumb, elbow on his desk.

'Damn! They've got him. What am I going to tell Chi-Chi?' Marco suppressed the rising dread and reluctantly reached for the phone.

As they drove through the gates, Jon saw the name *Glenbourne* discreetly
carved on a block of stone.

'Bloody hell, Emma! This is Marco's golf club! He only lives about
twenty miles from here. This place is owned by a Doh-Nai-Zen big wheel.
What are you playing at, for Christ's sake?' Paranoia clutched him.
'You've been conning me all along...' Images of being dragged in front of
Marco, of being tortured, then summarily executed rushed through his
mind as he desperately looked for a way out of the van, groping at the
door handles in mounting panic.

'Relax, Jon. We know all that. You'll be living in the main house, miles
from the golf complex. They'll never think of looking for you under their
noses. Anyway, the estate's owner just happens to be on our side.'

'Not the Duke?' Jon gasped, incredulous.

'Of course. You've already met him – Robin Buckingham, remember?
He's our mole.'

'Yeah, of course I remember him. But even so, sticking my head in the
lion's mouth doesn't exactly make me feel safe, to be honest.'

'As long as you remain undercover, it will appear as though you've disappeared off the surface of the earth. They'll never find you here. They
won't even begin to look for you in a place like this, under the roof of one
of their own.'

'Yeah, well. I've no options, have I?' he replied ruefully.

'No, Jon. No options.'

'I have to trust you. Put myself totally in your hands?'

'Yes.'

'I'm scared, Emma.'

Glenbourne was a Palladian mansion set in four thousand acres of walled
park and farmland. The main house was all marble and gilt columns, high
ceilings and tall windows. Pseudo-religious frescoes celebrating the lives
of the Buckinghams swirled kaleidoscopically over wall panels and concave alcoves; trompe l'oeil vistas of angels and cherubs welcoming family members into a blue-sky heaven strode majestically across vaulted ceil-

ing. Each time the old frescoes caught the eye, they seemed to sound a triumphant, resounding chord; an eternal *'Hal-le-lu-jah! Hal-le-lu-jah!'*

'The farming and golf complex enterprises supporting the estate will continue at a distance from the house as normal,' Emma told Jon, ushering him into his spacious quarters. 'The Duke has set up a publishing business as a cover, so all the comings and goings won't raise eyebrows.'

Jon went straight to the windows overlooking the formal gardens and orchards at the rear – softly swelling meadows beyond. 'Nice. Very nice,' he commented, turning back to look around. The rooms he was to call his home were extremely well-appointed with creature comforts.

'Glad you approve, Jon.'

'Why all the TV monitors?'

'As you'll be cut off from the world, you'll need to keep au fait with what's going on. We've networked through virtually all the world's satellite stations plus computer graphics, internet access and, eventually, video links with your family, if you wish. Whatever newspapers and journals you need will be delivered, too. By the way, all your personal needs will be looked after – meals, laundry, cleaning, the lot. As you're ostensibly in exile, Jon, we'll make your prison as comfortable as possible. Now, let's go down and look round the business end. After, I'll introduce you to your team.'

Downstairs was perfect. The old ballroom, housing computers and electronic equipment, was the heart of the complex.

'You really have done an amazing job,' Jon remarked, impressed.

She escorted him into a well stocked library and games room. 'If there's anything you or your team need, Jon, just ask. Accommodationwise, there are plenty of smaller offices for admin, and what used to be the dining room has been converted to a canteen, which leads on to a gymnasium – I'm told it's very well equipped. There's also an indoor swimming pool.'

'Wow! Do I really deserve all this?'

'Oh, yes! We regard you as our very own Prodigal Son,' she laughed. 'Come on, time for the team to meet their new boss.'

They walked into the ballroom and Jon performed a classic double take.

'Rob! Brian! What are you guys doing here?'

Rob still looked like an overgrown school kid and Jon felt such rising warmth that he could not help from embracing him, patting him on the back.

'It's a long story, Jon. I'll tell you later over a beer. I've got to thank you for kicking me out, you know.'

'Yeah' sorry about that,' Jon replied sheepishly, breaking away. 'I wasn't myself at the time.'

'Water under the bridge, old mate.' A grin illuminated his podgy face. 'It turned out you did me a big favour.'

He turned to Brian. 'How you been, Brian? How'd you get involved in all this?'

'Much the same as Rob, coincidentally,' Brian drawled, laid back as ever. 'After we left the company, we went our separate ways. Both got into charitable work; bumped into one another in Zaire, working for different NGOs. When we got back to England we joined Friends of the Earth together, working on GM stuff, then got ourselves loaned to this project. Funny old life. What goes around comes around, eh?'

'I suppose you had something to do with this?' Jon turned back to Emma to ask.

Emma shrugged, smiling.

'Let go, you fuckin' cow!' yelled a voice from Jon's left. He turned and nearly fainted as he saw the two muggers beaming at him.

'What *is* this?'

'Meet my muggers again, Jon. Two up and coming actors who'll be working on the team. I'm afraid our meeting was somewhat contrived as well.'

'Jesus, Emma. Why? I don't understand.'

'Had to meet you somehow. And it had to be on my terms so I could make sure you were genuinely on the run.'

Shaking hands, Jon felt abashed, apologising for the physicality of their first meeting. They assured him it wasn't as bad as it looked and that he shouldn't forget they were actors. He turned back to Emma. 'That was bloody cruel.'

'I hope you're beginning to appreciate – from the enormous lengths we've gone to – just how important you are to us, Jon.'

Emma introduced him to Elaine, a young, blonde woman.

'Hi, Jonny, baby,' she cooed in a perfect imitation of Lucia's voice.

'Don't tell me...' Jon groaned.

'Sorry, Jon. It was Elaine who telephoned you in the car. You didn't really believe that Lucia would help you – would show compassion – did you?'

'Well, I had hoped... How many more nasty surprises you got lined up for me, Emma?'

'Only a very small one – promise.'

Emma explained to Jon that the full team comprised of two programmer-technicians to set up and maintain the site; a designer-operator to help Jon in the initial design phase; six investigative journalists and researchers; then a group of activists under Rob and Brian and, finally, administrative staff, some of whom were to double as bodyguards and 'gofers'. The gender mix was roughly fifty/fifty and they would all live on the premises, full time.

'And we've strategically located sympathisers all over the world, aiding us on every level of security, research and inside information,' she added.

'Are all the team like you?' he asked.

'No. A few only. We've told the rest that you're a successful activist who's on the run from the CIA and that divulging your whereabouts risks everyone's lives. One of your responsibilities is to keep that subterfuge in place – for the time being. Anyway, they all have government files on them from years of activism – that's an added security bonus. Believe me, these are all totally committed and trustworthy people, Jon.'

'Glad to hear it.'

'Now, the house and grounds are protected with the latest surveillance equipment, as will be the site, but more so. No hacker could ever break in, or even track us down without our knowing it was happening,' she assured him. 'As an added safeguard, we've created a system of moving our server all over the world, using other computers randomly as temporary hosts, so they'll never track down the site's physical location, either.'

'You've got it all covered, then? Seems foolproof...'

'It is, as long as you don't give the game away. You're the only weak link. Big responsibility, eh?'

After supper, Emma took Jon aside to announce that she'd only be with him for another few weeks, so it was time to start on the detox programme.

'Will you be coming back?' he asked, alarmed, realising how much he would miss her.

'Possibly – in a few months' time. But the others will keep the detox programme running and be in an advisory capacity to you and the team. We have every confidence in you, Jon.' she added affectionately.

'So, when do you want to start?'

'Right now.'

'Okay. Tell me what to do.'

They went to Jon's room.

'Put this on, then just sit quietly with your eyes closed.' She handed him what he thought was a black plastic Alice band.

'What's this?'

'It's an electronic thought tranquilliser. We call it a 'Mind Trank' for short. It was developed by a couple of our boffins. It calms and blocks thought energy so the wearer can tune in to higher energies. It takes yogis and monks years of asceticism and disciplined practice to achieve what this little gadget does in seconds. So, put it on and let go of everything. Allow what happens to happen. Not that different to kiyomeru, although the experiences will be much more subtle – and cleaner. Are you ready?' He nodded. 'Then I'll call the others.'

It was as Emma predicted. The moment he donned the Trank, the incessant dialogue normally ruling his head petered out and he sensated floating in a wide, clear space. He became aware of two or three people entering the room to stand close. Within minutes, a swarm of butterflies seemed to enter his chest, their wings beating, vibrating to a high pitched hum and he relaxed into the experience. The others were physically stand-ing in front of him, yet all around him, appearing to glow brighter then dimmer, while emitting a range of single-note sounds that harmonised into a sweet, almost beatific chord.

After twenty minutes, he began to feel nauseous as darkness rose from the pit of his stomach, issuing from his mouth as a silent cry. He leaned forward and was made to parody puking; then his body began to shake gently. After another ten minutes, the sensations faded.

Emma broke the silence. 'Take off the Trank, Jon. How do you feel, now?'

'Weird. Light headed. At peace. Hard to describe.'

'Good. I shall ask you to do that every few days for at least six months. Then we'll re-assess the situation. And we need you to report all your experiences, feelings and dreams in between, if you can. Particularly if you feel you're losing control. Now for the small surprise I promised you.'

Jon groaned. 'Come on then. What is it.'

'I want you to fast twice a week.' A stunned silence. 'It will only be from midnight to six the following evening, but it's to be total. No food, no drink, no smoking. And no sleeping on the job. Don't look so shocked. It won't kill you.'

'But why? What's the point?'

'To discipline those lower energies, retrain that animal – and to teach you patience.'

Jon shook his head and exhaled resignation.

INTO BATTLE

www.grusum.org was launched two months later, the site's URL created by Jon.

'The 'g' and 'm' of grusum will be picked out in contrasting colours on all promotional and communications material,' Jon explained, presenting to the team. 'The aim is to totally reposition genetically engineered products and GM foods from potential life enhancers to life threateners, countering every devious technique used by our competition – a-k-a "the enemy".

'Our opening strategy will be to examine every single word and phrase the pro-GM lobby use, as well as our own. Have you all noticed, for example, how the apparently innocuous words "transgenic foods" are slipping into the media's vocabulary, in place of "genetically modified food"?' Jon asked. 'That's a planned strategy, for sure, and we're going to have to bust their euphemistic terminology wide open. The Labour Party employed the technique brilliantly a quarter of a century ago against Thatcher's government. Her party's Community Charge policy was re-spun as "The Poll Tax", a neat little sound bite containing an implied criticism – pay the tax or no vote. It ended up being used extensively by the press regardless of allegiances. Even Tory politicians found the words in their mouths while trying to defend their own policy. The arguments for were completely obfuscated and never got an airing and later, when the public reacted and took to the streets, the government was forced to think again. It must've been frustrating as hell for Maggie – and part of her eventual downfall.'

Jon instructed that from now on, at every opportunity – on the site, through press releases, articles, media interviews, news broadcasts – they must always present the pejorative 'mutated-gene food.'

Bang on schedule, towards the end of the year, the DNZ products were launched.

'Meet the competition,' Jon announced to the gathered team. 'Anyone fancy a bite?' There were no takers.

On the table lay a *gobar*. The brightly coloured wrapper announced that each pack contained the government's Recommended Daily Intake of calories, proteins, carbohydrates and vitamins – *a complete lo-fat, hi-nrg meal*. The product was eat-cold or micro-waveable, and could even be frozen and stored for months. Removed from the slip-on, vacuum-packaging, the gobar had the appearance of a tubular ice-lolly complete with wooden stick and domed top, and was divided into three distinct, fudge-like bands.

'Looks like a sort of party penis,' Jenny commented.

'No accident,' Jon assured her, laughing. 'Now, the top, green band is a starter. The middle, orangey one a main course, the pink a dessert. Apparently, a wide range of flavour combos are available.'

'That's pretty neat,' someone said. They all grudgingly agreed, nodding thoughtfully.

'I've got a box full here and I want us all to try one as our meal tonight.' A groan from around the table. 'Just one won't hurt – you won't get addicted *that* quickly. Even heroin takes a week or so. Anyway, we've got to know what all the fuss is about, if it works or not. "Know thy enemy", I believe they say...'

The multi-million pound media campaign hit the ground running the same evening – vibrant commercials made in dance-for-video style, reminiscent of a Kylie Minogue road show. Bright, mesmeric flashing lights; hand held, multi-viewpoint cameras; fast, rhythmic cuts; surreal, erotic body images – the routines performed by media-beautiful, multi-ethnic, androgynous dancers in their twenties, bedecked in street-cred fashion. The two minutes duration of seductive, free form dance was rivetted together by dynamic, contrapuntal percussion. The voice over shouted, 'Hungry? Go pop a gobar!', while in the corner of the screen, pulsing in time to the beat, the slogan *go-bar – more time to party* worked its subliminal magic.

The ads were screened simultaneously on every commercial channel at peak viewing times, and in every cinema in the UK. They would be repeated throughout the evening for weeks ahead. Similar campaigns, with national and linguistic variations, were running across America, Europe, Australasia and Japan.

The commercials were complemented by a massive, nationwide poster campaign. In the UK, the posters sported images of the same beautiful people driving in open-top cars, on the move from rave to party and back. Superimposed was the headline – *hungry? go pop a gobar* with the strapline, *gobar – more time to party* nestling bottom right.

The team asked for Jon's verdict. 'Very now, very street – parodying the drug culture – covertly, of course. Highly simplistic, but oh, so memorable. And with the kind of money they're spending on media, "go pop a gobar" will slip into the language within months. So – we've identified our Goliath and we've got our stone in hand. Now we just have to learn to work the slingshot and knock its head off.'

Global's masterstroke appeared to be nationwide marketing offering a free, pay-as-you-go, state-of-the-art, all-singing, all-dancing big-screen WAP mobile in return for fifteen wrappers. In reality, with that level of purchase, the phones, imported from Taiwan, cost Global virtually nothing. Each time they were switched on, one of an undeletable range of simplified, electronic ads for gobars was played out. Most punters felt this was a small price to pay and a million were sent for in the first month.

– *They pulled it off without me, eh…?* He was aware of a breeze of professional jealousy. – *Well, I'm going to spoil their fun. They're really gonna love me after this…*

As Emma predicted, the site grew painfully slowly at first. The main difficulty they faced was how to let the world at large know they existed and had something of interest to offer, while remaining totally invisible. To solve the problem, they developed a viral marketing strategy, created and worked on the hoof.

Small companies sprang up over night, renting rooms and office suites, supplying a verifiable address, appearing genuine. Then, once established, they booked advertising space in alternative magazines and on local radio, duly sending artwork and tapes.

'If any journal or radio station refuses to publish or broadcast, then you'll know you've crossed swords with Global controlled companies,' Jon warned the team. 'That means the bloodhounds will soon be close. Then, you immediately cut your losses and disappear.'

Traps began to be set for them – but aided by insider knowledge, they always managed sniff them out or slip the net.

They ordered print runs of thousands of leaflets which were handed out to young people in bars, dance halls and cafés through a complex chain of sympathisers, trusted friends and known activist groups.

'Use only cash to pay printers' bills. Settle up and disband overnight – sooner if you sense you may have been rumbled. Be disciplined. This way, you continually kept one step ahead.'

The most effective technique they discovered was electronic swamping.

Thousands of randomly produced numbers were text-messaged daily containing the site's URL and simple slogans such as, *WWW.GRUSUM.ORG 4 THE TRUTH; GOBARS R BAD 4 U; GOBARS –Y U R B-ING CONNED.* Similarly, social media sites were swamped with friends to friend posts, groups, pages – sending simple slogans through to full-length articles and anti GM videos.

'Anyone responding positively – store their name and address on a data base for future reference and mailings.'

Slowly, inexorably, the number of people visiting the site grew. When Jon one day had the idea of linking them with a popular music download site and YouTube, the numbers went exponential.

'There are so many of their people in the music biz and the media,' he told Jenny, 'this'll really screw them...'

'I simply can't get a handle on what's happening,' said Maria to the meeting. 'After the launch surge, we expected a dip then a gradual climb, but the graph is continuing to dive. It should be stable, at least, with the sort of spend we're throwing at this. All the research indicates that we should have been offloading double the number of units by now. It feels like we're dragging our anchor.'

Marco looked around the boardroom table at the other members of the action group. 'Any suggestions? Ideas?' he queried. They stared back blankly.

'Okay. Here's what we do. Eloise and Dominic, set up a region by region consumer consultation programme – use phone surveys, mailshot questionnaires and focus groups. Let's talk to people, find out why they're not buying. See if we've missed something, or if there's something out there working against us. Do you remember way back to when Wrangler spent millions on developing a range of men's clothes? And it bombed? There was that one guy in a videoed focus group. He said he wouldn't buy the stuff because Wrangler make good, tough jeans, not fashion wear. That was *key!* And everybody bloody missed it.'

Marco turned to Jeremy, Jon's replacement on below-the-line. 'I want you to set up something similar, but with retailers. See what they're hearing, what's the story on the street. Have punters got opinions, aversions, or prejudices about the product or the way it's sold? Did we miscalculate or miss something? Make it a free draw thing... win a holiday in the Seychelles, or a romantic weekend on the fucking moon for two sort of approach. Now, who's running our website and our pro-transgenics campaign?' Mansur tentatively raised a hand. 'There's something very fucking weird happening here. Whenever I pick up a paper or switch on the box, I read or hear people talking about genetically *mutated* foods, not transgenics. Now that isn't bloody, fucking good enough!' Marco shouted, banging his fist on the table, baring his teeth, galvanising his team the only way he knew. 'Do something about it! Now, all of you, get out there and bring this fucking project back on track. I want reports in two days and improvements in a week.'

Jon was reading *Campaign*. The article he was interested in revealed what Global Brand were spending on market research and focus groups. He read between the lines and felt a rush of excitement.
 – *Great! We are definitely getting to them…*

WINNING

Within a year, grusum.org was registering a million hits a week, but Jon's employers were not satisfied.
 'It's time to expand, to go global,' they announced. 'We need to set up sites in the US and all over Europe, Asia and Africa in as many languages as possible. Most of our visitors to date are academics, journalists, people of like minds – or the enemy trying to discover who we are and what we're up to. Basically, we're still only preaching to the converted. We need a worldwide debate – a million hits an hour, not a week!'

Jenny sat opposite Jon, observing him as he talked business with the only other team member left in the dining room.
 – *It doesn't add up, she thought. I can't believe he's an activist. Or that he's running from the CIA…*
 'Okay, thanks. See you tomorrow, Jon. 'Night, Jenny,' the other member called as he left the room.
 'More coffee?' Jenny asked, lifting the pot.
 'What's the time?'
 'Past midnight. Why?'
 'Can't. I'm fasting tomorrow, er, today. Sounds weird, I know but…'
 'Ha! That explains it. You're one of Emma's lot, aren't you?'
 'Bloody hell. How do you know about that? You're not one are you?'

'No. But my Dad is, and it's not congenital or inhertied, by the way.'

'I'm not a proper one either, but I'm sort of involved. Honourary, you could say. What did you mean by "that explains it"?'

'There's something different about you. You have this amazing energy and drive, you push people to their limits, yet you're considerate; understanding when people make mistakes; like you avoid conflict. I find that an unusual combination.'

'Christ! If you'd seen me in the past...' Jon replied, uncomfortable with her praise, yet deeply flattered. 'This fasting and the stuff I've been doing with Emma's people... It changes you. Things that were always hovering over me, waiting to bite, to drive me, they've sort of – gone.'

'What sort of things?'

'You know, getting in a rage, wanting to hurt or get back at people, feeling superior or inferior – it all sort of fades away. And now, most of the time, I can sense these same spectres in others; people bring them to work – I can almost see them. It's spooky.'

'Spectres?'

'Yeah. You know, if someone's work is being criticised and they react petulantly, I suddenly see their family culture – like a feelings film show. You know, a demand for perfection, or being told they're no good. Usually, their reaction has little to do with what's happening. It's just the trigger. They're really fighting the ghost of the parent firmly established in their mind like some eternal critic, and that blocks any appropriate response. So they lash out.'

'Yes, I see..'

'Trouble is, these little flare-ups are dangerous to the group's cohesion. I can't change people, unfortunately. All I can do is offer them face-saving handholds out of their self-dug pits.'

'Seems to work pretty well. I'd say we were a happy team. Cohesive.'

'Yeah, we are. The other nice thing is, sometimes I get that feeling that I had occasionally when I was sixteen. Like the world's full of wonder and promise; every moment an eternity to be savoured. It's as though there really is something benign, some thing or some force that actually... well, loves us. I suppose you find that strange...'

'Not at all. I grew up with it, don't forget. It's rare to meet someone who feels it too.'

'It feels strongest when I'm fasting – not at first, though.'

'What's it like fasting? Do you find it gets easier each time, or harder?'

'It gets easier to do, but harder to start, if you see what I mean.'

'No, I don't,' she laughed.

'Every designated fast day, I wake to what's become a ritual debate. Something inside me says, "Aw, c'mon. You're so busy today. You need the food energy; you got to think, so much to do. Maybe next week…" Then I have to use all my will power and negotiate with myself as though I'm dealing with a militant trade union – "Sure. I understand, but it's only for twelve hours. I won't push it hard. We'll have a rest at midday. And think how good dinner will be tonight…" That fight becomes more and more difficult.'

Jenny laughed. 'Reminds me of when I tried to give up smoking. And does your trade union co-operate?' she asked.

'Yeah, mostly. I usually struggle through the morning with low energy and a burning hunger in my stomach, wondering why the hell I'm bothering. A walk around the grounds at lunchtime helps to clear my head a bit. Then, by mid afternoon, if I'm lucky, I feel an extraordinary, new energy. Very different to normal. It's then that I have an overwhelming sense of… being looked after, protected, loved.'

'That's nice.'

'And a genuine self-respect, too. Not one based on wealth, personal success or position. Very little touches me then. I don't get irritated, don't feel lustful. It's as though I want for nothing and need nothing. Does that make sense?'

'I think so. Sounds like the ideal state to be in. It happens to me sometimes. It's as though I'm … authentic, somehow. Really me.'

'That's right. Funny thing is, I long for six o'clock all day, but when it comes I put off breaking the fast. Just sit there with a cup of tea, wanting to retain the serenity for as long as I can. That's the bit that gets better, easier. Bloody hell, I'm not making out I'm some kind of saint, by the way. These are all only fleeting moments.'

'You make it sound really lovely, though.'

'Doesn't always work. I do have days when I can't hack it and give up. Then of course, I feel really guilty.' He leaned back in his chair, musing. 'Break the fast. Very apt term. I feel so heavy after, it's like snapping from one life into another. You know, I'm beginning to understand what those old religious nutters were on about now…'

'Father, I need your advice. There is a website which we believe is adversely affecting *gobar* sales – this year's figures are a disaster, I'm afraid. I have to say it's an extraordinarily well-informed and well-conceived set up – and we can neither locate it, nor discover who owns and funds it. They are broadcasting increasingly defamatory information about Global Foods, transgenics – and even your companies. I'm worried they'll pick up on our arms involvement. Our friends will not be pleased if we become exposed.'

'You are correct, Marco. The Energy informs me of a nexus of power arraigned against us. I assume this website is at the heart of it and, no doubt, Lucke and his new friends are behind it.'

'I find that difficult to... What should we do, Father?'

'First, tell me what *you* think we should do. What are your proposals?'

'My gut reaction is to double the media spend and try to swamp it...'

'But?'

'If that were to fail, I'm concerned we would hold ourselves open to ridicule in the marketing world.'

'Yes, I see your dilemma.' Chi-Chi paused for thought. 'Find Lucke and you locate the site. I want you to use the proposed additional media money to finance an army of informers and private detectives. Activate our members in the police. Bribe, blackmail, coerce; everything and anything. This is the beginning of the end game.'

'What do you mean, Father?'

'Just don't let me down, Marco.'

Over the months, lack of sexual contact had become a problem for Jon.

'What shall I do about it, Emma? Am I supposed to celibate, or what?' he asked as she was preparing to leave after one of Emma's base-touching visits.

'It's up to you, Jon. There are some attractive, single girls on the team. Just do what comes naturally. Don't look so glum. You'll find a solution. I'll see you in a few months...'

Although some nights he felt tortured by randiness, he had not, apart from the deepening friendship with Jenny, engaged with any the women on the team. Jenny has made Jon realise that he had, in the past, only been drawn to women who were either victims, allowing him to bully then despise them, or aggressively demonstrative types who manipulated and dominated him. All black and white characters reflecting his endemic manic depression.

Jenny, he'd discovered, was not self-centred or self-loathing: had no neuroses screaming for attention, yet displayed vulnerability and a judicious honesty. She treated him as an equal, not wanting – or expecting – anything from him. Thus a mutual attraction began to build, but he told himself he didn't have the time for a relationship, or the energy to spare.

Occasionally, he had a wet dream. A dream in which he was making love to Lucia and he woke with a choking nostalgia. After, he wondered where she was and what she was doing as memories flooded back, saccharine sweetened by time, and he yearned for her again. The feelings lasted all morning, dissipating slowly, and only in relation to how hard he threw himself into work.

Yet, despite the imperceptibly mounting tensions caused by a loss of freedom and his self-imposed, monk-like asceticism, he realised he was feeling more and more alive.

– And, despite my little problems, strangely content to be who I am, where I am and doing what I do...

Jon was working at his desk when a shadow fell from his right. He reluctantly pulled from concentration and looked up at the intruder.

'I'm sorry to interrupt,' the man apologised in a mellow, cultured voice.

'No trouble. What can I do for you?'

'Robin Buckingham. We've met before.'

'Of course. You're the golfing Duke! Our host and pet mole. We met briefly in New York, and a few other places since.' Jon stood and took the proffered large hand, which was, he noted, both soft and callused.

'I suppose I am what is called a mole. The reality is a lot less exciting than in spy novels, though. I rarely get a chance to employ the duplicity I learned at Harrow.' They laughed together.

'Well, we think it's very courageous of you, and we're most grateful for the loan of your house. It certainly makes our work a lot easier.'

'My pleasure. I must say, the old place certainly looks different with this hi-tech makeover,' he said affably, looking round what had once been the ballroom but was now mimicking a Microsoft production facility. 'I hope you have everything you need?'

'Yeah, it's great – perfect. Can I get you anything? Cup of tea? Show you round?'

'Actually, I came to see you; got some very interesting information. If you have the time, could we perhaps discuss it over a walk – it is such a beautiful day.'

It was late April and spring was ripening into summer under an expectant blue sky, the sun hot on the skin between intermittent gusts of wind. Horse chestnuts and hawthorn shimmered, layered in brilliant, lacy white, while ash and oak swaggered, sporting pristine, new leaves.

'When you were thinking of changing sides, who approached who?' Jon asked as they walked through the formal gardens.

'Emma and her people contacted me. Through them, I saw a way to stop the insanity without revealing my hand – and putting my life at risk. God knows how Emma and friends knew I was ready to turn. I agreed to help them and they decided I'd be of far more use working from the inside. So, here I am.'

'You must have been a member for some time before that.'

'Yes, I was. Been a member of Doh-Nai-Zen since the fifties. But my ancestors, great grandfather, grandfather, my father and I were all involved in what went before. When Chi-Chi came on the scene he simply pulled the disparate groups together, gave the whole kaboodle an identity.'

'So, what actually made you turn against Doh-Nai-Zen?'

'I began to realise that the Energy was malignant, that it gained its power by usurping mine. Later, I discovered their plans to enslave people with this addictive foodstuff of theirs. Then the final straw – the realisation that their tampering would eventually destroy our farms, our animal stocks, the countryside. Simply couldn't go along with that. Realised if Chi-Chi and his henchmen were allowed to have the kind of control they really sought, we'd surrender something so inherently beautiful, so fragile and subtle, the world would never be the same again.'

They walked towards the orchards, down an incline and through a five-barred gate; the apple blossom sugaring the jagged trees gushed a scent that tasted, in the back of the throat, as pinkly sweet as candy floss.

'Take these orchards,' Robin continued, sweeping his hand in a wide curve, 'They're a good example of what I am referring to, a miniature symbol of the world I do not wish to see impoverished and destroyed. They were handed down to me by my forefathers and now, my responsibility is to husband them and to pass them on intact to future generations.'

'They are rather beautiful. What varieties are they?'

'Oh, Worcester Permains, Bramley's Seedlings, Blenheims and Egremont Russets. Then there's Lord Lambournes, Newton Wonders, Tydeman's Early and Peasgood's Nonsuch. That's just the ones I can remember. They all have such magical, evocative names, you know; and each variety has its own unique flavour and texture; its own colour, particular shape and season. To my mind, this diversity reflects our Creator's munificent nature. By the way, did you know that there were once over four thousand varieties of apple grown in the UK alone? And that only nine are commercially produced today?'

'No, I didn't. That's terrible.'

'Chi-Chi's world would reduce that further – to one laboratory vat of apple essence. A designer apple. Something that will never have known the earth, sunshine, wind and rain. And they'd do the same to human beings, to nature herself, if allowed. I couldn't sit back and watch that desecration happen.'

'What about feeding the masses, though?' Jon asked, playing Devil's advocate.

'Without big business interfering – cartels in all but name, fixing prices, controlling distribution and so on – and the obscene wastage of EU agricultural programmes – I genuinely believe that small farms, such as this, working in concert, could feed the nation adequately,' Robin replied, gesturing, indicating the expanse around them.

'There's fifty odd million of us living on this island. Could small-scale farming cope? Do we have the expertise still?'

'No, probably not at the moment. Barley barons, the agri-chemical industry and factory farming have seen to that. And they've mostly destroyed the soil. It's nothing but a growing medium now, thanks to years of nitro-phosphates. Like bloody blotting paper, so we need more and more of their damn chemicals to grow increasing amounts of substandard food. Terrible. But if the will was there, we could revitalise the land and eventually feed the nation properly. And the same could be done all over the world'

They walked on in silence, each pondering, until Robin commented, 'It's sad, you know. I grew up here, learnt my farming skills under my father and my grandfather. There are still a few men working for me; men I knew when a boy. Knew their fathers and grandfathers, too. But most of them were seduced into the factories, moved away to the new towns. And now of course, with technology taking over their jobs, they've all been made redundant. They're treated like obsolescent work units, not as humans. What a topsy-turvey world we've created, eh?'

'The monkey trap again.'

'Sorry?'

'Something Emma once told me. But it comes across as though you're a small 'c' conservative, anti-progress...'

'Don't mark me down as a Luddite, Jon. I'm, not against progress, per se. Many scientific, technological and medical breakthroughs benefit us enormously. And that's how it should be. I've no desire to retreat back into the middle ages. It's when things are thrown so badly out of balance for profit that I make a stand.'

'You mean the balance of nature, I assume?'

'Of course. That pre-ordained, in-built balance that's evident throughout the whole universe. Just imagine all those billions of years after the Big Bang – all that dust and gas swirling and gathering, forming into elements and compounds, then galaxies, stars, and planets. And then, that extraordinary moment when life began. What an amazingly creative urge was at work there. And now, after millions of years, our earth still swings around the sun, accurate to the second, giving us our years, our seasons – as well as spinning every twenty four hours to give us day and night. Every living thing is begotten in that finely tuned, multifacetted equation. I do not believe we have the right, and ultimately the intelligence, to interfere with that: to fly in the face of that delicate, divinely inspired balance. It's madness, Jon. Madness.'

'Well, I couldn't agree more. We're doing our bit to stop it here.'

'Of course, of course. That's what I came to talk about. I've got some really interesting photos to show you. Something you may be able to use...'

'Hi, Yvonne. How ya doin'?' Jon asked the image on his VDU.

'Pretty well,' she responded, her lips slightly out of sync with her words. 'And you?'

'Yeah. Good. How are the kids?'

'They're great. Wendy and Tina are here, back from Uni, dying to talk to you. Natalie's doing her PhD in the States, but she's recorded a message. She's doing really well, apparently, and loving America. Nicholas is a computer freak. He's not sure he really understands who you are, but he'll come to the screen in a minute. He's trying to find out how all this technology works. '

'You're looking good.'

'Thank you. I'm a working woman, now. Have to look my best.'

'Are you happy?'

'Very, Jon. I really enjoy my job. I've re-qualified as an accountant, you know, and I really love it. Actually, I've got a lot to thank you for. Particularly for helping me find myself. And for the money.'

'Yeah, well. I'm sorry it had to be such an ordeal. I hope you've not been hassled by Marco and his gang.'

'No. A few visits and veiled threats. And I'm aware that we're followed around most of the time. Quite exciting, really. But they get sloppy watching our mundane routines. I sometimes see them asleep in their car. It's so funny. And I'm certain they haven't even bothered to track us here. A weekend at my mother's is pretty innocuous.'

'Yeah, well, don't get complacent. You never know...'

'I won't, Jon. Anyway, your new friends are very efficient.'

'Yes, they are, aren't they,' Jon agreed with a smile.

'Will you ever tell me what this is all about?'

'When it's over...'

Two nights after Robin's visit, Jon was lying on his bed, half asleep. A persistent knocking on his door and Rob's voice shouting, 'Hey, Jon, you gotta come and see this,' dragged him back to consciousness.

'Whaat? What's going on?'

'Hargreave's doing an interview with the Minister.'

Jon raced downstairs to hear the TV set announcing, '...interview recorded earlier today, I asked the Minister for Agriculture about the growing storm concerning the Government's signing the green light agreement for worldwide, mutated-gene food culture production.' The team give a rousing a cheer at the mention of 'mutated-gene food'.

The image on screen cut to a plump, fresh faced, assured looking man wearing a dark business suit. He sat superimposed against a backdrop of the Houses of Parliament.

'Minister,' the presenter started, 'You're quoted as saying that, "There is no evidence that merely shunting genes around could lead to unforseen problems". Can I put it to you that an absence of evidence is not evidence of absence...?' quoted with a sneering half smile implying, 'Get out of that, you smarmy bastard.'

'Let me put you right on that, Nathan,' the Minister began, patronisingly unctuous, employing the simple parliamentary technique of never directly answering a straight question. 'Recent studies have shown that it will become increasingly difficult for the world to feed itself. The development of GM food cultures has been a technical triumph, supported by my government in alliance with governments worldwide, as a prudent

257

investment in our future. The risks involved are much less than that which is hysterically being bandied around in the alternative media and, frankly, any risks are far outweighed by the benefits for humankind and...'

'So you admit there are risks?' the interviewer interrupted, throwing a curve ball.

'Nathan, the Wright Brothers took risks when they tested the first aeroplane, but today you quite happily commute backwards and forwards across the Atlantic at six hundred miles an hour, in five hundred ton Jumbo jets flying at thirty thousand feet,' the Minister replied smugly, returning the ball with a deft backhand.

'Would you eat mutated-gene food culture products?' Nathan lobbed back.

'As you well know, government scientists have carried out exhaustive tests that prove...'

'Would you eat them?'

'That prove that there is no...'

'Would you eat them?'

'Nathan, Nathan,' the Minister sighed histrionically, as though dealing with a recalcitrant schoolboy. 'Serious scientific opinion – as opposed to medieval, alternative mumbo-jumbo – holds that these food cultures are as safe as traditionally grown foods and there is absolutely no risk whatsoever to humans or the environment.' The Minister sat back, hands together, convinced he had delivered an unreturnable smash shot to the far corner of the court.

'Show him the pictures, show him the pictures,' Rob was shouting at the screen in anticipatory delight.

'Well, if that's as you say, what about this...?' Hargreaves held up one of the photographs supplied by Jon's team that day. 'And this, and this...'

On screen there appeared a succession of images; hideously mutated plants bearing grossly distorted fruit; over-size insects with bulbous abdomens, supernumery legs and antennae; birds with abnormal wingspans, malformed beaks.

'These photographs were taken in the countryside around mutant-gene culture facilities,' Hargreaves voice-overed. 'The following video was taken inside.'

The amateur video footage portrayed on-going and failed experimental cultures. Vats of living cattle flesh, tubes draining waste or pumping nutrients: fluid-filled glass retorts holding deformed, just-alive creatures, eyes staring from gross heads, anthropomorphically sad, seemingly begging for death.

'What? Where did you get these? They're highly classified! Why wasn't I told?' the Minister was stammering, getting to his feet, ripping off his microphone in anger – confused, thrown off track. 'You've bloody kebabbed me, Hargreaves! I'll finish you for this,' he screamed, losing control. The Minister was totally unaware that at that very moment he was making history, creating a seminal, TV classic as wincingly painful as Kennedy's assassination, as evergreen as the first lunar landing, as satisfyingly poignant as a tearful Thatcher leaving Number Ten. A clip that would be run and re-run for many years to come.

Nathan Hargreaves lounged with an almost angelic smile on his face as if to say, 'Moi? What have I done?'

The team were whooping and cheering, jumping up and down, hugging one another and dancing in circles. It was their first major coup, a PR triumph and the culmination of three years hard work.

'Now we've got traction, we'll go for the jugular,' Jon said quietly, to himself. 'Let the press know about the addictive genes next. Man, I think we've got the bastards on the ropes...'

STRIKE BACK

'Still no good news, Father, I'm afraid. But I have done all you asked. The trap is primed. All we need now is one lead, one stroke of luck, one error from him and he's mine.'

'I see from reports that *gobar* sales are still not improving. In fact, they are declining.'

'Yes, Father. Have you any orders, any suggestions?'

'Just let the project simmer for now. Especially after that TV debacle with the British government. I want you and your team on the Lucke case one hundred percent. Absolute top priority. This is now life or death. The Energy feels wounded, Marco. This has got to stop.'

There was a knock at the door.

'Come in,' Jon called.

Jenny entered, saying, 'I've brought some urgent stuff from Emma. She says it should be given to you straight away.' She handed the papers to Jon.

He scanned them briefly. 'Hmm. That's good news. Apparently, there've been no Doh-Nai-Zen meetings for a while. So we're really getting to them. Right. Thanks a lot, Jenny.'

'See you later, then.'

'No, don't go. Stay and have some tea. I like talking to you.'

'Tea would be nice. I'm just about finished for the day, and exhausted.'

Jon busied himself in the kitchenette, chatting to Jenny as he worked, finally bringing tea on a tray. He sat beside her on the sofa, poured tea and handed her a cup. 'You know, I don't know a single thing about you outside the office.'

'I could say the same about you.'

'What are your interests? What would you do if you weren't working here?'

'I'd paint portraits. Actually went to art school, you know...'

'Really? So did I... University of Kent. Did graphics, though. How about you?'

'St Martins – Fine Art. I'd like to paint you one day. Try to capture that rugged look of yours and your contrasting soft-centre. I find that intriguing.'

She leaned forward and touched his face, her fingers exploring. Jon held his breath.

The atmosphere between them changed gear, both feeling the sweet vibration. He took hold of her exploring hand and examined it, turning it over, bending forward to brush her fingers with his lips. They simultaneously reached out to place a free hand on the other's shoulder, gently massaging, stroking, staring unembarrassed into each other's eyes, allowing the love to flow. Then they kissed; long, drawn out, mutually enjoyed. They broke apart, relaxed into one another and sat saying nothing, his arm around her shoulders, her head on his chest, each savouring the fragrance of the other, the contentment, the peace. It felt that they had all the time in the world, that there was no rush. All seemingly communicated without words, as time passed, the sun sank and darkness crept into the room.

'I suppose I'd better go?' she said, eventually, as a question, giving Jon the lead.

'Yeah,' he sighed, taking his arm from around her. He leaned across to click on a table lamp and Jenny stood, blinking and stretching.

He studied her youthful figure, her pretty face set in tumultuously thick, brown hair. He still reverberated with the experience of her proximity, her femininity, the long unfelt intimacy.

– *When this is all over, she's the one...*

'Goodnight, Jon,' she said, turning towards the door, thinking exactly the same.

''Night, Jen.'

Although Jon had access to all forms of electronic information and entertainment and could be with his new friends as much or as little as he pleased, the lack of real-world interaction began to forge a cloying frustration.

'I feel like a rat in a cage,' he told Nigel, his latest mentor. 'Is it possible, do you think, that I might be allowed out into the big bad world for just one night, at least? I'm beginning to get the psychic equivalent of bed sores.'

'It would be better if you could hold on a while longer,' Nigel responded affably, puffing on his pipe.

'Why? The project's working well and we're pulling two million plus hits a day worldwide. We're in partnership with virtually every NGO that exists and funded by every major foundation in the world that has no Doh-Nai-Zen connections. Our magazine sells a million copies a month, gobars have been withdrawn from the market, not a single pack on the shelves anywhere in the world, and mutated-gene culture has become an international swear word.' As Jon recited the litany, he paced restlessly up and down the room. 'What's more, there's a global debate going on and the UN have taken up the fight. Any minute now we expect the go-ahead on mutant gene foods to be rescinded and an all-nation ban on further experimentation – and there are no MG crops or cultures growing outside of hermetically sealed laboratories nowadays. And as far as we know, Doh-Nai-Zen has disbanded and disappeared. We get no reports of meetings or of any activity whatsoever. So, what's the problem?' he concluded, turning to face Nigel, certain his argument was irrefutable.

'We still have to be circumspect.'

'Bollocks,' Jon retorted, irritated.

'You know how devious they are. Their disappearing from the scene could be a ploy. We cannot take chances. However, what you're feeling is of concern to us,' he added. 'We'll discuss it and get back to you.' Jon knew it was only a placatory gesture.

He cooled off and returned to work, but the concept of time-out would not leave him alone. He felt he'd earned a break, deserved one, and

Emma and friends were being overcautious. He became concerned for his mental health, worried he was getting weird, going gaga again. He obsessed over visiting the outside world and the need for relief grew to exaggerated proportions, becoming the single most important thing.

– *I just want to feel like feel like a human being for one night, that's all.*

– *Shit! Now I'm turning into the Elephant Man...*

Over the next days, he nurtured a seedling of a plan. The biggest problem was he had no money. He hovered in the office observing the protocol surrounding the petty cash box, soon realising there was no way he could get access without arousing suspicion. He needed an innocent looking stratagem.

'Hey, Rob. I'm doing an editorial on the IMF – going up tomorrow – and I urgently need a graphic of money – all the archived stuff is too old hat. I thought I'd do it my self, the others are too busy on the Highgrove feature. I can use the digital camera and design it as I go, but I need lots of money. Got any spare cash on you?'

'Sure.' Rob fished a handful of Euros from his trouser pocket. 'How much do you want?'

'How much you got?'

Around nine, he left the supper table saying he was off to watch a film in his room. The team members left chatting waved goodnight and carried on with their conversations.

After changing clothes, he slipped out through the empty kitchen into the garden darkness. He had studied the surveillance system and knew there was a narrow corridor, a blind spot, through which one could pass undetected. He followed the memorised path, climbed the wall and dropped nimbly on the other side. He heard a car driving up the hill noisily changing gear and flattened himself against the wall. It passed by, the driver blind to everything except the road tunnelling through headlight beams, and Jon set off, walking briskly in the direction of the nearest town.

The air was sharp, soon to be frosty, and prickled the lining of his nose as he breathed deep. With eyes becoming blurrily accustomed to the night, he could just make out the grassy banks and bunched hedgerows lining the road. Above them, trees sprouted their black, crackling crowns across an indigo sky spattered with mischievously twinkling stars. To his left a crescent moon smiled a lopsided grin. He felt alive, striding out, warming his body, revelling in his physical strength and health.

After his long incarceration, freedom acted like a psychedelic. Just being outside of the walls was exhilarating and Jon performed an ecstatic dance in the middle of the road as he walked. It occurred to him that the freedom to go anywhere you pleased, within the limitations of another's privacy, was, or should be, a basic human right. He experienced a sudden anger because this had been denied him for over four years.

The anger led him to a deep empathy for those wrongly imprisoned – political prisoners all over the world, and all of those that have suffered wrongful imprisonment since civilisation began. It was, he became aware, an evil abuse of power and wondered if taking a person's freedom away unjustifiably, wasn't on a par with – or worse than – taking their life.

'Well, it all boils down to the same thing,' he mused, as he approached the the outskirts of the small, local market town.

Glimpsing a small pub, once three terraced farm labourers' cottages now knocked into one, he headed towards it. Outside, white plastic tables squatted emptily, sunshades in parenthesis, chairs drunkenly tipped, the multicoloured fairy lights festooned over the entrance colouring their surfaces. To his eyes, made achromatic by his condensed media world seen flat and airless on computer and television screens, populated by Tom Thumb size characters, the pub looked alive and human. It's air of festivity magnetted him in. He lifted the brass door catch and entered; warm air cuddled up to him like an old friend and he breathed the unmistakable pub odour of wood fires, alcohol and cleaning fluids. There was noisy chatter and laughter coming from the Public Bar on his right. He pushed open the swing door and stepped inside. One or two people stopped talking and stared at him briefly as he made his way to the bar. Seeing nothing out of the ordinary, they resumed their animated conversation.

'What's your poison, squire?' asked the landlord, playing his stereotypical part.

'Double whisky, and a pint of... ' Jon scanned the array of taps and pointed to a ubiquitous ale. 'Benskins.'

'A pint?' the barman scoffed. 'We don't call them pints any more. Where've you been hiding, me old China?'

'Sorry. Old habit,' Jon muttered, annoyed at his slip. The barman shook his head in overacted disbelief, raising his eyes to the ceiling, winking at the smirking locals perched on bar stools nearby. The tacit in-joke was that outsiders were weird, unable to follow protocol. Thus they could feel safely superior.

The barman reached above the bar for a half-litre glass, placed it under the tap and squelched the pump handle. Jon relished the sight of the amber fluid sloshing up the glass, forming its foamy head. As he handed over his money, Jon took a mouthful. The nutty flavour burst onto his tongue awakening a thousand memories of carefree nights out with his old mates. He downed the whisky in one gulp, his eyes watering as it scoured his gullet. He slid the glass back towards the landlord.

'Same again, please.'

Carrying both drinks, he found an empty chair near the blazing wood fire and sat keen-eyed, but invisible, like a zoologist on a field trip, observing the pub clientele in their natural habitat.

He had no feelings of condemnation towards them, but it soon occurred to him that Emma and Marco were probably right from their different perspectives. The people around him appeared as flotsam and jetsam, being washed this way, that way, in the huge ocean of existence, manipulated by currents they were totally unaware of. People without a thought in their heads as to where they'd come from, where they were going, or of the continuous battle for supremacy that was waged in them and around them.

They were mostly men, ruddy faced, stocky labourer and artisan types – farm workers, builders, plasterers, truck drivers – the alcohol already in their systems animating their banal conversations – football, soap operas, local gossip, smutty innuendoes. They reminded him, in the dimly lit bar, of Van Gogh's painting *The Potato Eaters* – it's subject matter the peasant family Vincent had lodged with for a time, while a trainee preacher.

– It's funny, he mused. *They even looked like potatoes – lumpen, warted, earthy – and that's all they lived on. And a potato is a root crop, grown underground – and they were ignorant peasants – completely kept in the dark. So, old Vincent knew. No wonder he topped himself. It was all coming at him faster than he could process it. Think I know how he felt…*

His mind continued to wander as he drank.

– They behaved exactly as their grandfathers, though, knowing nothing beyond the land, backbreaking work, birth, illness and death. But they were in tune with the seasons and nature. Their lives centred around the village church and belief in something greater than themselves. They were God-fearing folk…

The people around him in the pub were worse off in many ways, he decided.

– They're materially better off, but know nothing of nature and life and death – keep themselves at a sanitised distance from their mortality because they're scared of the truth… He sighed.

– If only it were possible to have the best of both worlds. To achieve a perfect balance between existence and essence…

He finished his drinks and walked back to the bar for refills.

'You're not from these parts,' the landlord stated, drawing Jon's drink. 'Haven't seen you in here before.'

'No, just passing through. Nice pint, that, and can I have another whisky chaser?' He downed the whisky and, picking up the brimming glass of ale, returned to his seat, his head already swimming with the long unaccustomed alcohol.

The men at the table next to him were hauliers, arguing about the price of fuel and he tuned reflexively into their loud-voiced conversation.

'Fuckin' government ought to knock at least a Euro off,' one was remonstrating. 'Bloody French have got it made. And they're fuckin' laughing at us. It's disgusting.'

'Yeah, bloody right,' concurred another, 'How can yer compete with the Frogs and Krauts? I'm paying a fuckin' fortune in tax and diesel. And we're bloody subsidising them.'

Jon failed to notice alcohol performing its dangerous double-magic of narcotising reticence and stimulating confidence. A rising camaraderie propelled him longingly into the men's cosy circle.

'Actually,' he slurringly interrupted, 'the tax on petrol and diesel ought to be trebled. As it stands, the taxpayer is subsidising your industry.'

'You what?' one of the men asked, astonished.

'Think about it. The cost of maintaining roads, repairs to buildings: the effects on the environment and on people's health – all caused by heavy traffic and fossil fuel emissions, and all paid for by us, while you hauliers rake it in…'

'Who the fuck asked you to butt in?'

'You cheeky fucker.'

'Yeah. You looking for a bunch of fives, mate?'

'Gentlemen, there's no need to take umbrage,' Jon smiled winningly, he assumed, 'I was merely trying to make the point that…'

'How'd you like your fucking point shoved up your arse, cunt?'

The last speaker, a giant of a man playing out the role expected of his brawn, stood, grabbed Jon by the lapels and hauled him to his feet. As if in a dream, Jon reflexively head butted him. Blood spurted from his nose and he staggered back, pulling Jon with him. As they went down, the table, chairs, and drinks smashed and clattered noisily to the floor. Then

265

the other men were on him, punching, kicking, dragging...

Jon was outside, in the dark, lying on the ground on his back, smiling to himself, alcohol still coursing warmly and anaesthetically through his body. He heard the men raucously shouting from the pub door.

'Don't fucking come back, or you're dead.'

'We don't want your sort round 'ere. Now fuck off.'

'Fucking prat!'

The door slammed and quiet descended. Inside the bar, the men swaggered and slapped one another on the back, ordering drinks all round.

Jon lay and looked up at the swirling stars.

– Strange. The whole universe seems to be centred in my head. So where will my consciousness go when I'm dead and my brain no longer works? P'raps I'm not my consciousness; p'raps it's like sight or hearing, only a tool that other energies use. Maybe that's why you never know where you've been when you wake up. Something else was using your awareness for a while...

Forgetting the thought the second after it presented itself, he got unsteadily to his feet. He sniffed and wiped a trickle of blood from under his nose. He worked his jaw, which was painful but not broken. There were a few bruises around his chest, but he knew his heavy overcoat had probably protected him.

'They could have given me a real beating,' he told himself. 'They're not bad blokes, really. Just feeling like victims – and needing to get back into what little control they have. My fault. Shouldn't have tried to make 'em look small in their local, I suppose.' Feeling forgiving and drunkenly amused, he made the first faltering steps of the journey home.

Inside the pub, the landlord was making a call.

'Sergeant Wilson, please.' A pause. 'Bob? It's Harry at the White Hart. Y'know that bloke you was looking for? I think he was in here tonight.'

Early morning, two days after his night out – the effects of the hangover and semi-beating finally forgotten, Jon strolled into the office. He had found it difficult to sleep that night, ideas buzzing in his head, concepts flying in thick and fast, stacking up, waiting to touch down, his head a mental Heathrow.

Through the tall windows he noticed the day was diamond sharp, the pale sky a playground for scudding white clouds whipped fibrous by turbulent, ten mile high winds. In the garden, the last daffodils blared yel-

266

low fanfares. The tops of the fruit trees down in the orchards were surrounded with pastel puffs of organic smoke, pink and white and the palest of greens. Overnight, it seemed, nature had cured itself of an incapacitating depression and awoken full of hope.

Not many of the team were at their desks yet. In an adjacent office he saw Brian watching the news on a monitor and poked his head round the door to say, 'Morning.' Brian acknowledged with a raised hand. Jenny entered the main room carrying the morning's post.

'Hi! Let me give you a hand with that,' he offered, feeling helpful, pleased to see her, thrilled by the warmth in her greeting smile.

They chatted as she sorted through the mail. 'That new Hillier retrospective at the Tate Modern looks interesting. Do you fancy going to see it with me – if they'll let me out soon?'

'That would be nice. When?'

'I've requested leave. Waiting for a reply. Next week sometime?'

'I'll look forward to it. She's an installation artist, isn't she?'

'Yes. Is that okay?

'It's not my style, but I like to keep abreast. So keep me posted.' She handed him a package with his name on.

'Thanks. I will.'

Brian interrupted, shouting from the doorway.

'Jon, you'd better take a look at this morning's news...'

Jon clicked on a nearby monitor, sensing the urgency in Brian's voice. A newscaster was talking to camera.

'The Duke of Buckingham was found dead in his London apartment late last night. Early reports indicate suicide. A spokesman told our reporter that police are studying a note and do not suspect foul play...'

The blood drained from Jon's face and he felt nauseously giddy, his mind racing.

– Bastards! Murdered Robin. Shit! They must know about this place. We're in danger. Gotta get away...

On instinct, his eyes flicked to the package in his hand – a small, cuboid parcel, the logo of their computer suppliers, addressed to John Bradford.

– Bradford? That's not right... A faint click and whirring inside. Within a millisecond he knew.

'GET OUT!' he screamed, shoving Jenny towards the door. She looked startled at him, uncomprehending and didn't move. 'GO! GET OUT OF HERE!' he screamed at her. *'IT'S A BOMB!'*

The tiny part of his mind unaffected by terror calculated, at computer speed, a course of action. He held the package in front of him like a goal-keeper taking a drop kick, knowing he could kick further than he could throw. His foot connected with all the strength his up swinging leg could muster. He felt a sharp pain and knew he'd probably broken a toe. The parcel began its arcing trajectory towards the high windows.

It happened in slow motion. He saw the parcel bursting through the window, glass beginning to fly.

– *I got away with it...*

There was an orange flash and a wave of heat. A giant, white-hot medicine ball slammed into his chest flinging him against the wall. He felt as though he was coming apart. Pieces of computer and office equipment came flying at him, peppering his face and body: A filing tray, clearly marked 'Out', cartwheeled in the air, across the room. It seemed to speed up as it approached, suddenly lamming into his head.

– *That's ironic...*

His brain cut to black.

SURVIVING

Silence. Nothing. Then a surfing, a riding up into awareness; a waking from sleep, not comprehending who or where you are. His consciousness unfolded like a flower at dawn.

He was receiving no sensory information whatsoever, yet was fully aware. He could feel the shape of his body, but had none of the usual background sensations of breathing, heart beating, muscles twitching, saliva flowing, stomach gurgling. Neither did he feel emotion and anxiety, nor experience the tumult of his thinking mind. He just was.

He knew he was moving, but was unable to work out why, or even how he knew. Neither could he tell in which direction. Backwards? Upwards? The sensation didn't scare him, or even feel particularly strange. Just different. The movement came to a stop. He still couldn't work out if he were up, or down, or where?

'Now this is odd,' he communicated to himself wordlessly, thought free.

An image unfolded in front of him – or was it below? – not seen, but perceived. Slowly, very slowly, it took form and he realised it was a planet; then he recognised the Earth, observed from thousands of miles in space. Not physically seen with biological eyes, reflected light waves focused onto a retina through a cell-constructed cornea. No rods and cones zipped bioelectrical impulses to be deciphered by a living brain. This was a seeing by direct experiencing, one where there was no division between observer and object. He sensed the world as a shimmering, blue and white crystalline sphere; a living, breathing entity, floating on an energy field, calmly bobbing like a beach ball on a gentle sea. It lay concentrically at the heart of larger spheres of differing energies and translucent colours with no name.

'A hierarchy of material, vegetable and animal. Someone told me about that once.' He hovered on the edge of an even larger sphere, sensing there were many, increasingly larger spherical layers beyond.

He spent a hundred years exploring the manifesting sensation, yet a second later was wondering what it would look like from the other side – and he was immediately observing it from that position. He discovered he could flick back and forth to any vantage point he wished before he even willed it, yet he never seemed to move – he somehow became another part of a greater self.

Understanding grew, and he merged with it – became the understanding. He was part of a grid, a network of individual but wholly connected energies encompassing and connected through the layers, back to the World.

'Interesting. I can shift to wherever I want because I am part of something and yet I am that something as well... both node and nexus.'

The network rippled in welcome. He graciously acknowledged, rippling back. The next second, a century later, a sparkling light captured his attention and immediately he was fused with it.

'Welcome, Jon,' Emma communicated. He experienced recognition, but no surprise.

'Where is this place? It feels... awesome.'

'The coarse, outer regions of universal consciousness, Jon. The human level. A projection point from which nodes of awareness enter life on Earth, to occupy a foetus and become an individual.'

'Right. Remember now. Why am I here, though?'

'Because the body you normally inhabit is currently on an operating table, down there, being patched up. You're technically dead at the moment.'

'Yes, of course. Glad it's over. Glad it's all true. Being here feels like paradise.' The network of energy vibrated with him in pleasure, rippling like a sail in the wind.

'It's not heaven, Jon. There are many, many layers of reality to experience before you arrive home. You're a young soul.'

'Know that. Are you dead, too?'

'No, Jon, not yet. All humans exist on this and all other planes, including the earth. Being aware of it, or not, depends on what controls your consciousness on Earth. Listen carefully, Jon. It's not your time. You must go back.'

He ignored her, only interested in the vortex of pure being, a crescendo of love emanating from the outer layers beyond where they hovered.

'Jon, pay attention. There's still a great deal to be done. You're very important right now,' Emma interjected more firmly.

'Is there? Am I?' Jon hummed dreamily. The pull was more insistent now, ecstatic. 'Don't want to be an "I" any more. Want to rejoin the universe – a billion, billion simultaneous orgasms. Pure love. Let go, Emma. Want to go home, back to the source. Back to creative bliss... Please, Emma. Let go...' He begged and cajoled, desperately seeking to undo the clasp that prevented final release.

'No, Jon! You're going back now,' she stated firmly. 'Apparently the surgeons have been successful. I'll come and visit you soon, in hospital...'

Jon was tumbling upwards, diving into a vat of suffocating molasses; boiling hot molasses that scalded and stung and gouged and bit. He wanted to shriek it away. He dreamed he was being tortured, gratuitously punished.

'Stop! Don't! *I don't know anything.* God! It hurts so much. Help me, please, please,' he screamed, but no words left his mouth.

'Mr. Lucke, Mr. Lucke, can you hear me?' He opened his eyes and winced. He was in a brightly lit, whitely clinical room, lying on a bed. Dangling tubes terminated inside his body as though he were a broken marionette. A tiny green screen to his left created a continuously unfolding mountain range synchronised to the rhythm of a monotonous, beeping beat. He watched a bubble rise in what appeared to be a freezer bag of frozen meat hanging above him. A woman in a blue dress and white pinafore stood over him looking worried, a little hat perched on her head. He thought she was a dinner lady and he was back in school. His throat was so dry he couldn't swallow or speak. A plastic mask covered his nose and mouth and he had difficulty breathing. A suffocating panic crushed him and he struggled to sit up, frantically sucking air. A red-hot poker was thrust into his stomach. He experienced agonising pain, emitted a silent scream and the black, boiling molasses came again.

Over the next weeks, between alternating hazes of mind-dulling anal-gesics and searing pain, the story unfolded little by little from visiting doctors and attendant day and night nurses. He learned that his instinc-tive reactions had saved his life – just. Jenny and Brian, and two others had been killed, the ballroom wrecked, the house badly damaged. He had died in the operating theatre, his vital life signs stalling, fading, the oscil-loscope flat lining, surgeons and assistants galvanised to hectic mode, injecting stimulants, applying jolting electrodes. But they managed to resuscitate him, brought him back from the edge of death. He was still in intensive care, he has been told, and not yet off the danger list. The news about Jenny and Brian devastated him.

– *It's all my fault, all my fault...* he agonised, wishing and wishing he was dead again, weeping soundlessly, tears soaking his pillow.

Later he was told his left arm had been removed. It had been mutilat-ed beyond current microsurgery technology. They doubted they could save his right eye. His other injuries were serious, but no longer life threatening – broken ribs, fractured pelvis, a removed ruptured spleen. His face and remaining hand would be permanently scarred by second degree burns and he had a broken toe – but he'd been lucky, the visiting consultant surgeon told him poker faced.

'Lucky? Lucky Lucke, eh? Bollocks,' he croaked at the consultant, his voice still hoarse from anaesthetics and the tubes that had been thrust down his throat. He managed a sardonic chuckle, and then wished he hadn't as pain seared through his body again.

'You'll be in hospital for ten to twelve weeks and will need more oper-ations. After that, you must expect at least another three months inten-sive physiotherapy. There is counselling available if you want it.' He knew he would decline the offer.

He drifted in and out of sleep, hardly aware of day and night. Sometimes in the early hours, stark awake under the dim-red glow of the intensive care ward's lights, the only sounds the whirring and burbling of pumps and drips, he was so overwhelmed by loneliness he pressed the buzzer to summon a night nurse.

'Are you all right?' they asked in hushed voices.

'Just uncomfortable,' he told them hoarsely.

'Shall I fluff up your pillows? Wash your face?'

'Please,' he replied, adding, 'Can I have a drink of water?'

'Yes, here, I'll help you sit up.'

These small acts of human kindness, made conspiratorially in the middle of the night, comforted him. Just to know there was another human awake, aware of him, tending him, kept him hanging in there for another few hours and, like a child after a nightmare, he managed to settle down to fitfully doze, temporarily reassured.

After a month of the crushingly boring, deadpan hospital routine, three more operations and suffering the debilitating effects of anaesthesia, he was taken from intensive care into a private room. Security guards came and went, acting as sentries outside his door or chaperones in his room with rare visitors.

Two CID officers made an official call. He told them he had no idea who could have been responsible, that he hardly knew Robin Buckingham and could see no possible connection between the purported suicide and the attempt on his own life, despite Robin being his landlord. They didn't believe him.

'It seems odd to us, sir. The morning Sir Robin is found dead, his house gets blown up.'

'Coincidence?' Jon suggested.

'It'd be a first in my thirty years on the Force.'

'Maybe Robin's enemies wanted to make doubly sure?'

'Er... Thank you for that, sir. Well, we'd appreciate it if you could really dig deep. If anything springs to mind, perhaps you could give us a call?'

'I doubt there's anything.'

'Very good, sir. Don't go anywhere in the meantime. We'll be back.'

'You know where to find me...'

– *What a pointless charade...* he thought, not caring if they were Marco connected or not, or even if their visit implied Doh-Nai-Zen itself was being investigated.

Members of the team called in, bringing cheering news. They were re-established in a new location and back online. The site continued to thrive and their hit rate was back to what it was before the attack. Thanks to the latest, digital fibreoptics technology, new ultra-wideband, interactive, internet TV could now be enjoyed in every home in the land – the broadcasting revolution they had been longing for. They were all still outwardly keen and eagerly awaiting Jon's return.

'Heads are beginning to roll,' Rob told him enthusiastically. 'We're *win-*

ning, Jon.'

He feigned interest but had no heart for it. Their presence reminded him of Jenny and Brian, and he surrendered to an enfeebling, soporific sadness, becoming maudlin.

– *So life's still taking things away from me...*

– *That's because you deserve nothing...*

Tiring easily, unable take in more information, he nodded off and they tiptoed from the room sheepishly.

Most of the time he felt useless. It seemed he had no interest in the world and felt the world reciprocated tenfold.

'Why the hell didn't Emma let me die?' he asked no one. He tried to recapture the ecstasy of his near-death experience. The memory was already in tatters, as one dimensional as a fast fading dream.

His wife and children came to visit. They were visibly upset when they saw him still with drips and tubes attached, pale and disfigured, invoking disturbing thoughts of beached and dying sea creatures. The trend in hospitals was to leave most wounds undressed and he presumed, with his face all scabs and stitches, his missing eye loosely covered in a white square of lint, stained orange at the edges, and with one arm, he looked like Frankenstein's monster. Nicholas, the son he barely recognised, hovered behind his mother.

'Say hello to Daddy,' Yvonne gently cajoled him, trying to usher him towards Jon's bed. The boy stared, frightened, embarrassed, wishing he could press a button to change channels and make it go away.

'Does it hurt?' Tina winced. His youngest daughter was now a vivacious young woman with a similar slender body to the one her mother inhabited when she and Jon first met.

'Only when I play football,' he replied, trying to joke with her, forgetting she was nineteen now, not eleven. She frowned at him, indicating she would not accept condescension even from the infirm.

'Can we get you anything?' Yvonne asked.

'Yeah! Cigarettes,' he replied, attempting normality. 'They took mine away.'

'Thought you'd given up for good,' she scolded.

Wendy and Natalie, now in their twenties, entered and hovered at the end of the bed, rent by emotion. They squeamishly hurt for his brokenness and were still worried he might die. But they were also angry with him, ostensibly for leaving their mother, but more because they knew instinctively – despite being too unworldly yet to fully comprehend – that

273

he had, by walking out on his wife, ruined their trust in the male sex forever.

'Hi Wendy. Hi, Natalie,' he waved at them. 'How ya doin?'

'Okay,' they replied almost in unison.

They were both muscularly curvaceous and knew how to dress. They had grown to be attractive, confident women.

'How's life?'

'Good,' they replied.

'Got boyfriends?' he asked.

They looked at one another and giggled, reminding Jon of when they were kids. A rush of warmth made him smile. He felt the scabs around his face crack.

'Well, watch yourselves,' he quipped, 'And make sure they wear condoms.'

'Dad!' they admonished him, looking around in embarrassment, checking no one had heard. They acted shocked, but were secretly pleased to be accepted into the adult world by their father, a middle-aged, male stranger.

Jon began to be exhausted by his attempts to joke and banter the get-together along as though he were the host at a wake. They were all under intense stress. Too many years of their relationship were missing. Individually, they had moved on, but as a family group they were emotionally stuck at the very moment of parting. The leaning back to the past was too painful a contortion. He asked the girls if he could have a moment alone with their mother. They agreed with alacrity, blowing kisses, Nicholas scurrying after them like a schoolboy at going home time.

'Look, is everything okay?' he asked Yvonne, earnestly when the others had left. They were both aware of not having been in one another's physical presence for over five years.

'No need to concern yourself, Jon. We're all right – really.'

'You still got some of the money I left you?'

'Plenty. It was sweet of you to do that. I'm grateful.'

'You were entitled to it. And more, actually.'

'Yes, I do know that, now, Jon.'

'I'll find out if there's any left and you can have it all.'

'I have more than I need, Jon, but you can put it in trust for the children, if you like.'

'Good idea. Anything else?'

'No, everything's fine. I still have no inkling of what you've got yourself

274

into, though. Don't think I want to know, really.'

'Have you moved house yet?' he asked. 'Do they still pester you in any way? Have they threatened you or anything?'

'No, no and no,' she replied, laughing. He noted a new zest in her, a subtle shift in manner, reflected in her dress, in her hairstyle: different phraseology, a new confidence. She was looking good, sleek again, her eyes alive, and he sensed there was a new man in her life.

'You're okay, then?'

'No need to worry over me, Jon. I'm very contented. You just get well. I'll come and visit again if you like.'

'That would be nice,' he mumbled, then began to nod off. Yvonne quietly left the room, also relieved to be dismissed.

Time continued to pass, but at the pace of waiting for a delayed flight. Then suddenly, summer had arrived outside the hospital windows, but it meant little to him. He heard the bustle of people living out their lives in the city below. It was as incoherent and as irritating as a neighbour's radio heard muffled through a wall. The hospital's humdrum routine had become his whole life. He lay in and on his bed propped up on pillows, sat in the easy chair, or paced around his room, occasionally shuffling to the hospital shop in dressing gown and slippers, walking a drip-trolley by his side. Radio, television, books all had no taste, reminding him of having 'flu when he was a kid – the aftermath, when food tasted like cardboard. His life appeared truncated and as flat as a postcard.

He was attempting to adjust his vision as a monocular man. He had no sense of distance, or depth, sometimes missing a footing or bringing a glass or a forkful of food too fast to his face, slopping the contents down his pyjamas. When the nurses cleaned him up, he felt disabled.

'Mr. Lucke, you're really not trying,' the exasperated physiotherapist told him.

'What's the point? I'm a bloody cripple. Can't even dress myself.'

'Mr. Lucke! Really! We don't use words like that any more. People with *far* worse injuries than yours live perfectly normal lives. Your so-called disability is more to do with your attitude than your physical state. It's totally in your mind.'

'Alright, I'll try to imagine an arm, then,' he whined sarcastically. The physio shook her head in frustration. 'Can't you fit one of those computerised arms I've seen?' he asked.

'No, we can't, I'm afraid. Your arm has been removed at the shoulder.

Prosthetic technology is not that advanced. There has to be some remnants of muscle and ligament.'

'I suppose I ought to be glad it was my left arm, not my right.'

This sudden gladness took him aback and he was surprised by his own re-burgeoning human spirit, which could feel good about such a small thing amidst seemingly crushing adversity.

A few days later, he awoke to discover that his depression had lifted, only then realising that he had been depressed. He was hungry, too; observed himself laughing and horsing around with the nurses, glancing admiringly at their female forms as they bent and strained, remaking his bed. He peeked down the front of their uniforms hoping to catch site of a brassiered breast – a fourth-former again with a new, young and attractive female teacher.

And then Emma came to visit.

'Well, well, well! You certainly don't look dead to me,' she announced, sweeping in, her presence brightening the room.

'Emma! God, it's good to see you! You're a sight for sore eyes – or should I say sore eye?'

'Love the eye patch. You look like a pirate.'

'Yeah, and look,' he laughed, indicating his folded, empty pyjama sleeve tucked into his jacket, 'You ought to see my Nelson impression.' He stood, took a magazine, rolled it as a pretend telescope and brought it to his eye patch.

'I see no ships,' he cried theatrically.

'Only hardships,' they said in unison, Emma groaning. They laughed together, not at the old joke, but in pleasure at each other's company.

'How do you feel about the arm, really, Jon,' she asked when the laughter had faded, concern in her voice.

'I haven't felt much about anything for the last three months,' he replied, sober again, 'but the funny thing is, I can still feel it there. It's kind of uncanny.'

'It's a well-known phenomenon. You're sensing the original energy matrix your physical arm formed around. Our whole bodies are like that. The matrix is the part that transmogrifies into our next world when we leave this – assuming it hasn't been degraded by extreme behaviour. But you know all about that now.'

'Sort of. It's all just a hazy memory. Can't believe it was for real.'

'Well, I can assure you it was. I was there.'

They sat and talked for several hours. The interaction worked on

Jon like a miracle drug and towards the end of the visit it seemed as though life had been breathed back into him, re-igniting both his humanity and raison d'être.

'I'm really looking forward to getting back to work now,' he said animatedly.

'That's good,' Emma replied. 'But you won't be going back to the site. Your work is completed there.'

'What am I going to do, then? Any ideas?'

'Several. In a few months time, you're going to start on a new project. We want you to help set up a Trust...'

'What? Sitting around all day dishing out money to worthy causes? Sounds kind of dull to me.'

'Not causes – a cause. The Trust will help fund a series of new university Chairs, Peace Studies, Spiritual Regeneration, things like that. Then there'll be bursaries and scholarships for students; lecture tours...'

'Oh, come on! You gotta be joking. I'm no academic. Something more in your line, surely?'

'No joke,' she replied. 'If you think about it, you've had real experiences, seen things that even Popes and Brahmins don't get to see. It's experience that defines a man, Jon, not learning. You'll be a real ambassador – and a star lecturer. You know you could become a folk hero if you wanted? A cult icon – the Che Guevara of the internet.'

Jon mulled this over, but instinctively realised that if he accepted such a role, his life would never be his own again, that he'd be public property. It would be extremely hard work, too. Interviews, books, public appearances, TV chat shows, the Press – he wrinkled his nose at the thought.

'No. Not for me, Emma. I'll stay anonymous.'

'Fine. But what about the Trust? I'll be working closely with you – as your guide and mentor.'

He liked the idea of working with Emma again and grudgingly agreed to at least think about it.

'But before that, there's something of monumental importance you have to help us with.'

'I'll do what I can, my impoverished physical state willing. What is it?'

'We're going to abduct Chi-Chi...'

'Balls! Now you gotta be joking!'

'No. Dead serious.'

'Why, though? What's the point? I thought things had gone off the boil.'

'Don't you watch the news in here?'

'Not if I can help it.'

'He's currently fermenting trouble all over the world, as we predicted. There are serious conflicts in Africa, India and Russia; The US is on the verge of war with the World Moslem Alliance and China with Russia. They're all talking of withdrawing embassy staff. Things are perilous, Jon.'

'If he's behind it all, couldn't you just assassinate him or something?'

'I wish it were that simple. The Energy connects them all through Chi-Chi. If we killed him the link would merely shift across to Marco and the others who'd then share power. Our aim is to cut the direct umbilical connection to it's living host, to drive it away – for the time being. With no direct access to a human of Chi-Chi's calibre, the Energy will be set back decades – until another Chi-Chi is born and comes of age.'

'Exactly how are you going to achieve this minor miracle?'

'We'll do an intense detox course in his presence while he does kiyomeru. That's the only way we'll gain inner access to his direct connection.'

'And you think this egocentric, ruthless killer will just go along with this?'

'No. That's why we have to kidnap him and sedate him first.'

'That's impossible, Emma. He has bodyguards, servants, twenty-four hour surveillance – the lot. Nobody gets near him. Do you actually have a plan?'

'Not as such. We're working on it. Waiting for the right opportunity.'

'You're crazy. And anyway, why do you need me?'

'Orders from above, Jon.'

'In other words, you've no idea?'

'No, but I can make an informed guess.'

'And what would that be?'

'Because you know the kiyomeru energy, and it knows you. Plus, you have both detox experience and the inner strength.' Seeing Jon's sarcastic look, Emma added, 'Okay. I admit it's hazy, but we have no alternative.'

'Emma, it's lunatic. Impossible. He's just too well defended. And then there's the sheer strength of the man to contend with. If he got within ten yards of me, he'd rip me from limb to limb… What's left of them.'

'We'll tie him up, or something.'

Jon gave a snort of contempt.

'There'll be a way, Jon. We just have to find it.'

'I'm sorry, Emma. I can't help you. It's too dangerous.'

'We can't force you, but I'd like you to think about it, at least. We really do need you on this. Look, I'll come and collect you when you leave hospital next week, and we'll talk some more. I've found somewhere for you to stay.'

Jon stared towards the half-opened window. The azure blue sky seen beyond the white curtains flapping in a light breeze reminded him of another life; innocent, carefree, time-abundant. After some minutes, he turned back to face her and announced, 'I'm sorry, Emma. I can't do it. It's too much to ask. I simply haven't got what it takes any more.'

SHOWDOWN

For three days and nights, Emma and Jon had been sitting in the hotel foyer or their room, wandering in nearby Hyde Park and up and down Park Lane, posing as a couple and taking turns to sleep.

That moment, as they drank coffee in the hotel's restaurant, Emma was wearing a discreet earpiece connected to what could have been a small I-Pod. It was, in fact, an electronically non-detectable, state-of-the-art surveillance gadget plumbed into Chi-Chi's personal telecoms network. They were monitoring and analysing every call into and out of his suite, waiting for the one they wanted, the chink in the armour, the crack in the wall. When it came, Emma almost missed it.

'Mikho? It's Julia. Marco is sending Enrico over to collect Chi-Chi. He has something to attend to and will have to drive to the meeting separately. Please pass on his apologies.'

'Sure. How long?' Mikho enquired.

'ETA an hour from now.'

Straining to control excitement, Emma turned to Jon. 'This is perfect. The chance we've been waiting for. It's now or never.' Anxiety puffballed in Jon's chest.

Over the next fifty minutes, she worked feverishly, making calls, pulling together the already in-place strands, forming an extempore plan, organising the rest of the standby kidnap team – and nurse-maiding Jon who was becoming increasingly nervous.

'Jeez, Emma. If just one tiny thing goes wrong... '

'Jon, it's going to be okay. We'll be great. You'll be great. Trust me.'

Emma's mobile rang. 'Right, thanks.' Then to Jon, 'Marco's car is approaching. Go to ours. I'll join you in a moment.'

Emma made a call. 'Miss Mikho? It's Reception. Your car and driver are here... Yes, I'll ask him to wait.'

The Bentley swept into the pick up area. One of Emma's colleagues, a young Japanese girl, Mikho's exact double, walked down from the entrance and tapped on the front nearside glass. The chauffeur leaned across the passenger seat towards her while lowering the window.

'Good afternoon, Enrico. Would you drive to the side entrance, please? We'll pick Chi-Chi up there. Too many people in Reception for discretion this afternoon.'

He nodded assent. The car moved off to begin its fruitless wait. An identical green Bentley with the same number plates slid smoothly into its place, its driver in full livery indistinguishable from Enrico's. The car stood purring awaiting its passenger.

The lift doors opened and Chi-Chi and the real Mikho swept out accompanied by two bodyguards. As they processed to the main exit, the ever-vigilant guards' eyes darting from left to right, a woman wearing the hotel uniform approached the party saying, 'Excuse me, Madam. There's an urgent fax requiring your attention at the reception desk.'

Mikho looked cross. 'Can't it wait? We're about to leave.'

'It's from Mr. Brancusi, Madam, and he specifically asked if you could sign and have it re-faxed before you left for the meeting.'

'Oh, very well.' Then to the bodyguards, 'Help Chi-Chi into the car and make sure he's comfortable. I'll only be a few minutes.'

They concurred and escorted Chi-Chi through the entrance doors. One jogged swiftly down the steps and round to the Bentley's offside passenger door, standing left hand on the waiting car's roof, right hand tucked inside his jacket under his lapel. He scoured the hotel forecourt with trained eyes. Seeing nothing out of the ordinary, he relaxed and nodded up to the other guard, then to the driver of their own car which was drawing up behind the Bentley. Continuing to look from side to side, the other guard escorted Chi-Chi down the steps, opened the rear passenger door and ushered him in, shielding him with his body. He closed the door and both bodyguards stood tall, scanning the area, waiting for Mikho. They were both bored, their reactions dulled by what had become a routine dumbshow.

The chauffeur hit the interior locks and released a clear gas at the flick of a switch. Chi-Chi slumped back in his seat, comatose, a smile on his face. The driver floored the throttle and the car shot forward into the Park Lane traffic, triggering a blare of horns. One guard was spun to the ground, the other staggered back, drew his gun, aimed, thought better of it and thrust it back into a shoulder holster. He turned and ran to his own waiting car and leapt in. Mikho rushed from the entrance screaming and waving her arms. The bodyguards' car lurched forward, wheels screeching on white smoke, doors flapping like wings, one guard still trying to scramble aboard. As the car entered the traffic, a Mercedes sports car rammed it from the side, bouncing it onto the pavement, scattering sightseers and shoppers.

As Emma and Jon drove by, they caught sight of the guards standing frustrated beside their trapped vehicle, surrounded by affronted pedestrians, while the Mercedes driver, a colleague, play-acted the irate foreigner, waving his arms, remonstrating loudly in Arabic.

'Slow down, Emma. Take it easy for Christ's sake,' Jon pleaded, stretching rigidly in his seat, his one arm across his chest, hand-clutching the panic strap.

'Sorry, Jon. Got to get Chi-Chi home before he wakes up.'

All three were seated in a bare, dimly lit room. Several of Emma's colleagues stood nervously at an open door sporadically talking in hushed tones. Jon and Emma sat side by side, facing Chi-Chi, who was still unconscious and strapped by his arms and feet to a heavy, wood and metal chair bolted to the floor.

The plan had worked – all the car swaps had been in place, waiting as arranged. No police, traffic wardens or bystanders had seen a heavy-set, fast asleep Japanese gentleman being transferred from one car to another. Chi-Chi has been successfully abducted, spirited away and hidden in a safe house to the west of London.

'We missed our vocation, Jon,' Emma laughed. 'We should have been kidnappers.'

Jon did not find Emma's lightness helpful. He was nervous, knowing the worst was to come.

'He'll wake soon,' Emma told Jon. 'Then we'll begin.'

The minutes passed. Chi-Chi opened his eyes, looked around the room assessing his situation. In seconds he knew exactly what was happening. He tested the leather thongs holding him, realising if he used all the strength available to him, his body would snap before the straps, and he relaxed. Inwardly he relished the impending battle, certain he would be victorious. He stared at Jon, a cold contempt in his eyes.

'So, you are alive, Lucke,' he stated in perfect English.

Jon turned his head away, unable to bear Chi-Chi's gaze. Chi-Chi focussed on Emma.

'How strange my enemies would entrust my attempted nemesis to a woman.'

'Gender is hardly an issue,' Emma countered, 'but I'm glad the irony is not lost on you.'

'You think your so-called God of Love is stronger than mine? Well, you are mistaken, as you will discover. So, let us cut to the chase. I don't suppose you will release me?'

'No,' Emma replied. 'I think we should start with a level playing field.'

'Admitting your physical deficiencies immediately puts you at a disadvantage,' he sneered.

While engaging with Emma, Chi-Chi was again projecting into Jon's heartland, prying, seeking out weaknesses, fears and anxieties.

'Emma, I'm not sure this is right. Are you sure we should be...' Jon stammered, suddenly afraid as ChiChi gained a handhold.

'Jon!' Emma snapped. 'Remember what I told you. He'll try anything and everything. Now, put on your Trank, relax into your feelings – and bloody stay there.' She turned to the others in the doorway. 'Close the door. We're ready to start.'

Jon did as he was told. Within seconds his anxiety diminished and his inner world expanded. The room faded then disappeared as his awareness slipped into another dimension.

He was hacking with a machete through a dense, torrid jungle, sweat prickling his back. Creepers and wide-leafed plants snagged at his heels and slapped his face. He tripped and stumbled, cursing. He started to pant with exertion, swatting in vain at the cloud of insects buzzing in his face. The scenery around him flickered and dimmed like a television set with poor reception. Suddenly, he heard an ear-rending roar and on the periphery of his vision saw a leaping leopard. His hand shot up, reflexively clasping the animal's throat and he was knocked to the ground with the force of the pounce, the machete flung into the undergrowth. They rolled to a stop, the leopard above him, his hand still clasping its neck. He locked his arm and the animal snarled and snapped at his head. He could smell its hot, feline breath; saliva flecked from its mouth, spraying his face as the animal writhed from side to side attempting to break Jon's grip, clawing the air, slashing at his face. He held it firmly wondering from where his extraordinary, one-armed strength stemmed. He stared defiantly into the animal's eyes and the illusion stuttered, became blurred and finally shrank to a white spot. Surprised, he got back to his feet.

– A taste of Chi-Chi's anger... a voice echoed in his head. Thinking he knew now what to expect, feeling more confident, he set off again. The jungle flickered all around, a path opening before him as he walked. He continued until he broke out into a stuttering mirage attempting to organise itself as a wide plain. Thirty yards ahead, the conjured image of a fully-grown, male rhinoceros confronted him, its spiteful eyes glowering. It snorted and pawed the ground, then charged towards him at full pelt. The ground trembled under Jon's feet. Aided by an awareness of its illusionistic nature, he controlled a spasm of fear and with an immense effort of will slowed time to a crawl. He watched the animal inching towards him, seeing every muscle ripple, every shift of bone and flesh under the leathery skin, hearing each footfall as an explosion. He eased himself to one side. The creature brushed past and disappeared.

'Gotcha! I'm getting the hang of this...'

Emma was immediately by his side. 'We're just skirmishing, Jon. Don't lock on to thoughts and keep aware...'

Monkeys. Thousands of gibbering, teeth-baring, vicious monkeys. They dropped on all sides, attacking singly and in groups, scratching, biting, mauling.

Jon and Emma stood back to back, hitting out, ducking, pulling off and throwing aside. Inexorably, the monkeys built around them, clinging on until they were both forced to the ground under their weight. He could feel coarse hair in contact with his body, needle-sharp teeth and claws gouging his flesh, their pungent monkey smell filling his nostrils. He panicked as he fought for breath, losing control, sliding down into the illusory dimension. He started to faint away...

'Jon,' Emma shouted. 'Do as I say, now. Stop fighting. Empty your mind.'

He did as he was told, sensing the urgency in her voice, just managing to stay conscious. A sense of calm benevolence pervaded his body transmuting to a deep gratitude for life. The monkeys screamed and ran in disarray, thrashing back into the jungle, climbing trees, vine-swinging into the distance, tails between legs.

Emma allowed Jon no time to think. She was up, pulling him to his feet. 'Come on. Follow me. Now!'

On the horizon Jon caught sight of a dust cloud kicked up by a stampeding herd bearing down on them. As they ran side by side, the thunderous roar and trumpeting bellows grew louder. Thousands of stampeding, elephantine creatures were bearing down on them. Ahead, a wide chasm opened, a white-water river running through it hundreds of feet below.

'Just jump, Jon,' Emma cried, catching his hand.

Together, they leapt and sailed across dreamily. Jon turned in midflight to watch the creatures plunging, lemming-like, over the precipice's edge, down into the ravine.

They floated across, landing gently on the other side.

'What's that noise?' Jon asked, hearing an approaching drone, reminiscent of squadrons of bomb-laden aircraft.

A swarm of giant hornets blanketed the sun as they dived to the attack. Jon discovered an automatic weapon in his hand. Back to back, side by side, he and Emma fired into the swirling mass. Hornets' heads exploded, spurting yellow-green fluid; ripped wings and torn legs dropped from the sky, piling around them. A hornet slipped through their arc of fire, dropping its abdomen, aiming its sting at Emma. Jon turned, saw the drop of clear liquid forming and began firing in panic, spraying bullets everywhere, finally catching the creature in its midriff. It gave a howl and crashed to the ground, cartwheeling, splintering, finally coming to rest at Jon's feet.

'Nice shooting,' Emma grinned, casually blasting at a remaining hornet about to land on Jon's back. Suddenly, the attack was over. A brief respite, then immediately, a Tyrannosaurus Rex, as tall as a house, lunged towards them, its jaws clacking hideously, its talons slashing the air.

'Follow me. Do exactly as I do,' Emma cried at his side. She took his hand again and they ran at the creature, flat out. Ten yards, five yards, one yard... He could see the monster's scales swarming with lice, smell its dung heap breath... He flinched and shut his eyes, anticipating the collision...

They were back in the room with Chi-Chi who was slumped in a trance, still strapped to the chair.

'Is it over? Have we won?' Jon asked ripping off the Trank.

'No, Jon. That's just Chi-Chi's opening gambit.'

'Christ, I thought we'd had it when that T-Rex jumped us. How did we get out of that?'

'I've no idea, Jon. My experiencing is completely different to yours. Mine's all about homunculi and jinns. Remember, it's all illusion, all in your head. Now *we* have to go on the offensive. Ready? Let's go...'

Jon replaced the Trank and and his head drooped, eyes closed. His interior space slowly expanded, transforming into a smooth-flowing river in full spate. He heard a rising roar and ahead two mighty rivers confluxed then flowed as one. He and Emma swelled and glided until they slipped over the edge of an immensely wide and deep gorge – a Niagara of psychic energy plunging tumultuously into Chi-Chi's inner world.
After a nauseous whirlpool of noise and confusion, a breaking through, then sudden quiet.

Jon found himself walking alone down a dimly lit corridor, doors to his right and left. He rattled the handles and pushed against each door in turn, but they were all locked. He noticed light spilling from a half-open door far ahead. He ran to it, pushed it wide and entered. His twenty-year-old self was sitting on the edge of a bed back in college digs, yawning, rubbing eyes, waking up.

In surprise, he merged with the image at the exact moment a tiny spore floated into its mind, landed on fertile soil and mushroomed into understanding.

– When I die, I'll go from living to nothing. Exactly like before I was born...

A charge of adrenaline exploded in his gut, fear ripping through his body.

– Not like sleep. There'll be no time, no dreams, no waking – ever again. Not even blackness. And there'll be no me to be even conscious of the nothingness. I'LL CEASE TO EXIST...

Over the next minutes he lived out the concentrate of the weeks that followed the seminal moment, re-experiencing the real-life suffocating terror, pain and anguish he had suffered over twenty-five years before.

He could barely sleep, eat or function. Sometimes he sat in his room, head in hands, rocking backwards and forwards on his bed, oblivious to everything but the manifest horror of inevitable non-existence. His mind had no control over the spiralling thoughts, each new wave fuelled by gushing adrenaline. His mind tormented him, persistent as a shambling wino dogging at your side.

'What a shit trick. We're given conscious awareness and then, not only is it taken away forever, but we have to fuckin' be there, watching as it happens. You lie there, feeling life slip away, experiencing the descent into non-existence. And it could come now, in half an hour, tomorrow, next week, next year... Every breath, every hour, every day takes you nearer and nearer... Some day you'll clean your teeth for the last time, make love for the last time; go to bed and never get up, or get up and never go to bed again... And when it comes, you're going to shit yourself stupid, become a gibbering jelly waiting for consciousness to snap shut, for fuck-ing ever...'

'Jon! Jon!' A voice was calling his name. 'Listen to me. You were right all those years ago. Death is the end. All that afterlife and heaven garbage, including your so-called near-death experience – nothing but self-delu-sion. All induced by your endocrine system and a few imploding brain cells. No different to the so-called transcendence experienced under a psy-chedelic drug, or induced by self-denial and asceticism. It's all meaning-less. Merely a safety valve created by evolution to ensure human mental health and survival. Another form of dreaming, that's all.'

Jon struggled to escape the persistent monologue, but it filled his con-sciousness, held him rigid, and there was no escape.

'Only through Doh-Nai-Zen can you postpone personal extinction, Jon. And then only for a double life span – a hundred and forty years maxi-mum, plus or minus – and that's it. Death. Total annihilation. How could a mind survive death, Jon? It goes haywire even without food energy. How could a personality survive without a body? Without memories? Emotions? How could anything organic survive cataclysmic putrefaction? It's all delu-sion, Jon. Fairy tales told by witch doctors, whipping up fear to keep the masses under control. Will o' the wisps and phantoms... And you would give up an extended life of non-stop pleasure for a phantom?'

'No! I don't believe you...' He thrashed and writhed, desperate to pull from the all-embracing grip.

'Yes, Jon. It's true. One second you're alive, in the world, experiencing the sweetness of life, the next – nothing. Forever. There-will-ne-ver-be-a-noth-er-you...' the voice sang in syncopated swing time, roaring with laughter. Jon started to weep, a body-warping frustration threatening to snap him in two.

'Jon – Don't – listen.' He heard Emma's echoing voice. It sounded far away and strangled as though she too were struggling. 'It's only – Chi-Chi – attacking – where you're vulnerable. Try not – to connect.'

'She knows nothing, Jon,' he heard Chi-Chi's voice counter. 'She's as deluded as you are. But you have seen the truth, experienced the reality of the Energy. It's all yours, Jon, for the taking. Would you surrender a hundred years more of life – full-blooded, hedonistic life with everything you desire – for an afterlife that doesn't exist? There is only one Heaven, Jon. And it's here on Earth. Miss out, and that's it. No second chance. Just another poor, deluded, one-off fool. Give up this nonsense. Come back to the fold. We'll start again, together. You can take Marco's place as my Chief Acolyte...'

'No! No! No...!'

Using all his strength, Jon shook off the persistent tirade, hurtled from the room and ran down the corridor. Bursting through the door at the far end, he found himself in a small park surrounded by tall, classical buildings. He collapsed onto a bench, breathing deep, eyes closed. A brief respite while he searched for the solid ground of conviction.

'It's been a long time, Jon, my old friend.'

Startled, he looked to his left. A monk-like figure with tonsured hair, brown habit and rope sash was sitting beside him, a well-thumbed Bible on his lap. The man smelled unwashed, unhealthy, and Jon jerked back, disgust in his nostrils.

'Do I know you?'

'You should, Jon. I have been your constant companion for most of your life. When we were tiny children, you took me in, housed and fed me and we grew up together. We've been virtually inseparable.'

'Who are you?'

'I have many names, Jon. Brother Guilt, the keeper of your sins; Brother Self-Loathing; Brother Self-Justification; Brother...'

'What are you talking about?' Jon shot back testily.

The monk opened the Bible. 'Let me show you, Jon.'

Jon stared in fascination as a moving collage of recorded images paraded across a double-page spread. He saw himself as a child, watching his parents argue, feeling again the dread as his sense of personal security evaporated – and that somehow he was the cause. In surprise he watched and re-experienced the misery and sense of parental rejection when they ignored him, pushed him away. Then he observed himself bullying his younger brothers; stealing from his mother's purse; then at school being admonished for a misdemeanour – 'It wasn't me, sir. I was standing on the corner and I saw him do it...' – followed by a procession of the deceipts and dirty tricks he had played on friends and the hurtful comments and thoughtless put-downs – everything tainted with the over-familiar hot sickness in his guts.

Staring at Jon, fascinated by his distorted-face reaction, the monk declared, 'Ah! The extraordinary, paradoxical pleasures of guilt. On the one hand you feel so bad, so full of sin, feigning hair-shirt and ashes; while on the other, it feels so satisfyingly *delicious* knowing, no matter what, you're damn well going to do it again, and again – and yet again. Take your little penchant for betrayal...'

On the page, Jon saw his wife and children, then Brian and Rob, then the Brancusis and Chi-Chi. Emotion tore him apart as he observed himself sitting laughing, talking earnestly with Jenny... The images dissolved and Emma's face materialised, smiling warmly, nodding understanding during a therapy session.

'You'll betray her, too, Jon. Just like all the others. You're a Judas.'

'No, no, no...' Jon moaned, rolling his head violently from side to side.

'And what about the people whose deaths you've been responsible for, Jon?' On a fresh page he saw the brown coated foreman clutching his chest as he spasmed on the factory floor, images of the man's family at the funeral, kids crying, wife pale with the horror of impending penury and loneliness. Then his father lying in his coffin.

'You broke his heart, Jon, with your intellectual bullying.'

Then images of Brian and Jenny being ripped apart in an explosion, flayed strips of their flesh slapping against a wall, leaving blood trails as they slide to the floor.

'And all because of your weakness, Jon, your stupidity...'

'*Fuck off!*' Jon screamed, making a grab for the monk's throat.

He was alone, clutching at nothing, an unpleasant odour hovering in the air. He slumped back on to the bench, bowed his head and sobbed quietly to himself, feeling the hot tears dribbling down his face.

'I can't go on with this...' he choked out between sobs. 'Make it go away.' Fear tore at his insides. He felt close to hysteria, desperate to run and hide, but was again held rigid.

From the corner of his eye, across the park he was stunned to see Lucia running up the steps of a building with a neo-classical facade. He called after her. She turned and waved to him then disappeared inside. He got to his feet and was immediately climbing the same steps, then running into a marbled foyer. He stood, looking around, wondering where she had gone.

'Hi, Jonny, baby.' Lucia cooed, slinking towards him. She wore black underwear and stockings. He mentally staggered, grunting under the sudden weight of desire. 'I've really missed you, Jonny and I need you *sooo* bad.

I wanna fuck you right now.'

She draped her arms around his neck, pressed her body tightly against his, curling a leg behind his back. He breathed her never-to-be-forgotten, sweat-tinged, perfumed smell, immediately experiencing a pulsing erection. He wrapped his arms around her narrow waist, pulling her closer, collapsing into her, dizzied with nostalgia and desire. He lost all sense of self, lusting to pull her taut body over him like a coat of flesh, aching to clamber into her womb, to devour her, to become one with her, to never lose her again.

'She's everything. All I've ever wanted. I'd do anything to have her back again...' he moaned, swooning, staring drunkenly into her eyes.

'I've always loved you, Jon. Why did you leave me?'

'I didn't. I...'

'It's all behind us now. Come with me. Forget everything. It'll be like the old days, just you and me, making love forever...'

'Yes, yes. Oh my God, I love you. I want you...'

Still staring into her eyes, he felt himself sliding down into the cave of her, into darkness, his only sensation the throb of sexual desire. On the cave floor, the roof, the walls, all around he saw thousands of entwined, squirming, mating snakes, glistening and hissing, radiating lust. As if slapped across the face, he recoiled in revulsion, pushing her away.

'Get away from me!' he screamed, forcibly brushing her aside. She staggered back. For a second he saw shock and surprise, then sadness on her face; then it distorted in anger. She screamed and charged at him, fangs bared, forked tongue flicking. He stood his ground. A spherical pulse of energy expanded around him. As the pulse and the Lucia mirage came into contact, there was an implosion and she disappeared.

Echoing all around him, Chi-Chi's ethereal voice resumed. 'All right, Jon. I understand.' This time the voice was softer, cajoling, seductive. 'But, tell me, what do you really want? I can give you anything in the world you desire. Is it this...?'

A ghostly film show flickered to life. He saw himself sauntering into the Vanity Fair Oscars party, the main guest among a thousand select others. Male and female celebrities approached him, fawning, hugging, kissing, desperate to make his acquaintance, to be part of his in-crowd. A rush of feeling – superiority, arrogance; a knowing that with a whimsical click of his fingers he can have anything or anyone, anyway he wanted.

'Or this...?'

A vision of a ticker-tape parade, Jon seated at the rear of a cruising, open-topped Cadillac, waving to cheering, idolatrous New York crowds – a hero's welcome.

'Or even this...?'

As the mass of goose-stepping troops levelled with the balcony, they looked up and left as one. On a given command, they brought their right arms sharply to their chests. He returned the salute, standing proud in a sharp, white, medal bedecked uniform. Overhead, a formation of jets flew past at five hundred feet, rolling their wings, drowning out the crowd as it chanted deliriously, 'Long live President Lucke, President Lucke, President Lucke...'

Jon ripped down the mental screen shouting, 'I don't want any of this. Leave me alone! I JUST WANT TO BE ME!'

'Let's explore the nature of this 'me' you want to be, shall we?' Chi-Chi persisted, unphased by the rebuttal, not missing a beat.

A chain materialised, wrapping itself around Jon, pinioning his arms and legs. The next second he was in a dungeon. At the centre stood a glass tank in which Emma was imprisoned, similarly bound. The tank was slowly filling with water and she bucked and writhed, staring wide-eyed at him, mouthing, 'Help me! Help me!'

'I must destroy one of you. Who shall it be, Jon? Just say the word and you can take her place. Or you can turn your back and walk from here a free man.'

Jon broke out in a sweat, seeming to teeter on a thin ridge, struggling for balance. In the valley to his left he sensed the horror of drowning; the claustrophobic panic, the red-hot chest pain; the final choking inhalation, water sucked deep into the lungs; the terror, the agony, the red blur – then nothing.

Swaying over the drop on his right, he observed himself walking away carrying the secret burden of his cowardice for life, self loathing an unshakeable Siamese twin.

– What to choose? his mind screamed. – The most intense terror for minutes, then death; or slow-release torture for the rest of my life...

Spasms of mental anguish and indecision ripped him. The water in the tank reached Emma's face. She pulled her head back, forcing herself up on her toes, hungry for seconds more of life.

'What to do?' he sobbed aloud. 'I don't want to die. But I can't leave Emma. But I don't want to die, I don't want to die, I don't want...' A sudden clarity, and he realised there was no conflict. He knew exactly what to do, what he would always do.

'Let her go,' he shouted to the voice. 'Kill me instead.'

A white explosion and Jon and Chi-Chi were standing six feet apart in an empty room. Despite the slavering Doberman head and the full Samurai ceremonial regalia, a slender, curved sword held in both hands, he knew the chimera facing him was Chi-Chi's essence.

With surprise, he became aware of having two arms again, a similar Samurai sword held pointing at the floor.

'What a pathetic fool,' the Doberman head sneered. 'You could have the whole world – and you turn it down. For what? A delusion! At this precise moment in time, you represent everything I despise in the human race. You are a cess-pit of mawkishness, sentimentality, pseudo-morality and spurious religious belief. And a traitor – the lowest form of life. Scum. Filth...'

Jon waited for the invective storm to die out, not reacting, feeling unusually calm. Chi-Chi raised his sword above his shoulders and took a step forward, bracing himself, legs apart shoulders aligned, pointing in Jon's direction.

'I'm going to cut you to ribbons,' he snarled, 'And toss your remains to the dogs of oblivion.'

Again, Jon did not respond. They were only their arms' length apart, staring into one another's eyes, each waiting for the first move.

They waited. Time passed. Flashes of light, sudden noises and peripheral movement... Jon concentrated on Chi-Chi's eyes knowing one blink, one nanosecond of concentration lost and he was finished. Knowledge from some ancient source ordered him to concentrate hard, informed him that the moment before he struck, Chi-Chi's pupils would dilate in micro-millimetres.

Time passed. They waited and they stared. Jon felt phantom sweat trickling down his forehead, into his eyes. The desire to blink became overwhelming and he knew that during such a fractional time-lapse, Chi-Chi would strike, would be victorious. Jon gradually, imperceptibly, shifted the burgeoning strain of concentration from his will, trusting the sweet energy he felt pulsing and growing inside, allowing it to take command of his hands and arms. The physical discomfort eased and was replaced by a fresh sense of composure. He experienced oneness with the sword, with Chi-Chi, with all life, with creation.

They waited and stared, Chi-Chi's eyes projecting contempt, humour, disdain, arrogance. Jon stared back, his eyes bland, unreadable.

Chi-Chi's eyes twitched. Immediately, a screamed war-cry and a lightning fast pulling back and hacking movement as he made his move. The sword was arcing towards Jon's neck, its polished surface glinting. Jon could hear its keening swish through the air. A surge of power coursed down his arms. In one unbroken movement, as fast as a spark, Jon's stepped to the right – at the same moment his sword came up and across...

He heard a faint snick. Chi-Chi's stroke missed its mark and his sword clattered to the ground. Jon watched in amazement as Chi-Chi staggered as though drunk; his Doberman's head wobbled then fell heavily to the floor, bounced once and rolled aside. Seconds later, the body slowly collapsed in on itself like a demolished high rise.

Emma was beside him. 'This is the moment, Jon.'

Chi-Chi's husk began to jerk and convulse, emitting giant sparks and flashes of energy. A gigantic snake of brightly lit energy whipped and thrashed into the sky connecting to the materialising apparition that filled Jon's visual field.

'Do it now, Jon. Don't be afraid. Sever the connection,' Emma urged.

Jon approached the snake of energy. He was shaking with fear, knowing he was facing something so primordial, so powerful. Bolts of lightning crashed around him, exploding into myriad sparks. For a second, he lost concentration and a spark arced into his body, throwing him to the ground, pain gouging his body.

I would have created heaven on Earth – given you unlimited power, infinite pleasure and you choose the mundane. You are not yet ready. My time will come... ' a voice boomed, reverberating on the air.

Jon leapt back to his feet, raised the sword and cut through the cord with one blow. The Energy wailed and the cord whipped back, snaking into space, retreating to a pinpoint of light. It glowed brightly for a second, spluttered, then disappeared.

Another jolt of searing pain and Jon passed out.

LETTING GO

'Get up, Jon. Get up!'

As he came round, disoriented, wondering why he was on all fours on the floor, he became aware of Emma shaking him gently. His head throbbed and he felt nauseous, a trickle of blood oozing from his nose.

'Ah, shit! Feel terrible. Wanna be sick...'

Emma helped him to his feet. He leaned on her as she guided him back to his seat. He collapsed onto it, head lolling.

Opposite, Chi-Chi had slumped down, still strapped into his chair. He looked like an old man taking an afternoon nap, snoring gently, a dribble of saliva down his chin.

Jon looked up. 'He's not dead then?'

'No, of course not. Merely, shall we say, spiritually castrated.'

'What are we going to do with him?'

'Just leave him. We'll let Marco know where he is. They can come and collect him. Come on now, Jon. It's all over. We did it, *you* did it, and now it's time to go.'

'Mr Brancusi? The person you are looking for is at the following address…' She gave the address slowly and clearly, then switched off the mobile. Jon was amused to see it was one of the old *gobar* freebies. As they crossed a humped back bridge, Emma slowed the car, wound down the window and tossed the mobile into the river below. They drove on in silence. Jon was so tired he felt as though he was melting into his seat. His eyelids fluttered and drooped and in the darkness, cradle-rocked by the car's undulating momentum, lullabyed by engine whirr and tyre hum, he drifted into an exhausted doze, his aching body gradually growing deliciously numb. Headlight flares and the rip and rush of passing cars conjured a collage of fragmented images. His mind sank by degrees into unconsciousness as ethereal voices began to weave and whisper through his dreams.

Another dimension; a spherical space. Nothing but a gentle, insistent voice.

'Listen well, Jon and remember…'

He sank further into sleep.

'The most crucial thing in life is to act appropriately. It may be appropriate to be angry, or to hold one's fire; to fight, or to walk away; to give a beggar all you have, or to give nothing. Knowing what to do and exactly when at any given moment is of the essence. The block to recognising an appropriate action is ego. Ego rules whenever you feel hurt by criticism, pleased by praise, happy or sad. It rules when you feel affronted, cocksure, anxious, fearful, jealous, depressed; when you feel better than, or less than, another; when you feel I am right, they are wrong. To live outside of the rule of ego, it is essential to be one's authentic self – the real 'me' you claim you want to be.

'As a grace in kind for the service you have rendered, you are to be blessed with a taste of your true self. This blessing will eventually bring inner peace – and huge responsibilities besides. It will not bring wealth or position.

'Soon, you will go to the authorities with your story. You will be pilloried and punished for your involvement, but you will discover you have the courage to face whatever befalls you. Your reward will be inner contentment and a sufficiency for the rest of your days.'

Jon jumped awake, immediately chasing after the fast receding revelation desperate to pin it down.

– *What was it? Try to remember. Something about appropriateness, finding my true self...* He reawakened fully, yawned, and stretched up in his seat, the revelation already forgotten by his conscious mind.

'Where are we?'

'On the M25. We're going back to my place. How are you feeling?'

'Good, thanks. Refreshed.'

'I'm glad. Have you thought any more about the Trust, Jon?'

'Umm...' Surprised, he suddenly realised that it was something he wanted to do.

– *Perhaps it won't be so bad. It'll be a change thinking of others instead of myself...*

'Actually, I've been thinking. I probably will take up your offer. I've got nothing better to do.'

'That's good news, Jon. I'm sure you won't regret it.' Emma's smile, unseen by Jon, announced her delight.

'Perhaps I ought to sort things with Yvonne and my kids, too. Get back together? If she'll have me...'

He stared unseeing at the lamp lit carriageways rolling towards them, mildly surprised at the positivity of the strange new feelings arising within.

– *Talk about a change of heart...*

Then a rush, a building sense of emancipation, a freshness, a virginality, as though newly born...

'I've just realised something, Emma. I think I've let go of that bloody banana at last. I'm out of the monkey trap. I'm free.'

It didn't occur to him that his arm had been ripped off in the explosion – and the ironic bi-sociation passed him by...

★ ★ ★

Silence; Michelle humming; David and Juanita sitting side by side in the dark.

'That seems to be all, David,' Michelle says after having allowed a dramatic pause.

'Right. Thanks. Close and refile and bring up some lights.'

'That was amazing, David,' Juanita says, sitting up, stretching, rubbing her eyes. 'Like I said earlier, it all rings bells – is that correct English?'

David nods it is, 'A bit archaic, but accceptable.'

294

'It triggers memories, then. Things that happened about ten years ago? I faintly remember there was something in the media, something very similar unfolding.'

'Yes, you're right.. But all that political skullduggery and stuff is just background. The novel's really about redemption – that's probably got more to do with the real me.'

'Anyway, I really enjoyed it. Thank you. I assume it's finished?'

'Well, more or less. I have some notes pulling all the loose ends together – a sort of coda. Not sure whether to include them or not.'

'Do you want to read them to me? I'd be interested.'

'You sure have stamina,' David laughs.

He walks to his desk, limping slightly with a dead-leg after sitting for so long, and pulls print-out pages from a draw.

'There's not a lot. Tell me what you think...' and David begins to read.

CODA

After a final stir, he tipped the pan's steamy contents onto a plate and carried it to the patio table. A freshly opened bottle, a salad and a lit candle welcomed him. He sat and quietened himself, making up a form of grace, thanking his God for life and food – a nightly ritual.

Nowadays, Jon felt his personal God as a presence – outwardly resplendent, residing in sunsets and mountain peaks, cloud formations and the plumage of birds. Inwardly, his God's close presence, experienced only when he was thought and emotion-free, reminded him of lying sleepily in bed at night when he was a child, hearing his parents' muffled voices and the occasional boom of the radio downstairs.

– You just felt so safe and protected as you snuggled down under the security of a heavy duvet, warmed by the heat of your own body... he remembered.

– Then you could delve, exhilarated, into your darkly rich, seemingly infinite imagination, while the rain and wind rattled and buffeted your bedroom window...

He began to eat, savouring each mouthful as a blessing, watching the stars emerge as the sky's brightness control was gradually turned down. The difference between England's polka dot sky and the Colombian stellar blizzard still amazed him. With no light pollution and crystalline air, the number of visible stars seemed to have multiplied a thousand-fold – overnight.

Replete, he pushed his plate aside, poured himself the last of the wine and lit a cigarette.

Sighing, he stretched languidly and yawned, his one arm behind his head, cigarette dangling from his lips. The food essences vibrated voluptuously through his body and he slid towards a delicious doze.

'Despite everything,' he announced to the darkened sky, 'I'm an incredibly lucky bugger.'

Snippets of the past began to play out, jerkily and disjointed, as though filmed by a handheld camera. Unedited sequences flickered like old, long-cherished home movies; fragmented images; short, abrupt scenes; over-long camera pans. A cocktail of emotions flowed; anger, happiness, remorse, embarrassment, nostalgia. He thought of his ex-wife, his children when young, of Emma, Marco, Lucia...

– *God. Lucia. Wonder what happened to her...?*

He'd met her briefly once, by chance, in a hotel foyer in Switzerland, long after her failed marriage to the politically bankrupted Morgan Lampton. She'd looked both rich and raddled, like an ancient filmstar.

'Lucia?'

'Do I know you?' she slurred.

'Jon. Jon Lucke.'

'Oh, Christ! Jon fucking Lucke. Bloody Hell! Should I be talking to you? Aren't I supposed to despise you? Can't remember why, though.'

'How are you?'

'Drunk. And sick. I'm dying you know.'

'I'm sorry to hear...'

'Ach! You don't give a flying shit. No one does – except me.'

He ordered coffee and tried to make conversation, skirting around their intimate past.

'How's Sonia?'

'Dead, I hope. The fucking bitch.'

'And Marco?'

'Fuck knows.'

'What will you do?'

'Told you, I'm sick. Cancer. On my way to a hospice. I'm going to die a fucking horrible death.'

She'd seemed drugged, her words staccato, as she skipped from subject to subject.

'Remember why I hate you, now. Grassed us up; a fucking Judas. Why, though? Actually, don't hate you. Feel nothing. You're nothing. Never were...' She was talking to herself, wrapped in bitterness; one moment frenzied, the next narcotically calm. 'You fucking destroyed us. No you didn't.

You couldn't. Didn't have the guts. Something else...'

She slipped into a world of her own. Jon stood and made his polite excuses. She flicked a dismissive hand without looking up and he walked away...

★ ★ ★

'Do you think I should include that?' David asks Juanita.

'Yes, I think you should. What about the rest of them? What happened to them all? It would be nice to have a conclusion.'

'There's a few more ideas and notes. Do you want to hear them, as well?'
Juanita nods and David begins again...

CODA PART 2

Deeper memories began to surface, recalling the frenetic activity around the time of the confrontation with Chi-Chi. Genetic engineering and bio-cultures had been eventually banned following an international agreement, signed by every single government in the world. The full horror of the biological chain reaction they would have initiated was more potent than nuclear holocaust scenarios.

Then, shifting uncomfortably in his seat, Jon recalled the humiliation of court and prison – the price he had to pay to be true to himself as he'd vowed he would. He had gone to the authorities with the story, bulldozing past any Doh-Nai-Zen member standing in his way. Without Chi-Chi, they lacked teeth, somehow, totally at a loss, like headless chickens running round the yard. And, by then, even Marco's contacts in the highest places couldn't stop Jon and the ensuing process of law.

Marco was arrested and charged with the murder of the young man in Streatham. His QC argued self defence, but Jon's testimony regarding the preparations and detailed description of the act was believed by the Jury and augmented by one survivor picking Marco from an identity parade. A guilty verdict was returned and Marco had been sentenced to life imprisonment.

At a later trial, Jon was given ten years for his knowing complicity, commuted to five on appeal. He served three and a half before being released with a new identity – for his own protection.

After the sensational trials and subsequent global media coverage, anyone with a connection to Doh-Nai-Zen was removed from directorships, or any position of power. Marco and Chi-Chi were stripped of their assets

297

and their whole empire collapsed.

There was to be a public enquiry but the whole thing was eventually papered over. Apparently, Marco knew too much about too many people, and there were powerful pockets of resistance to the infant new order. So, agreements were reached and deals were cut and, so Jon heard, Marco would probably only serve fifteen years at His Majesty's Pleasure.

– Money has always had powers of persuasion, Jon mused. Always will, I suppose. Perfection is not for this world...

The leaked images of experimental culture facilities had been the beginning of their undoing. It was an insane step too far and, by force of public outrage, the media become involved, followed eventually – and reluctantly – by governments worldwide. And by then, virtually every home in the Western world had access to the internet via their mobiles, tablets, TVs – and internet broadcasting had become live and interactive, involving anyone that cared to enter the debate. A virtual, global community manifested – a true social media network – with public opinion being monitored hourly.

The nature of politics, commerce and broadcasting, particularly news broadcasting, changed dramatically. It was an even bigger upheaval in communications than the invention of printing or the telegraph.

Everything was laid bare, for a time. There would never, ever again be successful cover-ups, bullshit, propaganda, political skulduggery and terrorism – or so everyone thought. For a year or two it was as though the whole world of ordinary people had tacitly undergone therapy, experiencing catharsis, or the numinous. They emerged open, honest, phobia free, hungry for the truth: as though humanity was one step up the ladder towards merging with the universal consciousness.

– It didn't last long.... he chuckled to himself sardonically.

– Those dark forces never give up...

The forest fire that had raged in high places had simply burnt itself out, merely purging the ground for the next generation of self-servers to sprout.

– The new wave promises to be worse than ever. Where are you, Emma, now we need you...?

He rarely saw Emma after the Trust was up and running. She had worked closely with him, nurturing, encouraging, teaching, making sure her fledgling could fly before it was she, the mother bird, who'd left the nest. After, she worked on projects around the world under a variety of pseudonyms and they'd just drifted apart, lost contact.

Some nights he dreamed of her. Dreamed of lying in her lap again, like a child in the womb.

"A thousand twangling instruments will hum about mine ears," he quoted to himself. Like Caliban, he cried when he awoke, begging to sleep again. Cried with a thick, breath-catching nostalgia for her and for a spiritual world he had once had a tiny taste of and will know again one day; one day soon, no doubt.

'But not too soon, please,' he added, chuckling. It was almost a prayer.

Despite the personal cost, Jon felt privileged – glad to have been involved, glad to have helped Emma's group to make a difference. In reality, he was grateful there had been no accolades, that he was unfêted and anonymous still.

– *No, I'm happy with life as it is because I am, at last, free to read and write and think and be myself...*

His bookshelves were lined with theological works on Christianity, Islam, Buddhism, Taoism, Hinduism, alongside volumes of ancient and contemporary philosophy. He read them for pleasure, comparing his own vicissitudes and flashes of enlightenment with those of the world's greatest minds and souls.

– *You've been graced with experiential certainty...* he told himself. He knew now there were as many worlds as there were people – each of us creating our own according to the sensory and attitude filters we have adopted in order to manage the terrifyingly awesome deeper reality to which we belong.

– *The physical world is only a cipher – a veiled, codified, wrong-end-of-a-telescope reflection of what truly exists. That's all we need to know. Once we understand that our individual world is a self-wrought illusion, we stop buying into it. If we fail to grasp this truth, we're sucked into delusion. Like poor old Chi-Chi and Marco. Poor deluded mutts...*

He occasionally wondered what had become of them both. Chi-Chi he knew, died some ten years ago – not exactly in poverty but a lot poorer than he was – living among a gaggle of followers in Chile, a husk of a man finally, by all accounts. And Marco? After his release, he disappeared.

– *Probably dead, too, by now. They were all so very old...*

* * *

'And that really is about it.' David pauses, awaiting a reaction.

'What do you think? Is it enough? Too much?' he asks Juanita, before realising she is asleep.

Deciding not to wake her, he collects a blanket from his room and covers her lightly. As when tucking in a child at night, he cannot resist kissing her forehead.

– *She looks so beautiful. So at peace, almost childlike...*

– *Perhaps I could get used to this relationship business again...* he tells himself, feeling a rush of affection.

Not tired, he walks out onto the verandah. It is much cooler now and he turns up the hurricane lamp, sits and lights a cigarette. A balmy breeze brings the subtle scents of citrus fruits and wood smoke down the valley. It is quiet, apart from buzzing insects and the hissing of the lamp weakly illuminating the verandah. Ten kilometres away a dog begins to bark.

He stretches languidly in his seat and shivers, wondering if he should fetch a sweater, or perhaps retire for the night, after all. He shivers again and decides it is definitely time for bed. He feels stiff suddenly and his legs ache.

– *Getting old, I guess...*

At that moment, just as he prepares to stand, he becomes aware of a gun barrel touching the side of his head. It doesn't make him start. It merely nudges into his awareness the way a dog wanting attention gently nuzzles your hand.

– *The muzzle nuzzles...* David thinks, amused, smiling. He hears the safety catch being released and knows who it is before he even speaks.

'Hello, Marco,' he says staring ahead and then laughs.

'What's so funny, Lucke?'

'Well, you know, of all the verandas in all of Spain, you should walk on to mine...' a misquoted pastiche in a poor Bogart imitation.

'Now you're a comedian, eh?' Marco sneers.

'And because it's a case of "Speak of the Devil...". I was just thinking about you.'

'Well, you'd better start taking this seriously. I'm here to kill you.'

'Yep. That's serious, Marco: but why? What's the point now?'

'Because I despise you. I rotted in jail for fifteen years because of your betrayal. The only thing that kept me from insanity was the thought of, one day, being able to wipe you off the face of the Earth.'

'Go ahead, Marco. I'm sorry I won't be able to give you the satisfaction of my begging for mercy, though,' David replies phlegmatically. 'Or screaming, or fighting. I've been too near death to be that scared of it any more. Actually experienced it, thanks to your little present. It's got to happen one day. And one day's as good as another, as they say.'

'No problem. I'm not interested in your emotional state. I just want revenge, pure and simple. It's a dish best served cold, remember? First, I would love to know why you did it. What motivated you? Who bought you off?' Marco walks round to face him, taking a seat, training the gun on David's chest.

David is shocked. Even in the dim light of the hurricane lamp he can see

Marco has aged more than the fifteen years since he last saw him. He looks ancient, like a hundred-year-old – one who's had a tough life. He briefly wonders how a centenarian made it up the mountain – he heard no approaching car. Marco's hair is thin and prison-grey, his sunken and wizened face skull-like. The skin round his neck is loose, wrinkled like a turkey's crop, his hands bony and liver-spotted, the knuckles grotesquely swollen with arthritis. He looks thin and underweight, bent and bowed down. The lustre in his eyes has long evaporated with the charm.

'Why did you throw it all away, Lucke.'

'I didn't throw it away, Marco. I bloody *escaped* it.'

'You destroyed my life, my family, my career, my business interests. Everything,' he snaps, ignoring David's answer.

'Are you sure it was me, Marco?'

'If it wasn't you, who the fuck was it?'

'Well, I didn't make you team up with Chi-Chi. He was the megalomaniac and you were the one who killed that kid – and others, as far as I know. And, anyway, I didn't topple you off your throne, either. The world did that. You weren't exactly flavour of the month, were you? You brought it all on yourself, getting involved with bio-genetics, politics, arms sales – all the world's evils. I guess you all assumed you were invincible. How wrong can you get!' Marco is busy feeding his hatred, saying nothing. David adds, 'I just did what I had to do, and it happened to get in your way.'

'Like I said, I'm not interested in your views. I just want my revenge.'

David begins to worry about Juanita asleep in the house.

– Have to keep him talking; think of a way round this...

'How did you find me, Marco? I've changed names, got a new identity, been living incognito for years...'

'It wasn't easy. An old friend in government helped. David O'Connor, eh?' Marco suddenly laughs sneeringly.

'What's amusing *you*, Marco?'

'Talking of names, do you know why I selected you in the first place?'

'I believe I was some kind of experiment, someone once told me. You and Chi-Chi needed some peasant blood to thicken the gruel flowing in your old, aristocratic veins. Something like that.'

'That's an extremely ill-informed pastiche of Chi-Chi's true motivation,' Marco responds testily. 'The reason I chose you in particular was because of your name. Did you study Latin at school, Jon?'

'Couple of years. Forgotten most of it now. Why?'

'Your surname – Lucke. In Latin it's faustus. Jon Lucke – Doctor Johan

301

Faustus. You were to be my very own Faust. You were my and Sonia's play-thing, our private little joke. You were going to sell your soul to the Devil and go to Hell, metaphorically speaking. And you did sell it with astounding alacrity and extreme avarice.'

'Yeah, well, I was a little naïve in those days,' Jon understates.

'And then you somehow got it back, you jammy little prick, and it didn't cost you a penny,' Marco spits out, angry now, beginning to work himself up into a frenzy of vindictiveness, losing the calculating coldness.

'Didn't it, Marco?' asks David, tapping his missing arm. 'I've got a record as well, you know. And lost my family, my old life...'

'Good – and you're going to lose a damn site more than that, now,' Marco says, loathing in his voice. 'I'm going to blow your fucking head off.' He raises the gun and takes aim.

'You wouldn't shoot a one-armed man, would you, Marco?' he asks, gig-gling at the assonant pun.

Violent anger flares and Marco is propelled to his feet, raising the gun, threatening to bring it crashing down on David's head, barrel first.

'Shut up, you insufferable... scum sucking... *idiot!*' he hisses. Words fail him as he chokes with rage. He slumps heavily back onto his chair as though his legs can no longer support his weight.

'Sorry,' David mumbles, trying not to laugh again, looking down, fighting the involuntary chest contractions. 'Once an ad man, always an ad man. I can't help it. Just happen to love stupid puns.' And he laughs again, unable to contain it.

Marco re-points the gun at David's head, and he sees Marco's finger trem-ble on the trigger. Hilarity dies away like a spent flare. A shudder snakes through his body. He shuts his eyes in anticipation and immediately feels calm again.

– *Shit. I hope Juanita doesn't come running if she hears a shot...*

Ten seconds pass... Twenty seconds... He opens his eyes. Marco is still sit-ting staring, the gun still pointing.

'What are you waiting for, Marco?' he asks softly, almost kindly.

'I – I don't know. This is absolutely crazy,' Marco stammers, shaking his head. 'For so many years I've been nurturing my hatred, longing for revenge, vowing to blow your brains out. And now I've got you in my sights, I just can't do it. My hatred's evaporated, just like that. Stupid. What the hell's happening to me?' He sounds scared. He puts the gun on the table, his head in his hands and begins to sob, his body shaking.

David gets up and goes to him, placing his arm round Marco's shoulders.

'It's okay, man,' he soothes, 'Everything's going to be all right...'

Marco clutches him around the middle, turns his head into his midriff and weeps. David softly strokes the thin, grey hair covering Marco's skull, feeling grace teeming like soft summer rain, rinsing through them both.

After five minutes, Marco's crying subsides and he sits back, pulling a dirty handkerchief from his jacket pocket. He wipes his eyes, noisily blows his nose and stands.

'I'm sorry,' he murmurs, 'Forgive me for my weakness.'

'That's all right...'

'I wasn't talking to you,' he snaps. 'I was talking to Chi-Chi.'

Marco picks up the gun, turns and walks away without another word, down the path, through Jon's orchard, towards the dried riverbed. He disappears into the darkness after fifty metres.

David falls back into a chair, realising his legs are shaking and his throat dry. He puts a fresh cigarette to his mouth and one-handedly strikes a match. He is bringing it to the cigarette tip when, for a second, he thinks he sees a flash of bluish light out of the corner of his eye and then hears Emma's laugh. He holds the position and his breath for a few moments... then shakes his head.

'Nah. Just my imagination.'

He lights the cigarette and snuffs out the match with a practised flick of the wrist, inhaling deeply at the same time. He picks up a half glass of grape juice, raising it in a toast.

'Here's to you, Emma. Wherever you are.' He finishes the drink in one mouthful and relaxes back into the gentle night.

In the distance he hears the sharp crack and reverberation of a single pistol shot. Dogs begin to howl up and down the valley. He sighs, shaking his head, knowing immediately what it means.

'Damn. I'll have to sort that out in the morning.'

– No. Better do it now...

'David, David! Where are you? What was that noise?' he hears Juanita calling sleepily from the house.

'Coming, Juanita. Don't worry, it's all under control.'

– Now how the hell am I going to explain this...? he wonders, standing, heading indoors to find a torch...

#0128 - 300416 - C0 - 210/148/16 - PB - DID1440490